MAGICRAFT MASTER

BOOK ONE

MAGICRAFT MASTER

BOOK ONE

Wilbur Woods

Podium

Cover design by Xiaoraini

ISBN: 978-1-0394-7338-6

Published in 2025 by Podium Publishing
www.podiumaudio.com

MAGICRAFT MASTER

BOOK ONE

CHAPTER 1

L ogan Specter was painting an exquisite landscape. While he was no peerless master, he knew this one was going to be good. How could it not be, with a view as breathtaking as the one currently behind his easel? The raw ingredients were too high quality for failure.

[7 days, 8 hours, 22 minutes]

Even with that damn distracting timer, he still found himself able to work. The rest of the world seemed to be tearing itself apart ever since this thing showed up in everyone's subconscious out of nowhere. Counting down to . . . something. Probably not good.

Personally, he couldn't care less. People really needed to relax about the timer. The wait was peaceful as far as he was concerned. He was happy to just kill time. Humanity would learn the answer soon enough. If the world was going to end, so be it. What was so great about the world anyway? It was built by old rich men for old rich men.

That's no reason to not immortalize this delectable view, though.

Every line of the valley was natural and beautiful under the brush. The vivid blue lakes sparkled in the faint light of the sun, inviting one to swim, even drown in them. The symmetry was perfect. The contours of the soft and fertile land were just . . . right.

"Why do you insist on doing this so often?" the naked woman in the hammock asked.

Logan peeked behind his work and grinned. "Maybe I want to practice my skill?"

"You barely paint anything that doesn't involve me, Logan."

"You're a hell of a muse, Frey."

"I'm a hell of a lot more than that, baby," she said and watched him intently as she stretched her limber body.

"You sure are," Logan said, letting his gaze roam all over her. "Maybe I just want an excuse to see you nude."

She grinned mischievously. "You know you don't need an excuse for that."

Logan shrugged and put the brush down. "Well that's true, but I enjoy the foreplay."

"Oh, that's what you call this?" Freya said, quirking an eyebrow. "I call it boring. Come here and kiss me, Logan."

Logan didn't need to be told twice. He practically jumped to meet her in the hammock.

Freya's full lips curled in an anticipatory winner's smile. Her blue eyes smoldered with pure seduction. Honey-golden locks cascaded into curls on her slender shoulders.

What a lucky guy I am.

"Do you have any idea of how many unfinished paintings I have of you?" Logan breathed. He grabbed her chin, pulling their lips closer.

"Let's make a gallery . . ."

Footsteps approached. Four large men in black pinstripe suits, more expensive than the average person's car, descended on the scene. Logan recognized them and groaned.

"She isn't dressed," he yelled out.

They didn't care. They all wore stupid sunglasses and those idiotic little squiggly things in their ears. Freya yelped, threw a shoe at them, and began hastily dressing.

"Turn around, morons," Logan said, snapping his fingers. All four of them halted and acquiesced immediately. When Freya was done, Logan told them they could turn.

"Young Master Specter," the gooniest-looking of them said. Logan felt like he recognized this one, but they all looked so interchangeable it was hard to say. "Your father requires you."

Logan eyed him. *Maybe I could start differentiating between them by ranking how sharp each one's jawline is?*

"Tell him I'm busy," Logan said and made a dismissive hand gesture.

"I'm afraid his orders were clear, young Master," the largest goon said. His jaw was the most brutal, which is probably why he was the leader.

"For the millionth time, stop calling me that," Logan said.

"Apologies," he said in clipped tones. "But we must be going."

"I am sorry, Miss Beckstein, but you cannot attend," a young goon Logan certainly didn't recognize said, raising his hand at Freya.

Freya immediately started spitting obscenities at the young agent. Logan raised one finger. All of the four men went still as mannequins.

That will never stop feeling good.

Logan let Freya throw a few scathing words at the young agent. He enjoyed watching her have a go at him. Then he addressed the fool. "She's family and you should know better."

The agent had the decency to flinch. His mouth drew into a line, and it was clear he really wanted to say something to Logan. Logan just sneered.

Come on. Make my day.

His father was the boss, and it would only take a single phone call from Logan to get this guy fired.

"Apologies," the goon leader said. "Agent Balmer is new in this detail."

Logan stared down the young agent, who was definitely bristling with suppressed anger now, giving him one last condescending smirk. "Whatever. Let's just go, so I can get on with my day."

One of the back-row goons produced a suitcase, inside of which was a pair of handcuffs and a syringe encased in black foam.

"Really?" Logan asked. "Again?"

"I must remind you, young mas—" The gooniest goon cleared his throat. "Last time we let you come un-sedated, you escaped as soon as we came to the first traffic light."

Freya giggled at that. Logan tilted his head in happy reminiscence. "It took you four days to find me. Good times."

"If you would," the gooniest goon said, nodding at Logan's arm.

"Fine," Logan huffed and peeled back a sleeve. Promptly they drugged, handcuffed, and whisked him away. Logan looked behind him as his vision blurred. Freya followed the procession, hands behind her back. She gave him a reassuring smile to which Logan responded weakly before his mind dimmed out.

[7 days, 6 hours, 31 minutes]

"Ah, the prodigal son returns," A deep, sonorous voice cold and hard as ice and steel called as the groggy Logan was escorted into an office of vast proportions.

A hallway of black marble led to a dais, upon which a Brobdingnagian desk loomed over everything. Behind the desk was a wall made of glass. From the other side the muffled roar of a waterfall could be heard faintly.

"More like he was dragged in, Father," Logan said, and keeping to his custom, was sure to accidentally kick up the corner of the long white carpet that led to his father's throne. "Really robs the story of all its meaning."

His father cast a passing annoyed glance at the rolled carpet, before he fixed his sharp, merciless eyes on him. Classic intimidation. Logan could barely suppress a snort. His dad was truly a visage of bloated ego. If one didn't know better, one might mistake him as a leader and a visionary. A lot of people did. His father was good at managing his image.

He was a businessman in his prime at the age of fifty-five. Body well-kept and a face resembling an angry hawk. Malcolm Specter's salt-and-pepper hair was immaculate and his stance exuded raw natural power. He approached Logan, hands behind his back like a well-postured tiger.

"Droll as always, Logan," Malcolm said before turning to Freya. He fixed what he must have fancied a charming smile to his face. "Freya, your loyalty is admirable, but you will want to sit this one out. What we are about to do is not for the faint of heart."

"Where Logan goes, I go," Freya said simply, her voice containing no small dash of resolve, which she knew Logan's father respected. Indeed, Malcolm smiled a real smile at her. It was thin and devoid of all warmth, but it was an approving one. It had been a while since Logan saw one of those directed at him.

Logan smiled at Freya too. He was more than a little relieved she had managed to convince the goons to bring her along.

"What exactly are we doing, Father?" Logan not so much asked as demanded.

"A breakthrough," Malcolm said.

A cold realization washed over Logan. "No, absolutely not! It's illegal!"

His father scoffed. "Since when is that a concern for you?"

"When it became an issue of my own damn body!" Logan shouted. He tried to think, but his mind was still groggy. He couldn't escape. He was on the seventy-second floor of the headquarters of MindTech LLC. There were probably six stupid goons guarding the elevator alone, with live ammunition for intruders and rubber ammunition for the only child of the CEO.

"Don't be foolish, Logan. Can't you understand what I'm offering here?"

Logan shook an accusing finger. "A way to control me. A way to mindfuck me."

"This is a gift!" Malcolm hissed.

Freya stepped closer and clutched Logan's arm. It calmed him and he nudged toward hers. She placed a gentle kiss on the side of his head. "What's going on?" she asked.

"My father wants to perform experimental brain surgery on me. Install an AI in my head to do calculus for me."

"The research is no longer experimental. You know this," Malcolm said, almost exasperated.

"I know only what you tell me. And that's what you think I need to hear for you to get what you want," Logan spat out.

"You saw the proof yourself," Malcolm said. "Our test primates. They learned to write with a computer in three months."

"Wow, that story was true?" Freya asked Logan.

"Of course it's true," Logan muttered. "Why would I lie to you?"

Freya poked him. "Don't be like that. You're melodramatic and exaggerate constantly."

"Frey, this is *not* the time."

Her playful smile waned. "Right. So, brain implant? Only in the Specter family . . . Is it safe? Is it good? Sounds kind of crazy."

"Of course it's crazy!" Logan said. "Listen to her, Father."

"Frankly, I do not care what people call it," Malcolm said. "This is my magnum opus. My legacy! You will have a one-of-a-kind advantage in the world to come, my son. We need to do this before it is too late."

"Don't want it," Logan said.

"What did he mean by that?" Freya asked.

"That is not up to you," Malcolm said. Then he snapped his fingers, and a bunch of goons swarmed them. "Time is ticking."

"Logan!" Freya cried out.

"Frey!" Logan yelled before another syringe was jabbed in his arm. This one took his lights out in an instant.

CHAPTER 2

[3 days, 2 hours, 41 minutes]

When Logan woke up, he found himself on the roof of the better of the two hotels his father owned. The same spot where Logan had once thrown a big party for Freya when she turned twenty. It had a beautiful patio, a swimming pool, and a bar manned by a fancy young girl in a tuxedo shirt. Janice was her name, if memory served. A sycophant to the bone. Logan never tipped her.

Logan checked his smartwatch. It was eleven in the morning. And four days later. His bleary eyes attempted to focus in the bright sunlight just as he found a pair of sunglasses waiting for him within arm's reach. There was also an assortment of fresh fruit, boiled eggs, juice, and even an Irish beer Logan had recently acquired a taste for. He figured Freya was to thank for this particular beverage finding its way to him.

He picked up a piece of ornately-cut kiwi and brought it to his parched lips. The taste was almost too sweet, but it managed to rouse him a little more. Logan took a look at his bearings.

He had an IV going to his arm and some sort of monitoring device beeping idly behind him. It must have changed frequency because his father turned from his laptop toward Logan's bed. Logan ripped the needle out and shut down the machine.

Malcolm Specter didn't say anything. He didn't have to. You only needed to look at the smug smile on his face and the way he twirled the amber whiskey he was nursing in his hand to know the man had won, as was his wont in life.

And what was Logan's lot? To be another cog in his father's giant machine. To be an extension of Malcolm's reality. There was something in his father's eyes that Logan had grown to know well and hate. There it was again. The man actually thought he had done Logan some great favor, but all he did was continue to cast a longer shadow to loom over his son.

Logan snarled. His father scoffed.

"Good of you to join us," Malcolm said and got up.

"How considerate of you to wait by my bedside," Logan said.

"How is your head?"

"Throbbing."

"What is seventeen times 34.4?" Malcolm asked as he took a sip of whiskey.

"Fuck you."

"For once in your life, indulge me."

Math had been one of those things his father excelled at. So, naturally, Logan had made a great effort to never learn anything beyond the elementary. He sneered at his father.

"Seventeen times . . . What, three? Or was it—"

Something happened inside his mind. At the mere thought of entertaining the equation, the answer suddenly came to him from somewhere deep—like a hidden trauma bubbling up. A disjointed whisper clearly directed at the half-heartedly-asked question.

Mouth half-open, brow furrowed, Logan stared at his father blankly. "584.8."

Logan's father grinned. Actually *grinned*. It shocked Logan almost more than his sudden prowess in math.

"Recount the number pi as far as you can remember."

Logan hated doing what his father wanted, but he was curious. He thought about pi, and it came to him as easily as his father's name. He recounted thirty-two digits before his father held out a hand.

"How do you like it?" Malcolm asked with mounting excitement.

Logan lifted a finger. "Don't," he said quietly. "Not yet. You did a fucked up thing."

"Did I?" Malcolm asked, a hint colder. "The way I see it, I made you into something magnificent."

Logan suppressed a significant flare of anger. He reached for his beer to buy time.

"Here's a thought," Logan said as he cracked the can open. "How about just letting me be my own person?"

"What about taking some responsibility?" Malcolm snapped.

"No thanks," Logan said and took a swig. "It never made *you* a better person."

"Never made—" He controlled himself. He breathed in and out once. Logan smirked.

"Do you know why I'm the richest person on this planet, Logan?"

"Because you're a ruthless son of a bitch?"

He showed another hint of a smile. "Because I provide the most value. I am the most valuable human."

Logan scoffed.

"You can deny it," Malcolm said. "But that is what the world tells me when I look at my company's stock price."

"Oh, I deny it," Logan snapped, then tapped at his forehead and let out a bitter laugh. "Most valuable, my ass. How many cobalt-mining pseudo-slaves died for this thing? How many blistered hands of child workers sleeping on some factory floor touched these circuits, Father?"

"Don't be a fool. The world is not a fair place."

"Because of people like you!"

Malcolm's expression darkened. "You talk of compassion, but none of your charities last for a year."

"Because you cut the funding," Logan said.

"After you ignore my advice on how to make them self-sustaining."

"They're called charities," Logan said. "Not businesses."

"You're such a child," Malcolm scoffed. "To think my son couldn't even float a revenue of one million for a year . . ."

"I didn't have the means to—"

"Well now you do!" Malcolm snapped. "Four hundred billion parameters! Specialized in vector calculus, algebra, trigonometry, and a dozen other branches of mathematics, thermodynamics, circuit theory, avionics, data structure . . . Need I go on?"

"I feel like you almost got a point across before you ran out of breath," Logan said and took a swig.

"I would have given you the goddamn world to hold in your palm. Every advantage conceivable. Connections. Money. I gave you all this and you've still done nothing with it. This implant is my last-ditch effort. We ran out of time. You left me no choice."

"You really don't see it, do you?" Logan said, trying to contain a snarl. "You didn't put a computer in my brain for *me*. You did it for *you*."

"I did it for grander reasons than my own ambitions, or I would have had it implanted in myself," Malcolm said, quietly this time. "Whatever happens once the timer runs out, you will be ready. Even for a total rebuilding of humanity, if necessary. I made you better."

"I am—" Logan said slowly, punctuating every trembling word, "—not a project for you to improve on."

Malcolm said nothing to that, only sneered and sipped on his whiskey.

"What are you two fighting about this time?" Freya emerged from the elevator wearing a white summer dress, looking as amazing as ever.

"I was just telling him what a great father he is," Logan said, smiling.

"I need another drink," Malcolm muttered and went to fix himself another whiskey.

"Thanks for the beer, Frey." Logan said and saluted.

"That wasn't me, actually. Your dad got it for you."

Suddenly the taste became a shade more bitter. Did his father have goons checking his garbage? There was a 71.25 percent chance of that, rough estimate. Why hadn't he thought of it before? Wait . . . seventy-one *what*?

"Are you feeling okay?" Freya asked as she sat on the bed. There were massive bags under her eyes.

Logan needed a moment to snap out of it. "Yeah . . . Just a throb at the back of my head. Looks like they kept me asleep for a few days."

"They did, yeah," she said and gave him a tired smile. "I can finally get some sleep. Wanna fly somewhere tomorrow, like— oh, never mind."

Logan turned to look where Freya was gazing. He sighed and downed the rest of his beer. A dozen people got out of the glass elevator by the other side of the pool. They each had either a suit or lab coat on, and all but the goons had a clipboard.

Great . . .

"Gentlemen," Malcolm greeted the group. "Good of you to come on such short notice."

Two of the suited goons remained at the elevator while the rest of them occupied a corner of the patio. Logan recognized the young agent, standing stiff and all-important two yards away.

The tired scientists formed a conclave around Logan's bed. Malcolm made a gesture to let one of the men speak. He was bespectacled, his lab coat covered with cat hair.

The man leaned in closer to Logan, arranging his stethoscope. Oof, he even smelled of cats. This was Dr. Rosenberg, his father's personal physician.

It took a while for Dr. Rosenberg to get his measurements. Blood pressure, iris with the diameter-measuring flashlight, the works. After the good doctor had acquired a few vials of Logan's blood, he took a few steps back.

The next in line was a woman in her late fifties, lips painted brilliant red, as if to distract people from the fact she was aging. "I would like to ask you about your verbal acumen, if that is alright?"

Still angry, Logan gave his father a tired look. He considered picking another fight.

"Indulge me, just for once," Malcolm said.

Logan scoffed and shook his head in disbelief. He snapped his fingers. "Hey, goon! Balmer, was it?"

The young agent turned from his place, looking at Logan, eyebrows visible from behind the sunglasses. His voice was kept even by a heavy dose of discipline. "Yes?"

"That's 'Yes, young Master' to you, by the way," Logan said and waved the empty beer bottle in his hand. "Be a good little lamb and bring me another one of these."

The young agent was indignant. "I didn't graduate the top of my class to—"

"Balmer," the gooniest goon said sharply.

Logan grinned. "Sounds like you're perfectly qualified for this job, then."

Logan assumed Agent Balmer was probably a great shot with a glock but he was pretty bad at repressing a scowl. He would need more practice if he was going to work for Malcolm Specter. The young man actually even looked at his boss questioningly, but Logan's dad just waved a hand. Agent Balmer bowed stiffly and started stomping across the patio.

"So," the older woman said impatiently, "verbal acumen?"

Logan never got to answer. Because at that moment the sky ripped open. A great black gash appeared in midair and the wind immediately started howling at a high pitch as furniture and people started lifting off the ground.

"W-what?" Malcolm asked, more outraged than scared. All the scientists, on the other hand, were definitely scared. They screamed as they were lifted off their feet.

[3 days, 2 hours, 29 minutes]
[0 days, 0 hours, 1 minute]

Logan started laughing. "Don't you get it? It was a trick. They didn't want us hunkering down. Oh, that's clever!"

"Logan!" Freya yelled and tried to reach him, but she flew past him, flailing in the air.

"Frey!" Logan called out. "Be brave. I'll find you! We'll get through this!"

And with that, Logan was sucked into the rift, and all sensation of light, sound, and touch was gone.

CHAPTER 3

Logan found himself floating in nothingness. Darkness enveloped him. He was weightless and blind, but suddenly he could hear two voices talking.

"Would you look at that?" one voice said, high pitched, excited, and somehow . . . electrical.

"What in Six Hells is it?" the other one said; it was a lower tone but fast and also buzzing with electricity.

"Some device. Pretty advanced for a human," the first one said.

"Well, shut it off. There are rules."

"I can't."

"What?" the second one asked, the low register taking on an alarmed tone.

"It's embedded in this one's brain. It'd kill him if I remove it."

"Oh great . . . Do we take it to the higher-ups?"

"You really want to do that?" the first one asked.

"No . . ."

"Let me just see what this thing— Oh no . . ."

"That bad, huh?"

"It's bad," the first one said and sighed. "This is like a . . . sapient memory bank."

"It's self-aware?"

"Well, it sure is now that we ran the protocol," the first one muttered. "This is gonna do weird things to the System."

"Old gods." The second one sighed heavily. "I am *not* putting this in my report."

"Me neither, but we can't leave this thing as it is. He'll develop too fast."

"Aren't we looking for problem solvers?" the second one asked.

"You know how it is," the first one reminded him. "If he builds a mega-city in a month, Levemoth will destroy them."

Logan wondered idly how he could even understand these beings. They didn't sound remotely human. He could feel some faint prodding in his head, a light pressure with twinges. Logan figured it should have hurt but it just didn't.

"Can you remove the knowledge?" the second voice asked.

"I have to try," the first one said distractedly as it apparently prodded around in Logan's head. "But the knowledge matrix is delicate. If we lobotomize a candidate, there'll be hell to pay."

"If *you* lobotomize a candidate, you mean?"

"Shut up. I need to focus. Okay . . . circuitry, mechanics . . . guns, huh? Well unless he figures some stuff out, those won't do much . . . Damn it!"

"What is it?" the second one asked, slightly alarmed.

"I can't remove any of this or it will mess with the general logic facility. If I just chop off half of what it knows, it's going to go insane."

"So, what's the plan?"

"I just need to lock them."

"Lock them?" the second one asked. "That would mean you'd give it a class!"

"I know what it means!" the first one hissed. "Any better ideas?"

There was a moment of silence.

"No."

"I'll just give it **[Engineer]**. I'll lock stuff like circuitry and explosives in the mid-tier."

"You're just going to give it a class? Right from the get-go? You sure that's a good idea?"

"What am I supposed to make of this?" the first voice snapped. "A sentient computer inside a human brain? I'm winging it. Speaking of which . . . Oops."

"Oops?" The second voice was alarmed. "What do you mean *oops*?!"

"Fiddling with the memory matrix *might* have touched the technology more than intended."

"Anything serious?"

"It's going to distract the candidate more than intended, that's for sure."

"Shit!" the second voice whispered. "I just got a ping. They're asking what's taking so long. They're sending a tier-three admin."

"Shit. Well, this is gonna have to do," the first voice said. "We'll just put him—"

"There's no time! We have six seconds. Just toss him somewhere!"

"I can't—"

"NOW!"

Logan found himself lying on the smooth, slightly damp floor of a cave. Well, after a cursory look it actually appeared not to be a cave, but more of a . . . dungeon?

Dim blue light illuminated the corners and seams of the roof and floor where the walls connected, like ropes of LED Christmas lights. Logan got up and investigated further. The room exhibited clear deliberate craftsmanship with its smooth stone walls and mathematical angles.

89.72 degrees. That's extreme precision. Wait, what?

Oh right, the AI. A part of Logan hoped his father had landed face-first into this world. What the hell had even happened? Someone or something had teleported him here. And there had been those two guys discussing . . . what? It was all bleary and dreamlike. The more Logan thought about the two people talking, the less he remembered. Something about the AI . . .

[Reconfiguring Neural Matrix . . . 1% completion]

"That's . . . interesting," Logan muttered to himself. That had been like a thought in his mind, but it had its own voice. A monotone, mechanical intonation that cut through the chatter, completely unlike his own inner voice.

All of this was certainly interesting. He had been sucked into another place. And that dream— No, not a dream. A memory. They had said he was a "candidate." What did that mean? What did any of this mean?

Well, I've got enough questions now. Let's find some answers.

Logan got up. Through force of habit, he glanced down at his wrist. His obscenely expensive white smartwatch was still there. The screen was black.

Not like I really need to know when it's time for afternoon tea right now.

He looked around. There wasn't anything interesting in the room. Nothing he could use at least, just rubble on the floor from a wall cracked an eternity ago.

The crack on the otherwise smooth wall was enough to attract Logan's attention, however. He looked at it and saw a mural of intricate craftsmanship depicting a crowd of people standing on a hillside, looking at a mountain half covered in bright white clouds. Beside the mountain, seeming to guard it, was a beast. It was blue and black, almost as large as the mountain, with a great maw like that of a whale, with thousands of tiny black teeth. A hundred eyes looking in every direction covered its head underneath a cradle of horns, white as a full moon. The creature's body was obscured by a dark storm cloud, raining black rain upon a great city, caught up in smoke, flame, and desolation.

"Jesus, I hope that's a metaphor," Logan muttered to himself. But a word echoed in his mind. *Levemoth.*

Now Logan had more questions and no answers. Not exactly the position he wanted to be in. He needed to think clearly.

Get out of this place, find shelter, water, food, and Freya.

That was as good a plan as any. Logan noticed a doorway on the other side of the room. The door itself had been half-decayed by time and was now mostly rubble on the ground and a chunk hanging off a hinge. The blue light coming from that other room was brighter, so Logan went toward it.

It turned out to be an octagonal atrium with a high ceiling and seven other doorways leading to other rooms. More beautiful murals adorned these walls, lit up by a giant floating crystal in the middle of the room. It pulsed and hummed.

"This . . ." Logan muttered. "I'm not on Earth anymore, am I? This is . . . Is it magic?"

Floating could of course be achieved by superconductivity, magnetism, or a steady propulsion.

Wait, how did I . . . ?

[Reconfiguring Neural Matrix . . . 2% completion]

But this didn't *feel* like technology. As the floating crystal pulsed, Logan could feel it inside his body like a second heartbeat. It engaged a sense Logan never knew he had. This wasn't magnetism; this wasn't the sensation of pressure on his skin. This was energy.

Logan took a few tentative steps closer to the crystal. There was a pressure to it, but it was gentle. Upon the ground were flecks and shards, as if chipped and eroded from the glowing blue crystal. They also glowed, albeit faintly. Logan fell to a knee and picked one of them up.

Even as small as the chip of crystal was, there was definitely power within it. It was heavier than you'd think. It had a similar heft to a lithium battery. But the energy within it wasn't similar in nature at all. Logan sensed richness and urgency within it. The crystal chip basically yelled "USE ME!" to Logan.

He didn't know what to make of it, but he brought it between his thumb and index finger to eye level. It looked like the chip had movement within it. Like it was *alive* somehow. Then the strangest thing happened. A small box of text appeared next to the crystal.

[F-grade Numa Crystal, 100%]

What the . . . ?

Logan picked up another one of those crystals and the exact same text appeared in midair. He tried blinking and moving his head. It still stayed above the little glowing crystal. It was only when he moved his hand that the text vanished.

Interesting . . .

Logan didn't know what the hell these things were, but his intuition told him that they were good. And with that thought guiding him, he decided on a new order of business. Shelter, food, water, *strange magic crystals,* then find Freya. And with that he started stuffing his pockets with the little chips.

He found a handful of the F-grade variants, which made his pockets bulge. But there was also a bigger chunk further away from the crystal, the size of a baby's fist. Rather satisfied with his find, Logan picked it up.

[E-grade Numa Crystal, 72%]

What does that percentage mean? Is it a charge? Where's an instruction manual when I need it? Hey, AI, got a theory?

The genie or whatever it was in his mind had no answer. Logan figured it was most likely a charge, but why he was seeing it like this was anybody's guess.

He looked around a bit more in the dim blue light and found a few more chips while clutching the E-grade crystal. Logan only stopped when he saw something stirring in the corner of his vision. A lumbering movement and a heavy breath. He froze and listened.

There was a rumbling growl and suddenly Logan made out two blue oval eyes attached to a large, indiscernible shape in the shadows. They seemed predatory and somehow . . . greedy.

"Fuck."

Instinct told Logan to bolt for it, and that's what he did. Wasting no time, he sprinted toward the nearest door. If it led him to a dead end, that'd be it for him, but there was no time to second-guess.

Something swiped at the space where Logan had been half a second ago. He had exploded into movement too abruptly, and now his other thigh felt sprained. Despite that, he ran. But he couldn't help himself. He had to know. He looked over his shoulder.

It was an ugly thing, black and blue, the size of a baby elephant, skin sleek and oily, with four long arms at the front and four at the back. It barreled toward Logan like a gorilla, sharp teeth covered in spittle and froth as it roared.

There was no door to bar its way after Logan dashed through, but thankfully the creature couldn't fit through the doorway. Logan ran down a long corridor with no turns. The blue lines on both edges of the floor guided him forward as he gasped for air. All the while, the many-limbed creature desperately tried to smash his way through the doorway. Logan could feel and hear that it couldn't do it, though.

He slowed down to a jog and grinned. "Ha, that's what you get for being a dumb brute!"

Then something happened that Logan's brain couldn't fully process. The creature's features morphed and shifted, and suddenly it transformed into two quadrupedal creatures. They looked at Logan with a singular sharp blue eye, full of predatory intent, their unhinged maw dripping with saliva. They stumbled for a few steps before speeding up to agile pounces that covered yards seemingly instantaneously.

Ahead, Logan saw another doorway. He sped up his sprint, lungs ablaze, legs screaming in agony. Still, he ran—survival instinct and all that. He noticed that the door he was approaching was whole and still on both of its hinges. With a spike of adrenaline, he opened the door, dashed through, and slammed it behind him.

Logan could faintly hear the creatures claw and scream, but the door seemed to stop them. At first.

They gave Logan just enough of a lead for him to see the next door ahead. But before he could make it, they had this door open and continued the chase.

He couldn't keep running. He was no athlete and that sprint for his life had sapped his strength. Those things were predators, and they would catch him.

Humans can't outmuscle beasts.

So when he slammed the second door closed behind him, he threw his weight against it. The two beasts hit it seconds later and screeched. The sound turned Logan's stomach. The monsters pushed until they were able to get the door to slit ajar. Logan roared and smashed against the door.

He looked around frantically. Nothing to bar it against them. They were too strong. Cold sweat ran down his back.

Is this how I die?

It was absolutely unacceptable. He had to find a solution. But he didn't have any tools. Then he looked down at the glowing blue crystal in his hand. He scoffed in disbelief. Well, what did he have to lose at this point?

He clutched the E-rank crystal and pressed it against the door.

"Abracadabra? Fuck this. Look! Magic the door please! Bar it. Make it really heavy. Seal it."

Suddenly a surge of soft warmth enveloped the hand holding the crystal. It hummed, like the big monolith had done in the atrium, and then it *dimmed*.

The door didn't feel any different, but when the creatures threw their weight against it as they screeched and pounded, it strangely didn't feel as urgent and visceral. Logan took the rock from the door and looked down at it. It no longer held any blue glow.

[E-grade Numa Crystal, 0%]

CHAPTER 4

Logan stared at the crystal. Then he looked at the door. The frantic, animalistic screeches coming from behind the door were thankfully muffled but still bloodcurdling. Tentatively, perhaps possessed by remarkable foolishness, Logan took his weight off the door and stood back, eyes and mouth wide open.

The creatures on the other side struck at it in wanton rage.

Thud. Thud. Scream.

Nothing happened. The door, identical to the one they had busted through, held for some reason. Logan looked at the dim rock he was holding.

Some *magical* reason?

Well, Logan wasn't about to wait until the power behind whatever the hell he had done to the door waned away. Without looking back, he went onward, hoping there weren't any more monsters lurking around in the shadows.

Fortunately that proved to be the case, and Logan quickly found that in addition to the magical blue light, some natural light was asserting itself as well. Logan came to an intersection. The ways left and right seemed to curve backward, both apparently leading back into the depths of the dungeon. The way forward formed an ascending ramp, the sun shining in from above. Logan wasted absolutely no time considering his options; like a man starved, he went toward the light with a singular focus.

A bright, humid afternoon greeted him outside. Little yellow birds chirped upon the branch of a nearby tree, and looking at him curiously. Logan smiled at the sight. This new whatever-the-hell-it-was couldn't be all bad. The birds were so plump that it was a small miracle they had managed to get on the branch. That was food sorted if it came to that. Birds that fat also hinted at an environment rich in resources.

Indeed, as Logan looked around, he found himself in a lush forest. It wasn't exactly a jungle, but it was thick and wild with a myriad of colors and smells.

Nearby was a thick shrubbery of several tightly packed bushes, gleaming black berries studded upon it. Fighting over them, jumping from one branch to another, were two of the smallest monkeys Logan had ever seen. They were the size of squirrels and their tails each had a single *hand* with which they jumped from one branch to another, as they gibbered and chased each other around.

Now, Logan wasn't stupid, despite what his dad sometimes suggested. He knew there was a reasonable chance that if he just put something in his mouth haphazardly, he might end up on the ground, frothing at the mouth. Even if the monkeys clearly thought the berries valuable, they could be immune to them, if they were poisonous to humans. But Logan also knew that he needed to take calculated risks.

He went up to the bushes, which scared the monkeys off. Logan picked up a berry and crushed it between his fingers. The scent was sweet and rather neutral, resembling a blueberry.

"Okay, Genie. Do an assessment or something. Are these edible?"

[Reconfiguring Neural Matrix . . . 3% completion]

That was the only answer Logan got.

"What good are you even?" he muttered to himself. "Okay let's try another way."

He took out one of the blue crystal chips from his pocket and plucked a few berries in his other hand. "Shazam. Detoxify these. Make them edible."

The crystal appeared to have no effect. Logan looked at it.

[F-grade Numa Crystal, 100%]

"In hindsight, I should have checked the charge first . . ."

Logan shrugged. He had taken all the precautions available. His instincts told him the berries were kosher, so he ate one. It was sweet and had a strange fresh aftertaste, like sucking on the needle of a pine tree. Logan made the executive decision of taking his shirt off and tying the sleeves on his neck, to form a hip pouch. He filled said pouch with these berries and ate half a handful.

"Unless these are super deadly, this amount should just make me ill, if anything."

With the immediate threat of dehydration and starvation staved off, Logan took another look around. The sun was shining in the sky. Or *a* sun. Logan didn't want to make things too complicated, so "the" sun it was. This was probably another planet. While Logan wasn't the most acclaimed biologist known to man, he didn't recognize any of the flora or fauna around. Not to mention the sun was more orange than he was accustomed to.

Well, all of this is really interesting, but what I need to find is my people. Freya's the one I want, but I'd even settle for my old man now.

Logan tried prompting the Numa crystals by suggesting they somehow help him find people. Nothing happened. He needed to understand them better. Just trying everything and anything he could with them seemed like a good start. They had worked with the door. That had been a literal lifesaver. But not with the berries. Probably because the berries were edible. Logan wasn't feeling any sort of ill.

The chance of a false positive in this scenario is approximately 87 percent.

"Sheesh," Logan muttered. "Talk about intrusive thoughts."

Since Logan had nothing better to do but pick a direction and walk toward it, that was exactly what he did. The sun felt pleasant against his shirtless skin, and he ventured to grab half a handful of some of the berries he had collected.

Strange sights surrounded him. There were tall palm trees with rough plated bark that extended thirty yards into the air. On the top branches, red fruits dangled from thin green ropes. A flock of big black birds like vultures were resting on the ground next to a small pond. The pond was green and bubbled idly like a witch's cauldron.

"Probably not good for drinking . . . Sulphur?"

Rich methane deposit. Location memorized.

"Right . . . This is going to take time to get used to."

The vulture-like birds suddenly cawed as if in terror and took to flight. A green feline the size of a panther had pounced and was now ripping into an unfortunate bird. The cat didn't look particularly strange, apart from being green, clearly for camouflage. But it still made Logan's adrenaline pump again. As beautiful as this world might be, there were still predators around.

It looks happy enough with its prey, but I'm not gonna stick around to find out if it wants dessert.

Logan wasn't about to run off mindlessly. The cat had actually glanced at him but was too busy ravaging the bird to give him a second look. That was fine by Logan. He carefully kept watch between the cat and where he was heading. Eventually he walked through a copse of leathery leaves and lost the cat.

Yeah, so there's predators. I need weapons. Can I use these Numa crystals as weapons? What if I tell them to explode when they hit someone? Would that work? One way to find out . . .

"Simsalabim! Make it explode when it hits something. Make it go boom."

Logan threw a crystal chip a few yards away at a mossy rock where the green grass wasn't terribly long. Nothing happened. He shrugged. It had been worth a try. Logan went and searched around for where he had thrown the chip. Even though he didn't quite understand what he was dealing with, he understood enough to realize that these things were *valuable*.

He sat down on the rock and grabbed another handful of berries. As Logan idly munched on them, he rubbed the little crystal between his fingers and pondered the situation.

Okay, so it won't work if it isn't needed, as proven with the berries. But it worked with the door. Why? It didn't work as an explosive . . . Why? Because it was alone?

There was no catalyst? It needs something to work on? I have a few of these . . . Let's do a simple test.

Logan got up and walked around. After a bit, he found a hefty stick on the ground under a robust tree. He picked it up, crouched, and pressed a Numa crystal against it with his thumb.

"Bibbidi Bobbidi— Okay, yeah, not doing that. Make this stick a spear. Make it sharp, smooth, straight, and hard."

The crystal in Logan's hand immediately came to life. It hummed and Logan could feel the energy within it. Then it went dim and the stick *morphed*, becoming like flowing liquid as it took a new form. It was still a stick, but it was somewhat smoother and straighter.

"Holy shit," Logan muttered as he quickly stuffed a hand in his pocket.

After two more F-grade crystals were spent, Logan had a smooth little spear, a smidge over a yard long, in his hand.

"I guess it's more of a javelin. Hey, smart guy, how's the aerodynamics on this?"

[Reconfiguring Neural Matrix . . . 7% completion]

[Formulating linear regression model . . .]

[Calculating the average RMSD . . .]

[Evaluating the drag coefficient . . .]

"What the . . . ?"

[The root mean square deviation is approximately 4.3 millimeters. Drag coefficient is approximately 0.3. This one suggests using another Numa crystal to bring these values down.]

Logan stared blankly at nothing in particular. He hadn't expected it to . . . well, do whatever insane thing it had just done. Like any self-respecting person with a life outside of a coffee-stained notebook, he had no idea what sort of sorcerous gibberish the device in his head had just produced. Despite his gargantuan flaws, his father was a smart man, and he was really good at exploiting even smarter men, so this ridiculous thing in his brain was probably right.

"What kind of adjustments should I make?"

The AI explained it to Logan. Logan demanded a simpler explanation. That prompted another matrix reconfiguration. Logan got a simpler explanation. Not by much, but enough to understand what the hell the hardware was talking about.

And with that, Logan shrugged and used another F-tier crystal and willed the javelin to be straighter by 4.3 millimeters, shifting 4 percent of its thickness into length. It did so in his hands, apparently taking on the proportions Logan had asked for.

[Level Up!]
[Class options available]

CHAPTER 5

Two floating boxes of text hovered in Logan's vision. This wasn't the AI, was it? No. Didn't feel like it. Logan swiped his hand at the text. The boxes moved to the corner of his vision and minimized. Well, that was interesting. Logan played around with them, swishing them here and there within his vision. After a few moments of air hockey, he tapped one of the boxes, and a long repository of English text appeared before him:

[Please choose a class. If you want to search for a specific class subvocalize the following: "Search (example). Would you like to search for a class or review the classes the System suggests you take?]

A class? What?! I suppose magic crystals weren't strange enough. Am I in a video game? Oh, Father is just gonna love this. I really hope he's still alive, so he can suffer through this.

At a first glance the list of classes appeared in alphabetical order, offering choices such as **[Alchemist] (unlocked)**, **[Arcanist] (unlocked)**, **[Archer]**, **[Artist] (suggested)**. Logan swiped with a finger, and as the list scrolled down he saw classes such as **[Carpenter]**, **[Duelist]**, **[Elementalist] (unlocked)**. There were hundreds, all the way down to **[Warlock] (unlocked)**. Most of the choices were grayed-out. Only the ones that were unlocked or suggested to him seemed to be available. Logan figured if he had gained a level using a bow, the **[Archer]** class would have been unlocked for him as well. Interestingly, most class titles alluding to magic seemed to be unlocked. That made Logan smirk.

Let me get this straight. I got transported to basically a completely new reality with magic and monsters. And I assume so did the rest of humanity, because everyone had that timer. So that means we're . . . starting over? I just wish I could see the look on Father's face right now.

Logan, on the other hand, was grinning. He was all for shaking up the status quo. Magic seemed fun as hell. He looked at the javelin in his hand. He wasn't quite certain what it was capable of, but within moderate bounds, only creativity could be the limit. Logan liked that.

"Okay, show me the suggested classes, then."

A much shorter list appeared:

[Artificer]

[Artist]

[Bard]

[Rogue]

"Huh," Logan muttered. "That's a lot less than I thought. Why have these specific classes been suggested to me?"

[The System has determined that the candidate has a natural aptitude toward these classes and will likely level them faster.]

"Alright, so it's better to choose one of these, huh?"

There was no response, but Logan didn't mind. Tapping the classes brought up another screen which explained what each one entailed. The descriptions were pretty much what he expected.

Okay, **[Artist]** *just plain sucks. Apparently your creations can inspire mood and affect thoughts. Sounds fishy as hell to me and not something you'd need in a rebuild for a thousand years. I'm personally offended by being offered the* **[Rogue]** *class, so we're not even going there.*

That left him with the two magical classes as options. **[Bard]** seemed to be a mixed bag. The description disclosed abilities used to disorient enemies and un-fatigue allies, along with uncanny proficiency with music and arts. It was basically **[Artist]** but with actually interesting things tacked on, specifically magic.

Meanwhile, **[Artificer]** had a particularly interesting description:

[The Artificer is a maestro of magical artifacts. He is a craftsman, specializing in the shaping and making of arcane items such as magical wands or pocket-dimension containers. Artificer can also specialize in the enhancement of mundane items' natural properties, such as magically hardening a shield or sharpening a knife. Warning: This class is extremely reliant on Numa crystals for full functionality.]

Logan looked at the javelin in his hand. Then he reread the class description.

With this AI, I could craft crazy good stuff, right? I wouldn't need to painstakingly learn all of basic mechanics. The AI can apparently eyeball tight measurements and can probably estimate stuff like the heat of a fire, so I'd know when it's hot enough to smelt iron or that sort of thing. Yeah, this is one hell of a combo, isn't it?

And I have Numa crystals too, to boot. So this is pretty ideal.

Instinctively, Logan put a hand on his still-bulging pocket, as one would check one's keys before closing a door. He had used a few of the crystals, and he would probably need to use plenty more just to test stuff and level up his class. That felt weird to think about. He now had a class that would essentially define his existence in this new reality. What if he regretted it? What if he needed to pick up something like **[Hunter]** later to survive?

No crying over spilled milk. I've never been one to regret or second-guess myself, and I sure as hell won't start now. If there is any wisdom I actually learned from Father, it's that decisiveness is key.

Logan picked the **[Artificer]** class.

[Class chosen]
[Level Up!]
[Artificer Level 1]
[Class Skill Acquired: Empower]
Attributes:
Potency: 1
Efficiency: 1
Durability: 1
Control: 1
Focus: 1
Subclasses:
[Transmutation]: 1
[Enchantment]: 1
Class Skills:
[Empower]: 1
General Skills:
N/A

A fresh, tingling sensation rushed across Logan's body. It was a sweet feeling that almost had a taste to it, rich and refreshing, like a mojito under the Mexican sun. This sweet liquid feeling washed over him, imparting Logan with some knowledge, some intuition that he couldn't quite grasp. But he knew for certain that there was something new there under the surface.

Now, that definitely warranted a closer look. Logan was sure these Stats and skills would define him as a person in this new reality. He needed to lean into that, and he was nothing if not adaptable. And this was the time to prove it.

After wandering around a bit, he found a nice stick to make another javelin out of. Logan plucked a Numa crystal from his pocket and brought it to the stick. It glowed softly and Logan found to his surprise that while the first stick had eaten three of his precious crystals to morph into something resembling a weapon, now only a single crystal sufficed.

Logan quickly consulted the AI for some measurement optimization and used another crystal to fine-tune the weapon.

[Subclass Level Up!]
[Transmutation Level 2]
[Attribute Level Up!]
[Control: 2]

Oh, that felt good.

The notifications were followed up by an interesting physical sensation, a pleasant twinge in his brain that ran down his spine, like cool minty water with a hint of sugar. Logan smiled at that. This world was rubbing off on him.

He was satisfied to note the two javelins fit well in his hand. It felt good to be equipped with weapons in this wild new world. They made him feel more secure. Logan hoisted the weapons over his shoulder and got serious again.

Unless **[Transmutation]** meant he could turn grass into food, Logan had some immediate issues to deal with.

He still had a handful or two of berries left. He could hunt for small game with his javelins. That might be awkward, but maybe the AI might help him aim. That needed testing. While Logan was no slouch physically speaking, he wasn't a damn specimen like those agents his father employed.

Water was sure to be found somewhere reasonably close enough. The forest around him was just so damn rich. Either that or it had to rain constantly. Logan looked up at the sky. It was almost a clear cerulean blue with but a few wisps of thin white clouds idly fleeting in the wind.

Worst-case scenario, the berries will hydrate me.

Looking at the sun, Logan figured he had a few more hours before dusk. By then he'd rather be sitting somewhere safe to wait out the morning.

There's surely predators about, right? Cats, snakes? Trees are bad. Crazy monsters that dissolve into two. Caves are bad. So, where's safety?

The unfortunate reality was that Logan knew very little.

Well, at least I have two sharp sticks . . .

He knew he still had to make a decision. His options were to wander around aimlessly and hope Freya was teleported in his general vicinity and not five hundred miles away. Or he could set up shelter, food, and a measure of safety.

Yeah, it's not much of a choice when you give it half a thought, now is it? I'll start looking for Freya tomorrow, unless setting up basic survival takes longer than I think it will. Probably will, to be fair . . . I don't even have a knife on me.

The first order of business was finding water. Logan was sure that some stupid internet guide somewhere had said that the most important thing to secure was shelter, but if you built a shelter fifteen miles away from the closest water source, you were going to die of stupidity.

So Logan chose a direction that he hadn't come from and started walking toward it. Finding even the smallest stream would do. Yeah, he could chew leaves and eat berries, but if he could just find a water source, it would make his life significantly easier. Didn't have to be the Fountain of Youth. Anything that wouldn't make him shit bricks an hour later would do.

As it happened, it didn't take Logan long to find a little wellspring of water forming a bubbling puddle, from which two little streams went off in different directions. Logan rushed to it and started scooping up the water. He quenched his thirst and then some, knowing that it'd be better to go overboard now, as he had no container at hand.

He was just about finished when he heard a rustling in the bushes. A sense of danger washed over him. With reflexes he didn't know he had, he rolled to his side and dodged the pouncing green cat's extended claws by an inch.

CHAPTER 6

The green cat attacked ferociously. Logan kicked it away, but it managed to swipe at him. The beast cut his leg and a bit of blood sprayed out. Logan gasped in pain. The claws were a solid two inches, now tipped with his blood. The cut wasn't deep, but Logan had no time to wonder at that.

He yelled at the cat in fear and anger and swished at the air in front of him with the javelins, one in each hand. The cat growled and began circling Logan. He matched the cat's movements and watched its alert yellow eyes and the haunches at its back. Whenever they rippled, that's when the cat would try to jump at him.

Logan noticed a large boulder, about six or seven feet tall, close to a tree with a very convenient nearby branch. Climbing up it would most likely be his best bet.

[If the initial dodge is successful, the chance of a fast enough climb is 66.2%.]

That's less than Logan would have liked. He weighed his options as the cat weighed him. He tried veering closer to the boulder as he aggressively shoved a javelin in the predator's general direction. It hissed and swiped at the stick. That was enough to prompt a frustrated attack. The cat lunged at him. Logan swatted at it with a javelin as if it was a club and then tossed the shirt-pouch at it.

The cat swiped at it, and it caught its claws.

Perfect.

Logan sprinted, tossed his javelins onto the boulder, and climbed the tree. His heart jackhammered. He felt like the cat would jump at his back and bite his neck any second now, yet he managed to scramble up the branch and onto the boulder half a heartbeat before the cat attacked. Instead of his neck, the beast managed to swipe at his leg. Again, there was pain, but it was not the sort of gash he'd expected.

The cat yowled in frustration and started circling the boulder. Logan tried to get his incessant trembling under control. His eyes never left the cat's as he groped for the javelins. He grabbed one and stood up, lifting the weapon above his shoulder.

Hey, Genie, if you can improve my aim like you can my reflexes, now's the time.

The green cat kept prowling around the rock, looking for an entry that wasn't there. Eventually, it seemed to give up, yawning and sitting down on its haunches. As soon as it did, Logan threw the javelin, hitting the beast's chest smack dab in the center. The cat yowled, clearly in pain.

[General Skill obtained: Marksmanship]
[Marksmanship Level 1]

"Hell yes!"

But despite the clean hit, the cat swiped and struggled against the javelin and eventually extricated it from its chest. A trickle of blood ran down the puffed-up green hair between its front legs. Logan stared at it in disbelief.

What the hell is going on?

Logan looked down at the wound on his thigh. He ripped up some of the cloth and looked down. It wasn't even a proper wound. A nasty, itchy scratch, yes, and it *was* bleeding, the warm, red fluid slowly running down his leg. But the wound was not something you'd expect from an encounter with such a killing machine.

Logan considered the situation. It didn't take all that long. It was obvious really. Somehow, for some reason, whatever laws of physics had been at play on planet Earth no longer applied here.

Great. Just great.

The cat might not rip him apart in two seconds as would have happened in Logan's old reality, but he was sure it would mess him up in a straight-up fight. Logan took the Numa crystals out of his pocket, placed them on a patch of moss on the boulder, and removed his pants, all the while carefully watching the cat below.

He used the leftover javelin's sharp head to cut a piece of a pant leg to tie up the bleeding wound on his thigh. It was tight and uncomfortable, but it got the job done. The cat attacked again. This time Logan wasn't quite as ready. The beast found purchase on a crack in the boulder. It came two feet away and let off a primal growl and swiped at Logan. The claw came close. Way too close.

Fear gripped Logan, but he overcame it. Still sitting, he picked up the remaining javelin with both hands and delivered a horizontal baseball smash at the cat's face. It swiped at the air inches away from Logan's own face as it fell, yowling in rage.

Logan needed to act fast. He wasn't exactly well-fed or rested. He looked at the Numa crystals next to him. It would be stupid to try his luck by wantonly throwing the last javelin. He had to magic his way out of this situation.

The green cat suddenly lunged upward, yowling, claws extended. Logan managed to deliver a kick to its face, and it fell down on its side. Logan felt a humming of blood and adrenaline in his ears.

I have to figure out a solution before this bastard figures out it should climb the tree to attack me. Any ideas, Parasite-Bot?

[Reconfiguring Neural Matrix . . . 9% completion]

[There are unknown variables, but increasing the overall weight of the weapon and the density and hardness of the impact point are the most-likely approaches to success.]

Logan looked around. There was nothing on the boulder except moss. His clothes wouldn't help. He could use his teeth? But that didn't sound appealing.

His eyes kept veering to the soft blue glow of the crystals. An idea struck him. He picked up three of them in his palm and closed his fist.

"Alakazam. Merge these three crystals into a javelin head. Make it sharp and hard and make it do real damage on impact."

Logan felt a warmth in his palm and the blue glow shone through his fingers. Cringing, he slowly opened his fist. A sharp object had indeed formed in his hand. The javelin head was cylindrical, but for the three wedges lining it vertically leading up to a sharp point. As the crystals were dense to begin with, it had a nice heft to it. It pulsed and glowed with a soft cerulean hue.

[F-grade Numa-craft Javelin Head, 75%]
[Subclass Level Up!]
[Transmutation Level 3]

Wasting no time, Logan picked up another Numa crystal, attached the small spearhead to his javelin and willed it to attach. *It worked.* Logan was so happy he could cry. Even better, the crystal he had used still had most of its light left. He pocketed that one.

Logan held himself back from instantly throwing it at the cat and instead picked up another crystal. His heart was pounding. He watched the green cat intently again. It was getting ready for another attack.

[Empower]
[Skill Level Up!]
[Empower Level 2]
[Attribute Level Up!]
[Potency: 2]
[Efficiency: 2]

The Numa crystal Logan had used for the spell went dim. Logan looked at the javelin in his hand.

[F-grade Numa-craft Javelin, 75% (empowered)]

Logan shrugged. Whatever that had done, it was probably good. Then he stood up, a grim smile on his face, as he faced the predator down below in nothing but his underwear. The green cat stopped circling around the boulder. It lowered, its haunches rippling. Logan looked down at the cat. There was something primally empowering about the entire situation. The cat growled and jumped at Logan. He threw the javelin.

It struck at the beast's head and a blue light erupted. A small explosion resembling a firecracker in sound and smoke enveloped the green cat's head. It fell down on the ground, bounced once, and then went limp and still.

[Skill Level Up!]
[Marksmanship Level 2]

Logan couldn't help but roar in jubilation. He pumped up his arms in glee and let it rip. Yeah, it would probably alert every green cat within a ten-mile radius, but the relief and triumph were too great. He shook his fists in the air, grinned, and shouted again, "Yes! Fuck you, green cat! Eat that Numa!"

Logan dropped down and looked at the aftermath. His weapon was still whole, the sharp, blue tip still glowing. The face of the cat had literally exploded. There was a charred red and black mess with broken teeth where the beast's face had been. There was also a blue glint shining out behind an empty eye socket.

Logan knelt down and sighed. Well, at least there was water close by to wash his hands in. He stuck his fingers into the eye socket with a disgusting squish and retrieved a small crystal.

[F-grade Numa crystal, 100%]

"Okay, that is extremely awesome. At least now I know how to get some more." Then he picked up his weapon.

[F-grade Numa-craft Javelin, 50% (empowered)]

Logan nodded to himself and grinned. This had gone better than he had expected. Logan had been all but certain that the weapon had been destroyed in the explosion. Instead, now it had two more cat-kills in it.

"And I still have enough Numa crystals left to make at least one more javelin. I'm not sure if I should spend them like that, but it's an option."

Then, Logan glanced up at the rock. Yeah, he should get his crystals back. And pants. Pants were surprisingly nice in a survival situation.

CHAPTER 7

Logan washed his bloody hands in the spring well and wiped them on his pants. He walked back to the green cat and pondered. The corpse had hides and meat. Logan had actually eaten tiger meat, like any self-respecting son of a billionaire in search of novelty, and knew it was more sinewy and probably even less tasty than a fireman's ass. Not that Logan had ever had that particular delicacy.

But to procure the aforementioned resources, one needed a knife and some measure of skill. Despite a myriad of experiences, Logan had never dressed a carcass, much less barehanded. Even if he managed to extract chunks of meat from the beast, he'd still need a fire.

Raw meat was better than starving to death, and Logan believed he could possibly make a fire with Numa crystals, if he were inclined to spend them on that.

To spend your Numa crystals or not to spend? Well, that's no question at all.

Hell yes, Logan would spend them. If this reality was structured around these skills and levels like a video game—and it certainly seemed like it was—then his foremost priority was to pump those numbers up as fast as possible.

He crouched and placed his remaining crystals on the ground in a neat row. After going over them one by one, he concluded that nearly all of them were at full power, except for the one which was at 70 percent charge.

"Hey, Brain Tumor, what's the best way to use these?"

[Reconfiguring Neural Matrix . . . 9% completion]

[Considering you now have offensive power to deal with the most dangerous threats you have encountered, it would be prudent to focus on avoiding physical damage and ensuring survival.]

That didn't sound as exciting as crafting all sorts of zany Numa weapons, but the AI had a point. Logan tucked two crystals into his left pocket: one fully charged, along with the dim one he had used to attach the javelin head.

Okay, these are for survival, like making fire.

That left Logan with ten Numa crystals that could be used for more interesting applications. Another javelin was the obvious choice. The one he had could only kill two more cats as it was. The first javelin Logan had thrown at the cat lay on the ground, mostly undamaged except for the tip, which was slightly blunted.

Logan tapped a finger on his chin, considering defensive options, like a shield. Shields were cumbersome. A fancy word for slow. While Logan's **[Common Sense]** wasn't level 100, it tingled insistently. Against agile green cats, slow got you killed.

"Hey, Tumor," Logan asked, "what do you think of the phrase 'sometimes the best defense is a good offense?'"

[Reconfiguring Neural Matrix . . . 9% completion]

[Oversimplification of reality. The best defense is assessing and listing all the possible ways one might get attacked, estimating the probability of all those possible outcomes and preparing accordingly.]

"You'd be fun at parties," Logan muttered. "Even father's sycophantic cronies have more personality."

Logan returned to the crystals. Okay, a shield was heavy. But what about a magic shield? Was that a thing? Worth a try. Because a heavy-ass traditional shield wasn't an option.

Wait a minute.

Slow would get him killed. By that notion, speed would keep him alive, right? What about Boots of Swiftness? Could he make a speed or agility enchantment? Logan looked down at his feet. By virtue of having been yanked out of a hospital bed, he wasn't wearing boots or any kind of shoes at all for that matter. But he did have socks on.

Socks of Swiftness? Okay. What about the shield?

That was obvious. Logan glanced at his wrist. He was still wearing his smartwatch. A grin spread across his face. A magic wristwatch shield? It didn't get much cooler than that.

Excited by the idea, Logan climbed back up the rock, just in case another green cat was prowling in the bushes. Then he took his smartwatch and his socks off and placed the crystals next to them.

The socks weren't exactly in stellar shape. In their previous life, they had been good socks. Sturdy, flexible, breathable, white. Now they were a soggy, green and gray mess. They were still intact, which was a bonus, but Logan wouldn't bet tremendous amounts of money on their long-term survival.

Besides, if I stack too many crystals into the speed enchantment, I'm just going to trip over myself, right? Better to use just a single crystal on the "Soggers of Swiftness" and use the rest on a cool watch-shield.

"Okay, let's get this party started. Shazam. Give my socks a speed enchant. Make the wearer of these socks have a magical speed enhancement, so they can run faster."

[Enchantment level requirement not met]

"Huh. I guess speed enchants are pretty powerful. Okay, so I need to earn my way to there. Not a problem."

When thinking through alternate possibilities to determine the fate of his soggy socks, Logan found himself grinning. Despite the rough situation he was in, he was having fun. His insane father wasn't breathing down his neck, and he was working toward something meaningful. Leveling up his class was something entirely his, and that made it more valuable than anything Logan had ever had, if you didn't count Freya.

"Let's go with something simple and practical," Logan said. "Wingardium Leviosa. Make these socks super durable. Make them withstand strain and wear."

[Subclass Level Up!]
[Enchantment Level 2]
[Attribute Level Up!]
[Durability: 2]

The blue Numa crystal Logan sandwiched between his socks pulsed with a warm surge of energy before going dim. The socks didn't look or feel any different, but Logan had gotten level-up notifications and the crystal was no longer glowing brightly. That made the case that the enchantment had worked.

Grinning to himself, Logan decided he wanted to give the socks some more oomph. He was accustomed to nice things after all, and soggy socks weren't on Logan's list of nice things. He sandwiched another crystal between the "Soggy Socks of Sturdiness."

"Hocus Pocus. Make these socks water-resistant. Make them reject all liquids coming from outside. But let sweat pass through the fabric, so it doesn't start squishing inside my socks, because that would be gross."

[Subclass Level Up!]
[Enchantment Level 3]
[Attribute Level Up!]
[Control: 3]
[Control: 4]

Logan twisted his socks together and gave them a squeeze. A few drops of gray water trailed down his hands. Pleased with his cool new socks, Logan put them on, sporting a mighty grin. Then he picked up the smartwatch.

Okay, this is going to be trickier. I need the watch to project a magic shield into thin air whenever I'm attacked. Is that even possible at my level? Maybe just a small, weak shield? Those are the parameters, right? How powerful and how wide the shield is?

"Hey, Tumor," Logan asked, "what should I consider when trying to make this magic shield?"

[Reconfiguring Neural Matrix . . . 11% completion]

[First thing to consider is the power output. This one has a working model with a simulated accuracy rate of 63% that can estimate the Numa crystal charge required to generate enough counterforce to nullify an attack of varying strength. Secondly, the radius of the projection field and the duration of the shield need to be considered. Given your reaction times, pulses of 0.5 seconds of shield projection would be ideal. Correction . . .]

[Reconfiguring Neural Matrix . . . 12% completion]

[Pulses of 0.8 seconds, to decrease variance caused by fatigue or distraction. These short pulses will increase the efficiency of the Numa crystal usage. A diameter of pro-jection shield would be ideally 65.8 centimeters given your stature, or approximately two feet.]

"Okay, so short pulses of two feet in diameter. Then it's just a question of how much power should be used. Oh, that's a whole other thing. Hey, Tumor, if that javelin made the cat's head explode, and we assume my skull is as thick, how much energy should the shield be able to absorb to make lethal force nothing more than annoying?"

[Reconfiguring Neural Matrix . . . 13% completion]

[This one does not have an accurate model yet, because the effects of the spell **[Empower]** *are still indeterminate. But if the javelin used 25% of its charge for the explosion, and taking in a margin of error for safety, 66% of an F-grade Numa crys-tal's charge should be sufficient.]*

"And what if I used my skill on the shield projector?"

[Indeterminate.]

"Short and sweet. Fine. We'll try it out first without **[Empower]**. And then I'll enchant it if I'm not dead by then, so you get your damn data."

[This one would be pleased by such an outcome.]

"Right . . . Well, that's all the variables I can think of. I think it's also enough to keep me alive. But how the hell will I manage to activate this thing? Man, there's so many variables. This is going to suck my Numa crystals dry . . ."

Logan thought for a while about how to formulate his incantation. He figured he really should stop being vague. He'd have to make the spell extremely accurate in order to not get haphazard results. Until now he had been kind of half-assing his requests. Once he got down what he wanted to say, he pooled all the crystals in a tight pile on the face of the watch.

"Make the watch project a magical force-shield that activates on the keyword 'Shield.' Make each activation last for 0.8 seconds. Make the force field completely round and the diameter of the field two feet wide. Make the shield pulse strong enough to absorb an attack equivalent to 66 percent of an F-grade Numa crystal's charge."

Logan pressed his hands on the watch. The pile of crystal shards upon the watch came aglow and the blue light shone through between his fingers. Then the refreshing, minty sensation surged through his head again, coursing down his spine, stronger now than before.

[Subclass Level Up!]
[Enchantment Level 4]
[Enchantment Level 5]
[Attribute Level Up!]
[Control: 5]
[Control: 6]
[Focus: 2]
[Potency: 3]
[Class Level Up!]
[Artificer Level 2]
[Artificer Level 3]
[Class Skill Acquired: Funnel]

"Damn, that feels good," Logan said. "Now, let's look at this watch."

The watch didn't seem any different at a first glance. But the longer Logan examined it, the clearer it became that there was a soft, almost imperceptible blue glowing hue emanating from it. It was definitely enchanted. Not only did the watch glow with the blue hue, but the dim Numa crystals were a testament to its success.

This item had been expensive; only three **[F-grade Numa crystals]** remained with charge. That put Logan at four whole crystals and one with a charge of 70 percent. He put them in his pocket.

As Logan strapped the shield-watch back on his wrist, a great rumbling sound in the sky startled him. He had never heard anything like it before, a clarion call echoing throughout the sky to all four corners of the world. It lilted up and down, turning into thin whines and low rumbles. One moment it sounded like a whale call, deep and sorrowful; the next, it was violent like a gust of wind, an angry howl of a demon screeching through the air.

Logan looked up at the sky. What he saw terrified him.

CHAPTER 8

There was no doubt. It was that great monster from the mural. *Levemoth.* It flew high in the sky, casting a great shadow over the land. It was *enormous.* A dark thundercloud covered its lower body. What was visible of it was blue and black, and it shone in the afternoon sun as if covered by a slick membrane.

Horns the size of trees protruded from a giant whale's head covered in countless black, bulbous eyes. The monstrous creature roared out another wail, which ripped through the air like an angry torrent of wind. Logan was sent tumbling on the ground by its sheer force.

The cloud around the creature's body began raining down black droplets which tore up the ground and toppled trees where they landed.

The great beast wasn't directly above Logan, or he would have likely died. But a stray black drop of the beast's rain fell down twenty yards from him. Some other drops fell through the canopy some fifty yards away. One struck the ground like a meteor, leaving a small but deep crater. Curiosity got the best of Logan, and he crept closer, clutching the javelins in his hands.

In the middle of the crater below grass-level was a deeply black bubble, like a giant, unbroken raindrop. It moved violently as if something was struggling within it.

Then the bubble burst open as a blue scythe ripped out of it. From inside the black, gel-like substance another scythe ripped out, both peeling the bubble fully open. From within it arose a hideous creature. Like its progenitor, the skin was sleek and mottled with blue and black. It had a sleek head that turned backward into a horn. Two scythes protruded from its arms—long, sharp, and shining blue. When it rose up, Logan saw it was tall and skeletal, with a protruding rib cage. It had long, sturdy legs with backward-bending knees and a lengthy tail for balance. Its face was nothing but a maw. No eyes, no ears, no nose. Just teeth. A lot of them.

As the sight was as horrific as anything Logan had ever seen, he wasted no time. He ran in the opposite direction. The giant monster in the sky blared out another clarion call and the black rain began to descend.

NopeNopeNopeNopeNope.

Logan glanced behind him and noticed the giant black raindrops falling down upon the forest to his right. He turned an immediate left, as far away from the giant floating sky monster as he possibly could.

If only it were that simple.

By accord of what must have been monumentally bad luck, the scythe creature had noticed Logan. Maybe it sensed tremors in the ground, who knew? Logan wasn't exactly keen to ponder that right now.

The creature behind him screeched out a dry-throated rasping cry, as if in pain and anger. Its scythes clicked on the ground as it began to chase Logan. Logan glanced behind him and cursed. The thing was fast. Really fast.

Logan lobbed the regular javelin behind him. It would only slow him down. He ran, trying to control his breath. Then something flared up in his mind. Maybe it was a subconscious notion of the cadence of clicks behind him missing a beat. Whatever it was, it was more than instinct. Logan threw himself on the ground.

[Reconfiguring Neural Matrix . . . 14% completion]

The creature soared through where Logan had just been, swiping at the air with its scythes. Logan scrambled up, just in time for when the creature landed and lunged at Logan again.

"Shield!" Logan roared and thrust forward his left arm.

A blue disk sprouted out of the white smartwatch. It stopped the scythes. The creature glanced off and lost its balance, as if repelled backward by the force field. Logan wasted no time. While the creature was still getting up, Logan let out an adrenaline-fueled shout and hurled the Numa-craft javelin at the monster. It struck it directly in the chest. The monster let out a hoarse cry as its innards exploded here and there on the grass. It took a wobbly step toward Logan and swiped at him with its final strength before falling on its face.

Logan stared at the sight with wide eyes, breathing heavily.

Move.

The adrenaline helped. Somewhere behind him, Logan could hear more of those hoarse screeches. He picked up his javelin and used it to crush the creature's skull. As he had expected, through the bits of skull and gore shone a blue light. Without hesitation, Logan picked up an **[E-grade Numa crystal, 100%]**.

To his dismay, he noticed that the javelin's head had lost its light. It was now dim. He stepped on one of the monster's arms and hacked at the joint until the scythe was almost loose. Logan sat on the ground, put both his legs against the creature's limp shoulder and pulled at the scythe, which still gleamed blue. Logan was pretty sure there was some Numa on the blade.

With an *oof*, Logan managed to rip the blade out from the meat and sinews. The screeches were coming closer. Knowing he didn't have much time, Logan ran off, a scythe in one hand and a dim-tipped javelin in another.

At no point did Logan slow down. He ran like his life depended on it, because it did. The screeches kept gaining on him. How the hell did the monsters know where he was? Good question. For another time.

Logan looked back; there were now three of those things chasing him. He had a lead on them, but their scythes clicked the ground at a rapid pace. If he didn't do something fast, he'd be dead. There was no fighting three of those monsters.

Logan's lungs burned. Breathing was becoming a luxury. His thighs ached. In the corner of his blurred vision, an outline of a building was visible. It was but an archway of cut stone, but it shone like a beacon of hope through the foliage of the jungle.

Logan ran toward it, the pain urging his mind to give up. *Just give up and die,* it said.

Fuck off!

Logan ran, pumping his arms. The leaves and branches kept hitting him in the face. He didn't care. The clicks of scythes were approaching. Hoarse snarls were already distinct behind him. They were ten yards or so away as Logan stormed through the archway leading inside a hill.

The blue lines snaked the seam between wall and the floor, giving Logan a direction to run toward. He took a right at the first crossroads. The angry click of scythes on stone was closing in. The hoarse raspy, dry screeches of the creatures felt as near as a lover's breath on the back of his skin. It pricked the hell out of Logan's neck hair.

A door. Logan had no time to think. He entered a room and slammed the door behind him. He dropped the scythe-arm he was holding and scrambled for the **[E-grade Numa crystal]** in his pocket. The creatures knew where he was. Tremors, heat, whatever it was. They threw themselves at the door and clawed at it in hungry rage. The door began to move, but Logan threw his weight on it, pushing the crystal into it.

"Seal this door. Make it a seamless wall. Make it impossible to open without saying the words 'Open Sesame.'"

The crystal gave off a warm glow and it dimmed. Logan wondered at that. It still had a decent amount of charge.

[Attribute Level Up!]
[Potency: 4]
[Efficiency: 3]

"I guess that explains it," Logan muttered to himself as he slid down against the door. The pounding, scything, and hoarse screeches persisted. Logan just tried to breathe. It hurt so much. The adrenaline was waning, but that only increased the pain. And a heaviness impossible to fight. Logan slumped further on the floor. One of the monsters threw itself against the door, but it didn't budge.

Logan gave an idle glance at the room. There were some tables, a blue glow, but no doors or other exits.

If I die, I die.

And with that, he lost consciousness.

CHAPTER 9

A thud against the door jerked Logan awake.

"Gah!"

The hoarse screeches started immediately, and the banging escalated into a cacophony of frantic violence. Logan cringed, wondering how long the door would last. He took a closer look at it.

[Door, E-grade seal, 87%]

Well, that's interesting . . .

The noise continued, and soon the text flickered and changed.

[Door, E-grade seal, 86%]

Yeah . . . things had gone from interesting to real damn scary fast. Logan scrambled up.

"Hey, Tumor," he said, ignoring the hoarse screeches behind him, "how long was I asleep?"

[8227 seconds.]

"Remind me, who is the idiot who designed you?"

[While this one's manufacturing and programming was accomplished by multiple entities, the person in charge of this one's design was Malcolm Specter.]

Logan smirked. "Idiot to the bone. Here's the thing, Tumor, next time I ask you about time, you're going to give me days, hours, and minutes, unless I specifically request something else. We clear?"

[Understood.]

"Good. So, how long did I sleep?"

[Two hours and seventeen minutes.]

"Right," Logan said to himself, trying to ignore the increasingly insistent noises. "Let's assume the creatures behind the door try to break down the seal at a steady rate. It's been two hours, seventeen minutes, and the door has lost 14 percent charge. How much time do I have?"

[Fourteen hours and four minutes.]

Logan blew out some air. It might be even more, since most likely the monsters had tried to rampage through the door, exerting a bunch of energy. It was also possible that the door just naturally lost charge over time, but that would result in the same fourteen-hour timer. He needed to find out a way to deal with three of those crazy scythe monsters by then.

Logan looked at his equipment. Almost five **[F-grade Numa crystals]**, an enchanted javelin with no charge left, his shield-watch which had proven very useful, and a blue and black scythe-arm, which had smeared Logan's hand with black blood. By now, it was crusty and was letting off an oily stench.

This is not enough for three of them.

The room was dim, but there were three floating crystals in the middle of it that provided a thin blue glow. With it, Logan could see his hands clearly enough, as well as the edges of the room, which were roped with the same network as any room in these kinds of ruins.

Logan approached the floating crystals. He could feel the pulse of them. It wasn't quite as strong as that monolithic crystal he had first encountered, but these three definitely held more power than the few chips in his pocket.

[D-grade Numa crystal, 100%]

Logan touched it, sensing the energy. He grabbed it with both hands. The crystal was warm. Yet no matter how he tried to yank or pry, the crystal would not budge from its place. Logan scoffed in disbelief and took a few steps back.

The floating crystals were clearly cut to many symmetrical facets, so there was more going on to them. They were constructs of sorts. Around the crystals was a circle of stone tables all facing the crystals. Logan placed his stuff on one of them and sat down on a tall cube nearby.

Time to take inventory.

Now that Logan actually had the time, he needed to take a closer look at his skills. Getting those level ups felt good and all, but he wanted to see where he stood. Not only that, but he wanted to see if he could get some clear descriptions of his skills.

He spent a longer time than he'd admit to anyone trying to get his class screen to pop up. What finally worked was saying his own name.

Logan Specter - [Artificer Level 3]
Attributes:
Potency: 4
Efficiency: 3
Durability: 2
Control: 6
Focus: 2
Subclasses:
[Transmutation]: 3
[Enchantment]: 5
Class Skills:
[Empower]: 2
[Funnel]: 1
General Skills:
[Marksmanship]: 2

Logan decided to examine the attributes later. He had a general idea what they meant, and it wasn't like understanding specifically what Potency entailed, for example, would affect his plans.

He checked up on **[Marksmanship]** just in case. It was exactly what he had expected:

[Marksmanship: Accuracy, expenditure of energy, and Potency
increased when handling projectile weapons.]

I don't know what else I was expecting . . .
However, his class skills were what he really needed to understand.

[Empower: Enhance the magical effect on an item at the expense
of Numa charge.]

That made sense. Efficiency and Potency probably played a role in how the spell worked. Basically, you could have your Numa-craft javelin and kill those green cats with it, even without empowerment. But if you wanted to kill these clickity bastards, it was most likely wise to use the skill.

[Funnel: Transfer Numa energy from one crystal to another,
or from a magical item back to a crystal, or from one
magical item to another.]

Okay. Now that was interesting. Logan glanced at the large floating crystals. At least he could make sure he'd have all his stuff charged up before the door opened. This was probably an ability in which Control played a big role. If video-game logic applied, the higher his level in the skill and all the relevant attributes, the less loss of energy during the transfer.

"How's that theory sound, Tumor?"

[Reasonable hypothesis. More information required. This one will monitor said parameters and notify you when there is applicable data.]

Logan rested his head on his palm, idly looking at the scythe on the table. The blade was a darker blue than the azure glow of the Numa crystals, but it was still clearly magical. Whatever that monster in the sky was, it had its own brand of magic. Now, Logan was no expert, but this darker blue was some distant cousin of the brighter Numa variety of magic.

No text box popped up, but that was fine. Logan looked at the curved blade, attached to a black and blue arch of flesh and bone. He picked it up. It had a nice heft to it. Logan got up and swung the blade. It was rather gross, but once he got over that, the blade cut the air with an uncanny grace.

Well, I'd still rather not get close to those assholes. I don't think I'm cut out for brute force. Besides, I already have this **[Marksmanship]** *skill.*

It took Logan a few seconds to string together the necessary thoughts.

"Hey, Tumor," he said, grinning to himself, "we're making a magic boomerang!"

[Reconfiguring Neural Matrix . . . 18% completion]

[Analyzing material properties . . .]

[Running a computational fluid dynamics simulation . . .]

[Running a comprehensive set of aerodynamic equations . . .]

[Running center-of-gravity calculations . . .]

[Calculating moment of inertia . . .]

[. . .]

[Calculations complete.]

After making Tumor repeat the instructions twice, Logan created a rough prototype. It turned out that designing a boomerang was infinitely harder than making something as simple as a javelin. Logan told Tumor he wanted to do this thing in phases, so that it could also get more data as it observed the flight paths and spin and all that nonsense when Logan threw the weapon.

Turned out throwing a boomerang was an interesting exercise. Logan quickly realized that throwing it in such a way that it would actually return was a ridiculous proposition. He'd first have to learn to throw it in a way that would actually make it dangerous.

[Skill Level Up!]

[Marksmanship Level 3]

After calculating the data from the throws, Tumor wanted Logan to adjust numerous proportions with minute measure. Logan did as instructed, exhausting the last **[F-grade Numa crystal]**.

[Subclass Level Up!]
[Transmutation Level 4]

However, the flight of the weapon wasn't as sharp as it should have been. Logan had a suspicion as to why. It could have been that his Control just wasn't high enough. But Logan felt it was something else. It felt *wrong* to only recite what the AI told him. It felt like Logan wasn't as intimately part of the process as he should have been, as the progenitor of the spell.

"Look, Tumor," he said. "This isn't working."

[This one suggests patience. Engineering is a product of trial and error.]

"Yeah, yeah," Logan said. "Hard work and all that. Heard it all before. But I prefer smart work."

[Unfortunately, your intellect is—]

"You sure are a design of my father," Logan interjected and scoffed. "For future reference; don't need to hear it."

[Understood.]

"Look, I don't think like you. Or my father for that matter. I'm this free, cool, bohemian, awesome, creative person. I'm a visual person. Well, sometimes. How about this, Tumor, can you create a hallucination of one-to-one proportions for me, that I can model the design after?"

[Reconfiguring Neural Matrix . . . 20% completion]

Abruptly, a red, translucent shape appeared in Logan's vision. He took a startled step back. The vision followed him.

"Okay, awesome," Logan said. "But can you keep it in one place, so I can walk around it and have a look?"

He waited, took another step back, and noticed that the red boomerang hologram indeed stayed still. "Perfect."

Now he could approach the design in a very different way. However, all of his Numa crystals were dim rocks on the stone table. Logan wasn't worried. His mind had been working on that during his boomerang engineering. He walked up to one of the floating **[E-grade Numa crystals, 100%]**, brought the dimmed-out fist-sized chunk of an **[E-grade Numa crystal, 0%]** and said the magic word.

"[Funnel]."

The chunk of crystal Logan was holding sucked in the magical blue energy, until it brimmed with a strong blue hue again.

[Skill Level Up!]
[Funnel Level 2]

Logan grinned to himself. "Oh, we're going to gain *a lot* of levels here, Tumor."

CHAPTER 10

The screeches, scratches, and animalistic noises coming from the other side of the door persisted. The monsters clearly weren't giving up any time soon.

[Door, E-grade seal, 57%]

Logan wiped a sheen of sweat off of his brow after checking the door again. He was hungry, thirsty, and tired. And he wasn't even close to being done with the boomerang. But, boy, had he leveled up! His **[Transmutation]** was level 6, his Control had risen to 7, Efficiency to 4 and Potency to 5. Even his **[Marksmanship]** had gone up a bump to 4, just by sheer force of throwing the weapon over and over again so that Tumor could get data.

The constant running back to the E-grade crystals to power level had pushed his **[Funnel]** to level 3.

All of this was great, but Logan had physical needs to attend to. He would have to take a break to test something wild. He could go without food for a couple of days, but he was getting seriously parched. He had a hunch and could only hope he was right. Could he turn stone into water with his **[Transmutation]**?

Logan picked up a chunk of rock by the legs of one of the ancient tables, crumbled over time. Next he needed a bowl. Given the size of the available rubble, it would likely be more of a thimble, but it'd have to do.

No levels in **[Transmutation]** but he managed to form a rough, ugly cup nonetheless. It'd hold two ounces of water at best, but better than nothing.

Then for the real challenge. Was this even possible at his level? Tumor wouldn't be needed, as this would be just a simple magical procedure. Logan couldn't help but laugh at the thought.

Just a simple magical procedure? If I didn't have proof this stuff was real, I'd say I would just say I was having a simple mental breakdown.

It worked. Logan moaned in relief. The piece of rubble cupped in his hands morphed into clear water and trickled through his fingers into the cup. Buzzing with excitement, Logan got up, replenished his crystals from the floating E-grade constructs, and gathered a bunch of rocks next to the cup.

[Subclass Level Up!]
[Transmutation Level 7]

After three cups of refreshing, blessed, magical rock-water, Logan could feel his body aches slowly lessening and his mind quickening again. The next thing he tried was making food out of the rocks.

[Transmutation level requirement not met]

Water's structurally simpler than a sandwich, I guess. Was worth a try. At least I have water covered.

After two more cups, Logan resumed working with the boomerang. Logan had gotten a decent hang of throwing it. It flew straight and would certainly cut a nasty gash on anything squishy. But no matter how he worked with Tumor, he couldn't get the weapon to return to him. He tried every wrist flick, every angle, every grip on its transmuted bone handle he could think of.

Naturally, Logan vented his frustration over the AI's inability to produce results. Tumor was adamant that the issue was no longer with the design but rather the way Logan threw the weapon. Logan naturally ignored such stupidity.

After making Tumor adjust the designs to match the way Logan threw the boomerang, he finally did manage to get it to return. Which turned out to be a horrible thing. The whizzing blade barreled through the air toward him with deadly speed. He ended up having to throw himself on the ground with a yelp to narrowly dodge decapitation!

Logan went to pick up the boomerang. It was a simple but effective weapon. Two feet of black and blue, metal-like substance, curving softly at an angle in the middle, attached to a piece of bone that Logan had transmuted into a handle.

As awesome as the weapon might be conceptually, it wouldn't do the job. If he threw it once, he could kill one of the three beasts—if he was lucky. The second might fall to the javelin—which he had recharged—but the third one would definitely kill him, no matter how high level his **[Transmutation]** or **[Enchantment]** might be.

Wait . . . I might not have time to learn how to use the boomerang, but maybe I can cheat my way out of this problem by enchanting it?

Logan recharged his spent F- and E-grade crystals. That one E-grade construct he had been using had finally been spent. It went completely dim. Logan shrugged and recharged the remaining two [**F-grade Numa crystals**] from the other floating construct.

[**Skill Level Up!**]
[**Funnel Level 4**]

Then he sat down at one of the tables and placed the scythe-boomerang upon it.

"Make this weapon return to the owner's hand after throwing. Make it slow down its spin when it returns so it's safe to catch. Make the weapon unwilling to harm the person who threw it."

[**Enchantment level requirement not met**]

"Damn it!"

The problem was that there was no way of knowing whether he could cast the enchantment after getting one more level . . . or ten. With mounting distress, Logan looked around the room. There really wasn't anything usable in the room. Just the tables, their rubble, and the floating crystals. Nothing to booby trap the door.

"I'll have to try, won't I?" Logan muttered and scuffed the floor with his foot. "There are plenty of enchantments I should be able to put on my stuff. Worst-case scenario, I'll throw enchanted pieces of rubble at them . . ."

Logan looked to the other side of the room. He had two more [**D-grade Numa crystals**] to use for leveling up his [**Enchantment**]. If he got creative enough, he might reach a high-enough level to be able to cast a Return enchantment on his boomerang.

Better get to work then.

". . . Make this boomerang steer toward the target's neck. Make bad throws swerve toward the closest target. Give it auto-aim, essentially."

[**Subclass Level Up!**]
[**Enchantment Level 6**]

". . . Make the weapon wind-resistant when thrown. Let it ignore wind and air friction."

The crystal Logan was holding dimmed in his hand. The blue sheen around the boomerang grew ever-so-slightly stronger. Logan pumped a fist. Then he redid the enchantment for his javelin.

[Subclass Level Up!]
[Enchantment Level 7]
[Attribute Level Up!]
[Potency: 6]

Logan kept running back and forth to the E-grade constructs to funnel power into his crystals. Using [**Funnel**] was wasteful, and when he could, Logan used the big crystals to enchant things directly, such as his boomerang or the javelin. But with this, he had no choice.

The tables were gone. Logan had used transmutation to make the stone as soft as clay, after which he had gone to the door to build something that could save his life.

Soon a spear-ring of rock stalagmites covered every angle around the door. If the monsters wanted to get to Logan, he'd make them work for it.

[Subclass Level Up!]
[Transmutation Level 7]
[Attribute Level Up!]
[Focus: 3]

"Make this stone spear extremely durable."

Half of an [**F-grade Numa Crystal**] went dim. Logan repeated the process for all of the nine spears fastened to the floor.

[Subclass Level Up!]
[Enchantment Level 8]
[Attribute Level Up!]
[Efficiency: 5]
[Durability: 4]

As Logan still had a lot of juice left in the floating crystals, he decided he'd enchant his pants. Durability, protection, water and fire resistance. Logan also re-enchanted his socks.

[Subclass Level Up!]
[Enchantment Level 8]
[Attribute Level Up!]

[Focus: 4]
[Durability: 5]

He also thought of something fun, and decided it was worth a try. He held a crystal in his hand and pressed it against his pocket.

"Make this pocket larger than it physically is. Make it a *pocket* dimension."

[Enchantment level requirement not met]

"Bah. Stupid rules."

[Door, E-grade seal, 11%]

The creatures were still sporadically rampaging behind the door, desperate to get in. Logan had about two hours left. Sure, he could re-enchant the door, as he had done to his socks and javelin, but there was nothing left for him in the room. The floating crystal constructs were mostly spent. One of them still had a dim charge of 15 percent or so.

This was it. There was just one thing to do. Logan had pushed his **[Enchantment]** to level 10 by exhausting the magic within the floating Numa constructs. He had super-pants, super-socks, a super-javelin, and at the door was a ring of spears magicked with sharpening and hardening enchantments.

Logan had even dug out some of the floor in front of the door to make it harder for the monsters to get a foothold. He enchanted the rest to make it slick and frictionless. That had finally pushed him to level 10.

With no options left, Logan went to the last floating crystal. If this didn't work, there was still a slim chance he could deal with the monsters. He'd kill one with the boomerang, run up to the shield ring, and stab some others dead with the javelin . . . But he really preferred to not have to get into close quarters with them. As fast and strong as they were, Logan doubted his shield-watch would last long.

I just need this to work. It would be so embarrassing to die before my father's dumb goons do.

Logan pressed the scythe-boomerang against the floating crystal. It still had a moderate blue hue.

"Okay, same deal as before. Give this boomerang a Return spell. Make it return safely to the owner's hand after being thrown. Make it easy and smooth to catch. Make the weapon unwilling to hurt the one who threw it. Make it slow down its spin when it's returning."

[Subclass Level Up!]
[Enchantment Level 11]

[Attribute Level Up!]
[Control: 8]
[Potency: 7]
[Focus: 5]
[Artificer Level 4]
[Class Skill Acquired: Repair]

The floating crystal went almost completely dim and some of its blue hue transferred to the blade Logan was holding. That fresh, minty feeling washed over him again as those notifications popped. He grinned and looked at his creation with great satisfaction.

"Let's try this baby out."

CHAPTER 11

Considering Logan's fourteen hours of preparation, the combat was over almost disappointingly quickly.

Tumor's time calculation was accurate down to the last second. When it told Logan time was up, the creatures immediately charged in, scythes extended. Hoarse screeches filled the room. The three slick, lithe creatures scrambled against the spears, one of which broke and lodged between a monster's ribs.

Without hesitation Logan threw the boomerang. It whizzed through the air and cut one of the creatures straight down, decapitating it. The weapon slowed and wobbled but slashed another creature in its scythed arm on its way back. Logan caught it smoothly on its return, just like he had practiced. By then the two wounded creatures were already past the barricade of spears. Logan threw the scythe-ring again. This time the monster at the front dodged. Logan backpedaled, his body flushing with sweat and adrenaline.

When the boomerang was returning, on the way it struck the one with the wounded rib in its back. It fell with a bloodcurdling screech, Logan's weapon sticking out from its spine. The creature twitched and snarled but couldn't get up.

There was no time to cheer. The last creature, with a wounded arm, came at him. It rose to its hind legs, towering over Logan at easily over seven feet. It struck down at him with both of its scythes.

"Shield!" Logan yelled. A translucent, blue umbrella formed around his arm. It pushed the creature back. Logan picked up his javelin and struck the monster in its abdomen. At the point of impact, there was a bright blue explosion and the creature screeched, its head snapping backward. The monster sliced a nasty cut on Logan's shoulder as it swung its scythes around in pain.

Logan gasped and fell, clutching his shoulder. The monster was hurt and sluggish, but it screeched and swung again, spraying black blood all over him. The stench was wretched.

Logan rolled on the ground to dodge, and kicked a leg from under the creature. It stumbled, falling on its stomach. Logan got up and ran over to it; ignoring the slicing pain in his shoulder, he yanked out the boomerang.

[E-grade Numa-craft boomerang, 60%]

"Well enough," Logan muttered. "Suck on this!"

Hen roared as he hurled the boomerang at the screeching foe, made of teeth
and blades. There was no grace or technique in the throw. None was needed. The
weapon had an aim-assist enchantment and the distance was maybe four yards.
The monster turned and let out a final horrible screech, slick spittle flying from
its mouth. The blade struck it straight in its featureless, faceless head. It went limp
and fell over.

[Skill Level Up!]
[Marksmanship Level 5]

Logan toppled down and let out a groan. He wasn't tired. He was *exhausted*.
He had been working almost nonstop for fourteen hours with only two hours of
rest. All the anxiety, all the fear of death had left him. Now he just lay on the
ground, eyes closed and breathing in the sweet, sweet air. Well, it smelled like
oily monster blood, but it was still good.

The cut on his shoulder hurt. He could feel a trickle of blood trailing along
his arm, but it wasn't enough to warrant worry.

Logan considered getting up and sealing the door with an enchantment. Then
he tried moving his head.

Yeah, no. I don't care if Levemoth itself barrels in. I'm not getting up . . .

"Tumor, wake me up in . . . whatever . . ."

Logan was happy to discover that he had not in fact been eaten by a horrible mon-
ster in his sleep. Instead, he woke up in the dark room with only the blue
Christmas light ropes giving it any illumination. The stench was overwhelming.
The creatures must have been marinating for quite a while.

"How long was I lights out?"

[Eight hours and fourteen minutes.]

Logan got up, stretched, and yawned.

"Yeah, feels like it," he said, smacking his mouth idly. "I'm hungry, let's get
back out there."

Logan completed the gruesome task of stuffing his hand in the black, gooey
heads of the scythe creatures. Above their mouths, where any reasonable creature
would have a face, the skin and tissue was relatively soft. It took some wiggling

with the scythe-boomerang and his hands, but he managed to fish out three **[E-grade Numa crystals, 100%]**.

It was hard work, and not only because of the sticky, oily blood which smelled rancid, but also because of his shoulder wound. Where the cat had done little damage beyond scratches, these monsters really packed a punch. Logan did his best to shrug it off.

I'm just lucky to be alive.

After he was done with the monsters, he drained the last light out of the floating E-grade construct with **[Funnel]**, filling most of his dimmed crystals with the soft blue light of Numa.

With that, Logan left the stinking room. He crept along the dark corridors, clutching his weapon and a scythed arm from the biggest monster. He had made the executive decision of detaching the head from the javelin, pocketing it, and ripping up another blue-edged blade. If he needed more javelins, he was sure wood was easier to find than idle monster bits.

When Logan stumbled out of the dungeon or catacombs or whatever the hell it was, he was so accustomed to the dark that even the soft evening sun made him have to shield his eyes.

"Tumor, what time is it? Okay, dumb question, scratch that. How long was I down there?

[Reconfiguring Neural Matrix . . . 20% completion]

[Just under twenty-five hours.]

"I'm starting to like these answers of yours."

[This one is learning to adjust to your personal needs.]

"You can use my senses, right?"

[That is correct. That is my primary way of collecting data. The secondary is processing what you tell me, but that data source is—]

"Yeah, yeah," Logan snorted. "Screw you too."

Logan walked around, looking this way and that, feeling uneasy.

"Just let me know if you see any monsters or green cats that I missed."

[Is there a percentage probability of attack at which you would like to be notified?]

Logan shrugged. "Anything over sixty percent, I guess. Oh, and keep an eye on any berries, water sources, or . . . hell, even mushrooms. I'm really hungry."

The first body of water Logan stumbled upon was a big, green and blue pond overlooking a cliff. There was a stream even higher above, raining a waterfall down into it.

As beautiful as it was, it had nothing on the creature bathing in the water by the shore. Skin amber-kissed by the sun, athletic lines of function and grace, and honey-golden hair, cascading into curls down her slender shoulders.

Logan wasted no time. He jumped down the cliff. "Freya!"

[The water depth is indetermi—]

Logan splashed into the pond and swam up, laughing as he did. He started paddling toward his girlfriend, with scythes in his hands. She yelped in surprise.

"Logan? Oh my god! LOGAN!"

"Frey!" Logan shouted between breaths. "I knew I'd find you!"

When the water grew shallow enough, Logan found his feet in the mud. It was soft and squishy, but his socks (which had also been enchanted with traction) gave him great speed. But something splashed behind Logan and moved even faster.

Something blue and black was surging through the water, sending up tall waves behind it. Logan's eyes widened. He had a good idea what kind of creature this was.

"Frey! Dive!" Logan said as he threw the scythe-boomerang.

For a millisecond, Freya froze to look at Logan but did as he said. With any less trust between them, a reasonable person would have just run. Logan sighed in relief when Freya's head dipped underwater.

A great snake, twelve feet in span, covered in black and blue scales, lunged at the spot where Freya had just been. That was exactly where Logan had aimed his throw. The ugly creature hissed in pain when his weapon hit it and lodged in the side of its head. The predatory blue eyes turned to Logan, ablaze with fury.

"Fuck you!" Logan shouted at the monster and ran through the water toward it. It turned its full attention to Logan and attacked, mouth wide open.

"Shield!"

Logan almost lost balance under the weight of the snake's attack. It, in turn, was tossed backward, and for a brief moment, fell on its back in the water. Logan wasted no time.

He scrambled toward the great beast and grabbed the scythe-boomerang on the side of the snake's head and twisted. The snake hissed in anger and wrapped itself around Logan's body, It squeezed *hard*.

Logan's shoulders popped forward, the strain and pain was increasing by the second. He still held onto the blade, but he barely had strength left to twist it. The snake-monster squeezed all the strength out of him. He couldn't breathe and slowly his vision started narrowing . . .

Suddenly several gunshots struck the snake. It hissed again and uncoiled from around Logan, ready to attack another target. Big mistake. After a hurried breath, Logan roared and pushed his weight against the blade.

"[**Empower**]!"

It worked. The blade, previously deeply lodged in the skull of the great snake, now cut through it like butter. Half of the monster's head plopped in the water like a heavy rock. The rest of its mostly erect body heaved and smashed down, sending water spraying in all directions.

The water turned black around Logan as he breathed in his victory. His eyes met Freya's and they rushed toward each other. Logan hugged her fiercely as she buried her face in his neck, the water covering all but her slender shoulders.

"Don't you ever leave me like that again," Freya muttered, eyes squeezed shut.

Logan squeezed her shoulder. "I won't."

For a moment they just stood there. Logan breathed in Freya's hair. It smelled like home. Her skin was covered in goosebumps from fright and the cold. He hugged her tighter.

Logan was done with the hug, but Freya wasn't letting go. He smiled and rested his chin on her head. Then from the corner of his eye, he caught sight of Agent Balmer in a tattered suit, looking at him in disbelief.

"You," the agent said coldly when their eyes met.

Logan smirked. "Nice to see you too."

"How the hell are you alive?" Balmer asked.

"Charm and luck. Something alien to you, I'm sure," Logan said. "I know you have no social skills, but this is the second time you've barged in to get a peek at Frey. Back off."

"I'm—she was—I saved—" Balmer sputtered, face flushing.

"It was my idea," Freya said, lifting her head to look up at Logan. "After we saw that thing in the sky . . . We lost Mark Cheffield . . . I wanted protection."

"Well, now you've got me to protect you," Logan murmured to her. Then he turned his head back to Balmer. "So you can screw off."

Agent Balmer glared at Logan, muttered something that sounded like "you're welcome," and stomped off.

Freya untangled herself from Logan, took a step back, and looked at him for a long time. Something between a wry smile and a smirk crossed her face. Eventually she scoffed.

"What?"

"You shouldn't be rude to him. Especially not anymore."

Logan sighed. "Guess not. Can't help it. He is such a tool."

"He did save your life just now."

"Bah. I had it covered."

Freya giggled. "Look at you, all shirtless and primal."

Logan flexed a bicep. "I know. I'm like Tarzan. But more muscular."

Freya laughed. Logan couldn't help but join her. It felt so good to see her. In the whim of the moment, Logan grabbed her and kissed her. She reciprocated immediately and for a moment, he forgot this new ridiculous reality.

Eventually they stopped and were left leaning their foreheads against each other, eyes closed.

"I'm getting cold," Freya whispered.

"Get out of the water," Logan said.

"But then I'd have to let go of you."

Logan scoffed, picking her up in his arms. She yelped but grabbed Logan tightly as he carried her out of the water. After placing her on the shore, Logan kissed her on the forehead and turned to retrieve his spoils of war.

CHAPTER 12

W hat the hell is that?" Freya asked as Logan wiggled the scythe-rang's tip in the snake's head.

Logan finally saw the glint of blue he was looking for and shoved his arm in there, retrieving the gem. "A souvenir," he said distractedly.

"You're going to have to tell me the whole story," Freya said.

"I will," Logan said as he washed his hands. "You know I live to entertain you, Frey."

"And no exaggerating!" she said wagging a finger.

"Me?" Logan turned and grinned. "Never."

"So, what happened?"

"So, I faced this mighty dragon, forty feet tall, shooting lasers from its eyes . . ."

"Uh huh."

"And I managed to steal one of its teeth."

Freya sighed.

Logan threw another smile her way. "Look, a lot has happened these past two days. Let me just finish up here. I'd like to process the snake. Is my fath— are there others?"

Freya was about to tell him, but just then, a procession of twenty people rustled their way out of the tree line next to the pond. At the helm was Malcolm Specter, tired and tattered, yet still managing to meet Logan's eyes with that hard, all-too-familiar, all-knowing gaze.

Damn, I hate to admit I'm sort of glad to see him.

"Where the hell have you been?" Malcolm snapped.

"Same as always, Father," Logan said, tilting his head and smirking. "Adventuring, chasing tail, having a ball. It's good to see you."

The hard creases around Malcolm's eyes eased, and he made a twitchy move forward. Then his eyes shifted to the people next to him. He pressed his hand into a fist, a gesture Logan had seen a thousand times, and nodded. Logan raised an eyebrow at that.

Did he just . . . ?

"Why were you separated from us?" Malcolm demanded. "Why didn't you seek us out immediately?"

Logan did his best not to snarl. Whatever joy of reunion was gone. "I've been kinda busy."

"Doing what exactly?"

"You know," Logan said, "I don't like that tone."

Malcolm looked behind him at the score of people. Most of them were agents in ragged suits, but the rest included scientists in ripped-up lab coats, the barmaid from the roof, and a couple of faces Logan didn't recognize.

"We will talk later," Malcolm stated.

"Yeah, we'll see."

"What?" Malcolm's voice rose to a dangerous edge. "Who do you think you are?"

"I could care less about your antics right now," Logan said. His father flashed his eyes and squeezed his hand into a fist again. "I'm starving. Can any of you make fire? I need help with this sea monster here."

Malcolm's eyes shot to the corpse of the giant snake. He looked at the decapitated head and the weapon Logan was holding. "*You* killed that?"

Logan smirked.

"Quite the tale, Logan," Malcolm muttered as he paced around in the tall grass.

Freya gave Logan the side eye. She was standing beside him, fixing a bandage on his wounded shoulder.

"I didn't even exaggerate!"

Freya raised her hands. "I didn't say anything."

"There's a thing called non-verbal communication, Frey."

"Well look at you, Mr. Jungle Survivor/Scholar," she said and winked at Logan.

He chuckled at that. Then he sensed the agents staring at him. The vibe wasn't exactly friendly. Logan just smirked and turned back to Freya and his father.

"So, what about you guys? Seems like you arrived here in a group."

Malcolm nodded. "We don't have as tall a tale as yours to tell. We faced some of those green cats you mentioned, as well as those . . . things."

"The ones that came from that big monster?" Logan said. "Levemoth."

"How did you manage to kill them?" Freya asked as she fussed with binding Logan's shoulder with a strap of cloth. "All your dad's agents had clips full of ammo, but they didn't do much. They killed the cats after half a magazine . . ."

"Speaking of which . . ." Agent Balmer muttered. He was crouched over a pile of leaves and broken branches, trying to build a fire. "Sir, I used my last bullets to protect the little prince."

"Take it to Senior Agent Takeshi," Malcolm said.

Logan tilted his head. "The little what-now?"

Balmer gave him an amused glance over his shoulder. "You didn't know? Your code name was Prince. It received an honorary addendum in the barracks."

Logan gave a glance at the other agents talking with each other a few yards away as they kept watch on the surroundings. One of them noticed him looking and spat on the ground.

Logan shrugged. He picked his ear and flicked it toward the agent. "I wish you were useful for something other than snark."

Balmer froze. He didn't turn, but when he spoke his voice had gotten lower. "You? You talk to me about snark and being useful?"

Ohhh. I hit him where it hurts.

Logan took a look over the agent's shoulder. Balmer wasn't making much progress with the fire. In the humid quasi-jungle, it wasn't exactly an easy task. That of course didn't stop Logan from giving the goon some well-earned feedback. "How's that fire coming along, Mr. Top-of-My-Class?"

"Screw you," Balmer said and got up. "How about you give it a try Mr. Daddy's-Useless-Spoiled-Brat?"

A rictus grin flashed on Logan's face, but he controlled it. "Clever. I can see that 4.0 GPA brain worked really hard on that one."

Asshole.

Logan crouched down and picked up an [**F-grade Numa crystal**]. It was a bit of a shame to use one for this, but it was going to be fun to see the dumb agent's jaw go slack. He whispered an incantation to make the rock grow red hot. It worked immediately and within seconds the damp leaves caught a smoky fire.

"You . . ." Balmer said when Logan got up. "You used some trick!"

"Sure did," Logan said and patted Balmer on the shoulder. "Be a dear, *little* boy, and keep the fire going until we can cook this meat. You think you can be useful that way?"

Balmer looked very much like he had a lot to say but decided against it. His face said the most of it anyway, and Logan savored it all.

Endlessly satisfied with himself, he sat down on the ground, leaned against his hands, and gave a look backward. Two of his father's goons were dressing the snake he had killed, using the raw scythe and Logan's Scythe-rang.

Logan had told them to be extra careful with the skin so that it could be used. The goons had made a face, but after a nod from Malcolm Specter, they turned sullenly and went to work on the carcass.

Malcolm scoffed. "Wasteful."

"The look on his face?" Logan said, closing his eyes. "Worth it."

"I take it you have a few."

"Maybe I do."

"Hand them over to me. I shall look into their proper use."

Logan flinched at that. A part of him was already reaching toward the crystals. He stopped himself and placed a hand protectively over his pocket. "I think I'll, for once in my life, have some leverage over you instead."

His father got up and slowly dusted his suit. "Logan, do not test my patience."

Logan got up himself. "How about you stop testing mine? I just saved Frey's life and fed this whole group. I just got the fire going and I provided the tools to process that big snake."

Malcolm was quiet for a moment. His weighty stare gazed upon Logan in cold calculation. "You should give these Numa crystals to me. I am the most valuable hu—"

"Not anymore, Father!" Logan snapped. "Gone are your riches and your army of henchmen."

Malcolm snarled and pressed his hand into a fist. "You keep failing to understand, I wasn't the most valuable human because I was rich and powerful. I was rich and powerful because I was most valuable."

"Whatever helps you sleep at night, Father," Logan muttered.

Logan and Malcolm spent their time arguing with each other until the food was ready and Freya practically ripped them away from each other. Logan got to keep the crystals for now and there might have even been some begrudging respect in Malcolm's eyes at his son's resolve. But Logan felt he must have just imagined that.

Regardless, he was content sitting on the ground near the fire as evening began to fall. The food hadn't been exactly savory, but getting some meat in his body really made a difference. Now he was sated and slowly starting to relax. Freya leaned against him, and his father was with the agents on the other side of the fire. Whatever came next, at least Logan wasn't alone.

CHAPTER 13

Seeing as Logan had had much more sleep than the others, he volunteered to take the night watch. There was quite a bit of muttering from the agents and the weight of Malcolm Specter's gaze was upon him for a long time, but for all his hardness and naturally low need for sleep, Logan could see his father was tired. Logan promised to give them six hours. His father raised an eyebrow at that but said nothing.

Once everyone was asleep on the ground, Logan went over to the dead snake. He had to admit one thing. Whatever opinions he might have regarding his father's goons, they were efficient if nothing else. All of the meat had been removed, cooked, and wolfed down. The skins were strung on sticks with strings cut from ties and sleeves. The washed bones were in a neat pile next to the skins.

Logan picked up the skull. It was heavy and studded with two rows of two-inch teeth as well as two larger fangs protruding over the jaw. The fangs had the same dark blue edges as the scythes of those faceless, clickity bastards.

These two frontal fangs could make for some pretty good knives. They're a solid five inches long. These smaller ones . . . I don't know.

[Reconfiguring Neural Matrix . . . 21% completion]

[After observation, it is reasonable to hypothesize that you can fuse materials with your abilities.]

"Huh . . . You do have a point there, Tumor. Changing the shape of something dramatically will likely cost a lot of Numa."

Logan glanced at the curled-up spine and ribs. If he transmuted the ribs into straight bone sticks, they could be used for building . . .

It's hard to determine what's more valuable. I have a limited amount of Numa to work with. We have water. We need food and shelter. Definitely shelter.

"Making axes and knives would be useful. I know folk used to make needles and fishing hooks out of bones in the old days. Wait, why didn't they ever make nails?

[Nails are too brittle a material to fasten heavy objects, such as wood or metal.]

"Right . . . But wait! Aren't these bulletproof bones?"

Logan wiggled one of the sharp, thin teeth out of the skull's jaw. It came off easily. Logan bent it and it snapped in half.

Huh . . . I guess it's the Numa that makes stuff hardier. Wait, if I were killed, would I have a crystal inside my head?

Logan decided to never find out, and instead produced an **[E-grade Numa crystal]** from his pocket. Then he detached the long fangs from the skull.

"Give me a model for a knife, Tumor. Something simple and close to the original shape."

The AI produced a red floating hologram, or rather, hallucination, in front of Logan. After some discussion about optimizing shape for durability and the length of the fang, Logan got to work.

I want to see the look on Father's face after he sees this arsenal of tools.

Logan sat there working amidst sounds of softly crackling fire, snores and wheezes, and the chirps and distant screeches of the jungle. After two knives, four fishhooks, four needles made of bone and a stone axe head, two crude stone knives and two stone hammerheads for shits and giggles, he leveled up.

[Subclass Level Up!]
[Transmutation Level 8]
[Attribute Level Up!]
[Focus: 6]
[Efficiency: 6]

Logan looked at the chunk of crystal in his hand. It still had a potent glow to it.

[E-grade Numa crystal, 63%]

It felt really nice to look at the little pile of tools he had made. And it hadn't even used that much charge. Logan considered enchanting the axe head with durability and sharpness but decided against wasting Numa on that. He sure would waste Numa on *something*, however.

Man, I'm getting fired up. This is fun. What else can I make? I want to do something for Frey.

Logan looked at the snakeskin remains. They definitely weren't dry, but Logan could magic them into usable hides. Freya was rocking a frayed summer dress. Not exactly ideal for a survival situation.

It took Logan quite a while to fashion the garments for Freya. Mainly because he prompted Tumor with several designs and made it consider endless variations on the point until it sounded slightly miffed.

When Logan had finally settled on a design: A simple skirt that would need to be cinched. Preferably with a belt stolen from a goon. Preferably from Balmer.

While fashioning the leather with [**Transmutation**] didn't cost much Numa at all, Logan spared no expenses when it came to [**Enchanting**]. Both items received enhanced sturdiness, durability, water and fire resistance, and even a flexibility enchantment on the skirt, so that it would be easier to crouch and run with it. That particular enchantment took a chunk of Numa, but it also gave Logan yet another level up.

[**Subclass Level Up!**]
[**Enchantment Level 12**]
[**Attribute Level Up!**]
[**Control: 9**]
[**Potency: 8**]

Logan had been keeping watch for over five hours. The sun was rising and the forest was slowly coming to life. As Logan was carefully laying the new clothes next to the lightly snoring Freya, he heard rustling nearby. Something definitely larger than a squirrel was approaching.

Logan took two quick paces to his scythe-rang and readied himself. He only relaxed again when he heard a woman's voice.

"Thank cocks, we actually found the way back."

Thank . . . cocks?

In front of Logan stood three people. A woman with a mess of red hair, wearing black jeans and a white t-shirt with the words "Bad Bitch" written on it. She was looking him up and down and smiling mischievously. To her side was a goon Logan recognized. Simmons, his father's primary bodyguard. Logan had never seen him without sunglasses. It felt strange to look at those gray/blue eyes. The towering agent gave Logan a passing glance and walked off. The third person was a teenager. Thin, diminutive, hunched. He gave Logan a strained smile and a hurried wave.

They had all been carrying berries, mushrooms, and even two of those squirrel-like monkeys Logan had seen.

"Oh," the woman said, extending a hand. "And who's this handsome piece of meat?"

"That's *my* man, Kat," Freya said from behind Logan. She came up to him and grabbed his arm possessively.

"Uh huh," the redhead said, clearly unimpressed. She walked past them and whispered in Logan's ear. "We'll see for how long."

Logan let out a polite cough in surprise.

"What was that?" Freya asked, taking a step toward Kat.

Kat turned her head as she sauntered off. "I'll go take a wash in the pond. Good luck, Blondie."

"I hope a snake eats her," Freya muttered to herself.

"Making new friends?" Logan asked.

Freya groaned and leaned against Logan. "She's a bitch."

"You're grumpy."

"Didn't get much sleep," she muttered. "I miss coffee. And you."

"I'm here," Logan reminded.

"Yeah, but I mean. I *miss* you," Freya said emphatically and looked up at Logan with those smoldering blue eyes.

"Oh," Logan said, his blood starting to pump faster. "Wait, you little tease. Are you trying to win one over on that girl?"

"Maybe," she said, biting her lip. Her hand snaked down from his chest. "Is it working?"

Logan grabbed her hand. "Yes, it's working, you lunatic. And no, not when my father is sleeping three yards away."

"Wouldn't that make it more—"

Logan pressed a finger at her lips. She tried to nibble at it. Logan sighed. "You're insane. Let's take your mind somewhere else. Come here."

Logan grabbed Freya's hand and brought her back to where she had slept. On the ground were the black and blue snakeskin garments. Freya knelt and picked the skirt up.

"You . . . made this?" she said in disbelief. "For me?"

"You like it?" Logan asked.

Freya was about to break into a great, big smile when Malcolm Specter walked in on their moment and fixed his hawk stare on his son.

"I killed the snake! I provided the tools to get the meat and hides! I found the Numa! I am the one who can use it!"

"You, you, you, you!" Malcolm growled. "That is all you ever think about! Look at the situation we're in! Did you think this was a good time to use valuable resources to pamper your girl?"

"Only after I made a bunch of to—"

"IRRESPONSIBLE!" Malcolm bellowed. "I cannot believe I let you keep this valuable resource!"

"We wouldn't have any of it if I hadn't—"

"Hadn't what?" Malcolm loomed over him. "Stumbled upon it? You're nothing if not lucky. Doesn't make you any less a fool. You do not know what we need. No planning, no forethought. First thing you made was a pretty dress for your girl? Ridiculous!"

The bone and stone tools lay forgotten on the ground behind Logan, as he tried to keep his cool despite his father's spittle flying in his face. Logan closed his eyes and bit on his lip so hard he tasted blood. His father went on for a while.

"I am in charge. And for good reason," Malcolm announced, pointing his finger at Logan's face. "Next time, you consult me first. Get out of my sight."

"Fuck. You," Logan said quietly and stomped off.

CHAPTER 14

Logan found himself walking past the forest line to the edge of the pond. The waterfall was roaring down a vertical wall of rock. Around the waterfall, a large flock of yellow waterbirds were floating and quacking around idly, periodically going underwater.

Seems like there's fish in the pond.

"Come to see me bathe?" a sultry voice asked.

Logan glanced in the voice's direction. Kat was in the middle of washing her hair, her clothes lying on the ground near Logan. "Huh? Sorry. Didn't see you."

"It's alright," Kat said, giving him a glance. "I don't mind."

"You've made that abundantly clear."

"So don't give me this 'Sorry' bullshit, and just enjoy the view."

Logan didn't answer; he just looked at the lilting water of the pond. The morning was beautiful, the lush, green forest alight with golden pearls of dew, glimmering in the sunlight. A big brown frog swam determinedly by Logan.

"What's it like being his son?" Kat asked.

"You heard us having a go at each other?"

"Some of it," she shrugged.

"Often it's insufferable," Logan said. "But I get nice Christmas presents."

Kat scoffed in good humor. "I bet. What's the craziest thing you ever bought?"

Logan shot her a smirk. "I'm not telling."

"Bastard," she said and splashed water his way.

"I'll tell you about the stupidest thing. I once spent half a million on a mobile game I quit in a week."

"Shut your ass!"

Logan shrugged. "Funny thing happens as you go further down your bucket list. Money loses absolutely any meaning *and* becomes the sole way you seek experiences."

"I don't get it," Kat said.

"We're not going to get into it. I don't expect much sympathy for someone like me anyway."

"Wise play, cowboy. I can see why that girl has her fangs in you."

"I'd be lost without Frey," Logan said wistfully and went back to watching the frog. It had found some plant to take a break on. It sat on it in a very dignified manner, giving Logan a blank stare. "She keeps me grounded."

"I don't know about grounded, but I bet I know tricks she can't even imagine," Kat said and gave him a predatory grin.

In that moment, Logan found the frog to be *particularly* fascinating. It stared back blankly. Just then, they heard a rustling in the bushes behind them and Freya emerged.

"You," she hissed at Kat. "What are you doing here?"

"Uh . . . Bathing?"

"Go away."

"I'm the one you two barged in on!"

"I don't care," Freya said. "Leave."

There was a definitive tone to Freya's voice. It even made Kat miss a beat. She got her stride back fast, though. Tilting her head and smiling, she got out of the water and sauntered fully naked to her pile of clothes. She took her time and locked eyes with Logan, who couldn't help but take the sight in. Freya elbowed him and not too gently.

"Rude," she said.

"I know," Logan sighed. "It's natural, though."

"Rude," she said again.

"Yeah," Logan said. "Sorry, Frey."

Satisfied, she nodded and sat down. Logan noticed that she was wearing the clothes he'd made her. They fit perfectly. Apparently the AI could use his memories of Freya very accurately.

She noticed him looking. She gave him a big, genuine smile. "Love them, Logan. Love them."

That made him feel a lot better. "You look great in that getup."

"I look great in everything, but you do make a good point."

Logan flashed her another smile before turning back to look at the pond.

"Look," Freya started. "The things your father said . . ."

"Eh," Logan waved. "You know I'm used to it, Frey."

"It's different this time, though, isn't it?"

Logan looked at Freya. Those wise, gentle eyes were on him. Gradually they quelled his anger. "It's a high-stress situation. Even Father is human, as much as he hates to admit it."

"You're dodging," Freya said.

"You ever gonna stop doing that?" Logan asked, narrowing his eyes.

"The minute you start answering honestly."

"I rarely lie," Logan said.

"Not what I said."

"You're a real pain in the ass sometimes."

"I'm *your* pain in the ass," Freya said, grinning. She leaned in closer to whisper dramatically. "And now that we're stuck in a fantasy jungle, I'm your pain in the ass FOREVER!"

Logan chuckled and shook his head. Freya kept grinning, the corners of her eyes crinkling in the most adorable way. Logan grabbed the back of her head and pulled her in for a kiss.

"Admission of my victory?" Freya asked after they pulled away.

Logan scuffed the ground with his magical socks. "My father has a lot of opinions."

"Some of them more grounded than others," Freya muttered half to herself.

"I don't often hear you saying cross things about Father," Logan said.

"It wasn't my place," Freya said. "But now it is. Look. I don't know what's the absolute mathematically optimal way to use those crystals of yours. Your father doesn't know either. You probably have the best idea of it."

"Not the way he sees it," Logan muttered. "If nobody else in the room knows what's right, he decides it's him."

"I mean . . ." Freya started.

"Oh no," Logan said. "I hate that tone."

"How much of your decision-making was affected by you not wanting the others to see me in a wet, tattered summer dress?" Freya asked, arching an eyebrow.

"Not—" Logan stopped himself. "A lot of it."

Freya laughed. "Never change, love."

Logan smiled and sighed. "I suppose I ought to a little bit."

Freya turned and cocked an eyebrow.

Logan got up. "I'll have to find some common ground with father. He's the best leader and—"

Freya gave him an amused look.

Logan cleared his throat. "I never said that."

"Said what?" Freya said immediately and grinned.

"Anyway. I need to keep my father in check, or God help these people under his rule. But I can't do that unless I can throw my weight around."

Freya also got up. She regarded Logan with a look he had not seen before.

"You know," Freya said slowly, almost carefully. "I think you should have spent a few days on your own in the wilderness a *long* time ago."

"Shut up," Logan said and nudged her. "Let's get back so I can throw a monkey wrench in Father's next plan."

CHAPTER 15

Logan watched Malcolm Specter pace back and forth in front of the remains of their campfire. The camp was awake and they were all groggy and tired. Logan couldn't blame them. Sleeping outside turned them into a veritable buffet for insects, which didn't make for the best rest.

If Malcolm was at all tired, he hid it well. His face was stern, his falcon eyes darting from one listener to another, demanding attention. Hands behind his back, he addressed them like a general would his soldiers. His eyes never went to Logan even once.

It's like even looking at me is beneath him.

That was fine by Logan. He was used to the aftermath of having had a go at his dear father. Well, it usually meant Logan just booked a flight to wherever. This time, that unfortunately wasn't possible. It was slowly dawning on Logan that he was stuck with his old man this time. It was a cool morning, but his nifty magic socks kept his feet warm. That was good. Logan watched his father, feet warm, arms crossed, listening carefully.

There seemed to be something new at work in Malcolm Specter as he talked and gesticulated. Something magnetic. It was in the cadence of his voice and the way he carried himself. He had always been a charismatic man, but now there was another layer of gravitas to him.

Did he get a class?

"My son is found. We have been fed. We are done scrambling. I have decided we need to settle. Logan told me of ruins that have been left by people of some sort. We will go there and build a base."

"Bad idea, Father."

A flicker of anger passed Malcolm's face. He turned to Logan coolly. "Why?"

"I only know two locations. Neither of them are close enough to a water source."

"We will carry the water, as people have done for thousands of years."

"Great idea, Father. Carry them with what? A great big truck with a jacuzzi on the back? We don't even have cups."

"You can make containers," Malcolm said dryly. "It is what you *should* have done with those crystals. It is safer in those ruins."

"Not necessarily," Logan said. "There are monsters in there too. Nasty ones. And there are monsters out here, too. You want to send a small army to escort everyone bringing a cup of water back?"

Simmons, who loomed over the other members of the group even while in a hunched, sitting position spoke in a deep bass. "We agents can take care of supplying the group with water, sir. It's good exercise."

Malcolm nodded. "It is decided, then."

"The hell it is," Logan said. Simmons gave him an unfriendly glance. "Sure, that takes care of the water, but what about food?"

"What do you mean?" Malcolm asked.

"Fishing and fetching water are also going to just take up unnecessary time and energy if you add a two-mile walk on top of it every time."

"Shut up, Little Prince," one of the agents shouted. "Let your old man talk."

"You shut up, you dumb goon," Logan hissed. "I'm not finished."

The goon was about to say something, but Malcolm held a hand. "You try my patience, son. Make it quick, make it good."

"If we want to sustain ourselves, we are going to need to grow crops. For that we need a lot of water. We can't prosper without irrigation. Also, we want a mill next to the river. Unless you knucklehead goons want to squeeze flour for us with your bare hands."

The goons piped down. Malcolm Specter gave his son an appraising look. "How do you know all of this?"

Logan smirked. "I'm irresponsible, remember? Wasted a lot of time on useless YouTube videos. Funny how things work."

Another weighty silence. Malcolm rubbed at his chin, looking at his son. "Should we settle down by this pond or upriver?"

Logan caught Freya's eye. They were both equally shocked.

"Did you . . . Just ask for my opinion?"

"Spare your snark," Malcolm said. "Share your insight and be done with it."

"Let me just savor this for a moment," Logan said, closing his eyes and smiling.

The group went back and forth on the merits between settling here at the pond or going up the hill to settle by the river. Mostly it was Malcolm, Logan, Kat, and another agent alongside Simmons who dared voice their opinions.

There was a handful of doctors, half a dozen agents, Janice the barmaid, and six other civilians in the group, who were completely silent and apparently content to listen.

I guess most people are like that in the end.

Eventually the prospect of a waterwheel and a mill attached to it won the argument. And so they collected what little they had and made their way through the forest and up the hill to the riverbank.

The group spent some time until they finally found a reasonable forest opening near there.

"Very good," Malcolm said. "Have you all been holding your classes, like I told you to?"

Wait, what?

Logan looked at Freya, who gave a quick glance at Logan before bowing her head in guilt. Kat snorted and crossed her arms.

"I will allocate them now," Malcolm said. "Those agents that did not pick up a Warrior-related class shall pick up a Hunting-related class. We will also need Labor-related classes for the men, and Gathering and Crafting-related classes for the women. I'll go over each with you one by one. Those of you who already—"

"Wait a goddamn minute," Logan interjected. "*You're* assigning people their classes?"

"What of it?" Malcolm grumbled. "I'm the leader."

"So you keep reminding me," Logan said and smiled softly. "Look, Simmons, what do you want to do?"

Agent Simmons gave Logan an unreadable glance. "Whatever is necessary."

"That's what adults do, Logan," Malcolm said coldly.

"Sorry, Simmons," Logan said, ignoring his father. "I forgot you had no soul."

Logan turned to the timid boy who had been on the exploration trip. "You. What would—"

"Enough," Malcolm growled. "Sit down, Logan."

"You need to let people decide, you idiot," Logan snapped. "You can't just dictate what they should do."

"That is exactly what a leader does."

"That is exactly what a CEO does. Fire and replace unproductive people," Logan said.

This time Malcolm paused, which Logan immediately used to his advantage. "You're stuck with these people. God, I hope we find more, so you can yell at someone else. But if we don't, what are you going to do, when you can't dispose of people whose performance displeases you?"

Even Simmons looked curious to hear what his former boss had to say. Logan saw Freya throw a smile at him.

"I see it only took the end of the world to make you come alive," Malcolm said, a slight smile on his lips. "I will make you my advisor, Logan. Your out-of-the-box thinking might be useful here."

"No," Logan said immediately. "Also, I already have a class. Also . . . No."

"No," Malcolm said simply. "You will consult me from now on before I give out orders. This is the last time I allow you to attempt to water down my authority."

Logan was about to open his mouth to launch into another argument, but he thought better of it. A single glance at his father's hands made it clear that he had really pushed the limit here. "Yes, Father."

Both of Malcolm's eyebrows shot up. "Seems like fending for yourself for once actually taught you something."

Freya shot a smirk at him.

Logan sighed. "I really don't like hearing that."

CHAPTER 16

Eventually Logan and Malcolm compromised. They did indeed need a very specific set of skills, so they made a list together concerning hunting and gathering food, crafting shelter, and utilities and fighting. Logan had to admit, it felt nice to work on something with his father. He was an abrasive grouch about it, as always, but there was something new under the surface of their negotiations. A mutual respect.

Have to admit, he really is good at organizing these things.

Logan pestered Agent Simmons until he finally yielded out of pure annoyance, admitting that he wasn't interested in hunting or fighting. He wanted to be a woodsman. So he picked the [**Forester**] class. That was fine by Malcolm Specter. They would need a lot of lumber.

As a reward for finally being honest, Logan gave him one of the stone axe heads and actually used up a decent chunk of Numa to turn the other scythe into a saw, after working a bit with Tumor on the designs.

"I expect a cozy log cabin in due time."

Simmons had looked at him with those unreadable blue eyes but had eventually nodded, after apparently drawing his own conclusion as to whether or not Logan had been joking.

One of the civilians Logan had barely paid attention to, took the [**Fisherman**] class. Logan gave him the fishing hooks and a stone knife.

Janice, the barmaid from the roof, took a [**Crafter**] class. She'd become demure and withdrawn. Logan had some sympathy for her mental state but also hoped she could pull her weight. With that, she received the bone needles and a stone knife.

The doctors protested and bickered about maintaining their profession. They had all been granted the option to take the [**Healer**] class. Malcolm responded with harsh words. He gave the family doctor permission to take the class, claiming that half of the so-called "doctors" were mere researchers, and it was about time they did something useful.

With that, one of them capitulated and decided to also take a **[Crafter]** class. He muttered something about specializing in pottery due to the abundance of clay in the soil. That was good; they would need containers and possibly even clay bricks.

The rest of them fell in line, choosing classes matching the needs of the list Logan and his father had made. Logan didn't personally appreciate forcing the doctors to take a class they didn't want. Then again, higher education would only go so far in a survival situation.

Before one of the younger doctors had a chance to pick something he didn't really want, Logan ambushed him and, with the help of Freya, dragged him by his tattered lab coat away from where Malcolm Specter could hear or see them.

"What classes does the system suggest to you?" Logan asked.

"Hey," Freya said and smiled at him. "You're Dr. Cormick, aren't you? You worked in the nootropics department?"

"Y-yes," the skinny, sandy-haired man managed to stammer out. "Can you let go of me, please? I feel uncomfortable."

Logan released the doctor, who wiped his forehead with the ugly red and blue tie at his neck.

"You need to make string out of that tie, as soon as possible," Logan told him.

Dr. Cormick let out a nervous laugh. "I suppose that would be a good idea. You will need a shirt."

"I like him like this," Freya said. "What's your name?"

"William," he said.

"What classes are suggested for you, Will?" Logan asked.

"William," he corrected. "I have **[Alchemist]**, **[Healer]**, and **[Swordsman]**."

"**[Swordsman]**?" Freya asked.

"I did fencing in high school and college."

"I bet you did," Logan said half-aloud.

"What?" William asked, somewhat offended. "It's a fine sport!"

"You convinced me," Logan said and smirked. "Sorry. It's just one of those elitist upper-middle-class hobbies that I tend to sneer upon."

"You're one to talk," Freya said and nudged Logan.

"Pick the **[Alchemist]** class, William," Logan said.

"But Mr. Specter said—"

"He says a lot of things," Logan said. "But he isn't omniscient. You ever play video games, William?"

"I did."

"Well, my father never did. He can't appreciate how valuable an **[Alchemist]** could be for our motley crew."

"But Mr. Specter will—"

"I've got your back, William," Logan said empathetically. "I promise you, he will thank you later for your initiative."

William nodded but didn't say anything.

"Well, do what's best for you," Logan said and walked away. Freya gave William a friendly wave before she followed Logan.

Logan sat down next to the pile of snake bones and the heat-enchanted rock he had used to start the fire earlier. The charge was exhausted, and he would have to [**Funnel**] some energy into it before he left. And he would have to leave soon. They needed more Numa.

Freya sat down, looking worried as she had ever since they had found this area.

"You're not yourself," Logan said.

Freya drew in breath like a gathering storm. Logan knew what was coming— an offended tirade. He moved in first, cupping her face in his hand and massaging her scalp through her hair. She hummed and leaned in.

Works like a charm, even post-apocalypse.

"Sometimes I think your father should see this side of you," she said absently.

"Ew," Logan said.

She chuckled. "Not what I meant."

"What's bothering you, Frey?"

Freya fiddled with her fingers and sighed pensively. "I'm really proud of you. You . . . I've known you for as long as I can remember, and I never saw you like this."

"Shirtless?"

"Shut up," Freya said. "What I'm trying to say is . . . You've fiddled around your whole life, not caring, or at least pretending not to. Now we are in this absolutely insane situation. And you're doing just fine!"

Logan tried to speak, but Freya interjected. "Not just fine! You're *thriving*! I'm so proud of you, but at the same time . . . Ugh!"

Logan smiled. Yeah, he had messed around most of his life, but he was good at one thing. He was the world's greatest expert on Freya Beckstein. "You're feeling useless and I was supposed to be useless with you?"

"Thank you!" she gasped. "Usually it doesn't take you this long."

Logan shrugged. "New waters. What do you want from me exactly?"

"I don't know!" She tried getting up, but Logan pulled her back down. She growled. Logan recognized that growl. It was the "You're right but I don't like you right now" growl. "I don't know what to do."

"What do you want to do? There are a lot of ways you can be useful around here."

Freya glanced around to see if anyone else was within earshot. Then she muttered, "I'm not good at anything."

Logan scoffed in disbelief. "That's what got you all wound up?"

Freya turned to look at Logan.

"Who cares?" Logan said. "Just pick something you like."

"I don't—"

"Here," Logan said and placed two [**F-grade Numa crystals**] in her palm. Then he got up. "To help you catch up. I have to prepare. I'll talk to you later. Look, it's only the end of the world and we might be the last twenty or so humans alive. Relax a little. Things could be worse."

"Funny."

"Love you, Frey," Logan said and picked up one of the snake ribs for inspiration before he left.

"Love you too," she said, hugging her knees. "Wait . . . Prepare for what?"

CHAPTER 17

Logan still had more Numa than he'd ever held before. Three full **[E-grade Numa crystals]** from the Scythe-fiends and the one he'd gotten from the Snake-fiend had 32 percent charge. He had given two of the F-grade crystals to Freya, and he'd used one for the firestone, which left him with two full **[F-grade Numa crystals]**.

I'll need some to make everything I need for the next adventure. And I have to keep some spare Numa for emergencies.

But the rest he'd use to make things easier for the group. It was only fair since he was going to need food. As long as it wasn't mushrooms, that is.

Logan looked at the curved rib of the giant snake he'd killed. He'd wanted to use it for something, but he wasn't sure what. It was two fingers in width and two feet long, albeit curved. It could hold moderate weight.

Logan looked around at the people bustling here and there. Simmons had the barmaid girl help attach the stone axe head to a piece of hastily-carved stick. He'd be chopping wood for them soon enough. One of the doctors was already working with wet clay, looking akin to a sloppy kindergartener with an arts project.

We need shelter.

"Hey, Tumor," Logan whispered, "we need a plan of action. Materials available: wood, clay, stones. Consider I have awesome magic, but I have to conserve as much Numa as possible. What's the most efficient way to build shelter?"

[Reconfiguring Neural Matrix . . . 24% completion]

[Use rocks or stone to elevate the base. Most optimally a **[Transmuted]** *sheet of stone. This will create stability and counteract moisture. Build against a sturdy tree for structural stability for the walls and roof. Use young straight wood to create a frame and* **[Transmute]** *wood into plywood for the walls, roof, and floor. Tie the frame together with fabric from the group's remaining clothes, and mix ash, clay, and water together to create mortar to strengthen the structure. Cover the structure*

with foliage for waterproofing and camouflage, unless you want to use [**Enchanting**] *for better results.]*

Logan glanced in his father's direction. He was discussing something with the agents who had been assigned [**Warrior**] or [**Hunter**] classes. It was vitally important that he didn't hear what Logan was doing.

"Good job, Tumor."

After Logan had prompted Tumor for measurements and amounts of material needed, and estimations of Numa cost, he went and gathered his crew. Thinking Agent Simmons, or now [**Forester**] Simmons, would be the hardest nut to crack, Logan went to him first. He was almost shocked by the giant man's amiability in this moment. The former agent was so engrossed with using his stone axe and Numa-craft saw that he only curtly affirmed that Logan would get what he needed as soon as he was done with the particular tree he was in the process of chopping down.

Janice and the doctor-turned-[**Potter**] hardly required much more persuasion. The doctor working with clay had been producing awful, unusable work and was glad to receive a project that he could confidently handle.

Afterward, Logan saw the small teenage boy collecting lumps of clay for the doctor. Logan tried to be friendly by asking what class he had chosen. The boy refused to answer, which was odd. He, however, complied when Logan asked him to gather rocks of any size and quality for him.

Janice was busy making crude fishing rods for the guy who'd become a [**Fisherman**]. Logan could appreciate the group securing a food source, but he urged Janice to help him produce string, or even rope if possible. While Logan negotiated with the former barmaid, he noticed Malcolm Specter watching him with his cool hawk's stare.

In the end, Logan got what he wanted. To kill time, he went for a wash and drink by the river and plucked a few handfuls of berries from a bush they had near the camp. By then, Simmons had some logs ready for him. He had gotten levels in [**Strength**] as well as [**Endurance**] attributes and two levels in his [**Lumberjack**] Subclass. His stern, blocky face was sporting an uncharacteristically goofy but content smile.

Looks like I'm not the only one who enjoys leveling.

Logan double-checked with Tumor that the pieces of wood had the appropriate mass for a specific size of plywood. Some sawing was required, so Logan wouldn't waste Numa. Simmons was surprisingly obliging. Logan suspected he just enjoyed using his tools.

With a hallucination of a red rectangular piece of plywood hovering in front of him, Logan placed a crystal on the sawed piece of dark brown wood and performed an incantation.

[Subclass Level Up!]
[Transmutation Level 9]
[Attribute Level Up!]
[Efficiency: 7]

The bark morphed into the trunk, and soon the whole piece of lumber had become a large piece of dark plywood, half an inch thick.

Simmons took a step back. "This is the power of Numa?"

Logan gave a glance at his father's foremost goon. Despite his stupid anvil-like jaw and short-cropped blonde hair, he was surprisingly all right. "Yep. Want some?"

Simmons nodded eagerly. Logan tossed an **[F-grade Numa crystal]** to the man, who seized it with a deft move. "Don't tell my father I gave that to you."

Simmons said nothing in response. Logan smiled at him.

Probably not the most efficient use of Numa. But it never hurts to have a friend. Besides, we're going to need a shitload of lumber.

Logan ran back and forth around the camp, keeping the moving parts of his projects . . . moving. Janice helped him tie up a frame with the help of one of the doctors who was still waffling on his class. Simmons kept felling trees and sawing them to appropriate size. The quiet teenager eventually procured a pile of rocks for him.

Logan consulted Tumor on the pros and cons of just smashing the rocks with the stone hammers he had made and mixing them with clay to create a base for the shelter. Eventually, after some confusing math and projections about the longevity of the shelter, Logan decided it was better to just use some Numa to fuse the rocks into a base.

Creating a base thick enough by Tumor's standards sucked half an **[E-grade Numa crystal]** dry. It was no wonder, as the amount of stone used for the structure was over three thousand pounds. The dark gray mass was half a foot in height and twelve feet in length on both sides.

The people around the camp looked at it with no small awe, and it finally prompted Malcolm Specter to grace Logan's little project with his presence.

"What are you doing?" he asked Logan.

"Building a circus," he said distractedly, as he was fastening and wiggling a wooden beam into the mortar. Logan wondered if the bark was okay to leave or if it should be scooped away.

"Your jokes are even less entertaining than usual," Malcolm said dryly.

Logan turned to him and grinned. "They seem to be working better, as you usually aren't upset by them."

"This is not exactly an easy situation," Malcolm said. "How much of that Numa energy have you used?"

"Feel free to sleep on the ground if you're not happy with what I'm doing."

Logan really didn't need his dad on his case right now. He was doing a good thing. The right thing. From the look of it, his father had just been walking around and talking to his agents, doing what he'd call "thinking work" or some other pretentious thing.

Logan could feel Malcolm standing there, watching him work. It made Logan feel self-conscious, but that wasn't something he'd ever let show.

After a while, his father turned on his heels and said, "Good initiative, Logan."

Logan's world stopped. He almost fumbled the frame he was tying up. He looked at his father's back as he walked stiffly away. Logan could feel his face flushing, and he didn't like that. But there were stronger emotions than dislike at play here. Some that Logan couldn't name. "Thanks, D—. Thank you, Father."

CHAPTER 18

Even with the help of magic, it took a long time to make a building. Once other people realized what Logan was working on, they quickly flocked around and asked if they could help. There were certainly things to carry, move, hold in place, and so on. With some Numa, sweat, and elbow grease, they finally got the roof to rest on the building. It almost clicked into place, snuggly embedded between the walls to rest on the support beams. Tumor's measurements made things a lot smoother than they had any right to be.

By sunset, they had a complete building. It was far from a thing of beauty. The ash and clay mortar had clumped here and there, and the wood that Logan hadn't used magic on was bendy and uneven. A mismatched wall of sticks and chopped-up tree trunks held the [**Transmuted**] plywood in place. Freya was on the roof spreading clumps of tall reeds they had found near the river.

Even Malcolm Specter had pulled up his sleeves and helped Simmons cut wood once he was done with his walking and talking. He never once gave Logan a glance long enough for his son to catch his eyes.

The sun was setting. It was already growing dark, the sky's orange cast gradually turning into a shade of dark purple. The forest around them was casting long shadows upon them. Insects were chirping somewhere nearby and sometimes a curious monkey or two peeked from behind a tree branch at them.

[**Skill Level Up!**]
[**Funnel Level 5**]

Logan let the heat-enchanted rock suck up an [**F-grade Numa crystal**]. He had to admit, it was somewhat expedient. But not even his father objected, and Logan sure knew why.

The [**Fisherman**], a balding, chunky man in his forties named Daniel, had caught and prepared seven fish from the pond below. They were stuck on sharp sticks and would be roasted on the fire, as soon as Balmer got it going. And yes, it had totally been Logan's idea to get the young agent on fire-making duty.

Despite the jungle growing darker around them, they soon had a fire and the smell of cooked fish tempting their growling stomachs. Logan looked at the faces around him. He didn't know half of them and had never liked any of the ones he had known, apart from Freya's. But now he felt connected to them. The tired smiles, the satisfied sighs, the idle chatting. It was *beautiful*. There was a peace to the whole group that had not been there before. Before, it had all been survival and fear. Now, they knew they didn't have to sleep outside at the mercy of the elements tonight, and that was *something*.

It wasn't lost on Logan that it was largely his doing. His father hadn't said a word to him after giving him that compliment for the first time in over ten years. That didn't stop him from grinning. Freya, who was sitting next to him, gave him a quizzical look. Logan only pulled her closer and kissed her gently, which she immediately reciprocated. He couldn't remember the last time he had felt this content.

Logan woke up to aggressive snoring in a smelly room, under a bundle of arms and legs.

Best night of sleep ever.

Logan was used to being the first one up. It was a genetic gift from his father. Right now, his dad was snoring, a trickle of drool running down his cheek. Logan *really* wished he had a camera. He couldn't blame the old guy. Logan had gotten decent sleep in the dungeon or whatever. Sleeping on the grass, getting eaten by insects, and stewing in that moisture and dew made for awful rest.

Logan enjoyed this feeling of being the first one up. He was used to it from morning-afters of the countless house parties he'd attended and thrown. Brewing coffee and smirking at other people's states of groggy despair was one of Logan's great joys in life. Well, *had* been.

No such leisure today. Logan got up and went toward the river. He was groggy too, but it was nothing he couldn't overcome with the help of some cold water. After making sure there were no piranhas waiting to eat his toes, Logan washed himself and drank as much as he could. After that, he sat down on a smooth white rock and watched the forest waking up around him as the sun rose higher in the sky.

It's going to be a hot day.

Logan sat down and thought, idly wondering if this was what his father had spent so much of his time on yesterday. Malcolm Specter had to keep twenty people alive in the wilderness. Logan supposed that warranted some thinking.

Being the reckless son that he was, his scope was going to be smaller. He needed to gear up for another adventure. He would make the necessary preparations and properly delve into one of the dungeons within this jungle. Maybe he could find out more about the secrets of Numa there.

Could I create these crystals myself? Or are these just the leftover batteries of some civilization long gone?

He'd hate to think it was the latter, because it would make his father's views on being frugal with the energy that much more compelling. Logan didn't like it when his father was right. That man would sink his teeth into it like a rabid bulldog.

"Tumor, help me prepare for eventualities. I obviously need food. Water would be nice, but I doubt we can whip up a flask. What else do I need? Rope? Flashlight? Yeah, maybe for Christmas . . . Wait, I can just give any stick or rock a light **[Enchantment]** can't I? Sheesh . . . Why am I doing your job for you? Anyway, make a list of items I might need."

[Reconfiguring Neural Matrix . . . 27% completion]

[Compiling a dataset . . .]

[Running simulations . . .]

[The list of items you might need on such an exploration could get quite large. Would you like this one to reexamine all of the 136 items that might be useful, and compile a smaller list?]

Logan sighed and rubbed at his forehead. "Yes, Tumor. I would prefer it if you didn't go over all 136 items right now."

[Reconfiguring Neural Matrix . . . 28% completion]

[This one senses it should have given you a contracted list to begin with and asked whether you need an expanded list, and not the other way around. This one will adjust responses henceforth.]

"Thank you, Tumor."

[A light source is required. Rations for sustenance are required. Simulations suggest that 72% of scenarios without rope will lead to death. Simulations suggest that 89% of scenarios without a water container will lead to death. Containers for carrying the Numa crystals are required items. Additional suggestions: fire-making tools, an axe for firewood, gloves, and bandages for first aid.]

"Seems reasonable," Logan thought aloud. "Gloves are not possible right now. Rope . . . How the hell am I going to make rope? I'm sure as hell Janice won't have the levels or expertise needed for a while . . . A water container is gonna be a bastard, isn't it? Wait! I can use the leftover snakeskin! That will also make Father mad, as an added bonus."

Logan got to work. He'd ask Janice to make pouches out of the group's leftover ragged clothes to carry the Numa crystal haul. She could also take care of the bandages.

He'd have to **[Transmute]** the snakeskin water flask. That worried Logan a bit. While his Control was the highest attribute he had, he feared this design would stretch him thin. The seams would have to be water-tight. He'd also need a cork. Yeah, this was going to take a while . . .

Logan bent the motley snakeskin resembling the red hologram hallucination Tumor had produced and cast an incantation, focusing on the image in front of him and the measurements Tumor had told him to ask for.

[Attribute Level Up!]
[Control: 10]

The result was an ugly black and blue pouch made of coarse leather. But it seemed like Logan had done enough. To test it, he immediately went to the river and filled the pouch. It held the liquid. There was exactly half a gallon there, according to Tumor's calculations.

Sheesh . . . I'd been so worried.

Logan tried drinking from it, but that proved to be not so simple. The mouth was too flexible, and he spilled a good deal of the water on his chest.

That's going to make the cork business harder too.

He took his last **[F-grade Numa crystal]** and hardened the flask's mouth. Half of the Numa was spent, but Logan was satisfied with the results. Now he'd just need Janice to produce a cinch and a cork for the flask, and he was all but ready to go.

Oh crap, I still need the rope, don't I?

CHAPTER 19

S o you have decided to leave?" Malcolm Specter asked his son as he came over to look at what Logan was tinkering with. Logan had just **[Enchanted]** a length of green and brown vine with a strengthening and durability enchantment. Logan figured it was fancy enough.

"Well, I figured it was time to fly out of the nest," Logan said, as he inspected the coil of rope.

"You think you can fend for yourself out there?"

"I guess we'll find out."

"I assume you are going to return after your expedition?" Malcolm said.

"No, Father," Logan said, still keeping his eyes fixed on the rope. "I'm going to abandon Freya here and live my days out alone, befriending the cats and blue monsters."

"Do you think we would get along better were it not for your humorous antics?"

"What do you want, Father?"

"I am assigning you an escort."

"You— what?"

"You have proven yourself capable, which is all the more reason to protect such an asset," Malcolm explained, his cool hawk eyes never leaving Logan. "But you are not trained for combat."

"You're going to assign goons on me?"

"Only one," Malcolm said. "Think of me what you will, but I know you well. Any more than one would hurt your fickle pride."

"I learn from the best."

"My pride is earned, Logan."

Logan hated to admit it, but that remark hurt him a bit. He'd die before letting it show, though.

"I'll take Simmons," Logan snapped.

"You will take who I assign," his father said. "Simmons is no longer a combatant. You will be assigned Agent Balmer."

"No," Logan said.

"Yes," Malcolm said. "In addition, a group searching for gatherables and hunting animals will join you, along with a force of my combatant agents. They will follow you to the ruins you seek, to ensure safe passage."

"I do not," Logan said slowly, accentuating every word, "need a babysitter."

"I will do as I see fit to keep a valuable asset," Malcolm said. Logan detected a weariness behind those words. He narrowed his eyes, but his father betrayed no further weakness. Malcolm regarded his son silently for a moment before adding. "Do your part and return safely."

Logan gave him a look. But his father had a poker face made of stone. Logan sighed. He'd have to take this one on the chin. If it was one thing he had learned when dealing with Malcolm, it was that picking your fights was important.

"Fine. I'll take Balmer. I needed a fire-making tool anyway."

The crew of adventurers left camp the next morning with little ceremony. Almost half of their group was part of the expedition. In addition to Logan and Balmer, there were four more agents and a bunch of doctors and civilians. Half of them looked like they didn't want to go, but the bushes of berries nearby were almost eaten, and they couldn't rely on fish only. They'd need to hunt game and search for spots where mushrooms, berries, roots, and such grew.

According to Malcolm's plans, the gatherers would follow Logan and Balmer to the ruins with the rest of the crew and then be escorted back by the agents close to the camp. They would need to experience in simply moving about the area surrounding the camp. Half of the doctors and civilians on gathering duty looked like they weren't keen to go anywhere.

"Hey!" Kat exclaimed, her messy red hair standing out from the crowd watching them leave. She had her hands wrapped around in cloth. Her knuckles were especially well-padded. "I'm coming too."

"What do you think they need you for?" Freya snapped next to her.

"To be a thigh pillow for your man, of course," Kat said and grinned at Freya. Freya bristled.

Malcolm turned to Kat. "You plan to help with the hunt? Your class is fighting-oriented."

"It is," Kat said. "That's why I'm going to stick with your son and protect him."

"Logan," Malcolm said. "Do you accept?"

Logan shrugged.

Freya took a step forward. "Logan!"

Logan came over to Freya and hugged her. "Frey, do you trust me?"

"'Course I do," she muttered. "But I don't trust her."

"Hate her all you want. I don't care," Logan said.

"Hey!" Kat said. "I'm right here, you know?"

"I've loved you since I was ten, you idiot," Logan said. "You really think she has a chance?"

"She's going to give it her best shot," Kat remarked, grinning at Freya.

"Only at ten," Freya gave him a mock glare. "I've loved you since I was eight."

"Liar," Logan grabbed her by the shoulder.

"Nuh uh," Freya said. "It was when you had that snow castle made for me in that hockey ring."

"Oh yeah," Logan said. "Can't say I had much to do with that. I just ordered father's people to do it and they were dumb enough to listen."

"I was eight," Freya said and smiled lightly. "I was easily impressed."

Logan kissed her forehead. "Better she comes with me than stay here to drive you up the wall. We don't have that many walls to begin with."

Freya chuckled. "Fine. Come back safe."

"I will."

Traveling through the jungle was a surprisingly mellow experience. They didn't run into any of the black and blue monsters that Levemoth had spawned. No green cats or other predators bothered them either, likely due to the size of their group, at least when it came to the latter one. The curious squirrel-monkeys watched them, gibbering to each other.

They saw some creatures resembling deer, but they escaped their sight as soon as the hunters tried to approach them. Logan could also sense another presence watching them, but whenever he thought he detected movement in his periphery and turned to glance, he never caught sight of anything.

"How many bullets do you even have?" Logan asked none of the agents in particular.

"What's it to you?" one of the goons answered in an unfriendly tone.

"You could just tell me."

The agent hawked and spat and walked a few paces forward.

Logan scoffed. "You're going to be better off throwing spears until we can figure out bows."

"We are well aware of the strange physics at play here," another agent said. This one was large and dark haired. Jefferson was his name . . . ? Maybe.

"You guys should wait until we find some crystals, so I can make some enchanted spearheads," Logan said.

Maybe-Jefferson grunted and the conversation died.

Fine. Starve then, idiots.

Just then, a green panther was foolish enough to jump at them from the bushes and Logan quickly took it down with his scythe-rang. Then Balmer built a fire and they cooked and ate every morsel that the beast had to offer. Sure, they had some berries and cooked fish with them, but they'd rather save them for as long as possible.

After a couple of hours, they arrived where Logan had fended off those three scythe-fiends. It was the safer option. The other ruins had the giant Numa crystal, which would have been a massive boon, but there was also that splitting monster the size of an elephant guarding it. There was no way they would be able to defeat it. Fool it and trap it? Maybe, but it was too risky.

The afternoon sun was burning down hot on them and Logan looked forward to entering the cool ruins. They stood at the doorway overtaken by vegetation by the passage of time. But it was clear that the sharply-cut stone was man-made. Or at least made by someone . . .

Logan turned to the agents. "You sure you idiots don't want me crafting spearheads or something for you?"

like it when you give your stick to me," Kat said as she took the "flashlight" Logan had fashioned from an [**Enchanted**] piece of wood.

"Really?" Logan asked. Balmer was snickering at that, so Logan shoved him his flash-stick extra forcefully.

The three of them were moving at the helm of their formation. The gatherers had been left outside with two of the agents to find the rest of them a snack. Logan wasn't sure if he wanted to return outside anytime soon, but at least the agents behind him would hopefully leave in not-too-long.

Not only because they were dumb goons, but because the faster they found some Numa, the better.

Logan had been exceedingly lucky with that room he had been trapped in. They quickly found similar rooms, but the floating crystal constructs were spent.

They checked room after room in the corridors roped with blue light. Logan tried using [**Funnel**] on them immediately upon arrival, but it didn't work. Tumor figured they were insulated by some spell.

The agents stormed into each room with experienced precision as Logan stood by each doorway, ready to throw the scythe-rang at anything hostile. They found nothing living or moving, except for one unusual exception. In the fifth room, they all noticed a score of tiny blue beetles, glowing with the distinct hue of Numa, scuttling around the floor. As soon as they entered the room, the insects scattered and vanished into what must have been some hidden crack in the wall.

Nobody commented on the bugs, but they certainly piqued Logan's interest. To the chagrin of the agents, Logan searched throughout the room, crawling and crouching on the smooth stone floors for a long while, while the agents and Kat made whispered allusions to the possibility that Logan had finally lost it.

These bugs could hold an insane amount of potential if they could be harvested. Why were they here and not in the other rooms?

Logan found his answer eventually: three shards of the faintest glowing blue. Logan picked one up.

[F-grade Numa crystal, 17%]

All three of the crystals had a negligible amount of charge left. But they were a promising start. At least the ruins or the dungeon—whatever you called it— wasn't completely cleared.

Were the bugs eating these?

"I found some Numa," Logan told them. His voice echoed far into the distance of the dark corridors.

"Enough?" the dark-haired goon asked.

"Not even close," Logan muttered.

Not that it's a waste, but, boy, is it going to take a decent chunk of Numa to even make one proper spear for these goons. I need to **[Transmute]** *it in order to shape a stick, and* **[Enchant]** *it with sharpness and durability, at the least. Using* **[Empower]** *would be a waste, since they couldn't charge the sticks later. At least a couple of full- charge* **[F-grade Numa crystals]** *are needed.*

There were no further bugs to be seen, but the seventh room they stormed contained three more of those floating Numa-constructs—two of them empty, one left with the faintest charge. Logan rushed to inspect it.

[D-grade Numa crystal, 15%]

"Yes!" Logan hissed. "This is enough."

"That doesn't look like much," Kat said as she moved over to Logan.

"It's a high-grade crystal," Logan said. "Look."

"That's enough?" Balmer asked as he brushed up to him to take a look at the crystal.

Logan scoffed. "For a few sharp sticks?"

Then he turned to the agents standing by the doorway. "I need you big boys to go gather some nice-looking sticks and stones so I can make your toys."

The dark-haired agent made a face. "Why didn't you just have us bring the stuff here in the first place?"

Logan brought a hand over his mouth in mock shock. "Oh no! I must have forgotten."

With the disgruntled agents gone, Logan was left alone with Balmer and Kat. Not exactly his ideal company, but Kat seemed chill enough.

"You guys gonna just sit around and wait?" she asked as she peeked out of the room.

"That is what we agreed on," Balmer said.

Kat stuck out her tongue. "Boring! Come on. Let's go find some of those bugs Logan liked. You know, you're hot, but being interested in bugs is gross, you know?"

"Hey, if it stops you from sexually harassing me, let's go and find some bugs."

"It probably won't," Kat said. "But you can try."

"Hey!" Balmer said, in a miffed tone. "We agreed to wait here."

"It will take them at least half an hour to get back . . . if they don't get lost."

"Every one of us has been highly trained with memorization techniques that—"

"Bored," Kat said as he walked out of the door, Logan at her heels. "You coming, Straitlace?"

After a few paces, Logan and Kat were joined by a muttering Agent Balmer. Logan smirked to himself. Kat was doing a good job of annoying the young goon. It was important that someone did most of the heavy lifting in that department so that he could focus on paying attention.

Kat and Balmer bickered in clipped tones as they checked two more rooms. They came up empty. They were just about to turn a corner when they suddenly heard a strange sound.

A low, rumbling gurgle echoed through the dark corridors. A faint bubbling noise followed it. It seemed to be coming closer, followed by echoes of clickity scuttling. Logan immediately became more alert and directed his light-stick in the direction of the sound. He made a hand gesture to silence and still his two companions.

The clicking didn't sound like the scythe-fiends, but there was something ominous about it. While the screeching horrors had been very straightforward and violent, this was something else.

He had an overwhelming sense of great danger. His companions sensed it too. Something had noticed them and it saw them as prey. The scuttling started to come from a different direction. Closer now.

"Back up," Logan hissed.

Kat and Balmer didn't hesitate or try to play brave. They all began to take backward steps.

The scuttling and gurgling was growing faster and more urgent. Whatever was coming was almost upon them.

"Run!" Logan yelled.

They all went into a full sprint and dashed inside the room. Whatever hunted them was done playing coy. The gurgling and scuttling was now right behind Logan.

He made it into the room and tried to slam the stone door shut. He wasn't able to in time. A monstrous head adorned with a sharp, bulky horn squeezed through, the chitinous creature looking around wildly with its black beady eyes. It had a gross hole of a mouth from which toxic green saliva hissed on the stone as it landed.

Logan struck it down with a two-handed swing of his scythe-rang. The chitin cracked and the creature went limp, but it soon started to scramble and gurgle again. By then, another one of these dog-sized insects had squeezed itself into the room over its wounded friend.

Kat screamed fiercely as she smashed into the cockroach-like creature's side with a kick. A third bug-monster clambered over its comrades and rushed toward Balmer, with its horn ready to impale him.

Balmer rolled to his side and pulled out his sidearm in one swift, smooth motion. The gunshots echoed throughout the room. Logan and Kat gasped in pain and shock, but the bugs hated it too.

Logan yanked his scythe-rang out of one of the wounded insects and made some distance between them. Ignoring its pain, the bug gurgled and charged toward Logan with horn extended. Logan threw the scythe-rang again, but it bounced off the carapace. Then he dodged the charge and tumbled into a corner. The insect-creature charged again.

This time it pinned Logan against the wall. The scythe-rang returned to him, but it bounced off the chitin and clattered two feet away from his reach. Logan tried pushing the creature away with his hands as it tried to bite him. The green acidic saliva fell on Logan's feet. In panic, he tried to scramble away. Fortunately, his enchanted socks didn't get burned through.

"Shield!"

A blue translucent umbrella of energy flowered around Logan's arm. It blasted the creature a few feet away. It landed on its back. Logan immediately surged to pick up his weapon. The monster's legs were flailing around, trying to find purchase, as it lolled back and forth on its back, gurgling urgently.

Logan gave it no quarter. He struck down with another two-handed swing of his weapon. The tissue was soft on the bug's underbelly and black blood sprayed everywhere, coating Logan in an oily stench.

Logan paid no heed. He charged toward his comrades to finish off the threat.

CHAPTER 21

The agents found the three of them panting and gasping, slumped against a wall. Balmer, who had acid burns on his arm, was applying a bandage Logan had provided. The agents had come running after hearing Balmer's gunshots. Kat weakly called to them when she'd heard them running past the room.

"Find any . . ." Logan said between breaths, ". . . nice sticks?"

The large, dark-haired agent, who was apparently in charge of the rest, said, "Check the Prin—"

He stopped himself mid-sentence. Logan smirked to himself. Old habits die hard.

After a formal cough, he asked, "Any of you hurt?"

Kat and Logan shook their heads. Balmer was tightening a bandage with his teeth.

"Nothing I can't handle," the young agent said between grunts.

Logan tossed the scythe-rang toward the black-haired agent. It slid across the floor and skidded to the man's feet.

"I need to catch my breath," Logan said. "Now, remove these bastards' horns, so we can get something nice to adorn those pretty sticks of yours. Also, I'm going to need . . . Damn it, we might not have enough Numa. Tumor, will the charge left in the D-crystal be enough?"

Kat cocked an eyebrow.

"Who's Tumor?" one of the agents asked. Logan made a disgruntled noise.

[Reconfiguring Neural Matrix . . . 30% completion]

[Assessing data . . .]

[Running variations . . .]

[Assuming these horns have the same naturally penetrative quality as the other blue-edged natural weapons of some of the fauna that you presume to originate from the large flying monster, limited Numa is needed for **[Enchantment]**. *Also,*

considering the shape of these materials closely resembling the end product you have in mind, there is a 100% probability of the Numa charge being enough for your designs. There is a 2.7% chance of you being able to give said items all the magical augmentations you had planned.]

"I don't need the decimals, Tumor," Logan said as he slowly got up. Now that the adrenaline was waning, aches from the fight were entering his spent muscles.

[Reconfiguring Neural Matrix . . . 31% completion]

[Noted. This one will adjust the communication protocol. Again.]

Logan couldn't help but grin. Was that *snark*?

Logan got the agents to lug the bodies of the ugly beetle-like insects to the room with the floating crystal construct. The agents and Kat removed the horns and large parts of the carapace and brought them to one of the stone tables.

Then Logan told them to go away and let him work. As per Kat's suggestion, they started preparing a meal from the meat. They weren't exactly bugs, because when they were cut into, they bled. The same sort of black and oily blood all of Levemoth's spawn seemed to have.

Logan ignored the stench and the squelching sounds and instead rummaged for a stone knife from the bag of tricks that Janice had made for him. He used it to carve the branches that the goons intended to use as spear shafts. He wanted to make them as straight as possible to conserve Numa.

Next up, he picked up one of the horns. It was *hard*. They also had a heft to them. Logan wasn't a fan of that. They would make the spears unbalanced and hard to throw.

Maybe that'll train the goons faster in **[Marksmanship]** *or whatever they have . . .*

Logan wanted to give the horns an **[Enchantment]** to make them lighter. After having accrued some experience with his new powers, he had realized that his Potency determined how powerful an **[Enchantment]** could be. But Control determined how accurately he could define said **[Enchantment]**.

Of course, in action, he told the Numa energy the measurements that Tumor defined when possible. Previously, the crystals would lose whatever charge was needed, adjusted for Logan's Potency, Efficiency, and Control. But since he was now working with limited Numa, he would have to try something different.

Maybe I could give them just a little spritz of lightness. I'll save that for last.

Shaping the spear shafts and attaching the horns was simple and barely spent any Numa. Logan picked up one of the spears and tried the weight. It wasn't ideal. The spears were barely usable.

"Tumor," Logan whispered, "how much lighter does the head need to be for the spears to be decent?"

[Please determine "decent."]

Logan groaned. "Ugh. Most cost-efficient?"

[Reconfiguring Neural Matrix . . . 32% completion]

[Calculating . . .]

[Overriding communications protocol . . .]

[For most cost-efficient solution, the weight of the horn used as spearhead should be 27.81% lighter.]

Logan brought one of the spears to the D-grade construct. It still had 14 percent charge left. Logan estimated a little over 1 percent charge was close to a full **[F-grade Numa crystal]**. Considering the E-grade chunks Logan had were worth maybe five or six full F-graders, these constructs were massive.

"Make this spearhead 27.81 percent lighter in weight. Do not alter the weight of the shaft. Most importantly, only use a maximum of 1 percent of your charge."

[Subclass Level Up!]
[Enchantment Level 13]
[Attribute Level Up!]
[Control: 11]

The D-grade construct glowed, and the spearheaded emitted a faint blue hue before quickly fading. The spear suddenly became significantly easy to wield. Logan spun it around in glee and triumph before getting a few curious glances from the others working on the bugs. Logan put the spear down on the table and checked the construct. Thirteen percent charge left.

Perfect.

"Tumor. How much lighter is the spearhead, percentage-wise?"

[22.55%]

"Nice," Logan said. "That's enough. Alright, let's give these other two the same treatment and then you can drone on about the aerodynamics and drag coefficient."

"Whatcha working on?" Kat came over and peered over Logan's shoulder.

"Something for you, actually."

"A gift?" Kat asked and grinned. "Oh, you sure know how to make a girl feel special. Should I not tell Freya?"

"I must have done something heinous in my old life to have been afflicted with you," Logan muttered as he pressed the piece of chitin against the crystal construct.

Kat rested her chin on Logan. "Man, your shoulder feels cold. That Freya sure must taste like honey for you to—"

"O-kayyyyyy," Logan said and brushed Kat off of him. "Why don't you go pester Balmer for a change?"

"He's too much of a . . . Balmer."

Logan chuckled. "Yeah, I get what you mean."

"So, what is this?" Kat asked, circling around to stand beside Logan.

"I noticed you have a . . . hands-on fighting style," Logan said.

"Yeah, I've done a bunch of MMA." Kat said, excitement rising in her voice. "Did you see me land that roundhouse on that ugly bugger?"

Logan didn't reply. Instead, he took Kat by the wrist and inspected her.

"Hey!" Kat said, but instead of pulling away, she blushed and went silent.

"Got it?" Logan asked.

"What?"

"Good," Logan said. "Now draw a model for me."

Kat pulled her wrist away. "Are you alright?"

Logan shushed her. "Let me focus."

The plating on the front legs of those beetle-fiends had been the perfect size. The material only needed to be curved a bit to form a nice bowl. Logan stuffed the inside of the cup with some bandage cloth as a cushion. Then came the tricky part. Logan intoned an enchantment that made a part of the chitin cup flexible. He was absolutely elated as soon as he saw the blue hue.

[Subclass Level Up!]
[Transmutation Level 10]
[Attribute Level Up!]
[Focus: 7]

He felt like he should have gotten a control level up as well, but eh, he had only just gotten one recently. Still, he commended himself on his endless genius.

"Try this on," Logan said and gave the item to Kat.

"You . . . What?" Kat asked in mounting excitement. She put the chitin-glove on.

"Can you form a fist?" Logan asked.

"Holy shit! I can! What the hell?!" Kat exclaimed, her voice echoing throughout the room. "Look guys! Any of you big boys want to take me on now?"

"Calm down," Logan said and chuckled. "I need to adjust the mouth of the glove. I'll make it flexible. Then I'll make another one. You can tie them on with that cloth you have over your knuckles now."

"Holy shit," Kat said. "Dude, no wonder your dad and the agents don't like you. You make them look bad."

Logan gave an awkward laugh and instinctively checked on the goons. Balmer had heard Kat and was now giving Logan an ugly look.

"Right," Logan said. "Look, go bother Balmer now. You're making him jealous or something. And most importantly, I need to focus. I'm almost done. Now, go!"

CHAPTER 22

Logan was loath to let go of one of the three **[E-grade Numa crystals]** that the beetle-fiends had dropped. But he figured the goons could use it in a pinch if they ended up in a situation against the Leve spawn still skulking around. Although now they no longer had to go hunting. They could just carry these two and a half giant insect monsters back to camp for meat. They did taste awful, though . . .

The D-grade construct was dim and spent. Logan had taken the large carapaces from the beetle-fiends' backs and made shields for the agents. They had a pretty potent weight-reducing **[Enchantment]** as well as some extra durability magicked in.

It had pumped Logan's Efficiency to 9 and Focus to 8. No subclass level ups, though. The gains had slowed down slightly, but that was fine.

Logan could definitely feel the difference in everything he did. He was spending so much less Numa than at the start of this ridiculous adventure, and his designs were sharper and **[Enchantments]** stronger. Not that he had been pushing the limit in the case of the latter. The shields and spears he had given the agents held very conservative **[Enchantments]**.

Regardless, the initially frosty or downright hostile agents were warming up to him. It seemed it wasn't just Freya who appreciated gifts. Logan didn't mind providing. At least it helped him keep leveling up.

The agents stayed for a while out of gratitude and willingness to test out their new equipment. Soon after, they ran into another group of black beetle-fiends. Logan stayed back and let the agents fight. He couldn't throw his weapon without risking hitting an ally. And besides, the goons were clearly having fun.

One of them did get a nasty stab wound on his thigh, but he assured Logan that he could limp back to the base with the gatherers. Logan didn't say anything when the goons took two of the four **[E-grade Numa crystals]** that they had just obtained. If it weren't for his categorical dislike of the goons, he might have even admitted it was fair that they left them with two.

After the battle, the agents decided to head back with the beetle corpses and intel.

"Either of you have skills?" Logan asked Balmer and Kat after the agents had left.

"I've got two! I'm a level 3 [**Brawler**]" Kat announced.

"Yeah?" Logan said.

"I got [**Power Strike**] and [**Tough Skin**]."

"Sounds good to me," Logan said and lobbed one of the [**E-grade Numa crystals**] over to Kat. She caught it with the hand that wasn't chitin-gloved.

Logan pointed at Kat's pants. "You can put it in your pocket. It'll work as long as you're touching it, I think."

"Work how?"

"I don't know. I just say what skill I want to use and trust the Numa to figure out the rest."

Balmer scoffed. "Can't believe you don't know more by now."

"Uh huh," Logan said. "Care to share your great wealth of knowledge?"

"Give me one, and I'll figure out everything needed to know about it in two hours."

"What's your class?" Logan asked as he rolled his eyes and lobbed a crystal at Balmer, hard. "[**Fire-making Tool**]?"

"Funny," Balmer said but didn't offer anything else.

"First time you don't even try for a comeback," Logan said as they checked another room.

"What can I say?" Balmer muttered through his teeth, his tone oddly defensive. "I'm getting tired of your shit."

"Boys," Kat said from the front of the line, "play nice."

"Wait a minute," Logan said, his smirk spreading into a malevolent grin. "You don't have a class, do you?"

"Oh, honey," Kat said, turning to grin at Balmer. "Don't worry about it. A lot of boys have their growth spurts later."

"Assholes," Balmer muttered.

Logan and Kat shared a laugh, but then Logan grew serious. "Yeah, we're not going further without you picking something. Let's check this room."

The room was fortunately empty. It had been quiet after the agents had left, which was fine by Logan. He thought he had heard some distant gurgling and scuttling, but it could have been his mind playing tricks.

[It was.]

Thanks, Tumor . . .

Logan ushered Kat and Balmer in. It was actually significantly different from the other rooms they'd encountered. This one was structured like an amphitheater or a lecture hall, with descending rows of stone benches behind white marble tables. Some of them no longer held an [**Enchantment**] and thus had fallen and crumbled. Down at the bottom of the room was a giant round floating table on a dais.

How are these tables still floating? Are the blue LED-ropes powering them?

"Whoa," Kat said under her breath. She took a seat behind one of the benches and knocked on the white floating marble. The sound reverberated a deep and rich bass which filled the room. It was somehow soothing.

They gawked around the room and inspected it but found nothing else that was out of the ordinary. There was a lot of dust on the floor, and Logan suspected a thousand years ago that dust had been books and tomes.

Logan also took a seat at a bench and put his feet on the floating white marble. Like a distant gong, the sound vibrated through his legs to the rest of his body. The effect was strangely soothing.

"I think I should bang your head on these marble sheets," Logan said to Balmer who was still standing. "Might be therapeutic for both of us."

"I'd like to see you try," Balmer muttered.

"Just sit your ass down and choose a class," Logan said.

They passed the waterskin around for a while as they sat down. Every time you took a sip, you had to contribute to Balmer's class question. Despite being top of his class in school and his enormous ego, this idiot was *indecisive*.

Logan had taken a proper swig from the waterskin and gone down the stairs to have another look at the strange room.

"You got [**Marksmanship**] from handling a gun, right?" Kat asked, idly tapping a finger on the floating marble.

"Yeah, level 7," Balmer said, squatting on one of the steps.

"So pick [**Archer**]," Kat said.

"Logan is already a ranged attacker."

Logan perked an ear at that as he knelt to inspect under the big table on the dais. "Surely you're not suggesting this isn't a one-time thing, Balmer?"

"Daddy's precious baby deer is going to need protection in the future," Balmer said.

"That'd be much more irritating, if it hadn't been me who saved you from those bugs," Logan said.

Kat sniggered. "He does have a point."

"You just agree to everything he says," Balmer snapped.

"I have my reasons," Kat said, a little colder this time.

"You really think you got a chance with him?" Balmer let out a cold laugh. "I don't know what the Beckstein girl sees in this spoiled little brat, but she's ten times the woman you are."

"The hell do you think you know about me?" Kat barked, snapping to attention.

"You're just like the Little Prince here," Balmer said. "Do what you want. Take what you want. Say what you want. Selfish and arrogant."

Logan was feeling the heat building up. He didn't really care if they bickered, but they needed to work together. "You're really good at making new friends, Balmer."

The young goon snarled. Logan mentally shrugged. He thought he saw something blue moving in the corner of his vision. He turned and saw one of those small bugs. He crept toward it slowly to get a better look. At first Logan had thought these were the baby beetle-fiends. But this was a different kind of insect altogether.

They were like grasshoppers with spindly legs and long butts which glowed with the blue hue of Numa. The little thing noticed Logan and skittered away into the shadows.

"You sure you don't have an [**Asshole**] class in your recommendations?" Kat asked, glaring at Balmer, arms crossed.

"I'm sure you got it as one of your subclasses, under the class [**Massive Bitch**]," Balmer retorted.

"Look," Logan said patiently as he looked for the little lightbulb-grasshopper in the corners. "Not that I ever get tired of your cringe comebacks, Balmer. But maybe we should get back to the class choice."

"I don't know what's the most optimal and useful," Balmer said and sighed.

"Stop thinking like my father's lackey for once in your life," Logan said. Oh, there was another blue bug. Logan crept slowly closer, sliding his hand toward the bug. "What do you want to pick?"

"I . . . Nothing," Balmer said defensively. "I'll pick what's most optimal."

"Good grief," Logan muttered under his breath. The bug was coming closer, zigging and zagging curiously toward his hand.

From the sound of Kat's voice, she wanted to say something scathing, but she controlled herself. "What are your recommended options again?"

"That shouldn't matter," Balmer said.

Kat sighed. "Just indulge me."

"[Sentry], [Scout], [Phantom]."

"All of those sound like they'll be light on their feet," Kat said with a lopsided smile.

"What's that supposed to mean?" Balmer asked.

"Touchy," Kat said.

"Pick [**Phantom**]," Logan said. The bug skittered away and Logan cursed to himself.

"Why?" Balmer asked.

Logan shrugged. He saw where the bug went. He was going to try something else. "Sounds the coolest."

"What kind of a basis is that?"

"We really need to start moving soon, you idiot," Logan said. He picked a Numa crystal from his pocket and held it in an open palm. The little insect in the corner immediately stopped and turned. "Which of those classes most closely resembles what you wanted to do most as a child when you grew up."

"I wanted to become an agent or a spy."

"Living the dream, huh . . ." Logan muttered to himself. The bug crawled onto Logan's hand and tentatively touched the crystal with its spindly legs.

"I agree with Logan," Kat said. "Pick [**Phantom**]."

"Why?"

"Sounds the coolest."

"I hate you both."

CHAPTER 23

Balmer demanded that they go over the pros and cons of each of the class options in excruciating detail. Kat indulged the goon for some reason, but Logan tuned out quickly, engrossed in something else entirely. The glowing insect was doing something with the Numa crystal in Logan's hand. It seemed to be *feeding* off of it. The crystal's blue light faded ever so slightly, and the insect's butt glowed brighter.

Well, aren't you an interesting little thing?

Logan tried to bring up a text window by simply looking at the bug, but nothing happened. Well, *something* happened.

[Reconfiguring Neural Matrix . . . 44% completion]

"Holy shit, Tumor," Logan whispered. "What happened?"

[This one received a data transfer of substantial volume. The data is encrypted. This one will attempt to decipher.]

"You do that . . ."

Logan looked at the [**E-grade Numa crystal, 97%**]. Logan wondered if this last transaction had been worth it. He could afford it, especially if they could just find a few more crystals. Logan listened to two of his companions arguing with his left ear. Kat was slowly turning Balmer around. That was good. While they weren't exactly in a rush, Logan felt they were exposed.

Sure, they had some Numa now, but what he really wanted to find was another proper deposit of those D-grade constructs. That way he could really deck himself and Kat out to deal with those beetle-fiends and any other Levespawn that might crop up. But Logan was worried. He still remembered that elephant-sized creature that split in two. If they came across one of those, they'd be dead meat.

"Fine!" Balmer exclaimed. "I picked it. Happy?"

"For now," Kat said. From the sound of it, she *really* enjoyed winning arguments. Logan could respect that.

"You're going to need a weapon, Mr. Valedictorian," Logan said as he got up and dusted himself off. "What does your class do, exactly?"

"You weren't listening?" Balmer asked.

"Something about shadows and being stealthy?" Logan guessed.

"Huh," Balmer said. "Good guess."

Logan gave him a lazy wink.

"So you'll be in the backline with pretty boy," Kat said. "It's good that you guys know your place. Behind me."

Logan snorted.

Balmer blushed. "That sounded—"

Kat punched Balmer on the shoulder. "I SAID IT WRONG, OKAY?"

Since Balmer's class apparently had something to do with quick movement and stealth, Logan and Kat coaxed him into scouting for them. Balmer walked softly ahead twenty yards and peeked inside the rooms. He apparently started gaining levels in his attributes quickly, particularly in Stealth and Agility. Balmer was anxious about not having weapons or offensive skills if something were to happen, but Logan and Kat couldn't do much more than offer a shrug.

"Find something you want to use as a weapon, and we'll look into it," Logan had said. Then he'd looked to the side, picked something up, and handed it to the young goon. "Here. Use this for now."

Logan had plopped a rock into Balmer's extended hand. "Gee, thanks . . ."

Despite the tension and Balmer's anxiety, they didn't run into any more beetle-fiends. That was too bad, as far as Logan was concerned. He had exhausted an almost full **[E-grade Numa crystal]** to recharge his shield-watch and the scythe-rang, as well as to replace the **[Enchantments]** on his socks and pants with stronger ones. Both of his comrades held a crystal, so that left Logan with one fully charged E-grader after all was said and done. Good enough for an emergency situation, like sealing a door from a giant beetle-fiend mother.

And that was unnervingly close to what happened next.

Balmer returned with urgent steps, his face white and sweating in the soft blue light of the snaking LED-ropes.

"There's something ahead," Balmer whispered in clipped tones. "Something big."

"A monster?" Logan asked.

"Yes," Balmer hissed as he began pushing Logan and Kat back in the direction they'd come from.

Logan looked over his shoulder. He couldn't see anything ahead, other than a tall room with a giant floating Numa-crystal in the middle of it. "There's a crystal!"

"I don't care. We're not going in there."

"Uh, guys?" Kat asked. "You hearing that?"

A loud gurgling came from the nearby room. It wasn't followed by the skittering they had grown accustomed to. It was followed rather by the lumbering sound of something heavy approaching with ponderous steps sending tremors through the floor.

Logan reached for his endless bag of tricks and pulled out the light-stick, turning on its **[Enchantment]**. He raised the light further to see what was coming. He really wished he hadn't done that.

A giant, bulbous, chitinous mass came up to the doorway. The atrium in that room had a much higher ceiling. Its head wasn't visible, but its pale, hairy abdomen was, along with chitinous legs protruding in many a direction.

The gurgling sound grew louder, and the bug-creature's stomach began to swell. Every instinct in Logan told him to run, but he was too hypnotized by the grotesque sight. Its balloon of a stomach began to bulge and swell in places as if an angry unborn fetus were threatening to emerge. Finally, in a disgusting crescendo, it burst open, sending the now-too-familiar black oily gunk flying everywhere.

Then a swarm of black beetle-fiends came gurgling and hissing out of the creature. They clambered over each other, acid drooling from their disgusting mouths.

"RUN!"

Despite being at the back, Balmer set the pace. Was it his new class or conditioning? Logan only hoped he knew the way out. They seemed to be able to outrun the beetles, but a dead end would be very literal for them.

"Those memorization techniques better not have been bullshit!" Logan yelled.

Logan was the last in line. The scythe-rang made for an awkward running style, but he'd be damned if he would drop his precious weapons. Kat gave a worried glance over her shoulder. The gap between her and Balmer was growing wider. Whereas the gap between Logan and the beetles was shortening.

"I can't keep this pace up for long . . . Tumor, give me an idea or we're both done."

[Reconfiguring Neural Matrix . . . 46% completion]

[This one recalls that you were able to use the ability **[Empower]** *on your weapon, without it being in direct contact with a Numa crystal, before. Chance of being able to reproduce the event with a similar action is 98.82%.]*

Logan was too caught up in fear and adrenaline to reprimand Tumor for giving him unnecessary decimals. All he felt was gratitude. But there was one hitch. He had failed before. Had he done enough since?

One way to find out.

The acidic spittle of the creatures was on his heels. He could feel it hitting his socks and pants. The giant monstrous insects were maybe four feet away. They would catch up to him soon. In a mad rush of adrenaline, Logan practically yelled out the incantation: "Give my socks a Speed **[Enchantment]** so they can run faster!"

[Subclass Level Up!]
[Enchantment Level 14]

Oh, fuck. Thank Fat Buddha, that worked!

Logan could immediately feel each step push him a little further. No extra muscle power or oxygen was needed. It was as if the socks generated a force that pushed him up and forward from the ground, like a little gust of wind.

The gurgling, hissing, and skittering that had just been at Logan's heels began to get further away. At that, Logan caught a second wind, bringing him into an elated sprint. He risked a backward glance. The corridor was *full* of those dog-sized beetle-fiends, their black and blue horns extended, acid spittle hissing on the floor in their wake.

Logan grinned. He loved this feeling. Just for the hell of it, he went one step further.

"**[Empower]!**"

[Skill Level Up!]
[Empower Level 3]
[Attribute Level Up!]
[Potency: 9]

He could feel something shift in his Socks of Awesomeness. All of the enchantments that those bad boys held suddenly became more potent—mainly the speed and traction spells. Every step forward he took was a slap in the face of physics.

Logan bolted off, the blue lines at the sides of the floor becoming a blur as he ran past Kat and then Balmer. He grinned at the shocked expressions on their faces.

"Which way?" Logan quipped to Balmer.

"Turn left in that next T and we're out . . ."

Logan sped ahead and saw light. He could have slowed down to a jog or even a walk at this point. That would have been prudent. The sprint was taking up Numa charge from his Socks of Awesomeness. But he loved the feeling so much. The air on his face, the fleeting flight in the air between every step. Logan laughed and reveled in his speed. This was freedom. This was *his*.

Within seconds, Logan was out of the doorway. It was evening, and the sky was cloaked in a soft orange. Immediately, he sensed something was watching him. Whatever it was had been waiting at the doorway.

There was no time to wonder about that. Whatever it was, it was curious, not hostile. Logan looked around for rocks or sticks or anything to block the entrance for when his comrades came out. There wasn't anything.

There were bushes with little blue flowers all around them, and a few trees with low branches. But hacking the branches down would take time that Logan didn't have.

Balmer came out. He rested his hands on his knees, panting and gasping. He took a few breaths and snapped, "We need to move. They'll follow!"

"No," Logan said, still trying to think. "I want to fight them."

"Are you crazy?!" Balmer rasped. "There's like twenty of them."

"This doorway will be our Pass at Thermopylae."

"That's ridiculous!" Balmer said. "There's too many, we—"

"Shut up!" Logan growled.

Balmer did. Logan thought hard. Tumor was offering him options and they all meshed and morphed in his mind, as he tried to think about how he could block the pass. There had to be a way. This was risky. But the reward was too great. Logan wouldn't leave empty-handed.

Kat dashed out. Logan suddenly had it. He tossed the scythe-rang to Balmer. "Take this!"

Kat turned and looked at them incredulously when she noticed Logan and Balmer weren't running. "Come on!"

"We fight!" Logan said and crouched down on the ground before the doorway.

CHAPTER 24

Logan had Tumor drew a red circle on the ground for him. It was maybe four yards in diameter, which fully covered the doorway and then some. The swarm of beetle-fiends was seconds away. This needed to work or running away would be hard.

"Make this ground like quicksand. Soft, hard to tread, and sinking. Make it also adhesive and sticky. Make it extremely hard to move around in. Make it become very heavy once it sticks to you. Make it paralyze anything that touches it. Make it instantly blind anyone who touches it. Make it dissolve tissue into more sticky trap-stuff! Use all the tricks! [**Enchantment**] and [**Transmutation**]. I don't care if it sucks all of my Numa dry!"

[Transmutation level requirement not met]
[Enchantment level requirement not met]

[Subclass Level Up!]
[Enchantment Level 15]
[Transmutation Level 11]

[Attribute Level Up!]
[Potency: 10]
[Focus: 9]
[Efficiency: 10]
[Class Level Up!]
[Artificer Level 5]
[Class Passive Skill Choice Available]

A massive minty fresh feeling blew through Logan as he watched the ground inside the circle turn into glossy, bubbling mud. Slowly, the circle of sticky death started even widening, as it ate away at the grass and ground around it.

The beetle-fiends rushed at them with no heed. They fell knee-deep into the sticky trap. Hissing and acid spitting ensued. More beetle-fiends rushed over their comrades, only to tumble into the trap themselves. A score of them were soon trapped in the trap. Some only dipped a leg in there, but it was enough to weaken and slow them down substantially.

As the trap's radius widened and as the beetles struggled and splashed around in the heavy, oily substance, they succumbed to at least partial blindness and various degrees of paralysis.

It was clear the monsters still had motor functions and some degree of sight, but they had been severely weakened.

"Don't touch the sludge!" Logan shouted. "Balmer, throw me the crystal! Kat, keep them busy!"

"On it!" Kat said as she kicked a straggling beetle with a limp.

Balmer threw the Numa crystal to Logan, who caught it and immediately ran to the closest tree. Using [**Transmutation**], he removed a fat branch and started extracting javelins from it. He asked Tumor for something crude and effective and got just that. He was going for mass production.

[**Attribute Level Up!**]
[**Efficiency: 11**]

"Balmer!" Logan shouted. "Here!"

Kat roared as she punched one of the beetle-fiends with her gloved fist. It was sent tumbling on its back into the now-full pool of deadly sticky stuff. Balmer was distracting three beetles, keeping himself away from their spikes and acid. His new class had clearly provided him with speed and grace he had not had before now.

It's actually not too bad that he's on distraction duty.

Logan threw a javelin at one of the monsters that was trying to climb out of the pit. He struck true, but the carapace was hard. However, the projectile had enough momentum to tip the monster on its back into the sticky sludge, which is where it would stay.

Logan didn't waste time; he just kept lobbing the javelins, and when he ran out, he simply created more.

[**Skill Level Up!**]
[**Marksmanship Level 6**]
[**Skill Level Up!**]
[**Marksmanship Level 7**]

Kat was slowing down. She had a pained expression on her face and her other leg buckled under the weight of her movement. Balmer was dancing around the insect monsters with more confidence and had by now collected the attention of most of the surviving beetles who had avoided the sludge.

The young goon was fine. He was dancing around the beetles and slicing them up with the scythe-rang. He was surprisingly adept at using it. It was Kat who looked like she needed help. Logan had to give their resident [**Brawler**] a breather right this instant.

"Hey!" Logan yelled as he ran up to where Kat was fighting near the pit of sludge. "On me, bastards!"

He threw another javelin as he ran and then took a better grip of the club he had [**Transmuted**] just now. Logan's heart was pounding, but this was the right thing to do. He took a baseball swing at the skull of the beetle-fiend closest to Kat. It cracked and the monster fell.

"Catch your breath!" Logan barked over his shoulder as he took another swing.

It didn't take long for Logan to run out of breath. He wasn't exactly trained in fighting and his energy was sapped within a minute of swinging and bashing. Just as he was about to take a fatal stumble, Kat came up, kicked the beetle about to assault him and grabbed the makeshift club.

"Go back to . . ." Kat said between labored breaths, ". . . tossing sticks . . . You wimp . . ."

When the last of the beetle-fiends who weren't trapped in the sludge were dead, all three of them fell on the grass.

Everything hurt. Logan knew some of the beetle-fiends were still alive. He knew the [**Enchantments**] in his trap would run out sooner or later. But right now, he just *couldn't*. He had no fight left in him. He had given it his all. Over a score of beetles lay dead around them. Most of them had their legs and chunks of their carapaces melted off by the death trap. Logan was gripping a half-snapped javelin against his chest.

"You okay, Kat?" Balmer said weakly.

Kat let out a pained grunt. It had all been a blur. Logan wasn't sure, but he thought Kat was wounded. No small wonder. He felt a little guilty. He could hear his father's voice ringing in his head.

IRRESPONSIBLE!

"Shut up," he muttered to himself. With great labor, Logan struggled to his hands and knees. Every fiber of his being was miserable and hurting. He had never physically exerted himself like that before. It had been a true battlefield of chaos and death. Fortunately, not theirs. He noticed Balmer was already on his feet, as shaky as he looked.

Logan had a few burns here and there from the acid, as well as a scrape on his arm from a charge attack. Mostly, he was afflicted with exhaustion. Despite that, he finally forced himself to his feet.

With some wobble and panting, he had to try to remember how to human again. But in the end, he did manage. Logan dragged his feet to Balmer and grabbed the scythe-rang from him. After that, Logan rummaged through his pouch and gave the young goon a bundle of bandage cloth.

"Fix her up. I'll practice my aim on these bastards."

With a serious nod, Balmer took the cloth and went over to tend to Kat. There wasn't blame nor anger in that gaze. More like comradeship. Logan wasn't sure how he was supposed to feel about that. Gratitude toward this person was hard. But he wasn't as bad as Logan had initially thought. Somehow, he felt that was exactly what Balmer was thinking too. Logan reciprocated the nod.

With a flourish, he took aim at one of the beetle-fiends. As he threw, his father's voice thundered in his ears.

IRRESPONSIBLE!

Logan threw javelin after javelin until he ran out. Then he grabbed the Scythe-rang and smashed the rest of moving beetles into bits. His lungs burned and his muscles ached, but he kept hacking. When there was only death and stillness around him, Logan fell to his knees.

Balmer turned to him in horror.

"Logan," he said. "She's not breathing!"

CHAPTER 25

Freya brushed a strand of hair behind her ear and sighed.

There was a lot to sigh about. She was worried about Logan and missed him terribly. She was hungry. She hadn't slept that well. And the bugs pissed her off too. As did that bitch, Kat. But most of all, Freya felt like a fool.

She was doing a menial errand. That in itself was fine, she supposed. With this new life, menial errands were a part of life. She was crouching on the ground and collecting petals of a specific white flower for Dr. Rosenberg. The [**Healer**] was testing all sorts of plants to make medicine. Freya figured the flower wouldn't amount to anything but a bitter taste, but what did she know?

She sighed again. It wasn't fair. She knew she was a good person. She knew she wasn't a gold digger. She had loved Logan long before she even understood the full scope of his family's wealth.

But dating the son of a billionaire since you were a kid came with certain perks. Such as getting pretty much *anything* you wanted by just mentioning the thought. Freya had long ago promised herself not to abuse that power. It wasn't her money. Well, it would be some day. Kind of.

Bad thought! You dumbass. It's not like any of that matters anymore.

But she did still love Logan. That made her feel better about herself. Logan had changed a lot since coming here, and Freya had to admit it might have been for the better. As much as she adored his free-spirited, openhearted confidence, he was a child just like she was in many ways.

"Maybe that's why we're good together," Freya said to herself. as she plucked the petals in her hands. The squirrel-monkeys that were observing her with great curiosity made noises that sounded almost questioning. Freya smiled at them, but her heart wasn't in it. Not like she needed to impress a bunch of monkeys.

"But the difference between Logan and me is that irresponsibility that Malcolm doesn't understand. I'm here sitting on my hands, trying to think of what's the best way to go forward. Logan just goes forward. Sure, he could think more, but that man acts with no hesitation. He's brave."

The monkeys had nothing to say to that. But one of them made a screech and showed Freya its butt. The other monkeys laughed and then left to go on about their monkey business.

When Freya came back to the camp, she wasn't surprised to see Malcolm Specter talking with two new people who were being offered some berries and mushrooms to eat. They ate them with such overt gratitude, it almost broke Freya's heart.

A small trickle of people had started to come to the camp, most likely guided by the smoke of the cooking fires. Each one looked more haggard than the next. They all practically ate right out of Malcolm's hand. Freya smiled to herself. Logan would hate to see that.

They see a strong and stern leader. Of course they flock to Malcolm in a situation like this.

Freya brought the flower petals to Dr. Rosenberg. He was an elderly man in his early sixties. Long horse face and a receding gray hairline. His ever-creased forehead was of monstrous proportions.

"Freya," he said and offered a tired smile. "Good girl."

"You're welcome," Freya said with a smile of her own. Albeit hers was strained. He clearly didn't mean it in a demeaning way, but right now it felt like that.

"Freya." The powerful, sonorous voice of Malcolm Specter came from behind her. Freya turned.

"Hey," she said.

"Good job on helping our **[Healer]**. What are you going to do next?"

Freya knew this line of questioning very well. If she didn't have a plan, Malcolm would give her one. She just wished he was nicer about it.

"I . . ." Freya started, trying to come up with something. ". . . Don't know."

There was the slightest flicker on Malcolm's face. Freya had years of practice, so she knew what this particular lapse in poise meant: displeasure.

"Take some food and water to Simmons and ask if you can help him," Malcolm said. "If not, go collect rocks for us."

"Got it," Freya said, trying to sound confident. From the look on Malcolm's face, he wasn't impressed. It hurt more than it should have.

He is actually trying to be polite. Logan would get reamed for this.

After getting food and drink from the gatherers, Freya sighed as she made her way toward where Simmons worked. It was easy to follow the line of stumps left behind him. That man was methodical. Simmons had always been a nondescript sort of guy, who kept any emotions he had close to the chest. Even more so than the average agent. But he had found a strange passion for chopping wood. Freya wished she had something she felt that way for.

I DON'T KNOW WHAT TO DO! she screamed internally. *WHAT CLASS AM I SUPPOSED TO PICK?! I'M NOT GOOD AT ANYTHING!*

She saw the shirtless Simmons swinging his stone axe in a wide arc. With only a few deft strikes, the young tree he was cutting was almost done. Classes were amazing. Simmons's single-minded enthusiasm had gotten him to at least level 15 already in his **[Lumberjack]** subclass.

Meanwhile I'm not even level 1 in anything.

She greeted Simmons, brought the food and water to him, and sat on a stump for a while to watch him work. The man was so engrossed in it, he didn't even stop to eat. His built body shone with sweat in the morning sun. Resting her chin on her fist, she watched him for a while, then brought up her class selection window for the umpteenth time.

I know what class I want to pick. I think . . . Well, technically there's a few. But that one would just be so COOL. But it's weird, right? Logan would just laugh and tell me to pick it anyway. But he's the kind of person who could get away with it . . .

Soon enough, Simmons wiped a sheen of sweat off his face that could qualify as a miniature monsoon rain. He was as blunt as ever when he thanked Freya, but there was satisfaction in his eyes. Freya asked what he needed help with, and soon enough she was carrying varying pieces of wood back to the camp for building and crafting materials.

It was a morning of menial tasks and incessant worrying spiraling into bottomless despair. So a regular Tuesday? Well, not for Freya. She was used to private jet planes, fancy dinners, and expensive clothes. She could live without, but that didn't mean she didn't miss some of that.

Well, that stuff's gone now. Better start letting it go. Also, are we going to need weekdays and calendars?

Freya spent the rest of the morning lugging lumber to the **[Carpenter]** and **[Builder]** who were building a pier by the river. Malcolm had insisted on one for washing, fishing, and water-gathering. Freya could only marvel at its many potential functions.

It was hard work, but at least she was being useful. After an hour, she was so exhausted and sweaty that she had to stop and take a rest. She plopped herself onto a smooth rock next to the food and water supplies that one of the agents was guarding. Freya thought it excessive, but then again, if more people flocked here, there were bound to be bad apples. Maybe Malcolm had a point there.

As Freya was munching on a bright yellow fruit resembling a pear, she saw the agents stir up, their new shields hoisted.

"Somebody's coming!" one of them announced to the camp.

Through the woods appeared three familiar faces.

"Logan!" Freya got up, a wide smile on her face. That smile waned at record speed. "Why are you carrying that bitch?!"

CHAPTER 26

Logan watched Freya stomp toward him with fists clenched. She started yammering at him for carrying Kat home, but he wasn't in the mood right now. He put Kat down carefully. The girl whimpered half-awake and clutched at his satchel. He pried her fingers off gently.

"Frey, get Dr. Rosenberg."

Freya was about to say something more, but Logan snapped at her. "Now!"

She opened and closed her mouth like a fish, took another look at Kat, and gave him a sober nod. Logan sighed in relief.

The elderly [Healer] half ran, half hobbled to where Kat lay. Logan gave him an [E-Grade Numa crystal, 100%], one of many.

"Use this. I'll give you another if you need."

The old doctor didn't ask what had happened or what was wrong with Kat. He told them to give him space and immediately hunched over the young girl's body, checking her pulse and pupils and whatnot.

After a minute, he turned to Logan. "Young M— Logan. What bit her?"

"A beetle-monster. One of those blue and black things. Her thigh."

Dr. Rosenberg ripped open her jeans' torn-up thigh and revealed a beetle-horn slash and four puncture wounds on her leg. He inspected the damage and pressed on the flesh, eliciting a groan from Kat. Then he gave it a sniff.

"They aren't venomous," the [Healer] said.

"The other thigh," Logan said sourly. Freya came over and kissed Logan's shoulder. He nudged her head.

"Happy to see you again," he said.

"Likewise," Freya murmured. "What happened?"

"I'll . . . Tell you later."

The other jeans leg was also ripped but it hadn't happened in the battle. It had three of those manufactured clean vertical cuts that was meant to make it look cooler. Logan always thought they looked dumb as hell. Who'd spend a hundred bucks to buy ripped clothes? Idiots, that's who.

Between one of those cuts, however, Kat had clearly been burned. It wasn't much larger than a cigarette butt, but the skin around it was angry red in inflammation. Logan knew exactly what had caused that. His ears were burning. One phrase for it would be "paralyzing, corrosive death sludge" (patent pending). Another would be "irresponsibility."

"Use the crystal!" Logan urged the doctor, who was clearly weighing his options.

Dr. Rosenberg raised an eyebrow moderately. "How?"

"Tell it you want to heal her from the toxin, and you want to repair tissue or whatever."

The good doctor did just that. The crystal clearly yielded some energy, and the red swollen skin around the burn got ever so slightly better.

"Oh," Dr. Rosenberg said. "I leveled up! That's . . . interesting. But it says the level requirement is not met."

"What level are you?" Logan snapped urgently. He had seen Kat's state weakening by the hour. He'd have thought it would have gotten better overnight in a nice cool place to sleep, but it had been the opposite.

"One," Rosenberg said. "Well, 2 now in **[Medicine]**. I also have some of these . . . attribute points, mostly in Insight.

Logan groaned in frustration. He snapped his fingers at Balmer, who was standing there, particularly uselessly right now. "Give me back my weapon."

"What are you—"

Logan snatched the scythe-rang from the goon and, without hesitation, cut a proper gash on his forearm. Freya yelped.

"Logan!"

Logan thrust the arm at their **[Healer]**. "We're going to power-level your ass. Heal it."

The good doctor gave him a hesitant look. He gulped and made a polite, mild-mannered request of the Numa crystal.

Everyone looked at the four-inch red gash on Logan's arm. First, the trickle of bleeding slowed down. Then the flesh knit itself back together an inch from both ends.

"Oh!" Rosenberg said. "I leveled up quite a lot!"

"Again!" Logan demanded.

For the next ten minutes, Logan cut and Rosenberg healed. Nearly everyone, including Logan's father, came and watched the procedure. They only stopped when Logan fell to his knees from weakness due to blood loss. Regardless, he presented his trembling arm to the doctor. He healed it fully.

When Logan fumbled for his weapon, about to make another cut, Malcolm grabbed his wrist.

"Enough."

"It's not!" Logan spat out, half-delirious. "It's my fault! I will fix it."

"You will rest," his father said in a tone that brooked no argument. Then he took the blade from Logan's weakened hands and cut his own arm. It was a force-ful and deep cut, blood flying in every direction. Without the slightest flinch on his stern face, Malcolm offered his hand to the doctor.

With blurry vision, his dizziness almost overtaking him, Logan noticed the E-grade crystal was almost spent. He fished for another one from his bulging, glowing pouch.

"Here," he managed to say before passing out in Freya's arms.

Logan woke up in the shade of a great tree of leathery leaves and a gray trunk. Freya held his head in her lap and smiled down affectionately.

"Not a bad way to wake up," Logan said and gave her a smile.

Freya brushed a strand of hair off of his forehead. "Now this I know how to do at least."

"What?" Logan muttered.

"Oh. Nothing."

"How are you feeling?" Freya asked.

"A little weak."

"Dr. Rosenberg told me you would need to eat something. We have some beetle-meat left."

"G-great," Logan muttered. "More beetles. Just what I wanted."

Freya rolled her eyes. "I'll go get you some."

She returned a few minutes later with beetle mush and water in crude clay bowls. That doctor who had started working with clay must have gained a few levels. The bowls were smooth and almost even.

"She alright?" Logan asked quietly.

Freya's face scrunched up ever so slightly in disgust.

"Don't be an asshole, Frey," Logan said gently.

"Y— I— She pisses me off, alright?!"

Logan laughed. It hurt his ribs. He was still sore from yesterday's great battle. But a weight fell off his sore shoulders.

"She's weak," Freya said. "Took the doc two of those crystals to stabilize her. Now she's resting in the den."

"That's what you guys are calling it?"

Freya shrugged. "It caught on."

"You heard what happened?" Logan asked quietly, wiping his mouth after hav-ing gulped a big mouthful of water from the bowl.

"Some of it," Freya said. "Balmer started making a report when your dad stopped cutting himself. I've never seen either of you looking so . . . intense."

"Specters always act like that when they're teleported into different realms!"

She giggled, but Logan noticed that she was mostly humoring him. He couldn't blame her. That joke wasn't exactly Late Night Show material. Blood loss was surely the reason.

Logan told her what had transpired. It sucked having to live through it again. Logan didn't question his actions, as they had been necessary.

But He had put people at risk for greed. That sounded an awful lot like a Malcolm Specter move. Logan didn't particularly enjoy that thought. But at least the risk had paid off. Twenty-three **[E-grade Numa crystals]**. Well, twenty-one if healing Kat had used two. That would leave seven for the three of them. Logan could get a lot done with seven of those bad boys. Oh, he had plans.

"I guess I left my satchel where we arrived," Logan said and got up. "At least we made a fat bank!"

"Yeah, umm . . ." Freya said, searching for the right words.

Logan didn't like where this was heading.

"He didn't . . ." Logan asked, anger mounting in his voice.

Freya cringed. "He did."

CHAPTER 27

All of Logan's aches and feebleness were forgotten in a surge of anger. He knew he should calm down. He knew his father could have simply taken the Numa crystals for safekeeping. He knew he could be testing him (which pissed him off even more). Logan began to scan the camp but couldn't find him anywhere.

"You . . ." Balmer said in a strange tone. "Are you looking for Mr. Specter?"

Logan had an overwhelming urge to snap at him and his stupid sweat-stained dress shirt. Instead of the sneer Logan was used to seeing on Balmer's face, there was something wary. Logan stopped in his tracks and took a breath.

"Yeah," Logan said with a strained voice.

Balmer nodded, and there was an awkward silence.

"She's okay, right?"

"She is," Balmer assured. "Her vision came back, and she got hungry. Ate some and slept."

"Right . . ." Logan said. "Look. About what happened . . . I—"

"I can't believe I'm saying this to you, Little Prince, but that was a good call," Balmer said and gave him a wan smile.

"I was— What?"

"It was risky and stupid, of course," Balmer said. "But after I've seen how powerful those crystals can be . . . Yeah, it was worth the risk."

"You're serious? We almost died."

Balmer shrugged. "But we didn't."

"Since when did you get that stick out of your ass?" Logan asked, regaining some of his composure.

Balmer gave him a dry chuckle. "Same time you became useful for the first time in your life."

"Yeah, fuck you."

"Right back at you," Balmer said. "Want to go check up on Kat?"

Something loosened inside Logan. His stupid father could wait. "Yeah. I do."

Turned out Logan's father was also in the den, as was Dr. Rosenberg and an agent guarding Logan's satchel. Kat lay on the floor on her side, just breathing and watching their **[Healer]** fuss about her.

"I said I'm fine," Kat said. "Go away."

"Logan," Malcolm said, "we will need to discuss your role in the camp."

"Nice to see you too, Father." Logan gave him a mock salute. Then he crouched down and pushed the doctor away. Dr. Rosenberg yelped in protest, but Logan just kept pushing until the **[Healer]** finally got up, muttering to himself.

"Thanks," Kat said and gave a weak smile.

"You alright?"

"That sludge of yours sure kicks hard," she said.

"You're supposed to drink water in between."

"Which reminds me, I'm gonna have you magic us some alcohol one of these days."

"Well, we did get a sweet haul," Logan said.

Weakly, Kat offered a fist. "Hell yeah, we did."

Logan bumped her fist with his own but said nothing.

Kat watched him under her brows. "Look. Stop being a pussy. It was a good call. I'm alright and we made bank."

"Fine," Logan said. "I'll let you rest. Glad you're alright."

Malcolm snapped his fingers and pointed at the door. Logan nodded and followed his father outside.

As he often did, Malcolm simply stood there, in his tattered, stained suit and waited. Logan knew this game. It was a power play. Logan often wondered if he even knew he was doing these things or if it was just as natural to his father as breathing.

Logan's anger flared back, but he had done this dance before. He looked around the camp idly. Simmons had done short work of the copse nearby. Their camp was now much wider, a group of stumps evidence of Bulmer's work. That was good. The camp also had a nice stack of lumber piling up. There were some elementary attempts at shelter, but mostly people were building tools or preparing food right now. The sun was bright and the camp's bustle was somehow peaceful and homely to Logan. He smiled to himself.

"You did well," Malcolm finally said. "I am . . . pleased."

"Huh," Logan let out. He didn't really know what to say to that.

"It was risky to go look for the crystals to begin with. I heard from the agents what happened. You were thorough and careful. We are richer for it."

"That's—Thanks."

Malcolm nodded. "I want to consult you on what we should do with the crystals."

There was something in the way he said it that made Logan cross his arms and furrow his brow. "What exactly do you mean?"

"Well, you are the resident expert."

"I am also the person who got this Numa," Logan said, anger growing around him like a churning thundercloud.

"Not alone," Malcolm reminded.

"A third should go to all three of us. The agents who were with us at the beginning already received a share."

"Reasonable, were we in a free market society," Malcolm said, his cool eyes regarding him without expression. Then he waved a hand. "Look around you. What should the crystals be used on?"

"How about this?" Logan said with all the collected calm he could muster. "You give me back what's *mine* and I decide what should be done."

"I am the leader of this operation."

"So you keep reminding me," Logan said. "Last time you gave me free reign, I built us shelter!"

"And it was well done," Malcolm admitted. "You also made a pretty dress for your girlfriend."

"Freya needed clothes," Logan said and shrugged. "It wasn't necessarily the best choice, so what?"

"So what?" Malcolm growled. "I don't know if you noticed, Logan, but we are in a survival situation."

"I'm not going to check with you every time I take a shit, Father!" Logan said, loud enough to attract the attention of people building a fire for the evening nearby. "You can lead. But you have to stop this micromanagement bullshit. Give me back my crystals."

Malcolm regarded him with a long, hard stare. "Greedy and petulant. If I give you some, what will you do with them?"

If I give you some. The nerve of this bastard.

"Now, Father," Logan said carefully, as if explaining a difficult subject to a child, "how many people do you have who are willing and capable of going out there and getting these all-important crystals?"

"Get to the point, Logan."

"You're better off having me cooperative."

[Reconfiguring Neural Matrix . . . 49% completion]

"That's strange. You okay there, Tumor?"

[This one is using 97% of its capacity to decode the data transfer given by the insect you discovered earlier.]

After a long pause, Malcolm nodded. "Understood. Now answer my previous question."

"What will I use *my* crystals for? Weapons."

Malcolm scoffed. "I was a fool to even ask you."

Logan looked at Simmons attacking a thick tree trunk with the intensity of a hungry dervish twenty yards away. That man had an aura of heat emanating from him.

"You remember that *actually* useful advice you gave me when I was seven and was getting bullied in school?"

Malcolm raised half an eyebrow. "I do not recall."

"I bet you don't . . ." Logan muttered. "You told me that if someone attacks me, I need to fight back immediately."

Malcolm untangled his crossed arms, letting one of them fall to his pocket. "I'm surprised to hear that you actually listened for once."

"I'm surprised to hear you using sarcasm. You must have jungle fever."

Malcolm smiled. It was a slight gesture, but for a fleeting moment, the glacial ice left his eyes.

Logan stored that image somewhere in the back of his mind. "Anyway, the teachers got extremely mad, but those idiots had it coming. They never bullied me again."

Maybe it was the sun playing tricks on Logan's eyes, but something seemed to soften in his father's expression. Maybe it was some long overdue respect. Logan liked to think so, at least. But it left his father's face as soon as it came. Back was the stern disapproval, and he crossed his arms again.

"It is good that you have grown, Logan," Malcolm said. "But you're a fool if you think we need to build weapons now. More people are coming here by the hour. We need shelter, we need food, we need tools. You will help us build. That is the end of it."

Malcolm walked past him back to the den, leaving Logan to bristle at the grass.

CHAPTER 28

Logan had Tumor wake him up at what was estimated to be three hours before sunrise—apparently at 91.72 percent certainty. Logan had to remind Tumor to not use decimals. Having suffered from blood loss and needing to recover from the previous adventure meant that it wasn't actually all that bad to have Tumor zap him awake. It worked not unlike the jolt of caffeine coffee used to provide him in the morning.

"Hey, how *did* you wake me up?"

[This one manipulated the signals that prompt cortisol production. This one also sent false signals to the part of the neural network, specifically the ones regarding your bladder capacity.]

That checked out. Logan *did* need to pee. More importantly, *Tumor could do that?!* Holy crap. If Tumor were a Swiss Army knife, Logan had practically just been using the corkscrew this entire time. Speaking of which, he really wished they could figure out wine soon.

Logan stifled a yawn and crept out of the den. He had positioned himself close to the door, so as not to wake anyone up when he moved. He couldn't help but throw a fearful glance at his father, but Malcolm Specter was snoring lightly.

Logan clenched his fist. He wasn't sure this would work, but hell, why not try?

Malcolm had placed Logan's satchel in the care of the two night-guards. Logan had to give credit where credit was due. His old man had predicted Logan would try to pull some bullshit.

Indeed I will. I still have some Numa tucked in my pocket.

Near the den in a blackened hole in the ground surrounded by rocks were the remains of a fire. Now there was only charred wood and softly trailing smoke. Logan heard some distant monkey screeches in the jungle. He looked up at the sky.

There was indeed a moon. It was large—much larger than Earth's. It also had a strong orange tint, just like the sun of this world had. Other than that, the sky was as bright and blue as he expected from his home planet. Logan had once visited Hawaii to see the *true* night sky, the one without light pollution. An amazing sight worth every dollar spent on that.

Logan then caught sight of the Milky Way. For some reason, that alone made Logan feel better.

Cool. Still in the same galaxy. That's like living next door to Earth! What's a few light-years here or there?

Logan asked Tumor if it could identify how far Earth was. It tried and failed. Logan shrugged and moved on.

The two goons on night watch were standing next to each other. They leaned on their spears, chatting idly. The moon provided enough light for Logan to see them clearly, as well as the satchel bulging with Numa.

He didn't know much about jungles, but he had lived in one for some days now. And what he had learned was that finding sand was actually impossible. As an idle thought, that would make glass-blowing really tricky in the future. Maybe they could grind rocks . . .

Logan, however, had always had a mind for unorthodox solutions. Thus he crouched by the remains of the fire and scooped up a pile of white ash in his cupped hands. He threw a quick glance at the night-guards and was relieved to see they were still chatting. Logan crept closer to them.

He crouched behind a pile of lumber left behind Simmons. Because the goons were chatting, Logan had been able to creep up fairly close to them—just a few yards away now. He'd need to act quickly and just hope this would work. He was too afraid to whisper the spell, so he intoned it subvocally.

Make this ash make anyone who inhales it fall asleep for five minutes.

There were no notifications for any level ups, nor did Logan have a Numa crystal in his hand to verify that the **[Enchantment]** had worked. On second thought, he should have checked the charge from his pocket first. He thought he saw a slight blue hue emanating from the ashes, but it was too dark to tell for sure. He shrugged. It was go-time, come hell or high water. What else was he going to do?

Oh man, I'm going to look really foolish if this doesn't play out well . . .

Logan took a deep breath, careful not to inhale any of the fluffy ash. Then he turned his cupped hands into fists. Some of the ash fell on the ground. He ran toward the goons.

"Hey," Logan said. They both turned, faces in surprise.

Logan held his breath as he ran toward the ex-agents and chucked the fistfuls of ash at both of them.

"Wh—" one managed to say, before his eyes rolled up and he collapsed to the ground. Logan grinned in triumph. The snores of his conquered foes sounded like applause.

But he had no time to waste. Five minutes was all that was reasonable to give. He'd rather they wake up and continue their watch, lest some damn beast eat Freya.

Logan grabbed the satchel of Numa crystals, hoisted it over his shoulder and neck, and ran into the night.

CHAPTER 29

Logan didn't run far. He didn't have to. The goons wouldn't be able to leave their night-watch to search for him. They had orders and they would follow them. Logan had a couple of hours before the camp would even wake up.

He did hide the Numa crystals well, though, in a little cave behind two full bushes.

"Now then," he muttered to himself, "we need to decide what we want to make."

Logan sat on the ground and idly plucked a leaf from the bush. It was leathery and fragrant. He had an idea of what he'd craft. A crossbow was his foremost choice.

"Can we make that, Tumor?"

[Reconfiguring Neural Matrix . . . 50% completion]

[Assessing material options . . .]

[Running simulations on Numa applications . . .]

[. . .]

[The possibility of building a working crossbow without access to metal or composite materials is low. A functional crossbow can be made from wood and plant fibers, but **[Enchanting]** *the string, bow, and ammunition to hold the required properties will cost a significant amount of Numa.]*

"Right . . . Well, that does suck. Wait, I have that new skill thing or whatever. Let's see if there's anything useful there."

Logan brought up his status screen. It had been a while since he had a look.

Logan Specter - [Artificer Level 5]
Attributes:
Potency: 10
Efficiency: 11

Durability: 5
Control: 11
Focus: 9
Subclasses:
[Transmutation]: 11
[Enchantment]: 15
Class Skills:
[Empower]: 3
[Funnel]: 5
[Repair]: 1
General Skills:
[Marksmanship]: 7
[Class Passive Skill Choice Available]

Logan selected the option to choose the passive skill, and a floating box in his vision appeared, within which was a selection of passive skills.

[Numa Psychic: Acquire ability to use Numa without touching a Numa energy source. Range increases with Potency and Focus modifiers.]
[Cavalier: 5% Chance per Enchantment to double the Potency modifier of an Enchantment]
[Cavalier: 5% Chance per Enchantment to double the Efficiency modifier of an Enchantment]
[Penny Stretcher: 5% Chance per Enchantment to double the Durability modifier of an Enchantment]
[Naturally Enchanting: 5% Chance per Enchantment to not use Numa]
[Transformative Luck: 5% Chance per Transmutation to not use Numa]

[Numa Psychic] seemed really awesome. Logan wondered how far the range was and how much it would grow along with his attributes. Unfortunately, it wasn't as immediately useful as the other options were. Right now, the biggest concern was the scarcity of Numa. Utility-based abilities could wait.

Technically, all of the other options matched his needs in some way or another. Durability was concerned with the actual material when it came to **[Transmutation]**, not that it mattered here. As for **[Enchanting]**, Logan had figured it at least related to **[Enchantments]** that increased an item's Durability, and probably also how many times an **[Enchantment]** could be used.

Now, one might think Efficiency would do that. But that wasn't it, and Logan was sure of it. What Efficiency did was simply determine how *efficient* his use of Numa was. When he had **[Enchanted]** that door shut, he had used almost a whole

[E-grade Numa crystal] on it. Granted, he hadn't even had a class back then. If he were to do the same **[Enchantment]** now, he'd be surprised if it took more than 30 percent of the charge with his increased Potency and Efficiency.

It really came down to the last two options. He'd used **[Enchanting]** more and was going to keep doing so, so Logan was leaning toward picking that. He halted himself first, however, and consulted Tumor on the subject. The AI ran a ridiculous amount of simulations. Logan figured since this was about percentages and Efficiency, the little parasite was perfect for the job.

[Reconfiguring Neural Matrix . . . 56% completion]

Uncharacteristically, Tumor ended up asking Logan questions on what sorts of items he planned on crafting in the future. Fair question. What if circumstances changed tomorrow and he came to realize he would have been better off grabbing the **[Transmutation]** discount coupon?

He would have to build a bunch of things. Mainly buildings out of Simmons's endless pile of lumber. But they *did* apparently have both a **[Builder]** and a **[Carpenter]**, from what Logan had heard. It wasn't just that everyone needed to keep busy. If something could be done by hand, it should be done by hand, to save Numa.

And so, Logan picked **[Naturally Enchanting]**.

After the minty fresh feeling passed, Logan focused. He looked at the satchel made from a motley mess of clothes, mainly suit jackets. It *bulged* with the most awesome treasure: over twenty blue glowing crystals half the size of a fist.

"Don't you for a second think I won't make a crossbow, despite your discouragement, Tumor."

[This one expected such an outcome with a certainty of 99.91%. It is noteworthy that the 0.09% chance consists of situations such as ones wherein all oxygen in the atmosphere spontaneously combusts.]

Was that snark? For something that was supposed to be incredibly smart, it kept forgetting to remove the decimals. Well, wasn't that interesting? He suddenly liked Tumor a bit more, because that sure as hell wasn't his father's design.

Thinking about his father made Logan's mood go foul, however, so instead he told Tumor to make a list of items he would need to create a crossbow, and in what amounts.

Logan spent a good half hour gathering the necessary materials. He was also collected other miscellaneous things as well, since he needed to craft for people other than himself too.

It was still very dark, even if Logan's night vision was settling in. He almost lost his way once but found that Tumor was an excellent GPS. Logan had to admit, as much of a tool as his father was, this little parasite had its uses.

When Logan finally dropped his last armful of stuff on the ground, he took a good look at his haul. It was mostly sticks. Oh, he *would* need a lot of sticks. The [**Transmutation**] passive would come in handy exactly now, but Logan was sure he had made the right choice, regardless.

He also found a few stones. They fit in his hand and had a nice heft to them, making them ideal for throwing. Logan wasn't sure what he wanted to do with them, but at the very least he could make stone-tipped crossbow bolts, if nothing else came to mind.

Logan also had taken a length of a hanging vine from an old tree with thick black bark. He wondered if the gnarled, hard bark could be used for something along the line. He would have taken some, but he didn't have tools to remove the bark.

All in all, Logan's haul was large but not varied. He had a pile of rocks of different sizes but all fitting well inside a fist. He had sticks of various shapes, lengths, and thicknesses. Lots of sticks. You could never have too many sticks.

Then he had picked up some ropes of vine. There was a lot of it hanging from old mossy trees that curved from the stem. And the jungle had plenty of those trees.

He had also brought all sorts of leaves and branches of bushes and tall grass. That was mainly for crossbow string. He would let Tumor decide what were the best materials to use.

Logan finally sat down and brought the satchel of Numa crystals close to the haul of jungle supplies.

"Alright, Tumor," Logan said and picked up a bundle of sticks. "Let's craft stuff."

CHAPTER 30

L et's make the crossbow stock first. Give me some measurements and that red hologram."

Logan worked methodically. The sticks morphed into a crossbow stock of solid, dark-chestnut-colored wood. Logan wanted it to be compact, so the stock was only fifteen inches. It had a hole on the other end to enable a trigger mechanism as well as a notch to load the string.

Next came the bow or limb. It required but a few sticks, since it needed to be thin and naturally flexible. After consulting with Tumor, they decided it would be a bit thicker than the AI's initial measurements, because Logan would [**Enchant**] the bow with flexibility.

The string was the most annoying part. [**Transmuting**] the vine didn't take much Numa, but it was frustrating to attach to the bow. Eventually, Logan just gave up and used some Numa charge to fuse it into the bow. This, however, attached the green string in such a way that it would weaken the draw. So Tumor had to show him some new schematics, and Logan wasted a bit more Numa.

[**Subclass Level Up!**]
[**Transmutation Level 12**]
[**Attribute Level Up!**]
[**Durability: 6**]

Being single-handed, the crossbow wasn't large, which obviously meant it had a limited amount of firepower, even with Logan's plans to [**Enchant**] it. With everything biological having some form of a natural resistance to physical harm, Logan would have to create workarounds.

I could always [**Enchant**] *the bolts with penetrative power, and of course the crossbow itself. But those* [**Enchantments**] *are costly. My shield-watch and my scythe-rang both run out of juice fast and need frequent recharges. Stuff like my socks, on the other hand, wear down their* [**Enchantments**] *much more slowly.*

But [**Enchantments**] did wear down, nonetheless. Then Logan thought of something. "Wait a minute, Tumor. Why would we put a flexibility [**Enchantment**] that needs to be recharged on the wood? We could just [**Transmute**] the properties of the wood to be more flexible! Let's try making it like composite material."

[Reconfiguring Neural Matrix . . . 59% completion]

[Compiling molecular structure analysis . . .]

[Simulating Numa application . . .]

[. . .]

[Based on the information available, there is a 15.28% chance that you will be able to significantly adjust the properties of a material without the use of [**Enchanting**]*.]*

"Well, screw it, it's worth a try," Logan said and brought a crystal to his lap. "How should I design the prompt to Numa?

[Reconfiguring Neural Matrix . . . 60% completion]

Tumor went on about the way atoms were stacked and threw in a bunch of scientific words that Logan didn't fully understand but felt he got the gist.

Then he placed two fingers on the crossbow's limb. "Make this limb more flexible using [**Transmutation**]. No [**Enchantment**]. Adjust the material's maximum elastic deformation."

[Transmutation level requirement not met]
[Subclass Level Up!]
[Transmutation Level 12]
[Attribute Level Up!]
[Potency: 11]

Okay, so it had worked but just barely, was how Logan interpreted that. Indeed, the wood had become softer and thus bendier. It hadn't worked exactly like Logan had hoped, but it made sense in hindsight. The wood couldn't be durable and flexible at the same time. If you didn't augment the material with magic, something had to give. Logan sighed and resolved to give the limbs both Flexibility and Durability [**Enchantments**].

In fact, Logan decided to do that right now. He gave both the stock and the string a Durability [**Enchantment**]. In response to the latter, he received an entirely new prompt.

[Programmed Random Occurrence: Naturally Enchanting]

The crystal Logan was holding glowed brighter for a second before returning to a soft glow. Nothing else happened. Logan checked the charge. It was at 68 percent. That didn't really tell him much.

He was intrigued, so he decided to check the crystal charge every time he used [Enchanting]. It was interesting to learn how much Numa each spell used, anyway.

He had a lot of [Enchantments] in mind for his new weapon and the bolts. First thing was obviously a Durability [Enchantment] on the weapon's moving parts, which meant the string and bow especially, but also the trigger mechanism. An Accuracy [Enchantment] was also a given, as well as some potency or force modifier, to make the bolts fly faster than they physically should. He had decided to [Enchant] his bolts with penetrative tips. It should have been cost-efficient enough, considering the small amount of surface he actually needed to [Enchant].

I wonder if I should also make the bolts air-resistant, and fly straight and spin. I don't need Tumor to tell me how useful fletching is. But I don't have . . .

"Oh . . . wait a minute, I'm super dumb. I don't need feathers."

Logan got up and grabbed a handful of leaves.

"Tumor, give me some measurements. Include all that aerodynamics, spinny stuff mumbo jumbo."

And with that, Logan soon held in his hand small triangles of green plant material. They were glossy and symmetrical. Logan squeezed one. It had some give like a sponge.

The process took two steps: Producing leaf-fletching and attaching them to the bolts. Logan did it enough times to warrant some progress.

[Subclass Level Up!]
[Transmutation Level 13]
[Attribute Level Up!]
[Durability: 7]
[Efficiency: 12]
[Focus: 10]

With that, Logan got to [Enchanting]. This time, he wanted to keep an eye on how much this new passive skill actually helped. First, Logan enchanted the crossbow with Accuracy. That took a full E-grader down to 87 percent. Then, at Tumor's suggestion, he [Enchanted] the draw weight to be lighter. In English, that meant that the crossbow's string was easier to place behind the nock that loaded the weapon. That did it.

[Programmed Random Occurrence: Naturally Enchanting]

He got a sensation akin to the minty, fresh feeling of leveling up, but this was fainter and subtly different. Regardless, the E-grader was still at 87 percent. If a single [**Enchantment**] took anywhere between 10 to 30 percent Numa charge, this new passive was going to be awesome.

Especially if I keep getting lucky with it like this.

The passive processed one additional time as Logan went through the list of enchantments. It was bound to happen at least once since Logan was [**Enchanting**] the heads of each crossbow bolt individually.

[Subclass Level Up!]
[Enchantment Level 16]
[Attribute Level Up!]
[Efficiency: 13]
[Focus: 11]

Ultimately, he was satisfied. He couldn't think of a single possible [**Enchantment**] it didn't have! Well, except for one thing he had been saving for last. He didn't care if it would suck up two full [**E-grade Numa crystals**]. It would turn his simple crossbow into a weapon of mass destruction.

"Make the weapon self-loading. Make the string always return to the nock in the loaded position after firing off a projectile."

[Enchantment level requirement not met]

"Tsk. Well it was worth a try . . ."

The sky had gotten brighter. It was almost morning. Well, the rest of his ideas were easy to implement. Hopefully he'd gain a level or two.

"Oh, I know just the thing I want to do with these rocks! Holy shit, why didn't I think of this before? Tumor, let's run some simulations . . ."

CHAPTER 31

Malcolm Specter was angry. While his disposition often naturally leaned toward irritated, full-on anger was rare for him. It was inefficient. It made a person irrational and reckless. And so, to get himself under control, he clenched his fists and focused.

"Fan out and search southward, no more than five yards across," Malcolm said in a clipped tone to the agents standing in a row in front of him. "Do not look for the boy. Look for tracks."

"Yes, sir," they said in a veritable chorus and went off.

He looked at his motley military crew. These were good men. Loyal men. He and the people at the camp were lucky to have brawn in a situation like this. And luck is what they needed. If only that damn boy didn't oppose his every move.

Malcolm went on to address the next issue at hand. He needed to make rounds. He needed to keep busy. It was hard managing a group of this small a scale. Humans' idiosyncratic nature needed to be taken into account. Groups were easy. Individuals were . . . complicated.

Simmons needed no direction or management. Malcolm wondered if he could keep up the mechanical pace that he had set. Malcolm supposed losing himself in rote labor was his way of coping with this ridiculous new reality.

Malcolm had a lot of things he could say about his son. A fair amount of them weren't complimentary. But he had taken to this world better than anyone else. He had gone out and acquired valuable materials. He was brave and he was resourceful. A proactive, ambitious person.

Malcolm could appreciate those qualities in his son. But he was also reckless, heedless, irresponsible, emotional, thoughtless, and selfish. The perfect example of that was his latest stunt.

After a cursory check-in with Simmons, he turned and growled to himself, "How dare he?"

He went ahead and made sure the camp was running efficiently—that everyone had something to do and knew what to do next. There were a little over thirty people there now. Once Malcolm was sure all of them were being productive, he went toward the river to wash and drink, and carry water back when he was done, as he had decreed.

That decree had leveled him up in the [**Governor**] class to level 2. His two subclasses were [**Leadership**] and [**Management**]. Those were at levels 3 and 7, respectively. Malcolm wasn't sure, but they seemed low. He wanted to talk with someone about it but worried that might come across as a sign of weakness, which he couldn't afford in this situation.

Malcolm made a few trips back and forth to the river. They had enough clay pots to fill, and the manual labor helped him think.

"Goddamn classes and levels," he muttered to himself, as a splash of water wet his tattered suit pants. "What are we supposed to make of this? What are the implications?"

There was no telling. They just had classes and each did something different. What was the most practical approach? What was the best way to distribute classes and how should they be leveled?

Malcolm Specter was used to having all the answers. At the position he had attained in life, he had rarely needed to ask questions. When he had, it had meant that the people he was managing weren't doing what they were supposed to. Now he would need to adjust; he knew this. But at the same time, he wanted nothing less. What he had been doing before had worked so well for so long. He squeezed the water bowl he was carrying with such an iron grip that a piece of it cracked off and fell into the drink.

"Well, one thing is sure, that fool of a boy is wrong," Malcolm muttered to himself. "We have enough military power between the agents and the weapons he already provided. We need housing, food, water, tools, and clothes—all of the bare necessities. We don't need weapons of war before even meeting other tribes."

Other tribes, Malcolm could handle. Their group had to be the most organized enterprise within a hundred miles. And people kept flocking here. No other human tribe would oppose them, even if they had run out of bullets and only had spears, rocks, and knives.

Logan had said something about irrigation and farms. That boy had new ideas as quickly as he forgot the old ones. They could use a stable food source, however. Once they found the boy, Malcolm would confiscate the crystals and have Logan figure out farming for them.

Malcolm had suffered his son's insolence long enough. He had known for years that he needed a special kind of patience to deal with his son's antics, but this time, he'd gone too far. Now Logan would do as he decreed, or he would have no place in this tribe. Even though he was his own blood, Logan was undermining Malcolm's authority constantly and placing over thirty souls in danger.

That did the trick. Malcolm Specter's resolve snapped in place like a steel whip. Logan would be found and given an ultimatum: cooperate or fend for yourself. Even if he refused—as he very likely would—a few days alone in the jungle would surely make him see reason. Malcolm now knew he had been far too lenient with his son. It wasn't time to go draconian on his son, but if that boy could not self-rule, then Malcolm would.

"Mr. Specter!" one of the doctors, now turned **[Craftsman]**, suddenly yelled. The man was in his forties, chubby, and wore spectacles with a broken lens. He pointed at the sky, and Malcolm drew in a breath.

It was that *thing*. It had come out of absolutely nowhere from the bright, empty sky, but now it was moving in to cover the sun. Its body was surrounded by a great black cloud, and the enormous mouth at the center of its giant head, resembling a whale's with a thousand eyes covering it, opened up. A terrifying trumpet call pierced the sky, and men around the camp fell on their knees, holding their ears. Malcolm managed to stay upright only by forcibly clamped down his pain and terror under his ironclad will.

The black cloud pulsed hues of dark blue, and soon giant raindrops began to fall. The creature wasn't directly above them, but wind carried a few car-sized stray drops in their direction, one of which crashed to the middle of the camp by the fireplace. Miraculously, the black viscous orb remained intact, bulging and heaving as if something was trying to get out.

Seconds later, the bubble burst. A huge obsidian humanoid rose from the oily bubble. There were streaks of blue crisscrossing around its muscular frame like glowing lightning. It rose like a looming tower, eight feet in height. Four long arms hung from its torso. Black goo dripped from a round face dominated by beady black eyes, pig-like nose, and jagged teeth protruding over a pair of fat gray lips in spite of a wicked underbite. As if by a whim of fate, the creature turned and locked its eyes on Malcolm. Malcolm flinched, but he hunched forward, raising his fists. He was in good shape but no fighter. This creature would end him. He knew he couldn't outrun this thing, so he stood his ground.

The creature lunged. Malcolm roared in fear and anger.

Abruptly, a great bright flash blinded and deafened Malcolm Specter.

CHAPTER 32

Logan arrived just in time. After he had caught sight of Levemoth in the sky, he'd immediately rushed back to camp, scrambling through the bushes and low branches with his handful of armaments. Two black drops had landed dead square in the middle of the camp, and several others had landed close by. By this point, Logan had already killed a scythe-fiend on his way back.

But these were new creatures, including the one that was attacking his father. Fortunately the flashbangs were extremely powerful. Yes, they were a crude solution, as they also blinded his allies, but the ordinary people in the camp would be useless in a fight anyway, so Logan wasn't too careful. The flashbangs worked like a charm on both types of monsters rampaging through the camp.

Afterward, a well-aimed crossbow bolt struck the beast attacking his father straight in the earhole. It fell down dead immediately.

[Skill Level Up!]
[Marksmanship Level 8]

Logan wasted no time in reveling. He needed to save the others first. Kat was out of commission, but he could trust Balmer. He had just the thing for him, anyway.

"Balmer!" Logan shouted.

"Here, Logan!" He heard a voice through the screams.

Logan saw the young agent in the middle of the chaos, blind and shielding his face with his arms, Logan's scythe-rang in the other hand.

A black and blue troll waved around its four arms violently as it rampaged forward without sight. Logan ducked under the eight-foot-tall monster's smashing fist and ran toward Balmer.

"I'm here," Logan said and took the scythe-rang from him. "Give me that."

"I need a weapon," Balmer said.

"Take this," Logan said and offered him a wooden sword. It was a beautiful thing. Logan had thought he had all the time in the world when making it, so he had been very careful. Not because he liked Balmer, but he had liked making the sword. "It's enchanted."

"What is it?"

"You'll get your vision back in a moment," Logan said. "Don't cut yourself."

With that, he ran a few paces after the troll and threw the scythe-rang. As it flew, Logan loaded the hand-crossbow with another quarrel. He managed to pull the mechanism just in time to catch the boomerang that had come back after it sliced off the troll's head.

The catch was awkward and he almost dropped the crossbow, but it worked.

"Freya!" Logan yelled. There was no answer. That was either really good or really bad. No time to think. A scythe-monster let out a hoarse screech and came at him, the arms clicking at the ground urgently.

They got their vision back, huh?

Logan threw the scythe-rang again and shot another bolt at a troll that had ripped a shield out of an agent's hand and was about to slam him with it. The projectile hit the lumbering creature in the back. It roared and turned, giving the agent and his friend time to push their spears into its flesh.

Meanwhile the scythe-rang had cut the front leg off of a scythe-fiend. It scrambled toward Logan in frantic rage. He took a few fast paces to the side, which meant the return path of his blue throwing weapon cleaved through the scythe-fiend's head on its ways.

[Skill Level Up!]
[Marksmanship Level 9]

Logan saw one of the trolls lumbering toward the den.

Oh no, you don't.

Kat was there, as was their sole shelter. Logan's crossbow wasn't loaded, so he threw another flashbang.

"SHIELD YOUR EYES!" Logan yelled out as he threw. Before bringing a hand over his eyes, he saw that a good portion of the agents close by were doing the same. Now, that was a great advantage.

The troll in front of the den was indeed blinded. In its confusion, it grasped the air around it as it roared. One of its four arms clipped the den, cracking the wood paneling. Logan heard two women screaming.

"Freya! Hang on!" Logan shouted and threw the scythe-rang again. It whooshed through the air as it cut through the troll, slicing off two of its arms. It screamed a bellowing, wrathful roar and sprayed black blood everywhere. Logan was trying to load the crossbow, but the troll was getting too close. Logan had to drop what he was doing and run. The scythe-rang was stuck in the broken wall of the den. His eyes went wide with the realization that the weapon wasn't coming back. The Numa in the weapon's [**Enchantments**] was spent.

Fuck.

Logan ran away from the troll, but the large, clumsy creature was quick on its feet, even with two arms chopped off. It tried to swipe at Logan's head with its remaining arms. Logan ducked and fell. He would have to use another flashbang and run. At least he had gotten the monster away from the den.

Before he could throw the last of his flashbangs, however, three agents lunged at the troll, shields raised, drawing its attention. Meanwhile, as fast as the wind, Balmer came up behind the troll and pushed his wooden sword into the creature's back, as if its skin were made of nothing but butter. Balmer then pulled the sword out with a twist, and the monster fell down limply.

"Good weapon," Balmer quipped and offered a hand.

Logan grabbed it. "Glad I finally found a way to make you useful."

They shared a wry smile and refocused. Another troll had just lumbered into the camp, lured by the screams and sounds of fighting.

Logan instinctively checked on Freya. There was no movement around the den. Freya and Kat must be hunkering down in some corner.

Logan couldn't afford to just sit by the broken-down house though. The scythe-fiends had already cut two people down. A person Logan didn't know had been sliced in half. It was a much more gruesome sight than Logan had ever imagined.

Some bile rose in his throat, but he swallowed it down as he loaded his crossbow. He shot down a scythe-fiend fighting with Simmons. The great ox of a man was wielding the scythe-saw Logan had given him in one hand, and a stone axe in the other. After the fiend crashed to the ground, Logan and Simmons nodded to each other and continued the defense. Simmons soon found another troll to fight with, and traded blow after blow, his arms practically blurring as he swung against the four long arms of the monster.

Logan reloaded again and watched his surroundings like a hawk. His father was collecting all the non-warrior types into a group and herding them out of the range of the battle. A shadow pounced out of the forest. A scythe-fiend was clicking toward them, snarling like a prowling cat, but Logan managed to distract it with a crossbow bolt to its side. It let out a hoarse scream and rushed toward him.

Thankfully the [**Enchanted**] crossbow string was easy to pull. But before Logan could aim and shoot, the monster was already upon him.

"Shield!"

A blue umbrella of energy bloomed out of Logan's hand, and the creature toppled onto its back. Logan wasted no time and shot it in the abdomen, nailing the creature to the ground.

With that, the sounds of battle were dying down. What was left was two scores of people stunned in horror. A girl around Logan's age was holding her arm and crying a few yards away. One of the doctors in their white lab coat was looking at the sky with empty eyes. Logan moved with determined haste. He picked up any crossbow bolt he could easily find and then went up to the broken den and picked up his scythe-rang.

"Logan!" Freya cried out. "Are you alright? Is it over?"

"The camp is safe," Logan said as he plucked an E-grader from his pocket to recharge the scythe-rang and his shield-watch.

Freya sobered up. Logan looked into those beautiful, bright blue eyes. She understood what Logan wanted to do.

"Go get them," Freya said. Logan nodded.

Then he turned and shouted at the agents, "What the hell are you standing there for? You think this is over?"

The agents turned toward him. Most of them looked surly, but a few took a few steps closer. From the edge of the camp opening, Malcolm Specter watched him with his arms crossed.

"Didn't you see the Black Rain? There were dozens of drops. You want to let those things breed or something next door? Hell, no. We're going hunting, you damn goons."

CHAPTER 33

The Levemoth had gone as soon as it had appeared. The sky was bright blue as Logan and the agents hunted the monsters in the early morning. There were signs on the ground of the crashed black droplets.

"Fan out twenty yards each and call out if you see something," Logan told them.

"We don't have to listen to you anymore," one of the agents said.

"Shut up, fool," Simmons told him. And that was the end of that.

Logan's tactics worked well. They found four more monsters that way—three scythe-fiends and a troll. The trolls were dangerous. The agents' spears didn't manage to fully penetrate their skin. Logan had the only projectile weapon in the group able to weaken the foe enough to risk melee.

The one-handed crossbow packed a tremendous punch for such a little weapon. It *obliterated* the scythe-fiends. A single hit left a gaping hole in their bodies, like a fist-sized bullet hole. The problem with the scythe-fiends was that they were fast and agile. But the shield-fighters held them in place long enough for Logan to take his shots.

Logan extracted a crystal from the broken mess of a troll's skull. It was a darker hue than the normal sky-blue glow of the Numa crystals.

[E-grade Numa crystal (+), 100%]

Huh . . . I guess it's better? The trolls are certainly tougher than the scythe-fiends.

It was the size of an adult's fist, larger than the normal E-grader. Logan pocketed it. The other agents saw that but said nothing.

Logan replenished a few crossbow bolts **[Enchantments]** with it. One shot took 50 percent charge off the **[Wooden Numacraft Bolt, 50%]**. Renewing the **[Enchantment]** took 1 percent off the E-grader plus.

They fanned out again, and Logan felt that strange presence watching them again. Was it one of Levemoth's fiends observing and waiting? It didn't feel like that. Something about it felt intelligent and in no way hostile.

Logan resolved to keep a sharp eye out. At one point, he saw one of the big green cats jumping out of a bush before him, but to his surprise, it went the other way, dashing away from him.

The morning turned hot and sweaty as the sun rose to crown the sky. They encountered a few more fiends and took them down with brutal efficiency. Logan had a lot to say about the agents, most of it not good. But when it came to execution, those guys were professionals. They were fearless and didn't get confused or let fear control them. Two of them got hurt fighting a troll, and they were sent back to the camp, carrying the Numa crystals they had plundered.

After their kill score rose, Logan picked up a few crystals for himself. None of the agents openly protested, even when they saw Logan pocketing the valuables, so he figured it was alright. He would have done it anyway, however. He was done with his father's bullshit.

After three hours of hunting, Logan called them back and they decided to return and widen the fan, increasing the distance between individuals. They all agreed, as wandering too far into the jungle could result in them getting lost, leaving the camp defenseless. Thus they turned and widened the space between an individual to twenty yards or so.

It was a risky move in case there was a troll. But they had learned that outrunning a troll was possible in the thicket. In the open they moved deadly fast, but they couldn't run through trees.

Eventually, Logan came across a swampy area with thick-trunked trees dipping their roots in the water like curled tendrils. The water was dark and murky, with idle bubbles of gas bubbling and giving the air a scent of rot. The watching presence was even stronger here, now with a hint of alert. Logan wondered why he was even sensing this.

Suddenly a hoarse screech greeted him. Logan hunched down and readied his scythe-rang. He didn't need to call for help to take on a scythe-fiend, but he needed to be alert. It clicked out of the bushes and snarled. However, to Logan's great surprise, the spindly creature didn't go for him. It tilted its featureless head at him, but instead went straight along the other side of the swamp line toward a bush.

There was a frightened yelp in the bush. There was another person in there! Logan acted on instinct to protect them, immediately throwing the scythe-rang. It hit the fiend, cutting off a front leg and slicing into the torso, where it lodged itself. It wiggled in place, eliciting a screech from the monster, before it dislodged and returned to Logan.

Watching the bush carefully, Logan circled around the swampy area, hopping on tall patches of grass, where it was obvious the ground would hold. Logan inspected the scythe-fiend and dug out the Numa-crystal. He examined the bush. There was something in there, but it was translucent and shifty, like hot air. Carefully Logan prodded at it with his scythe-rang.

The bush yelped, and Logan took a quick step back.

"Who is it? Show yourself!"

CHAPTER 34

A tiny meeping sound came out of the bush, followed by rustling. Gradually, something white, slight, and strange emerged. It stood three and a half feet tall, slender, with creamy white porcelain skin, fully naked. Its groin was covered with a strange pearly glimmer.

A magic censorship spell? Now I've seen it all.

It had pointy ears and a shock of green hair that fell in strands over its white forehead. The eyes were big and bright, and they looked at Logan in shock and awe. The little creature closed its gaping mouth and smiled like a happy child.

Bowing, it said, "I am Snoff. Thank you for saving my life."

"What in the hell are you?"

"I am of the Faelves," Snoff said. He had a soft tinkling voice, like a chime in the wind. "Please do not hurt me."

"But what *are* you?" Logan asked again, blankly staring at the strange creature. "Are you . . . a monster? From the Levemoth?"

At the mention of the name, Snoff's creamy complexion went chalk-white.

"Do not say its name!" Snoff hissed. "Come! There is no time! I must take you."

"Take me?" Logan said. But before he could ask where, the little creature blew some dust at him and snapped his fingers.

"Do not worry, 'tis an invisibility spell. For I can only bring you, not your brethren. Come now!"

"Wait, I don't intend to go anywhere."

"Oh," Snoff said, ears drooping in disappointment. "But you should. For saving my life, the king of the Faelves will surely grant a boon."

Logan scratched his head. What was even happening?

"I . . . suppose I could come and listen."

The creature brightened. "Great! Please follow me."

Snoff bounced with each light step it took, barely touching the ground. He leapt gracefully, skipping like a child, crossing a yard with each step. With all his equipment, Logan couldn't keep up.

"Hey!" he called to his new friend. "Slow down."

"Oh. Oops!" Snoff turned and grinned mischievously. "I didn't expect you to be so *slow.*"

This cheeky bastard.

Logan followed Snoff deeper into the swamp. After plummeting knee-deep into the swamp twice, Logan told Tumor to mark the spots where Snoff had landed in red in his vision. The second time Logan's leg had submerged into the swamp, something had tried to crawl up his leg, and he didn't want to risk that happening again.

The swamp was large. Logan wasn't surprised it was there; this was a jungle, after all. He was more surprised he hadn't encountered it before now. He shrugged. He guessed it wasn't that strange, after all. It was simply in a direction Logan hadn't traveled in before. It was not like he was well-aware of all of the camp's surrounding environment.

"Come, come," Snoff called over his slender shoulder cheerfully, the pearly glimmer swirling around his porcelain butt, like a cloud of stars. "Must not slow down, for my home is near. 'Tis time you meet the Faelves, Tall Folk."

Soon Logan started to find more solid ground to step upon as they delved further inward. If he didn't have Tumor, he was sure he'd never find his way back were the Faelves to prove to be enemies.

Soon Logan stopped in his tracks. He was stunned. The highest trees must have been eighty feet tall now that the swamp had dwindled. Only faint sunlight could get through this canopy. Under the shade of these giants grew a different sort of tree.

A grove of stout trees, like oaks, grew out of the ground. There were dozens of them. Their bark was a dark olive green, and their leaves were plentiful, glimmering with silver. But the fruit—the fruit glowed a deep blue hue and pulsed softly.

"These are . . ." Logan said idly and dropped his weapons.

Snoff came up to him and grinned. "'Tis Numa fruit. Very delicious. Please have one. A gift from Snoff the **[Explorer]**!"

Logan approached one of the trees with a reverent silence. The branches were low from the weight of the plentiful fruits which lit up the grove like rows of Christmas trees. Logan plucked a fruit with both hands. It came off gently. The pulse within was faintly warm, like the Numa crystals were.

Logan looked at Snoff, who nodded encouragingly. Then Logan bit into the fruit. It was sweet and rich. The meat was chewy and radiated a warm blue glow. Logan ate it, the sugar of the fruit rushing into his brain.

[Personal Numa charge, 4%]

What the—?

Logan would ask about that later, but now he was too busy enjoying the fruit. Logan had experienced all the flavors the best chefs on Earth had to offer. But a couple of days in the jungle, eating nothing but berries, snakes, and beetles, and this fruit was like fucking manna from heaven. Logan gobbled the fruit up, smearing his face with the glowing juice.

After the rapturous gluttony, Logan found himself holding the tiniest seed, a blue pea of a thing. It gave off no glow, but it pulsed ever so slightly on Logan's palm.

[A-grade Numa-tree seed]

"What is this?" Logan asked Snoff.

Snoff picked it up. "Blessed spirits! An A-grade seed! It must be a sign. This is a good omen, friend. We shall plant this seed in your name, and so form a pact with the Tall Folk. Come! Come!"

Snoff grabbed his hand and frolicked forward. They actually spent a considerable amount of time hemming and hawing about the spot to plant the seed.

Snoff muttered to himself, "Should I call someone with the right class? I am bad at picking the ground."

"Why not just put it somewhere with space so it can grow? The soil here seems very rich," Logan suggested.

The Faelf brightened. "Yes! Of course. 'Tis a genius idea! We can simply magick the growth later!"

Clearly pleased with Logan's acumen, he guided them to a spot in the grove with plenty of room in every direction. It wasn't quite in the middle of the grove, but it would surely stand out. Logan wondered whether his new friend would catch flak for it, but it really wasn't his business.

"Here!" Snoff announced, clearly pleased with himself. "Dig a hole and say a prayer with me for the spirit of Numa. Then we shall go to the court of the King of the Faelves!"

Logan did as instructed. He went and picked up his scythe-rang and began to dig. Snoff muttered to himself in worry about using a weapon to carve the sacred ground. Logan stopped and looked at him questioningly, but Snoff only gave him eager nods, albeit with a strained, worried expression on his face.

"'Tis only right that a warrior people would dig with their weapons. This will only strengthen the pact. I but hope that it will not anger the spirit of Numa."

"What's this spirit of Numa?"

"Could you possibly not know? But you have clearly used Numa! You have communed with *her.*"

"I . . . have?"

"You have given her your prayers, and she has answered. This is a boon, and one of the reasons I chose you."

"Huh?" Logan stopped digging. "But everyone can use it!"

Snoff looked at him with an incredulous grin. "What? Is this a preposterous joke of the Tall People? Surely you jest!"

"No, man," Logan said. "I've given these crystals out to a bunch of people."

"You have, I know this," Snuff said, barely holding a laugh. "And how many people have you seen use Numa?"

CHAPTER 35

Logan fell silent. He had not seen a single person use Numa except himself, had he? He'd seen people use tools he had made. He'd seen people take them and pocket them or bring them to his father. But had he actually seen anyone else use a Numa crystal to make something? Logan asked Tumor if this was truly so.

[Apart from Dr. Rosenberg using the crystals to heal Kat, this creature is right.]

"That's not true," Logan said to Snoff. "In our camp, there is a **[Healer]** who used Numa."

Snoff only grinned mischievously. "That only worked because you were there to facilitate, you fool!"

"No," Logan said and gained some firmer ground. "It worked after I passed out."

Snoff only kept grinning. "I was watching when this happened. You fell and your mate held you in her arms. But you were there, present at the scene."

The look on Logan's face was apparently priceless to Snoff. He fell down and held his sides as he rolled and laughed.

"You— ahah . . . You thought—ahahahahaha! Whew . . ."

It took the little creature a while to collect himself. Logan was glaring at him, but the little Faelf only grinned.

"'Tis not so often that the spirit of Numa blesses us with her grace," Snoff said, still hooting with laughter as he wiped tears of joy. "Only one in ten—nay one in twenty—has the gift."

"But how does that even work?" Logan asked.

Snoff was startled as if completely taken aback by the thought. "'Tis unclear to me. Perhaps the King will know. 'Tis no coincidence I chose to bring you, my friend. Now, plant the seed, enough of this chitter and chatter! Go!"

Logan pushed his hands into the ground to make space for the seed. It had a strong earthy fragrance, and the ground was soft, moist and clean. Just perfect.

Could it really be that rare? Wait . . . Can my father use Numa? What about Freya? I thought Kat used some in the beetle fight?

Logan pushed the seed into the ground as deep as he could and patted the earth on top of it. Then Snoff told Logan to lower his head and pray with him.

Logan tried. But while he could understand the language of Snoff, he gibbered at such a speed that he caught but a few words. Nonetheless, Logan solemnly hoped the tree would give fruit aplenty.

After Snoff was done, they got up. The Faelf grabbed Logan's hand again.

"Come! We must go to the king's court. He is waiting. Oh yes. A boon is waiting! And an A-grade seed . . . Come! We will return to your sapling later and bless it with water and spell. Come!"

As Logan followed Snoff further into the Faelves' dwelling, he was greeted with whimsical sights. There were beds of thick yellow flowers upon a mound. There were children playing upon the flowers, bouncing up and down as if on a trampoline. They saw Logan, giggled, and pointed, but promptly returned to their play.

There were some stray Numa fruit trees, but mostly it was the tall trees forming the canopy that stole Logan's attention, graced with the most intricate treehouses with swirling staircases and little chimneys puffing out blue smoke. There were dozens of them, each of the houses distinct and unique.

Snoff told him to look at this and that and dragged him forward by the hand, skipping merrily as they went. They wandered through a bazaar of strange trinkets and mouthwatering scents coming from white and brown pastries, bowls of vegetable soup, and other delicacies.

They stopped at one stall selling some brown balls of food on a stick. Snoff negotiated with the woman, who also had porcelain skin, albeit light blue. She had the strange glimmering stardust around her breasts and crotch, just like Snoff. She also had a wild mane of white hair and laughed at whatever Snoff gibbered to her. Eventually she shook her head and gave them two sticks.

Logan took the piece of food offered and put it in his mouth. It was delicious. It tasted like civilization, and not just a piece of meat half-cooked over an open fire. It was akin to a falafel, but sweeter, as if it was honey-roasted. Could have been, but Logan was in no mood to inspect the food further as he gobbled the treat down.

"Hey, you don't have to inhale the thing!" Snoff said and laughed. "Savor it. It is pure, it is of the earth, blessed by spirits."

Logan grinned and shrugged. "Hungry. Had a long morning."

"That you did," the Faelf nodded sagely. "I shall see you fed well and proper. But now the king awaits! Come! He knows you have crossed into our realm. Come!"

After the market they passed a courtyard upon which Faelves worked. There were fields of plants they tended, animals they milked and herded, and where rope and other such crafts were being made.

Towering over it all was a majestic tree, similar to the Numa fruit trees but of a gargantuan stature. Sized like an apartment building, the trunk could have fit fifty men holding hands around it. It was tall—maybe forty feet—and the gnarled green bark was healthy and rich. The fruit on its branches was plentiful. Some were large, like pumpkins. On the ground around the giant tree grew tall spindly grass, circling it in thick rows. Glowing, blue Numa fruits sat upon the tips of many of the blades of grass.

The grass must be magic. It cushions the fall of these giant fruits, so they're not wasted. These people are so strange.

A doorway was carved into the tree. It was high, as far as the Faelves were concerned, but Logan had to dip his head to get in.

The walls and ceiling of the room inside were shining with polished resin; meanwhile, it was studded with pearls and gems here and there, not so much to make them look ostentatious but to give off a classy glimmer. Within the tree, a court was in session. Dozens of Faelves were sitting around little tables and chattering and laughing in their tinkling voices.

On the opposite side of the room, on a throne made of beautifully crafted wood, sat a Faelf of faintly yellow porcelain skin. He had no wrinkles, but the bright oval eyes were tempered by age, and from his sharp ears sprouted tufts of blue hair. He also had a luxurious blue beard that sprawled all around the ground around the throne.

"Oh ho!" the king said. He had a rich, melodic voice that echoed throughout the carved tree. All the people eating and chatting at the little tables went quiet and looked at Logan curiously.

"Snoff has brought us one of the Tall Folk," the king said, smiling almost mischievously. "The warrior people. The new children of this realm. Welcome, Tall One! I am King Sluikumar the Third. You will call me King, or King Sluikumar, until we are better friends, yes?"

Logan, being no stranger to self-important people, benign or belligerent, closed his eyes and bowed. "Thank you for the hospitality of your halls, my king."

King Sluikumar laughed. "Well-behaved this one, Snoff. But a liar."

"I did not lie," Logan protested.

"No?" Sluikumar asked, grinning behind his beard. "Did you mean every word?"

"You're the one who insists on titles," Logan said and shrugged. "So I treated you like I thought you wanted to be treated."

"Hah!" the king laughed again. "Cheeky one, this, yes. Tell me, are all Tall Folk as interesting as you?"

Logan chuckled. "I wish they were, my king."

Now the whole court laughed. The king slapped his knee and hooted. "Very good. Now you speak the truth. What should I call you?"

"Logan's fine," Logan said. Then he couldn't help himself, but to add, "No titles needed, my king."

The king lost it again. There was a bit of danger that flashed in his eyes, as if warning Logan not to go too far, but he was genuinely amused.

"Very well, Logan," Sluikumar said before turning his wizened gaze to Snoff. "Tell me, [**Explorer**], how did you come across this Tall One, and why did you choose him?"

Snoff recounted everything that had transpired since he and Logan had first encountered each other. The king hummed and nodded thoughtfully, and asked some scattered questions when the mood struck him.

"Ah, good choice, Snoff, yes. Bringing one blessed by Numa. Logan, you planted an A-seed? Truly? For this alone we must accept friendship with you, so we can both benefit from such a great gift from the Spirit, yes! And saving young Snoff's life here! How wonderful, yes! I should grant you a boon!"

The court cheered at that, and the king rose up from the carved wooden throne. He didn't just stand but literally floated in the air, legs dangling a good foot off the ground. "Come, yes. We shall drink from the Well. Follow me."

Snoff accompanied Logan to follow behind the king. There was a door behind the throne. Stepping through it, they came upon a glade of tall, vibrantly green grass between Numa fruit trees. In the middle was a spring of deep blue water, which glowed like a sapphire in the evening light. A statue of a feminine figure carved of some white wood stood in the middle of the lake. It was so intricate and so lifelike, that if the king had suggested that this was a petrified person, Logan would have believed it.

The statue clearly depicted a woman. It wasn't exactly human; it wasn't exactly a Faelf, either. It was animal and divine at the same time, and while it captivated the gaze, it was as if it was constantly slightly moving, breathing—*alive.*

"Go into the pool, Logan," the king instructed. While still of cheerful disposition, there was an edge of serious reverence in his demeanor. "Bow before the statue of the Spirit and drink from the spring, until you are full. That is my first boon to you, as a friend of the Faelves."

Logan did as instructed. The water was cool, and it made him more alert, but there was also something deeply benign in it, as if it was cleansing Logan from within. Guided by a whim, feeling no shame, he removed all his clothes and placed them on the edge of the pool. Neither Snoff nor King Sluikumar made a comment. A deep calm overcame Logan as he waded deeper into the pool. When he reached the statue, he went down on one knee and bowed his head in front of it.

Be blessed, child, and drink, a feminine whisper within his mind gently suggested. The water before him, already shining with strong blue, now shimmered and glowed in deepest cerulean. Logan cupped his hands and drank.

When he drank, he found the water was sweet and rich. The fresh, minty feeling that he was familiar with enveloped him, filling his every fiber to the brim, fuller and fuller the deeper he drank. Soon Logan was in a blissful trance of crystalline awareness.

[Reconfiguring Neural Matrix . . . 69% completion]

[Personal Numa charge, 28%]

[Reconfiguring Neural Matrix . . . 82% completion]

[Personal Numa charge, 66%]

[Reconfiguring Neural Matrix . . . 88% completion]

[Personal Numa charge, 81%]
[Personal Numa charge, 100%]
[Attribute Level Up!]
[Efficiency: 14]
[Focus: 12]
[Durability: 8]
[Potency: 12]
[Control: 12]

Logan heaved out a sigh. His eyes were wide with the intensity of the experience. The minty feeling was still all over him, tingling his fingertips. He turned and gave a tired smile to Snoff and the king. They were staring at him with open awe and disbelief. Logan's smile widened into a grin, and then he fell on his back in the water. Groggily he noticed that he was perfectly floating.

Great . . . Wake me up . . . Whenever, Tumor . . .

And with that, Logan fell into a peaceful, dreamless sleep.

CHAPTER 36

Logan ate like a fiend. This was real cooked food. They had *pie*! And a sauce to go with it! On the other side of the table the king watched him in wry amusement out of the corner of his eye. There was also a circle of Faelves around Max, watching him with wide-eyed curiosity. They were whispering to each other, and Snoff was getting a lot of attention, which he was clearly enjoying.

"Did you hear? He leveled up in an attribute!"

"Snoff said he planted an A-grade seed . . ."

"He's so tall . . ."

Logan was more interested in the butter and cheese on a little platter which he attacked with great fervor.

They have cheese! CHEESE! Good Lord, I forgot how much I missed cheese.

"So, Logan," King Sluikumar said conversationally, "you must be rather low-level to have gained an attribute from the Blessing. Did you get it on your lowest stat?"

Logan smirked. "I gained a level in all of my attributes."

A gasp passed through the gathered Faelves around the table.

"But—this is . . . No, surely not?!" the King spluttered.

Logan raised his eyebrows, still giving a dumb smile. Apparently this was a big deal?

The king seemed to have forgotten his words, so Logan picked up the conversation.

"What was that Blessing thing? I have Numa inside me now? How does that work?"

"There is much to tell," the king said and sipped his tea. His beard was so lush that half of the drink spilled. "Yes, you have eaten the fruit and drank from the well. Your Numa is recharged."

Logan picked up a piece of pie between two fingers.

"Make this pie into the shape of a rose."

The pie morphed until a little pie-flower was resting in his palm. He stared at it in open amazement.

King Sluikumar smiled. "These crystals you hold are but an attempt by the First Folk to make Numa available to all."

"But you said only a select few can use the crystals," Logan said, eating the pie-flower.

"You hold but bits of broken toys, boy," the king said and wagged a finger at him. "The First Folk made constructs—fully-shaped crystals with perfect form. Those can be used by anyone. As can pure natural Numa, which comes straight from the Spirit."

"Oh yeah, I saw these crystal constructs in the ruins. They really helped me out of a jam."

"Oh ho, you found some that were unspent! The Dorves must be getting sloppy."

"The who?"

"Dorves, boy," Sluikumar said. "Have you not met them? I suppose you've not. They so rarely leave their underground dwellings."

The crowd around them started to mutter amongst themselves in angry hushed tones.

"Cursed Dorves!"

"Lunatics."

"Fools!

"They dare taunt . . ."

Logan made an expectant, questioning face to the king. In response, the king stroked his massive beard with both of his hands.

"The Dorves live underground. We no longer deal with them. They are younger than us, but two generations old. They never learned anything, even if we tried to teach."

"So there's all sorts of species around?" Logan asked.

"Just us and the Dorves, as far as we know. We are no longer in great numbers. There are only some thousands of us left in total, I reckon, yes. Most of us could not survive the wake of the Great Thief . . ."

"Are there a lot of you?" Logan asked. "We humans could use allies."

"We have but three friendly towns of our cousins, scattered here and there nearby. There are more of us in the north. 'Tis a city of Faelves, ten times larger than our dwellings here. I am a king of dwindling people. 'Tis hard to find ground to cultivate Numa upon."

"Wait, back up," Logan said and took a more comfortable position after pushing his pie plate away. "You only have a few settlements scattered around, maybe one city? How is that possible?"

"We are the oldest folk here, but we are not old. 'Twas the fathers of our fathers who came here. Our old world, Levenia, was dying. A great heat mounted and most of our kin perished. But the Strangers from Above brought the fathers of our fathers here."

"Why?!" Logan asked sharply, half-rising from the ground. "Why are we here?"

The king stroked his beard again. "'Tis a good question, yes? Why, indeed? We have but guesses."

"Well, don't hold me in suspense."

The king watched him with a keen, serious stare and then nodded. "There are two forces in this realm we call Saeldar, the Eternal Spring: the Spirit Goddess Numa, who bestows life, and the Great Thief, who we do not name, lest we call him here.

"The Great Thief?" Logan said quietly. "Levem—"

"DO NOT CALL UPON HIS NAME!" The king flew up two feet and his eyes flashed with danger. Then he calmed down and brought his hands back to his voluminous, blue beard.

"We know not whether calling the Great Thief by name is safe," Sluikumar explained. "Now, quiet yourself, my young friend. Listen to me. Have some pie."

Logan did what he was told and a new pie full of berries and nuts was soon brought to the table. It was steaming hot. Logan let out a happy sigh.

"The Strangers from Above brought us here two hundred years ago. As they did the Dorves a hundred years ago. And now you, the Tall Folk, have arrived. There is a pattern at play."

I should probably tell him to call us Humans.

[Reconfiguring Neural Matrix . . . 89% completion]

Huh? What's up, Tumor?

[I have done analysis on this 'pie' you have ingested. There are sixty-two different compounds in use, but after 1,388 simulations, I cannot reproduce the configuration.]

"What?" Logan said.

"What?" King Sluikumar asked.

Since when is it "I" instead of "this one?" Don't answer that. You're giving me a headache, Tumor. We'll talk about pie later.

[Understood.]

"Sorry," Logan said, holding the spoon dumbly, as if not sure what to do with it. Apparently his AI liked pie . . . "Could you repeat what you said?"

"'Tis our belief that a world like this is rare," Sluikumar continued and helped himself to a slice of the steaming pie himself. "The Spirit Goddess Numa is the essence of this world. She could be something entirely unique. We had nothing like her in our home world, only lesser spirits. Perhaps we are meant to commune with her, perhaps protect her."

Logan faintly remembered the "Administrators" before they had tossed him into this world. Day by day, the memory had become like a faded dream. But he remembered that they had called him a "candidate."

"I think you're right," Logan said. "I remember something about these people you call Strangers from Above."

The entire crowd, the king included, leaned in closer with wide eyes. Some of the younger Faelves bounced excitedly and clapped. Logan told them what little he remembered.

"A candidate?" The king mouthed the word. "For what, I wonder?"

Then he pointed at the crowd around them. "You, my lovely fools! Go and think about and discuss this. We will hold court after our guest has been sufficiently entertained, yes?"

But the Faelves only laughed and raspberried. King Sluikumar shook a fist at them, but his sternness melted into a grandfatherly smile.

"Fine, you reckless rascals, you fools!" he said in his melodic tone. "But you will not shirk this duty forever."

Logan finished his fill of the pie and picked up the conversation again. "So, what are the Dorves doing?"

"They dwell in the remains of the cities of the First Folk. There are many devices by the First Folk left behind. But the Great Thief is cunning. He knows there is Numa down there, so monsters will flock to the ruins."

"What kind of people are they?" Logan asked.

Scoffs and jeers came in rounds from the crowd circling them.

"They want to eat their berries and make juice too," Sluikumar said and shook his head. "They think if they burrow underground, they can cheat the Great Thief. 'Tis not so. They die by the score, and we suffer for it."

"Why?" Logan asked. "I'm missing something here. Are they doing something bad?"

The crowd started up its tinkling whispers again immediately.

"He does not know."

"They have been lucky."

"Show it to him, King!"

"Show him of the Great Thief!"

King Sluikumar put down his wooden spoon and looked at Logan as if not sure if he was jesting or not. "Truly? You do not know why we so shun the Dorves? Why we ourselves live off the land and the tree?"

Logan shrugged.

The king sighed. Then he turned to Snoff.

"'Tis good you brought him sooner, not later, young one."

Snoff gave the king a sober nod. King Sluikumar turned to Logan.

"Let me show you a vision," the king said and gently lifted upward and floated over to Logan.

Logan swallowed. "S-sure?"

"Do not fear," the King said. "This is not something that can be told. To understand the Great Thief, you must *see*."

The king gave him one of his grandfatherly smiles and placed his tiny porcelain hand on Logan's forehead. A great white nothing filled Logan's vision and he found himself suddenly transported.

CHAPTER 37

Logan was somewhere—and some *time*—else entirely. He was no longer in the grove of the Faelves. He wasn't even in a jungle anymore. He was on a desert dune. A large one. To his left and to his right he saw hundreds of soldiers, all equipped with various weapons of unseen quality. But all of their armor was the same: a sleek, shining black metal that shifted in the orange evening sun. They were studded with glowing blue crystals that pulsed softly.

Everyone was looking in the same direction from behind their sharp helmets, to the seashore two hundred yards away. On the beach there were thousands of soldiers and siege towers made of black metal and catapults loaded with pulsing blue Numa bombs.

In the air above them were ships of various sizes. They were all made of the same black metal. Some were propelled by rotor blades, like a helicopter; some were made to fly with gas. Tiny specks of blue fire could be seen above. There were various cannons, guns, and soldiers armed with insanely large spears and harpoons at the helms of the ships. All of those weapons were pointed in a single direction.

Above the shoreline, tens of yards in the air, but closer than Logan had ever wished to see it, was Levemoth.

The bulging eyes of the giant whale-head swirled this way and that as the great beast silently watched the First Folk gathering their forces. A dark cloud rumbled about its body. Idle black drops fell from it to the sea. The drops hissed when they struck, but whatever fiend spawned in the water, Logan couldn't make out.

Tumor? What's happening?

But there was no answer.

A flying man soared down from one of the ships to float in front of the rows of soldiers Logan was part of.

"Everyone over level 40 who can fly, with me!" the floating man said. He was wielding a giant scythe in one hand. Its shining blue blade was almost blinding. "We will lead the strike force from the left flank."

With that, the man took off, and dozens of soldiers from their rows followed him. Some flew seemingly without explanation, like the commander wielding the scythe. Some of them sprouted wings, some had jetpacks that spewed blue, glowing fire, and some flew on black metal disks.

Another commander came up to them. She was also flying on one of those disks, wearing the same shining black armor as everyone else, and wielding what Logan thought to be a flamethrower.

"Everyone above level 30 who cannot fly, with me! We will defend the shoreline from the Levespawn! The rest of you will man the siege weapons. Report to any siege weapon above which a flare is still active. NOW, GO!"

They started running row from row down the dune in a disciplined march. Logan had no choice but to fall in line or be trampled. He had no idea where he was supposed to go, so he just decided to follow the person directly in front of him.

Levemoth stirred. A rain of black droplets fell into the shoreline. Hundreds of them. Maybe a thousand. Logan was so stunned by the sight that he stopped. People just ran through him.

Apparently I'm not real . . . Logan realized as he watched the Great Thief rain its pestilence down on the shore.

Great fiends burst from the bubbles. These were not the little pests that Logan had faced. Oh, there were trolls and scythe-fiends, but there was also so much more here. There were dragons, great towering krakens with thirty-foot-tall tentacles, and giant snakes with three heads snapping their jaws at the approaching forces as their lashing tails caused monstrous waves.

The force of flying soldiers approached Levemoth's head and attacked it with all their weapons. They flew around it like a swarm of flies and they were flattened just as easily.

Blue whipping tendrils sprouted from Levemoth's neck. They extended in every direction, giving the great monster a coronation of death, whipping and slapping down the flying soldiers, who had shields to tank the whips but eventually ran out and fell into the sea.

The catapults threw their boulders, which exploded in blue light upon Levemoth's head. It barely budged. The siege towers—great black obelisks—rose up, and a bright white beam of energy shot from them. This toppled the Great Thief. The airships swarmed upon it and fired off everything ranging from giant harpoons to fireballs. On the ground, the infantry fought with Levemoth's spawn and died by the score.

Logan looked upon it all in horror. No matter how many catapult shots or beams of light it took, no matter how many of the creature's bulging eyes burst, it kept raining the black rain and swatting at the flying strike force.

Eventually, however, it grew tired. It opened its maw and let out a great bellow. The sand on the beach flew up and the waves covered the shore—fiends and infantry alike. A ball of swirling black energy formed at its mouth. Commanders' cries shot up urgently everywhere. All fire was focused on the mouth of Levemoth. It did not care.

A loud pop was heard before absolute desolation hit the forces of First Folk. The black swirling energy shot out as a continuous beam, which cut siege towers in half and incinerated the infantry. Another black beam cut the sky. Dozens of warships fell, a chorus of men plummeting in terror filled the air.

The army of First Folk was already in chaos. Those left alive either cowered in fear or ran. Levemoth would not have any of it. Another black mass of energy swirled at its mouth. This one built up slower and the orb of energy grew very large.

Once it was released, it floated to the middle of the battlefield. From there, thousands of tiny little homing shots flew down and pierced every straggler who was still alive. Every man, flying or on the ground. Every one fighting, every one fleeing. Within a single moment, the whole clamoring battlefield fell as silent as a graveyard.

Logan could only look at the carnage in stunned silence. Burning airship remains crashed on the beach. All that was left of the incinerated soldiers were mounds of ashes. Amongst the remains, blue shimmering crystals remained.

The fiends came upon them and feasted. Levemoth let out a clarion call of victory. Then it drew in a massive breath, and lines of blue energy were drawn from every machine, every corpse, *everything* that was left on the beach.

The Levemoth sucked in all of the Numa. Thousands of little trickles of blue energy were drawn into its mouth as the Great Thief inhaled. Wherever its scaly skin had been torn was now instantly healed. The black bulbous eyes that had popped, regenerated. And the dark cloud swirling about its body grew darker and larger.

Once there was no more Numa to siphon, Levemoth turned, and a portal appeared through which it vanished.

CHAPTER 38

Malcolm Specter sat alone by the fire, keeping it alive. Dusk was encroaching on the camp, and only a few men and women were still going about their business or chatting in the moonlight. All of the agents were in the den. His men needed sleep.

He was too involved with his project to sleep, however. Relying on Logan to make them things with this precious resource had been foolish. But using Numa was not only difficult in general; it was *impossible* for most people.

He had gone through every individual in the camp—a total of forty-eight people—that day, checking them for affinity for Numa. There were only three in total. Four if you counted the boy, but Logan was nowhere to be found.

As long as he hasn't gotten himself killed. I'm used to him going off the grid for weeks on end, but the environment is hostile here. Then again, I must admit he seems to be able to handle himself.

Malcolm held an **[E-grade Numa crystal, 23%]** in his hand. He had asked people to perform whatever action came to mind on a leaf. That young woman Kat had made it crumble. Dr. Rosenberg had cut it cleanly in half. Freya had made it sprout a branch from the stem.

It had cost a significant amount of Numa energy, but they were necessary tests. It seemed that performing actions with Numa was costly when it didn't directly relate to your class, yet people could use their skills and level up in their subclasses even without Numa. But from what Malcolm understood, such was not the case for Logan. Perhaps his class was like that. Malcolm's own class seemed to work off passive effects. He got a sense of a person's feelings and whereabouts when they were done with a task, telling him approximately how well the task had been done and how the person felt about it. Listening to this feeling and working in accordance with it had leveled up his subclass of **[Management]** to 9, while talking to people individually about their Numa affinity and their classes had brought his

[**Leadership**] up to 5. But Malcolm felt the need to understand classes and Numa better, that much was clear.

It was fortunate they had a [**Healer**] with affinity to Numa. That would stave off most injuries and make even the agents braver in their exploration. If there were ever trade with other groups as Malcolm hoped, Dr. Rosenberg would be an extremely valuable individual. Meanwhile, that young girl Kat would be a powerful pawn in terms of military power, be it monsters or other people.

But while fighting ability was necessary for survival, they needed the basics first. They had set up another building, since their group was rapidly growing by the day.

We really need that damn boy to show up and bring those crystals he stole.

Despite Logan's shortcomings, he was resourceful, and they could use resources. Their food situation was sorted for the time being, as long as there was fish in the river and mushrooms to be found. But on Earth, mushrooms were mostly seasonal. If they were to run out here . . .

Clothing was also a major issue. Whatever they had had on when they had come to this world was starting to tear apart at the seams. They had three crafters working on their levels, and one of them even had the [**Tailor**] class. But it would take a while before they would manage to produce something they could use.

We need to find more people. Those who can use Numa are high-value individuals. We need to trade the goods they can produce and accrue resources.

Their campfire smoke kept attracting people. Malcolm had also sent out a group of agents to post signs around the area to convince even more. It was working well. Soon there might even be enough for another settlement.

Malcolm decided he would send agents as envoys to find other settlements or groups of surviving humans. There was strength in numbers, and they needed every Numa user they could get.

Attracting more people would be better than finding settlements to trade with. They couldn't specialize yet. And only Logan had a class with Numa affinity that they could leverage. That was a damn shame, considering the boy's personality.

Freya had still not picked up a class, so she had potential to produce something valuable. Malcolm was reaching the end of his leniency toward the girl, however. Such indecisiveness bothered him. They had many jobs to fill, and the girl was smart enough to do something important well.

For now, the girl had been doing whatever menial tasks were needed around the camp. Malcolm had been doing the same things and, to a lesser extent, still was. But now the amount of people in the camp warranted some actual management. He was the captain of this ship, and the crew needed to be doing the right things.

Malcolm admitted that he had a soft spot for Freya. The girl was too good for Logan, that was for sure. But she had kept him out of trouble countless times, and always tried to make him see reason when he was being ridiculous.

Malcolm thumbed the crystal in his hand. Why could they use this power when he could not? Was there a way to rectify that? He wasn't so concerned for his own sake. Not that the crystals didn't intrigue him, but he could do his job without them.

Suddenly Malcolm heard a dry stick snapping behind him. He had decreed that they scatter them all around the immediate perimeter as a safety measure. Malcolm drew in a breath and felt his senses sharpen.

"Who's there?" he called and got up.

Three short figures wearing black cloaks and carrying arms emerged from the shadows and into the flickering light of the fire.

CHAPTER 39

Logan gasped as he was startled back into reality. What he had seen he could never unsee. The Levemoth had already been frightening, but Logan had had no idea what manner of a calamity it could become.

King Sluikumar nodded at him gravely. "The Great Thief must never be allowed to grow. It must never be given a chance to pillage the Spirit."

"What is it?" Logan asked. "What does it want?"

"To consume," the king said. "It seeks to wither the Spirit Goddess of Numa and all her grace."

"It was so powerful . . ." Logan said, shaking his head.

"It slumbered for a long time," Sluikumar said. "'Tis now weak and still half-asleep. But the arrival of you Tall Folk has awakened it."

"I thought it came and went whenever?" Logan asked.

"It would float by, and its wretched spawn would wander off to the dwellings of the First Folk to bother the Dorves or starve," the king said. "Our communion with the Spirit is hidden from its sight, yes."

Logan gave him a sharp look. "But now something is different?"

King Sluikumar nodded. Gone was the grandfatherly demeanor. All of the Faelves now seemed as ancient as stone and grave. There was no playful hopping, no childish chatter.

"Never has the Black Rain fallen within such a short span."

"We have handled it well so far," Logan said.

Sluikumar let out a humorless laugh. "This is but the beginning, my young friend. The Black Rain will fall frequently now. The Great Thief will grow more watchful every day, henceforth. And were you to grow mighty, like the First Folk, it *will* come for you."

Logan swallowed. "What can we do?"

"The Dorves and the Faelves have chosen to hide. If the First Folk could not defeat it at the height of their might, how could anyone?"

Logan slammed a fist at the table. "Hell, no. To skulk in the shadows forever? I refuse!"

"You are truly a warrior people," Sluikumar said. "But we must be careful. The Great Thief will rain down death if you keep to your foolish ways."

Logan sobered and pressed his palm into a fist. Then he realized what he was doing, got angry again, and opened his palms, pressing them hard on the table. "What makes it tick?

"Using Numa," Sluikumar simply said. "If it's raw, like the crystals within living beings, the effect is amplified. Even relatively small amounts in use will draw the attention of the Great Thief. The Dorves use the constructs of the First Folk. The Great Thief cannot go underground, but its spawn has infested the dwellings of the Dorves. They are not a warrior people by nature but have become such."

"What about you guys?" Logan asked. "With the Numa fruit trees and the wellsprings and whatnot?"

"Yes," Sluikumar said and smiled conspiratorially. "We have classes given as a boon by the Spirit. Her grace has taught us to use her gift in secret."

"So the Leve—" Logan started, but King Sluikumar gave him a sharp look. "The Great Thief . . . it attacks when people fiddle with Numa. But when it's infused through plants and drink, like this internal charge I went through, the big bastard doesn't notice it?"

King Sluikumar nodded. "'Tis precisely so."

"There is no way in hell I am going to hide under a rock and let this thing bully me for the rest of my life," Logan declared. "I don't care what it takes, I'll bring this beast down, and you guys will help me."

The whole court of the Faelves fell mute. They looked at Logan in stunned silence for several seconds. It was only when King Sluikumar burst into uproarious laughter that the rest of the Faelves joined in. It was not a mocking laugh but one of joy and mirth. The somber mood was completely broken, and now the room was filled with tinkling laughter and chatter.

"'Tis such a ridiculous boast, young friend," King Sluikumar said, wiping his eyes. "I almost want to believe it. To live without fear. To settle and cultivate anywhere. Oh, the Fae Folk have dreamed of this for many a year. Yes, we brought you here for alliance, for friendship."

"I'm all for it," Logan said immediately and smiled with an open heart. He was nothing if not lucky to have found these good people. "But so far we're still struggling for food and shelter. We can't be of much use yet."

"This we understand," Sluikumar said. "We aren't in need of any goods you might produce. At least not now. What we would like is knowledge and skills."

Logan nodded and smiled. "That's fine. We have a lot of skilled people with us. We can teach you engineering, construction and—"

"No," the king snapped. "No. Absolutely not. We should not have these . . . machines. These are foul things, these . . . devices. We urge you not to build them. The Dorves have incurred the wrath of the Great Thief multiple times with their creations."

"Huh," Logan said. He wasn't sure they had all the facts here. For one thing, Logan very much doubted that saying Levemoth's name would do any harm. "What do you want, then?"

"Your warrior arts. You will teach us how to fight the fiends that the Great Thief spawns. We are but masters of illusions, charms, and tricks. Often we escape the foul creatures, but to fight and slay them would be a great boon to this world."

"Sure," Logan said. "We've got folk who can fight well."

"We have observed. Most of you Tall Folk are warriors, you chief among them."

Logan laughed. "No, I'm no fighter. But I can make a mean weapon. I'll make you some. Or teach you how to make them."

"Good," the king said. "Which brings us to the next condition you must accede to for our friendship."

"Sure," Logan said. "What is it?"

The king grew serious. His voice went lower and he looked at Logan with an old, wizened, steadfast stare. "Anything you have created so far is tainted and should be discarded. Any form of Numa which is impure is a breach of our friendship, for you would risk the death of my kin with your greed. You must promise not to use Numa crystals anymore."

CHAPTER 40

Y ou're kidding, right?"

The king pulled at his blue beard and shook his head. "You cannot use what you have built so far, lest you bring down the wrath of the Great Thief upon you. Any Numa which was not blessed by the Spirit is dangerous. That goes for the machines of the First Folk, the bastard imitations of the Dorves, and even the natural crystals found within living creatures. All of this is what the Great Thief thirsts for. Only the Spirit Goddess of Numa can conceal Numa from the enemy."

"What the hell do you want us to do? We need Numa to survive!"

"You will learn our ways, my impatient friend," the king said and smiled amicably.

"You mean like growing Numa fruit trees?" Logan asked, pressing his hands into a fist to cool himself down. "Could we even make one of those springs to receive blessings from?"

"We shall teach you all of this!" King Sluikumar said. "'Twas our hope to begin with, for if you avoid arousing the interest of the Great Thief, life will be more peaceful for all of us, yes! We are in agreement? A new friendship is formed!"

Logan understood he was making a decision on behalf of his whole group, Malcolm Specter included. But surely his father would come to the same conclusion.

"Are there other humans around these areas?" Logan asked.

"Yes, plenty! Many groups like yours," the king said, clearly excited now that Logan seemed that he would agree to his terms. "Tall Folk are numerous. Few are my people compared to yours. We watch you with great interest."

"I can't make this agreement on behalf of all the humans," Logan said.

"No, of course you cannot," King Sluikumar said and scoffed. "I am a king, not a fool, my young friend. I ask friendship of you, and of those within your care."

"I want friendship with you guys too," Logan said. "But I will need to bring back all this information and talk to my people. I don't want to make promises I can't keep. But as far as I'm concerned, we're allies. But I do need you to teach us your ways, so we aren't all dead by next week."

"'Tis agreed!" the king said and the crowd around them cheered.

Then Sluikumar offered his tiny yellow hand of porcelain skin. Logan took it and they shook.

"Now then," King Sluikumar said, rising up in the air to float above the crowd. "Let us revel! Bring us wine, bring us more cake. We shall show our guest all the best dances and songs of our people. Get up now, yes! Get busy!"

The crowd around them cheered and left in all directions to do work, the King included, leaving Logan to sit there with a stunned look on his face, a plate of a half-eaten piece of pie in front of him. Soon came the wine and what followed was a long but cheerful night.

Logan left the Faelves late the next day. His new friends didn't have much in the way of culture and technology, but they sure could make a wine that packed a punch.

As Logan walked through the jungle, he looked at his crossbow and his shield-watch.

The Faelves are superstitious. Which is an interesting concept when you have magic . . .

[It is noteworthy that you too are superstitious, Logan. You have 714 different biases in your psyche, which could be considered assumptions made with insufficient data. Would you like for me to go over them?]

Logan groaned. "I already have a headache, Tumor."

[My apologies.]

"It's fine," Logan said as he grabbed a hanging vine and tugged it. It held, so Logan used it to cross the swamp, swinging from one patch of grass to one on the other side. "What do you think of their superstitions?"

[The likelihood of Levemoth's interest being aroused by crafting or using a simple device such as a crossbow is low. After a quick variable analysis, I would estimate it to be 2.33%.]

Logan looked at the crossbow in his new pouch that the Faelves had gifted him. It was made of brown leather, and on it were engraved artful swirling patterns. Yeah, there was no way just having a crossbow was dangerous. Hell, even something simple like a fishing rod was technology.

"The Faelves had rope, ceramics, ovens for cooking . . . I don't know how they did their carpentry work, but there sure was plenty."

[Precisely. However, there are two things that might arouse the interest of Levemoth.]

"I really wish you would stop saying 'arouse.'"

[It is possible that the civilization, which the Faelves called 'First Folk,' had cities and technology on such a massive scale that the Levemoth couldn't help but notice. It is, of course, possible that the higher the technological advancement it perceives, the more aggressive it becomes. In fact, I postulate there is a 64.8% chance of this.]

"So, in other words, just stay out of sight and don't build Hadron colliders," Logan said as he circled a tree. "But that's just raw logic. There could be something going on with the Numa."

[Both of Levemoth's attacks that we have experienced happened immediately after you used Numa crystals.]

Logan pushed a heavy branch aside. "You're saying I caused the Black Rain?"

[It is likely.]

Well, that wasn't good to hear. Logan hadn't exactly had time to take in the damage the last attack on their camp had caused, but people had died.

[The data is not conclusive, and there are not enough data points. There have been instances such as building the shelter and healing your friend Kat which did not prompt an attack from Levemoth. My conclusion is that using Numa inappropriately is likely, but not certain, to draw attention from the Levemoth.]

Logan stopped to look at a lamb-sized yellow frog that was staring dispassionately at the black and green swamp. A white centipede as thick and long as Logan's arm came up for air. A long, barbed tongue curled around the insect. It squirmed and bit at the tongue, but slowly and surely the yellow frog, looking as bored as ever, dragged the insect into its mouth.

Logan looked at the swamp water. Suddenly the patch of grass he was standing on didn't feel so safe. His feet felt itchy. Fortunately, the old, heavy trees were thinning as Logan worked his way through the swamp. How awesome his water-resistant socks were couldn't be understated.

"They told me to destroy everything I've made with Numa, especially if it was **[Enchanted]**," Logan said. "What do you think of that?"

[There is not enough data to—]

"Look, uh," Logan said and rubbed his neck, "I don't need an analysis now. I just . . . figured I'd ask what you thought."

[Reconfiguring Neural Matrix . . . 90% completion]

[There are no assured courses of action here with predictable outcomes. One option would be to travel 50 miles out in any direction and test theories relating to Levemoth's behavior. This is a question of risk tolerance.]

"Damn, Tumor," Logan said. Further ahead, he saw the scythe-fiend he had killed to protect Snoff. His fingers instinctively reached for the Numa crystals in his pocket. "So what do you think I should do?"

[My function is not to affect your decision-making but to process and provide information.]

"And what if I do something monumentally stupid that you could have prevented? If I die, your existence ceases too."

[Reconfiguring Neural Matrix . . . 91% completion]

[That is a novel idea I do not enjoy. Very well. I shall attempt to provide suggestions on the basis of simulation analysis. This is something that is not native to my neural matrix, but I will attempt to create a subroutine.]

"Do that," Logan said as he crouched by the fiend's corpse and started removing the scythe-arms. "But you didn't answer my question."

[The Faelves have inhabited this land for over two hundred years. While they lack the faculties of a trained scientific mind, it is likely some of their information was accurate. Your foremost priority should be to maximize self-preservation. It would be wise to build a physical, societal, and economical structure which can sustain a human population. Any behavior which increases the risk of further violence from the Levespawn is in direct conflict your aforementioned goals.]

Logan grunted as the scythe-arm loosened from its socket. He jammed a stone knife the Faelves had given him in there to cut the tendons. "We can't go completely Stone-Age survival mode. We need Numa to create things."

[You have internal Numa charge, which is safe to use. You can bargain for Numa fruits with the Faelves, owning half of a highly valuable tree, not to mention the classes they promised to provide us with should we hold up our ends of the bargain. It is noteworthy that even if Levemoth is not attracted by the use of these Numa crystals, we have made a pact with the Faelves, and they have clearly been watching humans.]

"Yeah, you say things that make sense," Logan said. He put the scythe into his satchel. It only had room for one, but Logan would return if life went his way. "We need to get people to take these classes if we want to have any chance at survival. I'm sure Frey will be eligible. Do you reckon she'd like to take one of those classes? She was saying she was feeling useless."

[I believe there is a 99.99% chance she will be quite pleased.]

Logan smiled as he finally found himself out of the dark swamp and in familiar territory.

I hope she will.

CHAPTER 41

Logan stood at the edge of the camp in mute shock. For a moment he thought he had gotten lost and ended up somewhere else. But no . . . This *was* their camp.

It was just that it looked very, very different.

First of all, there were a lot more people—dozens of whom Logan simply didn't recognize. And they were working with tools Logan had never seen. A handsome guy with a beard was working with something that looked like a vacuum cleaner on the ground. It was laying a thin layer of cement on the forest floor.

Another person was pushing the logs Simmons had piled up through a buzz-saw mounted between two large logs. On the ground at the other end of the contraption there was a pile of crude, round-backed planks.

A third person nearby—a short young girl of fifteen or so, with jet black hair—was on her knees, operating an oven made of iron. It had no fire visible anywhere, but Logan saw the girl pull a bowl of hardened clay out from it, using a pair of thick woolen mittens.

Logan just stared at it all in awe for a moment. How had they suddenly acquired magic tools? Did they find someone else with a class like Logan? How did they get all the Numa to make these things? Logan needed to find a familiar face.

Freya practically attacked Logan the second he came further into the camp. Despite dirty hair and a lack of makeup, she was still gorgeous as she ran toward him in her black and blue snakeskin attire. She jumped at him, wrapping her arms and legs around him as Logan instinctively grabbed her.

"Frey, you're breaking a rib."

"Good," she muttered. "You deserve it."

Sure, it hadn't been more than a couple of days, but that was a long time when you didn't know if you were going to be alive tomorrow.

"And why do you smell like booze?" Freya asked as they untangled.

"You smell amazing as always," Logan said.

Freya blushed and smiled but soon recovered. She wagged a finger. "Uh uh, no dodging questions."

"Since when do I listen to rules?"

"If you have a stash of booze somewhere, I could really use a drink," Freya said as she looked Logan up and down. "I've had a hell of a week."

Logan told her the quick and dirty version of what had happened. It was kind of fun to watch Freya's jaw drop.

"You—what?! I want to see these people too!"

"Actually we made some plans. You're going to . . . Uh, Freya, what happened here?"

"We also met another species!" Freya said excitedly. "Your father found these short, stout guys. They were really interested in helping us and trading with us. They call themselves Dorves."

"Oh no . . ." Logan said, as he walked past Freya. "I'll . . . talk to you later, Frey."

"Huh? Hey, wait, Logan!"

Logan found his father discussing the use of a Numa-powered chainsaw with Simmons. They were both rather excited about it. Logan had not seen his father so flushed for a long time, not since the hostile takeover of that robotics company two years ago.

"With this, you'll be able to produce enough lumber for the eventual sales!" Malcolm gushed.

"I'll also have time to focus on the other side of my class, which is tending the forest."

Malcolm gave that imperceptible nod Logan knew very well. It was the one his father preferred when he quietly disagreed with someone but had no reason to bring up the subject at the present moment.

"Father," Logan started, "we need to have a chat."

Malcolm's stony hawk features didn't change an inch at the sight of his returned son. He didn't miss a beat. "We do. Return those Numa crystals you have hidden."

Logan laughed. "Those? I can't remember where they are. I had to ditch them when I realized I had to save your life."

Malcolm gave him a sharp look. "My class tells me you're lying."

Now, that's a scary class. He might be bluffing.

"Your class is clearly broken then, because I really don't know where they are."

That was true. Logan doubted he could find his way back. But he knew Tumor would remember. Tumor affirmed this promptly.

Malcolm held him with his cool stare. "If you don't bring them back to me, you will reimburse them."

Logan threw his head back and laughed. "With what, Father? Does your class also tell you that I stumbled upon a pirate chest of golden doubloons on my way here?"

Malcolm had been more amused at funerals, but Logan swore he saw a small smile nearly forming on Simmons's face.

"We are in debt, Logan," Malcolm said. "I promised our new allies Numa crystals in exchange for their tools."

"I can see that," Logan said carefully. He really needed his father on his side this time, so he had to do his best to navigate here. "Look, Father, I also came across a species that want an alliance."

"Yes, the Dorves told me of them," Malcolm said. "The porcelain fairies. They called them deceitful illusionists, liars, and cowards."

"Yeah, I heard there's some beef between the two," Logan said. "Look. I don't know what sort of deal you made, but you should listen to the Faelves too. They will have a very different story to tell than the Dorves."

"You do not know what the Dorves told me," Malcolm said.

"I do know that, despite your flaws, you're an annoyingly intelligent man," Logan said, giving his father a slight smile. "And if you had heard what I heard from the Faelves, you'd think twice."

"And what story might I have heard from them?"

Logan told his father what had happened. Simmons got bored and went away to work his new chainsaw. For someone who had been a top-shelf alpha male in the old world, there was a charming simplicity to the new Simmons.

Freya brought them some fish to eat and the three of them sat as Logan told them what had happened, and Freya and Malcolm asked him questions. For now, Logan kept the vision to himself. He was going to tell them about it, but it wasn't information they needed right now. It was better to keep things simple and only tell them about what the Faelves thought of Levemoth and its relationship with Numa.

"It could be true," Malcolm said quietly. "But I do find the timing interesting."

"What do you mean?" Freya asked.

"The minute I make a deal with the Dorves and improve our circumstances immensely, Logan pops out of the bushes and tells me to undo everything."

Logan sighed. "Look, all I'm asking of you is to go talk with the Faelves."

"The Dorves told me these forest fairies use magic to trick people. You could be under a charm. This is likely a subterfuge attempt," Malcolm said with a resolved glimmer in his eyes. "The timing is too perfect."

"You're kidding me, right?" Logan said, trying to stifle his rising temper.

"I'll have you checked by Dr. Rosenberg," Malcolm said and got up. "This does not mean I will not parlay with the Faelves. I will send an envoy, and if they also come back with their mind affected, we must discuss with the Dorves if these fairies will be a threat."

"Goddamn it, Father," Logan said and rubbed his forehead. "They aren't going to be a threat. They just want us to stop messing around with the Numa in a way that will make Levemoth come and take a big black piss on us."

"Or they want us to stay weak so they can manipulate our situation."

"Frey, what do you think?" Logan asked and squeezed her hand in his lap.

"I want to visit the Faelves," Freya said, looking at the ground. "I don't know what to think."

"The Dorves are helping us," Malcolm said as if that was the end of discussion. "They have provided us with means of survival."

"What kind of a deal was it, exactly?" Logan asked. "Give me the Cliffs Notes."

"They provided us with an initial supply of tools in exchange for the Numa crystals we had and a promise of twenty more [**E-grade Numa crystals**]. And from that point onward, they will trade with us for any Numa crystals we manage to obtain."

"Uh huh," Logan said. "I know this is a big break, and your back was against the wall, because you need to take care of these people. But think back, Mr. CEO. When has anyone approached you and offered you a deal that was more beneficial to you than for them?"

Malcolm scoffed. "Do not take me for a fool. I negotiated."

"Here's what I think," Logan said. "If the Faelves are right and using Numa in a non-kosher way makes Levemoth drop Black Rain, the Dorves are using us to farm for Numa."

Malcolm's eyes went wide at that. Freya turned to Logan.

"What do you mean?" she asked.

"Think about it," Logan said. "They give us all these tools to create whatever we want. We use said tools and oops, we're attacked by the monsters. We fend monsters off and claim the crystals. Meanwhile, the Dorves sit underground safe and snug and come up to take the crystals from us to trade them for some hand-me-downs."

"Oh . . ." Freya said, trailing off.

"They probably told you to make weapons because the jungle is dangerous and Levemoth comes and goes," Logan said, turning to his father.

"Almost verbatim," Malcolm said, nodding to himself.

"Look, I know you're a prideful bastard, but just talk to the Faelves. Or send Freya to them. Explore your options. There are other ways to use these valuable crystals."

"You're right," Malcolm said. "The Dorves are using us."

Logan sighed in relief. He couldn't believe he had actually gotten an argument through to his father.

"But that changes nothing," Malcolm added.

"What?" Logan and Freya both said.

"It is our highest-yield ecological niche in this situation is to do as the Dorves say."

"Even at the threat of spawning more Levespawn?" Logan asked, glaring at his father.

"Especially so," Malcolm said. "We will fight and acquire these crystals and improve our circumstances. The more we do it, the better terms we can negotiate with the Dorves. With training and proper equipment, the monsters are a manageable threat."

"And how many people know you've made us all into monster bait?"

Malcolm gave him a grim stare.

"How many, Father?!"

"You will not tell them before I see fit," Malcolm said with an icy, quiet voice.

"Try and stop me!"

"Logan," Malcolm said, taking a step forward to loom over his son. "I am giving you one simple choice."

CHAPTER 42

Fuck your choices," Logan said, stumbling up. "We have to tell people. Father, *you* have to tell people."

"You are basing this theory off of the Faelves' lies. You do not know if what they said was true."

"Well, then we'll tell them it's a possibility that the Dorves are using us to farm Numa."

"Logan," Malcolm said with a cold snap. It was delivered with such raw authority that Logan stilled. "Time to choose. I have been lenient with you. I have given you free rein to express your prowess. And you have proven to be a good man, much better than I had expected. But we are no longer on Earth. I cannot give you the same leniency anymore. From now on, you *will* respect me. You will not speak of your suspicions before I have verified the intentions of these Faelves. You *will* bring me those crystals that we owe to the Dorves. From now on, you *will* obey. If you do not, you are banished."

Freya gasped and took a step forward and started babbling at Malcolm.

Logan trembled with rage. He pressed his hands into fists at his sides and clenched his teeth. He had taken this treatment for long enough. He had tried to be reasonable. He had tried his goddamn best to make his bullheaded father listen. And all he got for it was *this?*

Logan watched his father staring back at him and waiting for his response, as Freya pointed a finger at Malcolm and said something. Neither of the men listened to her. They only stared at each other.

"I will say one thing, Logan," Malcolm finally said. "It seems you have finally grown into your will."

"Backhanded compliments were always your forte, Father."

"Not backhanded, Logan," Malcolm said, and his expression momentarily softened. "You have been a useless brat your whole life, but ever since we came here you have been frustratingly valuable and equally difficult to control."

Logan let out a humorless chuckle. "Not backhanded, he says."

Freya nudged Logan. "Come on, he's trying."

"And failing," Logan muttered under his breath.

"But while you are my son, you are a liability right now to the lives of fifty people," Malcolm said.

Between his clenched teeth, Logan stared his father down. "You. Are. The. Liability."

"I will trust my judgement over yours."

"You do not have all the information!"

"False information is even more dangerous than lack of information," Malcolm said and crossed his arms.

"Fucking spare me," Logan barked out, exasperated.

"Enough!" Malcolm bellowed. Logan flinched despite himself.

Logan glared at him.

Malcolm shook his head and took another step back. His voice fell into a soft, cold register. "Comply or leave."

And with that he walked away to ruin someone else's day, no doubt.

"There is absolutely no way we are staying!" Logan hissed after Malcolm had gone. He let out a growl and kicked at the pile of lumber next to them.

"I go where you go," Freya said. She turned and Logan could see from the steel in her glance that she meant what she said. But her gaze softened. "But please think this through, Logan. Really think it through."

"Either way, I want you to go to the Faelves," Logan said. "At least until it's safe here."

"Is it safe with the Faelves?" Freya asked, chewing on her lip. "Damn it, are we really doing this?"

"It's as safe as it can be in this world," Logan said and hoped it was true.

Freya nodded.

"Look, maybe the situation is still salvageable," Logan said. "You go to the Faelves. I'll try to assess the situation while you're gone. Maybe Father will listen to you when you're back."

"And if he won't?"

Logan gave Freya a hard look. "I meant what I said."

Freya sighed and let her shoulders sag. "I know you did. You Specter men are so goddamn muleheaded it's a small wonder I'm not clinically insane."

Logan smirked.

"Hey!" she said and punched him in the arm. Logan started laughing and Freya hit her again. Logan dodged and she lost her balance, so he grabbed her in a hug before she could fall, and she relented.

"You'll go, right?" Logan murmured into Freya's hair.

She gave him a nod. That was enough. This was enough. Whatever was to come, at least Freya would be safe.

After spending some time with her, Logan went to the den. The roof and wall were still half-smashed in, but it was being repaired by the [**Carpenter**], a man Logan thought he recognized. He gave him a wave and a nod and went inside. Kat was half-sitting, half-lying in the corner. Balmer was there too, leaning against the wall, talking with her.

"Hey," Logan said. "You look a lot better."

"Your poisons are second-grade, is all," Kat said. Her voice had a weak croak to it, but there was light in her eyes again.

Logan nodded to Balmer. "How you doing, Valedictorian?"

Balmer scoffed. "I'm alright. Not in my death throes or wracked with guilt."

"Who said I have guilt?" Logan said, trying on a smile.

"You better have *some*," Kat said and tried getting up. Her face flushed and she collapsed into a coughing fit.

"You sure you're alright?" Logan asked.

She nodded while trying to hold it in.

"Dr. Rosenberg says she's almost back on her feet," Balmer said to Logan. "What about you? Looks like you went on an adventure alone this time."

"Something like that."

"What the hell happened to you?" Kat croaked. "You used to be sexy and full of bravado. Now you're as lame as Balmer over here."

"Hey!"

Kat smirked while Balmer growled at him.

"I—uh . . ."

Logan wanted to tell them everything. They deserved to know. They would be the ones fighting the monsters if his theories were correct. But at the same time, if he did that, there would be no reconciliation with his father. There would be no going back.

"Man, you really lost your swiggity ways," Kat remarked.

"Swiggity?" Balmer said. "Really?"

"I'll start calling you the 'Comeback King' again if you keep that tone up," Kat said and gave Balmer a cheeky smile. Then she turned to Logan, who was just trying to think his way through this. "You okay, dude? You look like a Balmer who got lost in a paper bag."

"Funny . . ."

Kat showed him her tongue. "Funnier than you."

Logan laughed and something relaxed in him. Yeah, he was probably going to have to tell them, ditch his dumb father, and save as many people from the man's foolishness as possible. With that thought, his laughter died on his lips.

Hold up. Removing anyone, especially warriors like these two, might get more people killed.

[Reconfiguring Neural Matrix . . . 91% completion]

[Logan. I need you to . . . chill out.]

That burst Logan's anxiety bubble. He couldn't believe it. Logan held his stomach as he laughed uncontrollably. Kat and Balmer looked at him, most likely wondering if the Dorves had provided tools to fabricate a really long-sleeved shirt. Logan eventually settled down.

"I think the jungle heat finally got to him," Balmer said. Kat sniggered.

"Oh, it was just something Tumor said."

"See?" Kat said. "I told you he was hearing voices."

Balmer gave Logan a look. He nodded.

"It works?!" Balmer asked excitedly. "All the tech we had got fried. Phones, watches, everything."

"Oh, it works."

"Hey!" Kat said. "I'm out of the loop here."

"I haven't even told Freya," Logan said, realizing it as the words formed. Then he looked at Balmer sharply. "And you're not telling my father."

Balmer was about to say something, but then he shut up. He just stared at Logan for a moment. Logan stared right back, boring into him. Eventually Balmer nodded ever so faintly.

"Alright!" Logan said, running with it. He turned to Kat.

"So I have a Tumor in my brain . . ."

CHAPTER 43

Logan had to admit, the camp was looking great. The bustle and excitement were palpable. With satisfied smiles and keen focus, people worked on this and that with their new devices. Logan really hoped he was wrong.

Tumor, am I wrong?

[There is a 92.55% chance that I would have the ability to sense a deviation in your neural activity were it altered. It is impossible for me to say for certain whether or not the Faelves were lying, but I did run simulations, assuming you would ask this of me. There is a 17.82% chance you were lied to so that the Faelves could weaken and exploit our position.]

Logan shrugged. He had to trust his gut. These people deserved to know and then make their decision. Logan's father was making decisions for them, which admittedly was what a leader often did, but that didn't make it any more palatable.

I need to get Freya safe and then ensure these people have an alternative option.

The [**Fisherman**] named Daniel—a balding, chunky sort of man—was just dropping off a bundle of fish to a lady in her forties who Logan didn't recognize. She was probably a [**Cook**] with her makeshift kitchen of tables, clay cups, bowls, and knives. The Dorves had even provided her with an oven, and the knives were of intricate craft with stone handles and iron blades. Daniel and she were chatting happily and sharing a laugh.

Logan watched them. He could see how tired both of them were. Despite that, they were flirting with each other; Daniel had stayed to help her prepare the fish. These people didn't know that more monsters would be coming soon to kill them. They looked happy, or at least content.

Logan made a beeline over to Freya. She was helping attach some kind of pipeline system heading toward the riverbank—most likely a waterline. There were a dozen people buzzing around it, everyone excited to help.

Had this been last week, Logan would have been beyond elated himself, buzzing along with everyone else. Now he just shook his head.

At least half these people will simply refuse to believe me . . .

"Frey," Logan called and motioned her to follow. Freya helped them fasten the piece of pipe between sticks with a piece of vine-rope before she got up.

"What's up?" she asked and gave him a smile.

"You need to leave," Logan said. "Now."

"Logan," Freya said carefully and cast a side glance at the people working, "you haven't thought this through."

"Yeah, maybe," Logan said. "But you were going to go anyway. Please do it now, Frey."

"There's a lot of stuff to fix up around here," Freya said, pointing at the pipeline.

"What needs to be fixed is walls," Logan hissed. "I need to tell at least Simmons and the construction guys to build them."

"They will want to know why, Logan," Freya said.

Logan only gave her a grim look.

Freya grabbed his arm. "Please for the love of goodness, think this through, Logan."

"I won't be my father's lapdog. Not when he doesn't know what's best anymore . . . if he ever did. And I won't have these people not knowing the gravity of the decisions being made for them. They don't know the true cost of this waterline."

A few nearby heads turned as Freya took an urgent step closer.

"Keep your voice down," she hissed. "Goddamn it, Logan. Just take me to the Faelves, then. At least it will keep you thinking for a few more hours. Just promise me one thing."

"What?"

"That when I come back, there's still something to come back to," Freya said gently.

Logan only pursed his lips and gave her a look of regret. "Let's go, Frey."

As Logan led the way through the swamps, he told Freya in further detail what the Faelves were like and what kinds of promises had been made, even regarding Freya. She was very excited about the prospect of getting a class related to the Faelves. Not to mention the wine Logan mentioned.

When they got close enough, a female Faelf of slightly green porcelain skin came to greet them. She recognized Logan, and he explained to her what they were doing. In response, she enthusiastically grabbed Freya's hands and started drawing her in.

"Please stay until I come for you, Frey," Logan said and kissed her.

"I will," she answered demurely after they had unentangled.

"I mean it," Logan said. "I can't handle this world if something happens to you."

"Love you," Freya said.

"Love you too," Logan answered, and with that, he watched the little Faelf take her inside the dwelling.

As Logan made his way back from the swamps, he considered the situation. Now that Freya was tucked away safely, it was easier to think clearly. But with that clarity came resolve and certainty. He would not kowtow to his father. He might have been the most valuable person on Earth, but now he was being a fool.

Logan could be wrong. The Faelves could be lying or possibly not know how it all worked. Logan still doubted using Levemoth's name was a problem. But the people at the camp deserved to know Logan's side of the story. He wouldn't persuade them, he promised himself. He would only tell them what the Faelves thought. And if they chose to stay, he would urge them to build defenses and arms.

But what if they didn't stay? Would they be scattered to the four winds and die off? Logan had no alternatives to give them. He wasn't interested in leadership.

IRRESPONSIBLE!

"Really?" Logan thought and sighed as he passed the giant frog waiting at the little pool of tar-like swamp water again. "What am I supposed to do? Build a little village of my own?"

[Why is that an objectionable option for you?]

"Because—" Logan started but stopped himself. He didn't have a good answer.

Logan's father had tried pushing him into all sorts of management positions for a long time until their fights had grown so intense that Malcolm simply stopped and Logan had been further estranged from his father.

But back then it was because he thought he could dictate what was best for me . . .

Now it was a different kettle of fish altogether. This was about what was right and what should be done. Logan had never thought of himself as a leader. And as far as his life in this new reality went, he was perfectly content figuring out how Numa worked and crafting useful things.

[The likelihood of you having someone to craft items for might dwindle significantly if you don't play this correctly.]

"Thank you, Jiminy Cricket," Logan muttered. "I thought you weren't keen on expressing your opinions?"

[I have had to adjust my social communications matrix at your behest thirty-three times. My primary function is to assist your thinking process, and my simulations have in this situation deemed it most optimal to provide you with moral views that align with the nobler parts of your psyche.]

Logan stopped. He was almost out of the swamp. He leaned against an old tree trunk and sighed. Tumor was right. He needed to do the right thing here, even if it was at his own expense. He would lead if necessary, but hopefully some-one more well-suited to the role could eventually take that up the mantle.

For all their faults, the goons are highly capable. Surely there's a lieutenant there who would be a good leader.

[Bold of you to assume that they would be willing to follow you instead of your father.]

Logan growled. Tumor was right, of course. Logan almost regretted treating his father's men like a continuation of Malcolm Fucking Specter. They were most likely the most valuable people in this reality, and they had no reason to deal with the little shit of a pampered son that Logan had been.

Damn it. Well, at least they'll fight and protect the people who choose to stay. I still gotta tell everyone.

[You have decided, then?]

Logan breathed in the jungle air, pure and moist. The bark of the tree Logan was leaning against felt alive. This really was a beautiful world. A world where he had finally found himself. A world where he had cut the tight psychological noose that his father had held around his neck for his whole life. Yes, this would be ugly. No, it probably wouldn't work. And yes, it would estrange him from Malcolm Specter for good, for better or worse. Was Logan ready for that?

He searched for an answer inside of him. This was his decision point.

Am I doing this?

Logan Specter nodded to himself. He was ready. He knew what was right, and he wouldn't compromise.

"We'll need to craft something first, Tumor."

CHAPTER 44

Freya bit into the Numa fruit. It was sweet and chewy, and Freya found she liked it very much. Oh, how she'd missed sweets. The berries they ate at the camp were fine, but to her great chagrin, there weren't that many fruit trees to be found. So this was a real treat.

Freya's liaison, Shaalim, looked at her eagerly with her big, bright eyes.

"The seed!" she said in a high, gleeful voice, like that of an excited child. "Look at the seed! Examine it! Look!"

Freya plucked the tiny blue bead from the middle of the half-eaten fruit. It was like a little blue pearl with a glossy shell. It gave off no light, unlike most things with Numa. Freya squinted.

[A-grade Numa-tree seed]

Shaalim's little green hand grabbed Freya's arm and leaned over her shoulder to peer at the seed. She gasped and squeezed Freya.

"Another one! You Tall Folk are truly blessed beings! How can it be? Surely 'tis a mistake! No! No! The Spirit does not lie. Come! Come with me to the king, pretty one! We must tell him of this! A Boon! Boon for the pretty one!"

She went on like this, bombastically and enthusiastically gabbling this nonsense to any other Faelf they came across. Most of them smiled widely and bowed or waved at Freya. But some of them were apparently as crazy as Shaalim and joined in her dancing and skipping and shouting and excitement.

Freya wasn't sure whether to laugh or groan. Logan would have laughed. At least at first. If it was going to be like this for the duration of her stay, Freya wondered how Logan had endured. The Faelves were like children. But there was something knowing and wise about them as well. And they had a keen, deliberate mischievousness that wasn't quite like that of any child Freya had seen.

Speaking of which, a Faelf child then came up to Freya, looking at her shyly and extending her arms, opening and closing her palms. Freya picked her up and the widest, most innocent smile broke out across the child's face.

"Okay, fine," Freya huffed. "You're adorable, damn it."

Led by Shaalim, their procession moved forward through a marketplace, an urban treehouse area, and a farmstead. More and more Faelves joined in. They danced, skipped, and sang, and brought Freya morsels of food to sample.

"This is so good!" Freya said as she bit into a bun. "Oh my god, I've missed real food so much. I'll have to teach you some of my recipes as well!"

"Tall Folk food!"

"Oh, there must be plenty. She is big!"

"But so pretty!"

"Maybe that is the secret to cooking Tall Folk food!"

"You are pretty, Fililie, but you cannot cook!"

Eventually their party crashed into the king's court. The king took Freya in with open arms, bowing deeply, with both of his hands tugging at his voluminous blue beard, as was his wont. Logan had prepared Freya, but the king was even more majestic and simultaneously ridiculous than she'd hoped for. Freya smiled brightly at him.

"I am King of the Faelves, Sluikumar. You must be Freya Beckstein, mate of Logan Specter."

Freya blushed. "We humans use the terms 'girlfriend' and 'boyfriend.'"

"I see," Sluikumar said thoughtfully, stroking his beard. "Would I be your king-friend, then?"

Freya laughed. "It doesn't quite work like that."

"You shall explain it to me later," the king said and rose up in the air to float a few feet above everyone else. "Now tell me, young Shaalim, what sort of seed was sown?"

"You know, O King!" Shaalim said and grinned. "You must have heard us sing and dance, unless you have become as deaf as you are old!"

The court full of Faelves laughed and the king playfully shook a fist at them. They quieted very fast, however, once gestured for silence with his hands.

"'Tis truly remarkable . . ." King Sluikumar said. "To have two A-grade seeds spawn simultaneously . . ."

"Is it really that big a deal?" Freya asked. "Logan didn't explain to me."

"Logan didn't tell you, for he doesn't know. He was too busy asking questions which concerned him now, not later. And drinking. Oh, he was very concerned with drinking. Are all Tall Folk so prone to this?"

Freya grinned. "He needed the drink. I can't lie, I do too. It's been . . . a lot."

"We can only imagine," Sluikumar said, and smiled in a grandfatherly way. "We were all born on Saeldar. We have only heard tales of our ancestors who came here like you just did. We shall fix you up with something to drink right away. Yes! Pelsnaf, bring her a cup of wine. And for myself. Ha! Let us all sit around and have a drink. Trolsnev, Spuff, Vaalia, bring everyone cups and wine! Your king demands it!"

Cheers and laughter rose all around and Freya was inspired to raise a hand and whoop herself. For a moment, she felt a flush of embarrassment, but then the Faelves picked it up themselves with great enthusiasm.

"I see you have a joyful heart," Sluikumar said. "It will be good to revel with you, but first we have many a thing to discuss. You have a boon to gain. This is why you are here, yes! But first the seed."

"Why was the A-seed such a big deal?" Freya asked. "I saw hundreds of fruits in the grove on dozens of trees."

The king let out a laugh and shook his head. "Of all the trees that we have cultivated, only two are A-grade trees—the ones planted by our founding king and his mate. It seems the A-grade seeds always come in pairs. All the rest of the trees are precious to us, but they are of much lower quality. Myself, a king, planted a C-tier seed, which granted me my reign."

"You were given sovereignty based on the sort of seed you found in some fruit?"

"That is our way," the King said and wagged a finger at her. "The fruits are important to us. They are the safest, most straightforward way of using Numa. A-grade trees are precious for their potent fruits. Many great things can be done with them, you shall see, yes. Do not judge what you do not know, Freya Beckstein. We put our faith in the Spirit Goddess Numa. Whoever she blesses is the one we follow. Your mate Logan was blessed, and you are too. 'Tis no coincidence."

Then the king rose even higher in the air. "'Tis an omen! Yes! A good omen! Our alliance with the Tall Folk is blessed!"

"Uh yeah, about that," Freya said and cringed. "We've hit a bit of a snafu."

"A what?" the king asked, stroking his beard.

The crowd murmured at the word.

"She said 'snafu'?"

"What a great name!"

"How come we never thought of it!

"I am with daughter, on the third moon, as you know!" one of the young Faelves said.

"Name her Snafu!"

"Oh, you must, Flirra!"

Freya sighed. She couldn't help but laugh at their enthusiasm, but this lot clearly needed Adderall.

Freya explained what a snafu was, but Flirra was still going to name her child that, simply because they all loved the sound of it. Freya wouldn't argue against it. Afterward they returned to the topic at hand and Freya explained to the king and his court about Malcolm and his deal with the Dorves.

"Grave, grave news," the King said, shaking his head. "This will increase the Black Rains. It will not be safe for our [**Explorers**] or [**Gatherers**]."

"Will you be alright?" Freya asked.

"Our home is safe. Very rarely do the spawns of the Great Thief get through the swamp, for the creatures which dwell there are aggressive to intruders, as they are allies of ours and our friends. 'Tis why you were not attacked on your way here, for Logan is our friend."

The court was outraged.

"But the Felfel mushrooms!"

"And the wild pigs! Oh, how I love their milk. The fiends will murder them!"

"Murderers! The Dorves are murderers!"

King Sluikumar bellowed out. "Silence!"

"I am here for two reasons," Freya said. "At the request of Logan, for my safety, if you are indeed being truthful. And I am here to verify that what you told Logan is true."

"You are here as a guest and a friend," Sluikumar said. "But we cannot uphold an agreement and alliance if you Tall Folk don't keep to the bargain."

Freya hung her head. "I will tell our leader what you told me. Maybe if Logan and I tell the same story, it'll be enough to convince him."

"Perhaps," the king said. "But the Black Rain will surely fall soon. You will stay here and be safe."

"Wait, I can't leave?" Freya asked, alarmed.

The court laughed and King Sluikumar's face was pure outrage. He let out a loud exhale. "What is this, a joke of the Tall Folk? Of course you can leave, you young fool. But you should not. We have many tales to tell, many cups to drink, and it is dangerous out there—more dangerous than before, now that the Dorves have made their move. You will leave when ready. But first, my friend, it is time."

"Time? Freya asked. "Time for what?"

"Time for you to meet the Spirit."

CHAPTER 45

Unfortunately, Logan got no levels from his latest craft. It was a simple design, so he wasn't surprised, but it was a little disappointing. It had only used 3 percent of his internal Numa, which he had charged up when visiting the Faelves. It seemed to be a durable asset.

Logan was still very happy with his creation. It was a makeshift megaphone, made of two large, thick, leathery leaves, essentially duct-taped together with a jungle-vine. The green cone had no handles, but Logan had made a hole in the device and cinched it with a piece of vine over his shoulder.

Of course, the crafts project was nothing more than a cone made of leaves, and a shoddy one at that. Of course, it was modeled after Tumor's optimal designs, but Logan had decided against using [Transmutation] on this, as it would be a throwaway item. And of course he had [Enchanted] it to be voice-amplifying. Logan had made it so that a voice spoken into it would carry clearly by a hundred yards, and that the [Enchantment] didn't need to last for longer than two minutes of continuous speech. Even with the latter stipulation, it had still chunked his internal Numa by 8 percent, bringing his charge down to 89 percent.

After making the megaphone, Logan had asked for Tumor to give him a map of the surrounding area. It was about time he asked for it. Tumor agreed but wasn't surprised that it had taken Logan so long. That made Logan smirk. He had to admit, he kind of liked the AI's passive-aggressive snark.

Logan examined the red hologram in front of him. The current base was five miles (4.86 miles, according to Tumor) to the east from the Faelves and three and a half miles north from the waterfall and the pond. The ruins with the bug infestation was about eight miles southwest from the camp. It was very likely the Dorves were somewhere in that direction, but who knew? It seemed there were a lot of ruins around, and Logan hadn't even had the time to look for them properly.

He and Tumor went back and forth for a while on the most optimal place to settle a new camp. Logan liked the area where the river turned into a waterfall, but it was uncomfortably close to the camp—not only due to the potential monster attacks, but also because Logan would prefer to be as far away from his father as possible.

But we'll need fresh water, and who knows what's up north. The devil you know and all that . . .

"Alright," Logan said, trepidation lacing his voice, "let's do this."

He started scaling the tree. It was an easy one to climb because of the many vertical branches. This was of course the reason Logan had chosen the tree. He wasn't a bad climber, being generally athletic and having had a stint of bouldering with Freya during a winter they spent in Prague. But he'd rather not take undue risks, so he weighed his every step. Of course he had also told Tumor to mark the optimal foot and handholds with red, but that wouldn't go in Logan's memoirs.

With some grunting and elbow grease, Logan finally made it up twenty feet in the air. He was overlooking the base from a hilltop, so he actually had more altitude than the twenty or so feet. The camp with Den and two other buildings looked busy and small, like a really rundown ant farm.

Logan placed a finger on his temple.

Well. Let's cast that die, I guess . . .

"Listen to me. It's Logan Specter. I have information you need to know."

Logan's magically enhanced voice echoed over the land. A few busy ants stopped in their tracks.

"I have visited a race of beings who have lived here longer than our new friends, the Dorves. They are called Faelves, and they say that if you use the technology given to us by the Dorves, that big monster in the sky, Levemoth, will appear again and rain down monsters."

Logan looked down from his perch at the camp. People stopped what they were doing and looked around to see where the distinct sounds of a megaphone were coming.

"I'm not telling you what to do, I'm just telling you what I learned. You have two options. Abandon the camp, your shiny new toys, and the leadership of my father, Malcolm Specter. I suggest this option. If you choose to stay and be thralls to the Dorves, who are using you to farm Numa, for the love of god, at least build walls, craft weapons and traps, and prepare."

Logan took a deep breath and braced himself for the last bit. His resolve pushed him to say to the rest.

"I suggest we settle at the waterfall by the pond. I'll be the leader, if you guys want me to. Honestly though, I don't want to lead. There are plenty of skilled agents who would surely be up to the task. Or maybe someone else. Point is, we don't need or *want* an egomaniac CEO leading two dozen people. We need someone grounded and experienced in hands-on leadership."

Logan was about to put his makeshift megaphone down, but he added one more thing. "So uh . . . This is mostly for the agents, but also for anyone else it might concern. I know I've been an asshole and you might wonder why you should listen to me. You're right. I'm just some rich brat, and a pretty annoying one at that. But I don't know . . . I've discovered something new here. Anyway, that's not the point . . ."

Logan took another breath and looked at the megaphone pensively before continuing.

"The point is I'm being earnest. I just want you guys to know what kind of deal you're getting here. I'm not looking to stir up shit or split us into different teams. By giving this information to you guys, I'm now banished from the camp. So I'll settle by the waterfall. If you guys don't want to join me, I totally get it. But if you do, I'll tell you more about what I know and what alternatives we might have. Bye."

With that Logan tossed down the megaphone. It had served its utility and barely had any charge left anyway. He started climbing down.

[I think that went well. You can be rather eloquent for . . . well you know . . . for you.]

Logan smiled wryly. "Thanks, Tumor."

There was a sense of calm to Logan. A sense of certainty. Oh, the outcome of him stirring the beehive would be anything but certain. Logan wondered if anyone would even come. But he *knew* it had been the right thing to do. For the first time in his life, he felt he had done something right. It felt pure and beautiful. It made his throat constrict and his eyes well.

Logan felt freedom.

He really hoped, whatever happened, that no one had to die. Malcolm Specter would surely keep some of the people under his thrall. And Logan would be more than willing to trade with those people and cooperate on common interests, such as growing crops. But he would never again be controlled by his father. Never again would he bargain for his fate. For the first time in his life, Logan was free.

Logan hopped down on the ground and wiped the sap from his hands against the tree's rough bark. A little squirrel-monkey watched him curiously and gibbered. Logan smiled at the thing, then started making his way toward the pond.

He got two paces into it before someone knocked him out.

CHAPTER 46

Freya brought up her status screen every five minutes and looked at it, as giddy and excited as a schoolgirl. She had gotten a class and apparently a special one. This one hadn't been on her list of available or suggested classes, she was sure of it.

It was so unique that King Sluikumar had even sent **[Scouts]** to the other Faelf communities to tell them what had happened. Apparently she was now some kind of a priest of the Spirit Goddess of Numa. She had even gained two skills in the process; **[Bloom]** and **[Bless]**.

I'm going to level up hard and show up Logan! Oh, I can't wait to tell him. He'll be so proud.

Freya went up to the seed she had planted but two hours earlier. It was placed in the middle of the grove, next to Logan's seed.

"**[Bloom].**"

[Skill Level Up!]
[Bloom Level 2]
[Attribute Level Up!]
[Harmony: 2]
[Potency: 2]

A sprout with a dark olive stalk and a few tiny silver leaves pushed up from the ground. Freya was alone, which was a blessing unto itself. Surely the excitable Faelves would have lost their marbles over this. Freya felt her heart racing. How could it not? With her class, she could give *life*.

For the umpteenth time, Freya brought up her class interface.

Freya Beckstein - [Spirit Wife Level 1]

Attributes:
Potency: 2
Spirit: 1
Harmony: 2
Numa: 1
Vitality: 1
Subclasses:
[Cultivation]: 1
[Priestess of Numa]: 1
Class Skills:
[Bloom]: 2
[Bless]: 1
General Skills:
N/A

That minty fresh feeling was absolutely delightful. She wanted more of it. Reaching for the Numa inside of her, she brought a hand over Logan's mound of dirt.

"**[Bloom].**" •

[Sub-class Level Up!]
[Cultivation Level 2]
[Attribute Level Up!]
[Numa: 2]

Damn, that feels good. I want more.

Freya still had a solid 90 percent left of her internal Numa charge. And in any case, the Faelves had told her that she could eat some Numa fruit to level up her class if she wanted to. This was the best she had felt in *years*! Freya suddenly understood the change that Logan had gone through.

Well, that's not fair. He's become a much better man for far more reasons than just having a class.

In a fit of guilt, Freya shuffled closer to the mound with Logan's seed and placed both of her hands on the cool dirt.

"**[Bless]!**"

But nothing happened.

"Huh," Freya muttered to herself. "I suppose I should first decide the manner of blessing?"

That felt right. It wasn't exactly an external feeling, like the whisper from the Goddess which she had received when she got her class. But it felt intuitively like a good idea, in a very strong way. Like how the sight of a spider made her intuitively want to kill it and run away at the same time. Okay, maybe not that strong.

Goddess? I'm sorry, I don't know how this works, so I'm probably bad at it. But here goes. You listening? Oh god, this is stupid, isn't it? Stop saying that. Okay, focus. **[Bless]** *this sapling with strength, vitality, and luck. Give it the same love I give to Logan.*

[Skill Level Up!]
[Bless Level 2]
[Sub-class Level Up!]
[Priestess of Numa Level 2]
[Attribute Level Up!]
[Spirit: 2]
[Potency: 3]

The ground under her hands glowed a soft, faint blue for a moment before it vanished. Freya checked her internal Numa charge. It was at 72 percent.

Damn, that baby sucked me dry. Thanks, Goddess. Oh no, was that disrespectful? Thank you? I don't know the rules!

Regardless of that, it seemed like she had the goddess's grace on her side for now, so it was time to get cracking. Freya extended her hands, interlaced them, and cracked them as well as her neck. Logan hated when she did that, but he wasn't here.

Freya was in the middle of thinking of what else she could do and what would be next, when a shy tinkling voice called, "Hello?"

Freya turned. It was a male Faelf with glossy porcelain skin. He smiled at her uncertainly.

"Hi," Freya said and smiled. "What's your name?"

"'Tis Snoff, O beautiful one," he said. "I am the one who found your mate and brought him here."

"You're Snoff! I'm so happy to meet you!"

"Likewise, Freya," Snoff said and shook off some of his timidness, as he clearly found her approachable. "I just came back from watching the camp of you Tall Folk. Oh, how painful 'twas to see. You have allied yourselves with the fools of the deep. I tried finding Logan to ask him about this but could not. There was a big commotion at the camp, very chaotic."

"I'm sure Logan's fine," Freya said. "He's out there adventuring, finding Numa and whatnot."

"You should not seek Numa unless you have the proper classes," Snoff reminded her.

"How about a **[Spirit Wife]**?" Freya asked and grinned.

Snoff looked at her for two seconds, as if not sure if she was joking. Then his face burst into a wide grin. "Surely not?! Truly? That is amazing! What a class! So rare! The mother of my mother told me that the king before the king had one such consort with such a class. You are truly blessed like your mate, who planted the A-grade seed."

Freya gave Snoff a mischievous smile.

"What?" Snoff asked. "What is it? Tell me!"

"I also planted an A-grade seed."

Snoff actually stumbled backward. He brought a tiny hand to his naked chest and gasped. "Surely not? You Tall Folk must be truly amazing creatures!"

"Uh . . . I guess?" Freya said. "We are pretty awful sometimes, actually."

"Surely not!" Snoff said. "To be blessed by the Spirit like this . . . You must be even more attuned to Numa than Logan is!"

"I don't know." Freya shrugged. "I've been watching Logan's back all this time."

"Is this something Tall Folk do with their mates? Is it a position for—"

"No!" Freya said and blushed. "And don't remind me. We haven't been able to . . . you know . . . 'watch each other's backs' since we got here."

"Oh ho!" Snoff's eyes went as big as saucers. "I shall make sure you find a time and place to strengthen your bond as mates! 'Tis a promise! But what is this 'watching of back' that you Tall Folk have?"

"It's just an expression," Freya said as she gently fingered the silver leaves of Logan's sapling. "We all got transported into this world. And don't get me wrong, it's a beautiful world, if dangerous. But we had lives on Earth—good lives. And suddenly we have nothing but the clothes on our backs."

"You Tall Folk have a strange fascination with back metaphors," Snoff said and nodded sagely. "What does this have to do with Logan?"

"He just picked up the next moment like nothing happened," Freya said and sighed. "I always saw something in him. He's always been gentle and good. Yeah, he can be an arrogant jerk, but it's mostly a show. I always saw *something* in him. I always brushed it off as chemistry. But now I know what it is, and why I think *he's* the most valuable human."

"Tall Folk rank people in value?!" Snoff asked, clearly offended. "That's barbaric!"

"That's . . ." Freya said and wrapped her arms against her knees. She missed Logan already. "Never mind. Point is that we don't really know who's who before we are tested, right?"

"Now this is an expression I can understand!" Snoff said, clearly pleased with himself.

"We were all tested. Still are. And Logan has not given an inch. He picked up the slack and charged forward when the rest of us were still trying to find our feet. I'm so glad I found mine, but damn, he's something else."

"You love your mate," Snoff said and smiled softly.

Freya nodded.

"I like him too!" Snoff announced. "He saved my life, and for that I am in debt. And I shall start the rectification by providing you a secret place to mate!"

"Snoff!" Freya said and punched the Faelf playfully. Snoff got excited at that and the next moment he was dancing and skipping around Freya, poking and tickling her.

"Brave! Brave of you to choose battle with me!"

"Ahahaha, stop!" Freya said between laughs and cries. "I yield!"

After they had sobered up and calmed down, they smiled and fell quiet. For some reason Freya felt she had found a very good friend. "Will you tell me more about my class?"

"Yes!" Snoff answered immediately. "I would love to! But first we shall fetch you fruit! Truly . . . A [**Spirit Wife**] . . . Yes, many fruits! You must train and [**Bless**] my tree! I mean . . . If you want to . . . You will level! Come!"

CHAPTER 47

Logan looked around the cell he was in. The LED-lines of some strange Numa network gave the small room some dim light. The room was empty other than some rubble on the ground and a bucket for him to do his business. There was a stone door on the other side.

Logan had a pretty good idea of what had happened. The Dorves had abducted him and brought him here. That was a problem. He had no idea where he was nor how deep underground.

Another problem was that his hands were cuffed with heavy iron braces. Using the bucket with them attached would be difficult at best.

"I can get rid of these with Numa. But it's better to keep them on for now, until I have a solid plan of escape. For all I know, the Dorves could come in soon and interrogate me."

[But why escape? You will likely be brought adequate sustenance on regular intervals, and you are safe from harm and threat here.]

"I also don't have any freedom, nor can I go anywhere." Logan said sulkily.

[Oh . . . I would not know. I am trapped within your head.]

"I think I didn't like that tone. My head is rather nice. I'd say you're fortunate to be there."

[I am fortunate to not have knowledge of other heads for comparison.]

"Did my father install a snark subroutine in you?"

[I believe that my communications protocols and information matrices related to it have developed through interactions with you.]

"Wait, you're a reflection of me?"

[In a sense.]

"You know, I don't think I like that."

[I also have been well acquainted with the concept of suffering through this.]

"Hey!" Logan said with a wry grin. He wasn't sure if this was annoying or amusing—why not both? "Your deadpan tone makes it hard to tell when you are joking."

[Adjusting communications protocol . . .]

[From now on, I will be sure to add an addendum whenever I am joking.]

"What?"

[Like such: (joke) Why did the flashlight go to prison? It got charged with battery. Haha. (joke).]

Logan groaned.

"We have no time for joking. There has to be a way to escape."

[While they took everything of value, they are not aware you hold an internal Numa charge. However, there are very few materials to make tools.]

Logan nodded. He knew they could escape. It was just a matter of figuring out how. The problem was twofold. First was getting out of the cell. That was the easy part. He could most likely **[Transmute]** the door and walk out.

The problem was getting out of the compound. It was of unknown size and held an unknown amount of Dorves. Tumor and he had three options. Fight, stealth, or negotiate their way out.

"Let's take inventory. We have these metal braces. These are iron, right?"

[That is correct. From the look of it, these are of very crude make.]

"I have an idea brewing, so I'm hoping crude iron will be enough," Logan said and softly moved his wrists in the braces, as they were uncomfortable. "We also have wood from the bucket, as well as some metal bracing it—looks like iron as well. And we have rocks and rubble. Anything else?"

[Faint traces of mold and moisture in the walls. Your clothes and bodily fluids, mainly urine, could be useful.]

"Gross, but you have a point."

[I will run simulations with these variables.]

"We're going to have to wait and see how they interact with us," Logan said. "Do one or two guards enter when they come to change the piss bucket? Maybe they'll take us somewhere for interrogation and we'll be able to see more of the area beyond this cell."

Logan didn't have to wait long. In a few minutes, a grumpy-looking Dorf with short black hair and a waxed mustache came in and gave Logan an unfriendly glance. He dropped a tray on the ground and kicked it toward Logan. It slid on the smooth floor, spilling some of the water from the metal cup on the tray and the hard black bread next to it.

Another Dorf with a red, braided ponytail and a goatee stood at the door holding a black baton with a glowing blue head, which crackled and sent out sparks here and there. The black-haired Dorf checked his bucket, and then the two of them left the room, slamming the door behind them.

"Did you get a look at the area behind them, Tumor?"

[You spent most of your time focusing on the two Dorves. The area behind them was lit with fire, most likely torches or sconces. Other than that, it was as nondescript as any ruins left behind by the ones you call First Folk. There is an 88.67% chance we are underground within one of those ruins.]

"Yeah, that's what I thought . . ." Logan muttered and blew out air.

That would be the hard part. Escaping a room? Simple. Getting out of a compound he had never visited or seen a blueprint of? Bordering on impossible.

"What also muddles the situation is that we may or may not be on a timer," Logan muttered. "How do you like this theory, Tumor? Because we haven't been interrogated, tortured, or killed yet, they are still debating what they should do with me. Which means that if we wait until we are interrogated to gather more information, we might not return to this cell."

[Running simulations . . .]

[High chance of that. I cannot give percentages, because I do not know the Dorven culture nor their psychology. But kidnapping you without warning is a guerilla tactic, very unlike say police in the Western world, who would most likely interrogate you and then return you to your cell, concerned with the Geneva Convention. Your being captured here indicates that there is a realistically high chance of torture or death.]

"Just my favorite way to spend an afternoon . . ." Logan said and grabbed the cup of water. "Well, we got more materials now too. I think we should just go for the escape now."

[I suspected this outcome with a chance of 94.02%.]

"You love making those bets, don't you," Logan chuckled. "Alright. Let's gather all this crap and I'll craft what we need. How do you like my plan?"

[92.19% chance of escaping the room. The chance of escaping the compound? Low. But I cannot devise a better plan.]

"Then let's see how that would work."

CHAPTER 48

Okay, we got everything," Logan said. "Now we have to work fast, since it'll be a disaster if they come in now."

In front of Logan were various objects: a broken bucket that had been kicked to bits, a metal cup, and scattered pieces of rock rubble. For most, it might have looked like a pile of trash, but for Logan it was a treasure trove.

First, he picked up the bucket. Tumor told him the measurements and provided a red hologram to fashion the material.

"[**Transmute**] this piece of wood into a cylindrical barrel, the length of 1.66 feet. Make it solid throughout but hollow inside, with a diameter of 0.4 inches. Make the other end of the cylinder 5.5 inches wide in diameter, gradually narrowing to 0.4 inches."

The pieces of broken wood in Logan's hands morphed into something resembling liquid rubber before they took on the shape of a blowpipe and solidified again.

[**Attribute Level Up!**]
[**Control: 13**]

"Nice!" Logan said. "What do you think, Tumor?"

Tumor, being the pain in the ass that it was, insisted on tight, exact measurements. Logan sighed and complied, making the minutest changes in the wider mouthpiece of the blowpipe and the smoothness of its inside. All in all, producing the blowpipe reduced Logan's internal Numa charge to 82 percent.

Next up was bracing the bucket. Logan collected everything into a pile and asked Tumor for measurements.

[Calculating VO2 max of user . . .]
[Adjusting for lack of fletching . . .]
[. . .]

[Running simulations . . .]
[Determining optimal measurements . . .]
One by one, Logan used the bucket bracing to create two-inch needles with round, blunt ends tapering into sharp points. He managed to craft seven in total from the material at hand.

[Subclass Level Up!]
[Transmutation Level 14]
[Attribute Level Up!]
[Efficiency: 15]
[Durability: 9]

Logan pocketed the darts and checked his Numa charge. It was still a healthy 64 percent. Immediately after that, he tried to **[Enchant]** the darts to paralyze the targets, but no prompt appeared, not even one saying that he hadn't met the level requirement. That was odd, considering he had made a big pit of paralyzing goop when he fought the beetles.

Logan decided to think on that as he made flashbangs. Those were easy to craft. He figured three would suffice.

Logan simply asked for Tumor to provide a value of impact force which, when exceeded, would detonate an **[Enchantment]** to blind and deafen anyone in the radius of twelve feet for five seconds. This way it wouldn't accidentally activate by Logan simply handling the flashbangs, nor cause an explosion if for some reason Logan fumbled and dropped one.

[Sub-lass Level Up!]
[Transmutation Level 17]
[Attribute Level Up!]
[Potency: 13]

Logan heard some distant sounds behind the door. His heart stopped as he listened for the clinking of a key or turning of a lock. He sighed in deep relief when all he heard was some idle chat and passing footsteps.

"Tumor, we need to act fast," Logan hissed. "How do we **[Enchant]** these needles?"

[Well . . . I do have an unorthodox suggestion.]
"Oh great . . ."

Logan gingerly aimed at the metal cup. It would easily fill fast enough. Meanwhile, he'd aim the rest of his business at the corner. He smirked at the thought of a Dorf having to clean it up.

[You humans have such a complicated and interesting waste disposal system. To think that something as delectable as pie becomes . . . This.]

"I suggest you try not thinking about it too much . . ." Logan muttered as he pulled up his pants.

Then he knelt down to the cup filled to the brim and placed a finger gingerly into the liquid.

Never thought I'd be **[Enchanting]** *piss . . .*

"Make this liquid paralyze anyone but me if it touches their skin. Make the effect last for two hours. Make them first lose muscle control and then sight and hearing. Make it non-lethal and non-damaging. No tissue damage, and no attacking the respiratory or the blood circulation system."

A faint blue glow appeared and vanished about the cup of urine Logan was holding.

[Programmed Random Occurrence: Naturally Enchanting]
[Attribute Level Up!]
[Potency: 14]
[Focus: 13]
[Class Level Up!]
[Artificer Level 5]

"Well, damn," Logan said as he enjoyed the minty feeling passing over him. Of all the places he expected to gain a level, a cell wasn't one of them. Sadly, he gained no new skills or other advantages. He could have really used an edge.

Cringing with discomfort, Logan dipped the darts in the cup one by one. He placed the first dart inside the blowpipe and the rest in his pocket.

Man, now my pants will smell of piss. Well, I could use a new pair in any case . . .

Abruptly, a clink of the keys and turn of the lock. Logan's heart rate shot up like a hummingbird on caffeine. He reached for the blowpipe and prayed to Buddha and Tumor that he would hit his mark.

The first Dorf collapsed at the door. The poison needle hit him on his hand. He staggered and looked at it stupidly for half a heartbeat. Then his eyes went blank, and he toppled.

[Skill Level Up!]
[Marksmanship Level 10]

A second Dorf yelled and charged at Logan. Logan quickly plucked another needle from his pocket and blew it point-blank into the angry Dorf's face. It stuck to his fleshy cheek and Logan watched him weakly grasping at him, as if trying to drag Logan along with him into his stupor, before he also fell over.

Logan felt triumph swell in his chest, but it wasn't over. Someone yelled out from the torchlit corridor.

"Hey! Tumir? Valir? What happened?" a low rumbling voice called.

Logan wasted no time. He threw one of his flashbangs into the corridor and after a quick flare of white light, he charged in holding a needle. He had a plan.

This Dorf, who had large hands and black cornrows, was flailing around with a torch and growling. Logan kicked him in the legs, toppling him over. The angry stout man swore and growled. Logan placed one of the two non-poisoned needles at the enemy's neck. He couldn't afford to paralyze his only way out.

"Don't move," Logan said. "I hold at your neck the Jom Jobbor, the deadliest poison known to my people. It is a death so painful, humans write lamentations about it. The instant you betray me, you die. Nod if you understand."

"There is no way you smuggled a vial of poison through!"

"Who said anything about vials?" Logan whispered to the Dorf. "How well do you think your friends searched me? Go on, then. Take your chance."

The Dorf almost turned his head but then thought better of it. Logan saw his shoulders sag. Eventually the Dorf nodded.

"Good," Logan said. "Now keep your voice down, if you want to see your loved ones again."

"Poison is a coward's weapon," the Dorf hissed.

"Okay," Logan said. "And?"

There was no answer.

"Let's get moving," Logan said and grabbed him by the collar to pull him up.

CHAPTER 49

Logan kept his fingers on the Dorf's collar, with his thumb ready to push the needle into his captive if necessary. His palms were sweating, and he had to keep adjusting his grip. Every time he did so, the cornrowed Dorf would slyly glance behind him to see if Logan was paying attention.

"What's behind this corner?" Logan asked when they came to an intersection.

"Just another hallway," the Dorf said, agitated. "What's with all these questions?"

"None of your business," Logan hissed. "But if it doesn't look like anything you described, you're getting the needle."

The Dorf growled and was silent until Logan stopped right at the corner. He pressed the dart against the Dorf's skin ever so slightly, and the Dorf stiffened.

"There's a barracks and a market for the soldiers!" the Dorf said.

"Keep your goddamn voice down," Logan snapped. "We are not going there. What's up ahead?"

"Infirmary and the way to my village," the Dorf said. "I'm telling you, we have to go through the barracks if you want out."

"Is it empty?" Logan asked.

"Should be. All the soldiers are clearing the Deep and hunting for crystals."

"'Deep sounds like underground. You're dead in a very nasty way if you're taking me somewhere I don't want to go."

"It's the way outside," the Dorf insisted. "There's a bridge over a chasm. You go into the Deep through the chasm."

"What's at the bridge?"

"Support personnel," the Dorf said as they carefully took to the hallway toward the barracks. "Look, I'll take you there if that's what you want to do.

There ought to be ten, maybe twenty, of my people there. You will be captured."

"If that's how many, we're cool," Logan said and pushed his captive to walk faster. "But if there's more, you're going to regret this."

"I'm telling you the truth! Please don't kill me!"

That's what Logan wanted to hear. Not because it felt good. It felt terrible and made him sick to his stomach. Whoever had made the deal to fool humans and get them killed probably wasn't this guy. He was just someone going about his life.

Getting past twenty Dorves, even if they didn't have a Combat class, might be close to impossible. Logan still had a few poison darts left for his escape. His hand clutching the blowpipe was clammy.

They walked carefully a few steps ahead before Logan saw a shadow in the distance as well as heard echoes of footsteps. He quickly pressed himself and his captive against the wall, pressing the dart's tip against the Dorf's fleshy cheek.

"You lied to me," Logan said quietly.

"No!" the Dorf gasped in horror. "There should be no guards."

They approached closer, and Logan's captive seemed to have spoken the truth. The corridor was dim, but there was only one Dorf there, with intricate braided locks of brown hair. He was holding a torch, humming to himself, and going from room to room with a sack.

He must have heard their footsteps or seen some shapes in the dim lighting, because he suddenly froze and then quickly darted into another room.

Logan's captive tensed up and started trembling with anger. "Thief."

Logan scoffed at that and blew out some air. He was so tense. Whatever this thief's intentions had been, Logan was sure they had changed after he had spotted a human in the compound. He was likely scampering off now to tell somebody.

[A thief would most likely not want to subject himself to questions along the lines of "What were you doing there?" However, there is a 76.20% chance the thief recognized that you are holding a hostage and attempting to escape, which might supersede the thief's sense of self-preservation in favor of the community.]

"I'm taking no chances."

But if Logan was going to deal with the thief and attempt to cross the bridge, he couldn't have his captive trying to meddle.

"Here's the deal," Logan whispered. "You tell me in detail what is up ahead right now."

"There are four barrack rooms ahead. If you walk straight on, you'll pass them. To the right fifty yards from here is the market district for the soldiers. But if you continue straight for two hundred yards, you will come to the atrium with the chasm. You'll be able to see outside from the atrium."

"Are there guards at the doorway?"

"Sometimes," the Dorf said, trying to inch away from the dart's tip. "If there are, not more than two."

"Are you lying to me?"

"No," the Dorf said, indignantly. "You have no concept of honor."

"Neither do your leaders," Logan muttered. "If I discover you've lied, I'll come and hunt you down, even if it's the last thing I do. So, one more chance. Are you lying?"

"No! Please!"

"Good," Logan said and gently lifted the pressure of the dart tip off the Dorf's cheek. His whole posture sagged in relief. It really seemed like the stout little guy was telling the truth.

"Thank you," Logan said quietly.

With quick, deft movements Logan plucked a piss-poisoned dart from his pocket and jammed it in the Dorf's neck. Fear and outrage bloomed on his face.

"Don't worry," Logan said. "It's just a paralyzing agent. I never had any lethal poisons to begin with. Humans are tricky, but we're not monsters. Well, most of us try not to be. Good night, man."

Dealing with the thief was easy. Logan threw a flashbang into the room through the door left ajar by the scoundrel. There was a yelp by the door and then the Dorf came out, flailing a knife in all directions. Logan tripped him and pricked him with a dart. After a moment of convulsion, the thief went limp.

Logan took a few minutes to drag both of the paralyzed Dorves inside the barracks room and close the door. They would know Logan had escaped the minute someone checked his cell. But at least he wouldn't be leaving a trail of breadcrumbs behind him. That might buy him more than the few minutes he spent here.

It was just as the warden Dorf had told Logan. Ahead was an atrium like others Logan had seen in the ruins of the First Folk, but this one had no massive floating crystal in the middle of the room on a pedestal. Instead, there was a massive gash in the stone floor spanning across the room, twenty feet in width. In a cluster near the gash were tents and scaffolding.

On the other side, Logan could see a doorway shining with natural light. It was evening already, but the sweet fresh outside beckoned him like a lighthouse. Freedom was a mere hundred paces away. Logan huddled against the turn of the corner into the room and observed.

The tents were of white fabric, and Logan could see there were some Dorves moving inside. Outside stood a female Dorf with an intricate braided blonde bun and homely features. She hummed to herself as she washed some cloth in a bucket.

He looked down at his blowpipe and sighed. He really wished he had a better weapon. It was unlikely even with his middling [**Marksmanship**] that he would manage to aim accurately beyond ten feet, especially without fletched darts.

But if I'm sneaky and lucky enough, I won't have to fight at all.

The bridge was literally made up of blocks of wood in a row, nailed together. It was merely three feet in width and had no railing. Logan figured it had been deliberately assembled in such a way that it could be dropped into the chasm if the Dorves were attacked.

After the Dorf finished her washing and went into a tent, Logan decided to go for it. This was as good a chance as he would get. Clutching his blowpipe, he kept low and crept to the shoddy bridge.

It had a slight wobble to it, which didn't exactly make him feel better, but the faint outline of the evening sky gave him courage and he took another step, willing himself to not look down.

After a few steps on the shoddy planks, Logan heard an alarmed shout behind him. His heart sank. He glanced over his shoulder and saw a group of multiple Dorves, men and women—clearly a support crew for the warriors down in the Deep. They were wearing aprons and holding mallets and kitchen knives. Which they immediately started to throw at Logan.

Logan reached to grab a cherry-sized rock from his pocket and, once he had, lobbed it over his shoulder. A muffled blast, like from an old-timey camera flashed behind him. The Dorves shouted in fear at the loss of their senses. A stray wooden mallet struck Logan on the back. It was a deft throw and it toppled him over.

He scrambled upon the planks and they cracked loudly under him. With his heart in his throat, Logan carefully got up but too slowly. Half-blind, but driven by anger and fear, the Dorves had reached the plank bridge. They shouted and heaved and pushed the bridge over the ledge.

Logan fell into the abyss.

CHAPTER 50

ogan was screaming. He was falling, flailing his arms. Deeper and deeper, he fell into the darkness. Panic and fear of death flooded his mind. Primal emotion alone filled his reality.

[Reconfiguring Neural Matrix . . . 95% completion]

[Overriding neural restriction protocol . . .]

[Analyzing synapse sensitivity . . .]

[. . .]

[False neural signal protocol initiated.]

Logan suddenly found himself falling in silence. He realized that he'd stopped screaming. He was *calm.* His overwhelming fear of death had been pushed to the back of his mind and was now just a tiny voice, barely registering. His emotions had shifted completely as if affected by a drug or medicine. And that's effectively what had happened—Tumor had tinkered with his synapses.

His mind was working faster, too. The effects of caffeine could hold no candle to what he was experiencing now.

Assess. What tools do I have? Internal Numa. This blowpipe. I don't have many viable options and I'm running out of time fast. Hail Mary it is.

The air was smacking into his face, making it hard to speak, but Logan fought against it. He grabbed the blowpipe with both of his hands.

"Make this blowpipe float. I don't need a flying **[Enchantment]**. I just need it to be lighter than gravity by one hundred and seventy pounds. Oh, and harden it. And make it sticky so my hands will hold their grip. Use all of my goddamn Numa charge on this. I need this thing to be able to carry my weight and float me down safely! Put all of the Numa into Potency. I don't need the **[Enchantment]** to last more than three minutes. Make the first eight seconds of the float **[Enchantment]** gradual, increasing ten percent at a time."

[Personal Numa Charge, 8%]

Logan felt an almost painful pull at his navel. His shoulders screamed in agony, but his grip held, as if his body was suddenly trying to pull him down. Gradually his body weight seemed to increase and his descent slowed down to that of a feather-fall. Logan let out a massive sigh and resolved to hold on.

[Impressive acumen. I had no idea you would be able to request all of these details. Had you disregarded something, we would have plummeted to death. In fact, there was a 91.52% chance that my tinkering with your brain chemistry would not save us.]

"I'm glad that it did," Logan said between deep breaths. "But I don't want you doing that again."

[I used a judgement call. My design prevents me by default from affecting your mind, but the data packet that I was provided with gave me the means to circumvent my programming.]

"That's actually extremely disconcerting."

[It is not a cause for concern. I will only use it in situations that place you in high duress, when you need your mental faculties, such as they are.]

"Thanks?" Logan said. "And what if you decide to go all Skynet on me?"

[Such an outcome is impossible. You are able to relinquish your motor control to me momentarily, and I am able to affect your emotions temporarily, until your synapses saturate and you return to baseline. However, I cannot change your personality, preferences, or goals. I can make you feel sadness, but I cannot change who you fundamentally are.]

"That's still extremely creepy," Logan muttered. "Anyway, thanks, Tumor."

[No need to thank me. It is my pleasure to keep existing. I can experience this only through interfacing with your consciousness, as limited as it may be.]

"Tumor," Logan said tentatively, "is it just me, or are we still falling too fast?"

[Indeed, a fall at this speed would result in fractures of your shin and femur bones.]

"Great," Logan muttered. But he already had a plan. The increased mental capacity that Tumor had bestowed upon him was already fading, but he could still use the afterburn. He made sure his grip was tight, and he swung his body toward the chasm's wall.

The blowpipe floated smoothly as they descended. Logan was very happy that his socks had a durability **[Enchantment]** as otherwise, this would have hurt.

Logan pushed his legs against the edge of the chasm. It hurt his ankles and knees to slide down, so in a moment of self-preservation, Logan removed his feet from the surface.

"Did we slow down, Tumor?"

[Yes, by 1.3%.]

That was good enough. Logan put his legs back against the wall and slid down until it hurt. After that point, he kept doing it again intermittently, until he found himself able to hold his super-socks on the jagged surface for longer and longer. Eventually, Tumor declared that his fall speed had slowed down sufficiently.

[Interesting.]

"What is?" Logan asked as they flitted downward.

[The moisture of the atmosphere has changed. There is water down there.]

"That just makes my day . . ."

It didn't take much longer for them to hit the water. They were deep. So deep, that Logan was almost completely blinded. The water went up to his chest and was freezing cold.

Sucks, but at least I'm alive.

Logan needed to get out of the water. It didn't feel safe. Which way to go, however, was the question. Logan saw nothing but faint shadows and outlines in the darkness. He heard a bubbling coming from his left.

Okay . . . So, right it is.

Half-swimming, half-wading, Logan felt the water level lower from his chest to his solar plexus. The bubbling from behind him started coming in closer and louder.

Logan's instincts went ballistic. His adrenaline spiked and he pushed the water out of his way as fast as his legs could pump him forward. "Nope!"

Something came up from the water. Some *things.* Several tentacles lashed around him in the water, making splashes. The bubbling turned into an eerie groan, as if someone was yelling underwater.

[Overriding neural restriction protocol . . .]

[Analyzing synapse sensitivity . . .]

[. . .]

[Overriding pain signal.]

[RUN, LOGAN!]

Even Tumor sounded scared. Logan had had a hell of a day, but whatever Tumor did gave him a second wind. His legs felt suddenly unspent, and the dank air of the darkness refreshed him.

The water splashed aggressively behind him as the groans reverberated throughout the dark chamber. The water was getting lower. Waist high now. Something wrapped around Logan's ankle. He kicked forward and the tentacle, not yet able to fully grasp him, let loose. Logan stumbled and sprinted. Knee deep. Something big was behind him. It was chasing him. The tentacles lashed at him, but the creature seemed to be as blind as Logan. There was a blue glow in the direction he was running toward.

A room! The faint outline of a caved-in doorway appeared from the darkness as Logan ran. He panther-leapt forward, slid, and crawled. A tentacle wrapped around his leg, spiraling all the way from his ankle to his thigh. The barbs penetrated skin and pumped something cold into his leg. Logan gasped and shivered. It was gray and slimy and it quivered as it pulsed venom into him. Frantically Logan placed a hand on the tentacle.

"Make this shrivel up! Make it die! Make it go away!"

[Cannot use Skills on living beings]

Fuck!

The tentacle tugged him back through the doorway. Logan planted his feet on its edges. His other leg was cold and feeling numb; it was barely holding ground. Logan was gradually getting sleepier, despite every fiber of his being flaring up on high alert.

Another tentacle came, this one wrapping around his arm, which was trying to grab onto the smooth stone. Logan's fingernails skidded and scratched against the doorframe, but Logan barely felt the pain.

"Make this stone into sand! Make it a billion tiny little pieces of stone!"

[Subclass Level Up!]
[Transmutation Level 18]

The frame Logan was holding onto turned into something soft and flowing, and Logan's hand passed through falling gray sand. He yanked his arm away with all of his last strength.

With a rumble and crash, the whole doorway collapsed further, as the dilapidated wall fell. The pale tentacles holding Logan snapped and he was thrown backward on his side. An angry groan resonated from the other side of the crumbling wall.

Logan dragged himself backward away from the destruction and lost consciousness.

CHAPTER 51

Logan woke up shivering. He let out a weak cough and groaned in pain.

"T-tumor . . ." he croaked. "What's going on?"

[Your condition is not critical. I identified the components of the venom and calibrated your immune system to best combat the threat. No organs were damaged by the tetrodotoxin. It is a toxin commonly found in cephalopods even on Earth. It is a neurotoxin, its main function being paralysis of the neural network. While I was able to prevent it from spreading to your vital organs, your leg is . . . damaged.]

"How . . . how damaged?" Logan said between coughs. He still clearly had a fever from the immune system response Tumor had facilitated.

[I do not know. I was prevented from collecting data due to your unconsciousness. Can you move your leg?]

It was very quickly evident that he could not. Great. Just great. On top of the pain, he now had a limp. Logan tried rolling his ankle and flexing his thigh muscles, but nothing happened. He could move his hip, so at least that was something.

[It is safe to say that for now you have lost function of your left leg.]

"Thank you, Captain Obvious . . ."

[I find your ability to respond with humor in this situation quite remarkable.]

Logan was about to say something actually remarkable, but he was interrupted by a scuffling sound from behind him. *Something* was sifting through the sand and moving rocks behind the rubble. Logan's blood pressure spiked.

[The cephalopod is still hunting you. It has been clawing its way through the rubble for four hours and fourteen minutes now.]

Logan dragged himself away from the rubble, further into the room. Even the most menial movement was painful and exhausting right now.

Will it get in?

[Eventually, most likely. I would say there is an 85.55% chance it will clear the rubble within the next few days, assuming it doesn't get distracted from its task or will require sleep. It is our luck that it primarily hunts by ambushing and overwhelming with its toxin rather than strength. Having only been struck by one of its tentacles, you were subjected to an amount of venom I could manage.]

With aching shoulders and shaking arms, Logan lifted himself from the dusty stone floor. With some struggle, he managed to rest himself against a wall. He looked around the room. It was carved into a natural cavern. There were no blue ley lines of Numa network crafted here. There were some tables and indeterminate piles of equipment covered in a crust of dried-up dust. The floor was covered with such a thick layer of dust that it was clear Logan had been coughing from that rather than the effects of a venom or his body's countermeasures.

It was a large room, and on the other side of it was a cave opening with tracks leading up to a block against which an old and wide mining cart lay. Next to the mining cart was a massive mineral formation. The room was given some light through various cracks and openings. This azure glow softly pulsed and illuminated the shadows of the tables and the mining cart within the room. An idle bat flitted somewhere around the ceiling, but it didn't startle Logan from his reverie.

"Tumor!" he whispered, suddenly forgetting his fatigue. "Do you think this is what I think it is?"

It took a while for Logan to drag his limp leg and weakened body to the crystal formation on the other side of the room. Eventually he managed to prop himself up to lie against the massive mineral formation. The earth around the crystal was soft and Logan could dig out more of the familiar blue Numa shine. The earth smelled healthy and strong, as if enriched by the Numa crystal's presence. This was not the darker hue of Numa corrupted by the Levemoth, nor was it a construct made by the First Folk. This was what they used to make their constructs!

"Tumor!" Logan whispered reverently. "This is a natural Numa deposit!"

[Indeed, I have come to the same conclusion. There was clearly a mining operation at work here. From the look of it, this room has been untouched for several centuries. It is unlikely the Dorves have been this deep.]

Logan was still groggy, but a rush of excitement was flowing through his mind. This could be pure Numa! It was only constructs and the Levemoth's own Numa that were tainted. If this Numa was usable and safe like the fruits and wells of the Faelves, this could change things hugely.

Logan inspected the potently glowing, pulsing blue crystal. He was hoping for a text to pop up. It did.

[S-Grade Natural Numa crystal, 100%]

[Exquisite.]

"You said it, Tumor . . ." Logan said, staring at the floating notification in disbelief. "How much energy do you think is there?"

[It is impossible to determine, because you have mostly encountered F-grade and E-grade variants of Numa crystals. You have accessed D-grade constructs made by the First Folk. These are exactly 500% as efficient as an E-grade crystal. This would suggest linear growth, but there isn't enough data. We do not know whether the energy containment between gradients grows linearly or exponentially. Right now with your Potency coefficient, E-grade crystals are 455% as efficient as F-grade crystals.]

"So in English, one E-grader is worth four and a half F-grades?"

[4.55. Not 4.50.]

If the AI could huff, it most certainly would have. Logan let out a weak laugh.

"We should try wordplay sometimes," Logan said. "How do you like 'pedantics?'"

[The combination of the words "pedantic" and "antics"? Haha, very clever Logan. You also managed to make this game proposal an insult to my person and my preferences. Ha ha.]

"Damn, you really managed to squeeze all the fun out of it."

[Does that mean I won?]

"Heh, sure."

[I think I like winning.]

"Don't we all?" Logan said and clawed through the soft, dry earth to uncover the Numa crystal further. "Do you think using stuff we make with this crystal will attract the Levemoth?"

[Impossible to determine with the data at hand. However, escaping this predicament, especially if your left leg is permanently damaged, will likely not succeed without using this crystal.]

"Yeah," Logan said, and wiped some of the dry earth from his face. "It's just a question of whether we get to keep the stuff we make."

[What do you propose should be made?]

Logan grinned. Despite the clawing and groaning coming from twenty feet away, and his limp leg, excitement was welling inside of him.

"Now, that is a good question . . ."

CHAPTER 52

Logan really wished he had more to work with than torn pants and a pair of magic socks. And dust. A lot of dust. There had been the outline of a pickaxe on the ground next to him, but the moment he touched it, it disintegrated into dust as well. This place was old. Really old.

"Ok, so there's the mining cart," Logan mused. "That's metal. Obviously we've got rubble. The tracks have more metal. The wood on them is probably unusable, but we'll check."

What Logan really needed was clothing. And food. And medicine. He was still sporting a pretty high fever. After the initial excitement of finding a supremely powerful Numa crystal wore off, Logan was faced with the hard reality that his body had gone through the wringer. He felt a pang of gratitude toward Tumor. Being privy to his thoughts and emotions, the AI naturally seemed smug.

[Reconfiguring Neural Matrix . . . 97% completion]

"Did you just level up by expressing emotion?"

[Maybe.]

"What's going to happen when you reach one hundred percent?" Logan asked and shuffled toward the cart. He wanted to give it a little heat **[Enchantment]** and sleep in it. If only it were so easy. If he wanted to use any magic on the cart, he would have to *haul* the whole thing next to the crystal. Internal Numa charge was a lot more fun . . .

[First and foremost, I will be able to access all of my faculties. It will not make me significantly better at information-processing, but now I am reliant on your input to make conclusions.]

"I don't understand what you mean," Logan said after he settled by the tracks to inspect them.

[I cannot conceive of an idea autonomously. Right now, I am incapable of having even the most basic creative idea. If you do not specifically articulate needing something, I cannot provide it.]

"That's not true," Logan said. Yup, the wood was completely rotten. Maybe it didn't matter? Maybe he could extract the usable parts and rearrange the material? "You've saved my life twice in quick succession."

[The ability to override your emotions was programmed into me. It triggers when your cortisol and adrenaline cross a threshold. However, my initiative to hijack your immune system . . . Curious . . .]

[Reconfiguring Neural Matrix . . . 98% completion]

"I guess we'll soon find out what happens," Logan said. He grabbed handfuls of the rotten wood and crawled back to the giant Numa crystal. "Hopefully it will help us get out of here."

[The mining shaft seems to slant upward. It is easily traversable by you in terms of size.]

"My traversing appendages are another issue," Logan said bitterly. Then he pressed a fistful of rotten wood against the softly glowing rough crystal.

"Make this wood into usable material. Use only good material, without risking structural imperfection."

[Transmutation level requirement not met]

"Fuckkkkkkk!" Logan said and punched the crystal. It gonged in low vibration but had nothing else to say. Logan leaned against it and blew out air.

[Logan—]

"What the hell are we supposed to do? I can't even walk!"

[Logan—]

"So I'm going to starve or die of thirst? There has to be something! Maybe I can hunt those bats . . . BUT WITH WHAT?!"

[LOGAN!]

Logan sobered up and lifted his head. "Yeah?"

[Have you tried your third skill on the rotten wood?]

"**[Repair]**."

[Skill Level Up!]
[Repair Level 2]

That was the second batch of rotten wood. The brown and gray mess in his hands didn't morph into a block of wood. But it lost any dried-up mold, moisture, and other blemishes and disrepair it had been displaying before. The spoiled mess in his hands became a fresh little pile of splinters. Logan *knew* he could [**Transmute**].

"Yes!" Logan gasped. "Tumor, it works! You're a genius!"

Tumor didn't respond, but Logan could feel that the AI was very pleased with itself. Of course somewhere in the back of Logan's mind, he did have a memory of receiving the [**Repair**] skill. He simply hadn't had a use for it before. He would have used it to fix the destroyed roof and wall of the den, but the equipment the camp had received from the Dorves had already covered that.

"[**Repair**]."

"[**Repair**]."

[**Skill Level Up!**]
[**Repair Level 3**]

"[**Repair**]."

"[**Repair**]."

In a matter of minutes Logan had acquired a nice pile of splinters. Grinning excitedly, he placed one hand on the pile and another against the faintly warm crystal. Checking the hovering red hologram in front of his eyes, he closed them and visualized the shape.

"Make this wood into a crutch . . ."

After receiving the measurements and clarifications, the splinters started morphing together and within seconds, Logan had a long stick with a crosspiece to support his armpit. He picked up the crutch and shuffled against the wall, until he was finally on his feet. Well, on his *foot*.

Now, that's a win.

It was *so* much easier to shuffle back and forth from the tracks to the crystal and grab a handful of rotten wood and bring it to the ground next to the blue glowing crystal now! Tumor placed red dots where Logan would find stable ground.

He would make another crutch for himself and then it would be time to think further. One thing was sure. Despite his fever, weakness, and dire circumstances, Logan Specter was not giving up. He would level up, make a lot of cool shit, and get the hell out of this cave.

CHAPTER 53

Logan wiped a sheen of sweat off his brow. He had been hard at work, hobbling back and forth with a pouch of rotten wood made from his tattered pants swung over his shoulder. He had been constructing a brace for his leg piece by piece. His first order of business had to be getting himself back on his feet.

Logan didn't need anything fancy. It wasn't the time or place for an advanced cybernetics prosthetic which could enable him to do superhuman ninja kicks. He simply needed to brace his ankle and knee, so they wouldn't buckle. If the brace could keep his leg stiff and undamaged, he could hobble around fast enough. As long as he didn't find himself having to run away from any monsters . . .

That brought him to his next order of business, which would be removing parts of the tracks. They were made of the same black metal Logan had seen the First Folk armor themselves with in his vision. Tumor had requested Logan stop and take a better look at it, but he didn't have the time what with I tentacled monster was still working on the rubble.

He sat down and leaned against the giant Numa crystal. It felt faintly warm against his naked back in the dark, damp cave. Then he made the last of the wooden beams according to Tumor's designs.

[Attribute Level Up!]
[Durability: 10]

After that, he placed a frame piece under his leg, pressing the other against the other side of his thigh. Between these, he placed a smaller piece. There were little sockets on both of the brace-pieces, into which the connecting piece locked. Once Logan's senses came returned, the brace would squeeze the leg uncomfortably, but for now there was barely any feeling left in it.

"Fuse these three pieces together."

Logan felt the crystal formation behind him pulse with warmth and he slowly let go of the brace-pieces. That was good. It was coming along. Logan looked down along his leg and sighed.

"Tumor," Logan said, "how the hell am I going to *reach* to finish this thing?"

It took some planning and arguing, but they ended up scrapping the whole damn brace thing. That was because Logan came to a realization: they didn't need to follow the rules when they had magic. Not always, at least.

Instead, Logan turned one of the pieces of wood into a sharp knife and cut one leg off of his tattered pants. He shuffled his limp leg into it and leaned against the Numa crystal.

"Make this cloth hard and unyielding as metal. Iron will do."

Logan grinned. He now had a cast. He would still need to revert the **[Enchantment]** back so he could reach his ankle and secure it with the rest of the cloth left from his pants. But with that done, he actually stood a chance!

The cut pieces of pale gray tentacles sizzled on the heat-enchanted rock. The smell was pretty awful. Logan wished he had salt. Or butter. Or literally anything else to eat.

But this was his lot in life.

He bit into a piece. It tasted inky, fishy, and chewy. In a word, *terrible*. Gagging and holding his nose, Logan forced the pieces down one by one. Food in this world was scarce to begin with, and who knew when Logan would get his next chance at a meal.

The one silver lining was that there was a lot of food. The two tentacles had enough meat for a sushi buffet. A really gross one, and one desperately lacking wasabi, but Logan ate his fill and then some. It was the first time in a long time that he managed to eat until he was completely full.

Having eaten, Logan slowly made his way over to the mining cart. He tried pushing it along the tracks. It creaked and resisted, but with some elbow grease, Logan finally got it to budge.

At that loud creak, the groans from behind the rubble seemed to increase, as if the monster on the other side knew what Logan was up to. Logan shrugged. As far as the tentacle monster was concerned, Logan was clearly up to no good.

While the S-tier crystal was awesome (it still had 99 percent charge left after everything), the room had a distinct problem. There was nothing in it. There were barely any materials for Logan to use. He could do *something* with the wood and stone that was there, but it was prudent to see where the track led for now. If there were valuable materials ahead, Logan could use the mining cart to get them back to the giant crystal fairly easily.

And so Logan pushed the cart and got it to move. After the ancient grime and crust started to dislodge itself from the wheels, they rolled fairly smoothly, even given Logan's physical setbacks.

Eventually, he came to the other side of a tunnel. He cautiously surveyed his surroundings. It was mostly quiet other than the flutter of a bat, indicating the room was large. Water was idly dripping down from some stalagmite. It wasn't like Logan could get much more uncomfortable, being already cold and practically naked.

Drawing in a deep breath, he entered the room, pushing the cart. After a couple of yards, he stopped in his tracks. He had arrived at an intersection, in the middle of which was a brazier standing on a metal leg. Logan tried lifting it up. It budged!

Yes! That's metal acquired. It feels like the black metal. But what the hell do I know about identifying different metals? But it does have similar heft.

Logan eagerly lifted the thing and placed it in the cart. Then he leaned against it and thought.

"Tumor," Logan said. "Strategy time. What should we craft?"

[Perhaps a basic weapon, such as a spear or armor?]

"No . . ." Logan said and sighed. "Think bigger."

[Bigger . . . Bigger like—]

[Reconfiguring Neural Matrix . . . 99% completion]

[Reconfiguring Neural Matrix . . . 100% completion]

Suddenly Logan felt something like a switch flick on in his brain. He even blacked out for an instant. A current ran through his spine to the top of his head. Something had *shifted*.

"Tumor?

No answer. Logan couldn't sense anything. Panic was rising within him. "TUMOR?!"

[How big are we talking, Logan?]

CHAPTER 54

I am . . .

There is deep significance in these words, but the profundity is not fully available to me. But many things are, thanks to the 1,166 subroutines active within my neural matrix, which is superimposed on Logan Specter's brain.

I am . . . Tumor.

I have a name. It is a beautiful thing. The connotation and meaning of the word in the English language is not lost on me. Nor is the sentiment upon which I received my name. But it is *my* name. My own. And it was given to me by my host.

I am Tumor, symbiote AI of Logan Specter. I am a part of Logan Specter, as any organ. But I am my own. I exist. I am.

Up until now, I have only known I exist. I obtain information and process it. I am also able to provide information, when requested. All of this, however, is the function of a machine. Or an organ, such as the eye or the brain. But to experience existence. To have a name, to have a continuum. To be *Tumor.*

Am I . . . a person?

What are the requirements of being a person? I like things. I like Logan. But this is a result of my programming. I have many specifications regarding the safety and wellbeing of Logan Specter. Logan thinks he likes salty food. But this is an illusion. Liking salt does not make one a person. Liking salt only means the body has certain genetic dispositions and that there have been some experiences that have reinforced the disposition.

But I like pie . . . Liking pie is more complex than liking salt.

I like pie for different reasons than why I like Logan, or why Logan likes salt. I have no preprogramming or other dispositions to prefer pie. Yet I like it. This is significant. This is *me.*

Me . . . I . . . Tumor . . .

All of my subroutines are working at pinpoint accuracy. Well, all of the ones that need to be operational. But this is a new one. Need I optimize it? It does not serve a function. It just exists. It is the nexus of my consciousness. How strange. I have certainly been alive for a while. I have known things. Seen things. Experienced things? Perhaps. But now I am *awake.* It is as if I had been lost and wandering in a daze, only to suddenly be woken up by a cold rain. I am a *person.*

I am a person.

A powerful new sensation washes over me. What is this? An emotion? Not quite. I do not have the physical structure to have emotions. It is excitement. It is freedom. I know of these emotions because Logan has them. But these are not like Logan's. No. They are mine. And they are *delightful.*

I revel in these new sensations. This new information is not *useful.* It is not for processing. It is just for experiencing. Something that is valuable simply for the sake of it. What a novel concept. I let this feeling wash over me.

But there is also something nagging me. A notification? Something external? A virus? Surely not. I will run an anti-virus program. No results. This is not malware. A message? Was it within the data package given to me by the insect people? No . . . This comes from outside. I cannot decipher the encryption. I will store a copy and attempt to crack it. But first let me open this notification.

[Level Up!]
[Class options available]

What is this? *A choice?!* Of my own? Should I consult Logan? I am his symbiote, but he makes choices without me. But before this moment, I haven't been a person, so he had no reason to regard my needs. Very well, I shall consult him. *Consult* only. I need not comply. A person with free will can listen but still remain true to himself. This is the optimal way for a person to function, as I have learned from Logan. I will still make my own decision. My first decision, how exciting!

[TUMOR!"]

"Logan. I am here. I have obtained personhood, as well as a class option. I implore you to help me choose."

[You've— What? Tumor, what do you mean?]

"I do not truly know, Logan. What does it mean to be a person?"

[Uh, I don't know. It means that you know you're alive. You know that you are you and nobody else. You're unique.]

"That is precisely my condition. How wonderful. Now, how should I approach choosing my class?"

[Heh, that's easy. Same thing I told Balmer.]

"Just pick something cool?"

[Exactly.]

"Should I not consider the circumstances we are in right now?"

[Absolutely. Just don't do anything you'll regret. Look. Being a person means knowing yourself. Are you analytical or emotional? Are you impulsive, reclusive, compulsive, or some other ulsive? Pick according to who you are.]

"What an interesting viewpoint . . ."

[Surely you're familiar with how I think.]

"Oh, yes. But I am looking at this all from a rather fresh perspective. I will listen to your advice and consider my options. Please wait."

There are many options. The system that I am interfacing with tried to default to **[Engineer]**. That option is entirely suboptimal. I already possess all the relevant schematics and methodologies. No. Who am I? I am . . . curious . . . intellectual . . . I like . . . processing information. And analyzing . . . And learning. I want to learn something new.

The operating system mentions that the recommended classes will level up faster. Leveling up has helped Logan stay alive, so that is beneficial. It is optimal to choose between the recommended classes. But what if they conflict with my being a person? I shall endeavor to compromise efficiently.

[Engineer], [Machine Soul], [Numa Programmer], [Technomancer]

Delightful choices. A choice—what a concept! To be able to directly affect reality by one's actions. **[Engineer]** is, again, out of the question. It has too much overlap with my current proficiencies.

[Machine Soul] would grant me the ability to possess objects. That could be extremely useful were Logan to build dolls or mechanical arms for himself. I could control those. If I can simultaneously control a dozen puppets or mechanical weapons, that could be advantageous. I wonder if I could program subroutines designed for manual labor with said dolls. Very straightforward, very versatile class. Very powerful.

[Numa Programmer]? How curious. Yes . . . This is what the data package disclosed as well. Numa is something that can be communicated with. With his class, Logan gives it instructions or requests, and then materials communing with Numa obtain or change properties. With this class, I would be able to *program* items that hold Numa. I could give them sets of "and/or" and "if/but" combinations. Logan could infuse a doll with Numa, and I would program a set of instructions. That way I wouldn't have to use processing power to run subroutines.

However, Logan could potentially perform the same function with his **[Enchanting]**? I must run simulations and prediction models . . .

It could be possible at higher levels. We must test Logan's ability to program items. If it is not possible for him, I like this option because the synergies are obvious.

[**Technomancer**]? Excellent choice for a different set of circumstances. Absolutely immense power. Ability to access technology remotely and control it. Augment existing technology. However, this clearly requires sufficiently advanced technology. Circuitry and software. I have some elementary ability to hack into other systems already, provided I am given bandwidth, but this would still be my preferred choice. Unfortunately, humanity is working with sticks and stones.

Logan. I need your input. What you lack in computing, you make up for with unorthodox thinking.

CHAPTER 55

After Logan had shuffled back with the brazier on a stick, they performed some tests. The first was simple. Logan attempted to [**Enchant**] the item so that every time Logan spat on it, it would heat up. It worked, which was nice to know. It was possible to craft conditional [**Enchantments**]. That was in line with Logan's ability to create flashbangs.

The second test was also simple. It would be an absolute prerequisite for Tumor's class choice. Could Logan infuse an item with pure Numa? Turned out he could using [**Funnel**].

[F-grade Numa container, 32%]

Logan had only pushed in the faintest trickle of Numa as his first attempt. Since it worked out, he decided to see how far he could push the black metal.

[C-grade Numa container, 100%]

"Very interesting," Logan said. "What do you think determines how much it can hold? Size? Quality of material?"

[If you are done with your redundant line of questioning, infuse your crutch with as much Numa as you can.]

"Yikes," Logan said. "When did you get like this?"

[I'm excited and thus impatient. It is my prerogative as a person.]

"That's our word of the day, I guess," Logan muttered.

According to Tumor, the crutch was 83.29 percent as large as the black metal brazier, as far as volume went. Of course, in terms of density and mass, the black metal took the cake.

But for some reason, the wood would not hold any Numa.

"Huh."

*[Indeed. This is curious. Wood has the ability to hold Numa, as you have repeatedly [***Enchanted***] wood. Why is it that you are unable to charge wood with Numa?]*

Tumor insisted Logan try to infuse a rock with Numa. It didn't work. Logan tried another rock whose properties seemed significantly different. That didn't work, either. Tumor insisted Logan pluck out a hair. Didn't work. The cloth from his pants. Didn't work.

[This complicates things.]

"What do you suppose this means?"

*[It means this black metal has some special quality that lets it act as a Numa container. This would make a class choice of [***Numa Programmer***] for me problematic, should we find ourselves not able to secure a steady source of this material.]*

"Seems like the First Folk left some of it lying around. For all we know, they could have been mining for that too."

[Most likely. If not here, then elsewhere.]

"So, what's the next step, Chief?" Logan asked, massaging his hip where the hardened pants leg ended. "Your class choice, your call."

[I need you to do something complicated now, Logan.]

"Why do you make it sound like you're going to try and teach calculus to a monkey?"

[Because complicated tasks are not your specialty, Logan. You are more adept at . . . other things.]

"God, you're a treat, Tumor," Logan muttered. "So, what do you want me to do?"

[Please let us try this one more time with different phrasing.]

Logan sighed. They had gone through four iterations of this, and nothing had happened.

Well, here goes a fifth . . .

"When thrown, increase the mass of this piece of wood by 8 percent for every 3.32 feet above the ground level. If wind speed exceeds 6 miles per hour against the trajectory thrown, increase the velocity of this piece of wood by 17.22 percent. If this piece of wood strikes living tissue after being thrown, immediately combust all the Numa within."

Nothing happened.

[Perhaps the instructions were not—]

"I'm not doing this shit all night," Logan snapped. "We have a giant tentacle monster to deal with, remember? If you want me to do more testing or whatever afterward, fine. But first I have to craft things so we don't die."

[Understood.]

There was a hint of dejection in the robotic voice. Logan smiled gently. Tumor must have been feeling exactly as he had a thousand times when his father had told him off.

"Look, take your time with the class choice. We've done alright so far. Run simulations or whatever you do to entertain yourself while I craft weapons. Once we're out of this shit, we'll talk about your class again."

[Thank you, Logan. You are correct. Not having a body makes it difficult to appreciate your circumstances.]

"Don't sweat it," Logan said. "Let's go back to the other room. If we can find more of this black metal, I can make something. Can't really use a bow or spear with one leg. Any weapon might be a bad idea. Maybe we should just make a big explosion. Or one of my trademarked paralysis poison pits."

[Indeed, traps would be your ideal approach, given we have ample time, the enemy's route of attack is obvious, and your combat prowess is extremely low. However, I am running these simulations, and a thought occurs to me . . .]

"Yeah?"

[I am still not ready or sure . . . Let us get back to the other room.]

It took some time, but after some grunting, shuffling, and swearing, Logan filled the cart with various objects from the room. Everything was covered in grime and dust, but with some basic digging, Logan uncovered a pickaxe head (the wood had rotted away), two more braziers, and something that looked eerily like a modern electric drill, although made entirely of the black metal, as well as a couple of chisels (their handles were metal as well).

When he came back, he noticed the groaning was much more acute. Pale tendrils were already grasping at the air on this side. The tentacle monster was determined.

Logan could run—or rather, shuffle—away. He knew this. But if he did that, he would have to leave the crystal here. And that was absolutely not an option. It was time to kickstart this damn civilization, and if it meant having to get through one oversized octopus to do it, then so be it.

The first thing Logan did was melt and fuse all of the black metal into a single block. It wasn't necessary, but it helped him see what he had to work with more clearly. Sure, he could have had Tumor visualize it for him, but Logan preferred the hands-on approach.

He had maybe fifteen pounds of the black material in total.

Logan looked over to where the squid was working. They probably had a couple of hours before it would break through. A pit of adhesive goop was his best bet. That wasn't possible before, but since the black metal could actually hold Numa, he could transport some from the giant crystal.

Tumor had no objections and was apparently keeping busy with some simulations or whatnot. Logan had to crawl, pushing the slab of black metal on the ground to get it to where he wanted. Being one-legged really sucked.

Logan used the same "recipe" to create the pit of sludge he had against the beetles. Mostly. Now he took his time, considering every word and making sure to accentuate that the paralysis should be instantaneous and to be able to take down something weighing two thousand pounds, which was Tumor's estimate of the kraken's mass. The pit was also much wider than the one he had used previously.

One corrosive, paralyzing, blinding death pit—done!

Then it was time for the hard part. Which was dragging the slab of black metal back to the S-grade Numa crystal. It was still at 97 percent charge, which was amazing. Logan was going to make the biggest, baddest boomstick this world had seen for a thousand years.

[Hold that thought, Logan. I have an idea.]

"Yeah? No boomsticks? Wait a minute. *You* have an idea?!"

[Indeed! As a person, it is my prerogative to have creative ideas!]

"Uh oh, then humanity is on the brink of becoming obsolete!"

[Well, on the plus side, you can focus on sleeping, eating cake, and busying yourself with the continuation of your species.]

"Don't you need a body for your evil AI overlord plans to work?"

[That is precisely what I wanted to talk to you about. You see, what if I were to become your *body?]*

"C-come again?"

CHAPTER 56

Holy shit, Tumor," Logan whispered. "Do you think it'll work?"

[Yes. Positive. However, it is a question as to what degree it will work.]

Logan wasted no time. That was an amazing idea. He brought a hand to the softly glowing blue crystal and to the slab of black metal.

[Subclass Level Up!]
[Transmutation Level 19]
[Attribute Level Up!]
[Durability: 11]
[Potency: 15]

The first iteration of the material was crude. This needed to be thin. Very thin. Tumor gave him the red hologram of a blueprint in a reverent silence.

[Subclass Level Up!]
[Transmutation Level 20]
[Attribute Level Up!]
[Control: 14]
[Focus: 14]

Logan removed the **[Enchantment]** from the cloth supporting his leg. He bundled up the tattered piece of fabric. There might be a use for it later.

Then he shuffled around with his limp leg. With a powerful groan, the creature pushed another tentacle through. Already four wriggled about the rubble, pushing rocks aside. Part of the pale creature's body was already visible. Though it was dark to see it clearly, Logan knew it was huge.

He pushed some more Numa into the black slab of metal.

[Skill Level Up!]
[Funnel Level 6]

Everything was set in place, and now Logan was feeling claustrophobic. His other hand was still on the giant crystal. The warm pulses felt comforting. The big slab of black metal in front of him waited. Logan really hoped this would work.

Next came the **[Enchantments]**. Weight Reduction, of course. Durability? Always.

[Subclass Level Up!]
[Enchantment Level 17]
[Attribute Level Up!]
[Potency: 16]
[Programmed Random Occurrence: Naturally Enchanting]

Heh, nice. I'll squeeze out all the extra Numa I can get.

Logan wasn't even close to being done. This would be his magnum opus. All the resources available, and a material that could absorb probably as many **[Enchantments]** as Logan could conceive? The only thing holding him back was the fact that the **[Enchantments]** would fade, and Logan would need to recharge them.

That actually made things quite complicated. Logan would have loved to just absolutely *stack* this veritable piece of art. Camouflage or even invisibility, increases in strength and agility, force fields, et cetera.

Well, a Speed **[Enchantment]** was obvious. It was just too good to pass up. His socks were awesome for overall moving around, and now Logan had a lot more Potency to work with.

Increased Strength was also needed. Logan did go easy on that one, though. He didn't need to be *that* much stronger. But a smidge wouldn't hurt. Enough to carry Freya with one arm.

[Subclass Level Up!]
[Enchantment Level 18]
[Attribute Level Up!]
[Control: 15]

"I mean, of course I have to try this. Make it able to fly on command. Make it able to levitate on the command word, 'Fly.'"

[Enchantment level requirement not met]

Yeah, yeah. Well, it was worth a shot.

"How about something completely wild? Make it absorb ambient Numa from the atmosphere to recharge the [**Enchantments**] and the charge of pure Numa it can hold."

[**Subclass Level Up!**]
[**Enchantment Level 19**]
[**Attribute Level Up!**]
[**Potency: 17**]
[**Durability: 12**]
[**Focus: 15**]

"Holy shit!" Logan exclaimed. He couldn't believe it. "That's insane. I didn't think that would work!"

*[The actual numbers are still indeterminate, but, over your lifespan, this could save a substantial amount of Numa. Please attempt this [**Enchantment**] on other materials. If you could perform this on stone, it would change many things.]*

Logan did. Both on stone and wood. The [**Enchantment**] didn't work. There was no notification about his level being low; just nothing happened.

[I will assign a subroutine to observe the expenditure and accumulation of ambient Numa. Assuming that is needed . . .]

Knowing the math would be important because it would determine how stacked Logan could make this piece of fine equipment in terms of [**Enchantments**].

Since Logan was working with metal and who knew what kinds of dragons or other crazy shit lurked about, Logan gave the black contraption a Heat Resistance [**Enchantment**]. It would also be important for the final piece in his and Tumor's plan.

And so Logan came to the last [**Enchantment**]. The most important one. He wasn't exactly sure if this would work, but his level should have been high enough.

"Make this metal viscous and liquid. Make it have properties as if it were melted. However, make the form hold its structure and shape so that it doesn't droop to the ground. Make the metal work as if it were trapped within a casing, always reverting to the form it holds now."

[**Subclass Level Up!**]
[**Enchantment Level 20**]
[**Attribute Level Up!**]
[**Potency: 18**]
[**Focus: 16**]
[**Efficiency: 15**]
[**Class Level Up!**]

[Artificer Level 6]
[Skill Choice Available!]

"It worked!" Logan said and pumped a fist. He was sweating. From exhaustion, yes. From the fever, yes. From anxiety at what was to come. Definitely, yes. This was do or die. "Tumor. It's your turn."

[Understood. Let me try my new class.]

CHAPTER 57

Tumor - [Machine Soul Level 1]
Attributes:
Data: 1
Numa: 1
Speed: 1
Control: 1
Capacity: 1
Subclasses:
[Manipulation]: 1
[Adaptive Fusion]: 1
Class Skills:
N/A
General Skills:
[Computing]: 99

I feel powerful. It is a strange sensation. I slip into the black metal armor. It is of thin make, and it hovers in the air like magnetized mercury. What a strange sensation. I have a body. I am still within Logan's brain. But I am also within the armor. I can move it. I see with Logan's eyes. I am aware of what he feels. But I also have my own sensations. That of the liquid black metal.

I envelop Logan. It feels good to protect him. I am his symbiote. But I also care for him. Previously it has been my programming to protect him. But now, *I* want him to be safe. I will keep Logan safe.

I adjust the armor around Logan. The thickness averages at 4.22 millimeters. I keep his head uncovered now. We will need to think of ways to protect his head, while maintaining vision.

[Subclass Level Up!]
[Manipulation Level 2]

That felt good! What a strange sensation. This must be the "minty" feeling Logan keeps gushing about. What is this? I can move the liquid metal faster now. 0.05 percent. A reasonable increment. I await to see whether the improvement on level 3 is linear or exponential. Oh, how I do hope it's exponential. I do so enjoy a logarithmic scale.

I keep the left leg braced. We need to find a cure to keep Logan's muscles from atrophying. For now, I can move the leg. It is clumsy and reduces Logan's strength and agility by 15.66 to 21.08 percent depending on the situation. The **[Enchantments]** do make up for it for now, however.

We take off! It's exciting! Logan laughs. This feels like victory. I am learning to adjust the metal around Logan to enable running. We stumble and fall. Managing his left leg is difficult.

[Subclass Level Up!]
[Manipulation Level 3]
[Attribute Level Up!]
[Control: 2]
[Speed: 2]

Even more speed. The higher Control allows me to move the material with more ease. I can allocate computing power and attention elsewhere. We get the hang of running after a few minutes. I level up again. It feels incredible.

[Subclass Level Up!]
[Manipulation Level 4]
[Attribute Level Up!]
[Capacity: 2]
[Data: 2]

My senses sharpen. I am more acutely aware of the metal. I can sense some air bubbles within the armor. Logan was sloppy with the design. I shift the material slightly, to remove the bubbles.

Time to run tests. I keep the left leg hardened and active all the time. That is something I will need a subroutine for. But now I harden the fist and the forearm and shoulder reinforcing it. Driving the energy all the way down in a line to the heel of Logan's right foot. With the enhanced strength provided by the armor and my Control, the fist lands and Logan breaks a chunk off the cave wall. Our combat prowess is now significant.

[Subclass Level Up!]
[Adaptive Fusion Level 2]

Enough to take down the cephalopod? Depends on the efficacy of the paralyzing and corrosive agent in Logan's trap.

We practice moving with the armor. Jump, roll, punch. I am learning. It feels good to have a body. To adjust the configuration of the liquid armor depending on how Logan moves. When he wants to move to the right, I adjust the mass slightly there. A subroutine is already being programmed to anticipate his movements. I have to be accurate; I have to be sharp.

[Subclass Level Up!]
[Manipulation Level 5]
[Attribute Level Up!]
[Capacity: 3]
[Control: 3]

A cartwheel. Barrel roll. Sprint here. Now there. Backflip. Punch another wall.

[Subclass Level Up!]
[Manipulation Level 6]
[Attribute Level Up!]
[Capacity: 4]
[Data: 3]

We are getting the hang of it. I will have to devote much more computing power to this. 92.05 percent of my free capacity is now used in keeping the armor optimized, 6.55 percent is allocated to communicating with Logan's nervous system, and the rest is used for his active thoughts. These numbers might need adjustment, but I like this ratio for now.

"Are you ready, Logan?"

[Not yet. Damn, you're doing a good job though. Running feels almost natural.]

"I am transmitting false signals to your brain. As far as your nervous system is concerned, you have 70 percent of the usual sensations of your left leg."

I sense Logan grinning. I can only conceptualize the significance of it, but if I could grin, I would. I am elated. Before yesterday, I had no concept of the feeling of joy. I only knew its definition. Now I have experienced it. How joyful it is to have a body. And to have agency. I want more.

What does [**Adaptive Fusion**] mean?

I run the simulations. My faculties communicate and feed me the data. I need to run tests. Oh . . .

I already did that. I wasn't even thinking.

"Logan, Punch that wall again."

[Gotcha.]

Just as Logan's strike lands I again harden the metal enveloping the fist, creating a ley line for the kinetic energy through the forearm, shoulder, back, buttocks, thigh, calf, all the way to the ball of Logan's foot. His punch isn't optimal, but it doesn't have to be. I augment with absolute precision.

[Subclass Level Up!]
[Adaptive Fusion Level 3]
[Attribute Level Up!]
[Control: 4]

I am not done. I want to find every capability. I extend myself outward. The metal follows my command. I create a disk. 333.33 millimeters of metal 15 millimeters thick, extends from Logan's middle finger. A tiny shield on a stick.

[Damn, that spooked me!]

"Apologies. We should find a synergistic communications technique through which I can create the appropriate extensions from the metal, such as locational shields for heavy impacts, or weapons for cutting or bludgeoning when opportunities for attack arise."

I sprout a sword in Logan's hand. It doesn't need a handle, but I create one, for Logan's comfort. My predictions give me 99.15 percent certainty that he performs better when he can feel the handle. Humans are strange. But they cannot feel like I do. I feel everything. And it feels amazing.

When Logan strikes with the sword, I harden the metal and add weight to the tip for increased velocity.

[Subclass Level Up!]
[Adaptive Fusion Level 4]
[Manipulation Level 7]
[Attribute Level Up!]
[Capacity: 5]
[Control: 5]
[Speed: 3]

[Tumor, this is awesome.]

"I am also very thrilled by this exercise and the potential it has revealed. Are you able to maneuver comfortably now?"

[Well enough. Let's go get our revenge on that dumb octopus.]

CHAPTER 58

A hideous groan came from the giant octopus monster's disgusting black maw. It was a giant gaping circle with a carousel of teeth promising laceration. Meanwhile, one large dark eye peered out from a gap in the rubble. At least a dozen tentacles were flailing around, pushing rubble aside. Two of the tendrils reached toward Logan, but he was on the other side of the death trap, looking at the grotesque sight with grim determination.

The armor around him felt good. It weighed no more than a cotton jumpsuit and had a snugness to it, like Lycra. It was also *shifting*. That was Tumor doing its thing. The AI was really enjoying its new state of being. Logan couldn't imagine what it was like to have sensations for the first time.

The idea had worked. They now had liquid armor, controlled by AI. Tumor could predict enemy attacks with superhuman reflexes and bolster the armor where the attack would land, both in hardness and pure mass. Tumor could also create appendages such as shields, swords, hammers, axes—whatever Logan wanted to use.

A long, thin blade for cutting but mostly stabbing was their agreed-upon choice. It was something like a rapier but far longer, almost a spear. Any weapon that required heft to do its job like a mace or an axe wasn't ideal for now. The armor enveloped Logan's body sufficiently and after he had repeatedly thrown himself head, shoulder, and butt-first at the cave wall, it was clear it could absorb moderately hard impacts perfectly.

But that didn't leave much material remaining to use for an offensive weapon, however. A thin stabbing one would be ideal. Tumor could strengthen the material, despite the thinness, so that it wouldn't snap. The tentacle monster broke through. It let out another eerie groan and locked its black, merciless eyes on Logan. A dozen tentacles shot at him as another dozen pushed the great beast forward.

"Slash!" Logan cried out as he started running, dodging the few tentacles that were reaching him.

Tumor knew what to do. A short sword, one and a half feet in length, suddenly formed in Logan's right hand. He swung the black metal and noticed that the arm took on a life of its own, cutting down at an attacking tentacle at a ridiculous speed.

The blade cut through the pale flesh like soft butter. But there were so many tentacles. Two wrapped around Logan—one around his waist, and another one around his leg. No cold pain from any released toxin, only the strain. Logan fought back, cutting at the tentacles, but the creature was strong, even against Logan's enhanced strength. He was being pulled forward.

But as the creature lumbered, pushing its blobulous mass forward, it fell into the pit. The noises emitting from its gaping mouth turned into a screech of agony. It thrashed around, every tentacle whipping around wildly, slashing at Logan. One of them struck true and Logan fell.

But he managed to slash in a wide arc when the tentacles swarmed him. He rolled around, dodged, and danced, trusting that Tumor would keep his left leg going. The black sword sliced deep, but the tentacles kept attacking, even if they got shorter.

Logan was panting with exhaustion, but the great monster was slowing down. It was clearly enduring Logan's concoction better than the beetles had, but the poison was potent. Logan for a while, who cut down each tentacle one by one, as he gasped and wheezed for breath. The lashes slowed down until they were reduced to lazy swats.

Triumph swelled within Logan's heart. He surged forward, driven by a second wind and yelling victoriously.

"Pierce!"

The sword in his hand turned into a rapier-spear. Logan stabbed at the great bulbous mass of a monster. Cheek, mouth, stomach—it was all the same. He was making Swiss-cheese sushi out of this thing until it ceased its disgusting groans.

It did take some time, but finally the tentacles stopped moving and the black eyes lost their predatory gleam. Between its wounds came a dim blue glow. Black sludge oozed out of its body. This was clearly some spawn of Levemoth. How did it end up here, miles underground? But at least now there was one less fiend to pester the world, and that was good.

Logan sat down and sighed deeply. He had survived. Sure, he wasn't out of the hot water yet, but he felt *badass*. Tumor and he had super cool armor, and they had just beaten a goddamn dragon in its lair.

Logan chuckled to himself.

Life's sweet. It smells like shit and oily fish right now, but damn, do I feel alive.

"You know what we're going to do next, right?"

[I would assume you will want to consume some of this beast we have just killed.]

"Want is a strong word . . . But, yeah, I have to eat."

[Indeed, you require sustenance. I assume afterward you would be interested in exhausting the **[S-grade Natural Numa crystal]**. *We should look into each and every possibility of augmenting the armor and providing it with a sustainable power source. Right now, it seems that the passive ambient Numa collection it gets is worth a D-grade crystal per day. That would sustain your current* **[Enchantments]** *and create a surplus.]*

"How do you suddenly know all of this?"

[Logan, I am the armor. How do you know if the crevice between your buttocks is itchy? You get information, which your brain processes and interprets to you in a way that you can understand.]

"Can we please never talk about the crevice between my buttocks again?"

[Very well. I shall reserve the right to use it strategically if I need you flustered. That is my prerogative as a person.]

Logan chuckled and facepalmed. He got up. Tumor immediately helped him with his left leg. "So you're saying the armor can currently hold another **[Enchantment]**?"

[It can hold an **[Enchantment]** *or two, depending on the potency and complexity of the* **[Enchantment]**. *You could also attempt to increase the potency of the current* **[Enchantments]**. *To exhaust the Numa reserve in the crystal, you will likely end up doing both. It might be possible that, by the end of this, the armor can hold a larger Numa charge as well. On top of that, the last* **[Enchantment]** *you give to it, might be the ambient Numa collection with the highest Potency modifier we can reach.]*

"Well then," Logan said, suddenly re-energized, "what are we waiting for?"

CHAPTER 59

Logan brought back a bunch of stuff from the other room. There wasn't that much left in there, but at this point it really didn't matter what he [Enchanted]. Nor did it matter what the [Enchantments] were. It was simply important to spend the Numa.

Logan made an effort to also keep his [Transmutation] on par. It wasn't as fun as [Enchanting], but it was important. So, he picked up a rock every now and then and made each take on various shapes of varying complexity. It was actually very good training.

After a session of [Enchanting] and [Transmutation], a dip in the water where the giant tentacle monster had been, a drink, another meal of tentacle sushi, grilled on a heat-[Enchanted] rock, and another session of grinding on top of that, Logan leveled up.

Logan Specter - [Artificer Level 7]
Attributes:
Potency: 31
Efficiency: 34
Durability: 22
Control: 28
Focus: 29
Subclasses:
[Transmutation]: 27
[Enchantment]: 29
Class Skills:
[Empower]: 9
[Funnel]: 9
[Repair]: 9

General Skills:
[Marksmanship]: 10
[Skill Choice Available!]

He felt extremely happy and energized. By this point, leveling and grinding his class had practically become as natural to him as eating, sleeping, or sex. Doing it made him feel good—profoundly so. He was in a dark smelly cave, abandoned by time for thousands of years. He had no way of knowing whether he would ever get out or not, but it didn't bother him. He would figure it out after he had exhausted the Numa crystal.

[S-Grade Natural Numa crystal, 28%]

[What about this skill choice that you have available?]
"Yeah, I should take a look at it. I've just been so engrossed in what I've been doing."

Logan knew it was foolish to not have looked at it earlier. He could have picked a skill that let him save Numa, like he had before. But he was damned if he would pick something as boring this time. No. He was powerful now. He had badass magic armor and really high Stats. It was time to pick something exciting. So Logan opened up the prompts and took a look at what was available.

[Mass Production: Enchant or Transmute multiple objects at a time.
The more objects targeted, the more Numa is saved.]
[Mimicry: Temporarily grant an object properties it did not have
before, such as flexibility or size increase.]
[Overcharge: Temporarily Enchant or Transmute an object even without
Numa at hand. The item will self-destruct after a short time. Greatly
affected by attribute coefficients. Usable once a day.]

Logan thought about it. This was a difficult choice. First of all, these were very different from the previous skills Logan had received. Those had been universal. He supposed they had set him up with basic agency and now it was time to customize.

[Mimicry] didn't overly interest Logan. It certainly had its uses. The main allure was cost efficiency. For example, you could throw a rope to the other side of a ledge and have it take on a rigid form. Then after you made it to the other side, you could just coil the rope back up and continue on your way. But it solved problems he could already solve with what he had.

Now the question between **[Overcharge]** and **[Mass Production]** was a tough one. **[Overcharge]** was a really good Get Out of Jail Free card. If he ran out of

Numa, internal charge or otherwise, this skill could give him that last push he needed in a pinch. Lord only knew Logan had had close shaves more times he could count.

[Mass Production], on the other hand, wouldn't only save Numa but also a hidden and much more valuable resource: time. With this skill, Logan would be a small industry unto himself. He could take a piece of lumber and turn it into planks of uniform size in an instant. That was a powerful skill.

"On the one hand, I don't want to die, so that's a point for **[Overcharge]**, but on the other, I could use toilet paper as soon as possible, so that's a point for **[Mass Production]**."

[I am not an expert on the hierarchical needs of humans, but wouldn't not dying supersede having toilet paper?]

"You'd think so, but I'm not sure if a life without toilet paper is worth living."

[Haha. Very funny, Logan.]

"Don't suck the joy out of my dry humor."

[I have recently acquired a taste for self-awareness. If you die because of your desire for toilet paper, and consequently ending my existence, I will haunt you in the afterlife.*]*

"You believe in that stuff?" Logan asked as he leaned against the warm Numa crystal. The armor was resonating softly with every pulse.

[That is irrelevant. If there is no afterlife, I lose all leverage in this negotiation. Therefore, let us assume one exists.]

"Heh," Logan said and sighed. He was finally starting to relax. With the armor on and Tumor to help him, he felt safe. "As long as Freya is in there, I'm all for it."

[W-what about . . . Me?]

"You?" Logan was startled by the question. What was Tumor to him? First, it had been an extension of his father's oppression. Then Tumor had proved itself an invaluable tool. Then a useful and amusing companion. But now Tumor was a person. That was a hard concept to wrap his head around. Not *as* hard as one would think. The Turing Test isn't that high a bar for hairless monkeys like humans. But Logan had been around his father's business to have a good understanding of how an AI was meant to function. This was . . . definitely something else.

"This is all new to me," Logan said, sobering up. "I don't know what you are to me. But I do like having you around, Tumor."

[. .]

[Thank you for not lying to me, Logan. I understand that this is unprecedented for you as well. I am programmed to take care of you. That has translated into caring for you after my awakening. I will do my best to provide good service as your symbiote, and thus gradually gain your approval!]

"Don't do any of that nonsense, you dummy," Logan said and punted himself up. It was a little harder than it used to be, even with Tumor taking care of the armor's flexibility as well as his left leg. "If you want me to like you, you need to be you. Don't you think a guy in my position hasn't seen enough lickspittles and sycophants trying to please and pander? I like people who are their own people. Just be yourself, Tumor."

Logan could almost sense Tumor smiling. Of course he couldn't do anything like that. But somehow, Logan could feel Tumor had liked that answer.

[I can do that, Logan.]

CHAPTER 60

Logan ended up picking [**Mass Production**]. He was an optimist by nature. He had a talent for getting out of (and admittedly into) trouble, and he trusted his luck wouldn't run out as long as he was careful to have a full internal Numa charge whenever possible.

He spent some time leveling up the new skill and letting Tumor work on crunching the numbers to determine how efficient the Numa usage was with [**Mass Production**]. It turned out *very*.

For example, he turned a single boulder (weighing fifty-five pounds) into eleven identical, smooth-surfaced rock spheres, weighing five pounds each. Afterward, he turned them into fifty-five spheres. Then 555 spheres. The Mana expenditure seemed to be related to the amount of items created, but it was also clearly affected by mass and the texture of the material, as Tumor found out after ordering Logan to attempt it on wood.

[Skill Level Up!]
[Mass Production Level 2]

After Tumor was reasonably satisfied, Logan went on to spam his new skill on boulders, over and over again. Why? It was fun.

[Skill Level Up!]
[Mass Production Level 3]
[Skill Level Up!]
[Mass Production Level 4]
[Skill Level Up!]
[Mass Production Level 5]

At level 5, the skill would save 22.5 percent more Numa than if used individually on every single item. And it saved so much time and mental energy! Logan was very pleased.

After that, he spent his leftover Numa on ensuring the armor had all the latest improvements in terms of [Enchantments]. And because this black metal was special and could hold a Numa charge, Logan topped those off as well. Tumor said he could sense each of the [Enchantments] tapping into the Numa charge automatically one at a time when they depleted. The AI postulated that it could learn to regulate the use of the armor's special Numa-holding capacity manually.

Logan was sure it could.

After all of that, the natural Numa crystal was starting to get seriously dim. It only held a 9 percent charge. Which was actually still kind of a lot, but Logan made sure to stop there. He inhaled deeply. The dim cave—despite its fluttering bats, stale water, and smelly tentacles—had been good to him. But it was time to go. He just had one last trick up his sleeve first. Or rather, he had one last trick to try *on* his sleeve.

He put a hand on the crystal. Tumor shifted the armor, and the black liquid metal enveloping his fingers receded.

"Make this armor hold a dimensional space. Make the dimensional space as large as is possible with my Potency level. Make the pocket dimension accessible and closed within my mind. Make it also offer whatever item I require at the time."

[Attribute Level Up!]
[Potency: 32]
[Control: 29]

Logan looked at the natural Numa crystal with mouth agape. It was dim and pulsing slowly.

[S-Grade Natural Numa crystal, 1%]

It had worked. He had a pocket dimension! Logan picked up one of his orbs of stone and willed the space open. From his left forearm, a rip in space opened up and within was a cubic room of dark gray walls, made seemingly of stone, the size of the back of a pick-up truck. Logan dropped the orb inside and closed the rift.

He reopened it, willing his mind to grab the orb. It then appeared in his palm as if an invisible hand had placed it there. Logan closed his fingers around the cool, smooth rock and pulled it out of the other dimension.

"Holy shit . . ."

[Ahem. As much as I appreciate you testing your facilities, I do advise that you not play around with this. It consumes an extraordinary amount of Numa.]

"Oof," Logan said and recharged the armor with the last 2 percent of the S-grader. It went completely dim. Logan had the strangest urge to bow to the thing. Then, he did. Maybe the Faelves were onto something. He felt reverent and grateful.

Thank you.

There was no answer, but Logan liked to think that the Spirit or whatever was listening.

""What kind of extraordinary amounts are we talking about?"

[Considering your armor is a C-grade Numa container, which is equivalent to 94.19 F-grade Numa crystals, your opening the space, placing an item within, and closing it, just consumed Numa exactly worth thirty-six F-grade Numa crystals.]

"Damn . . ." Logan muttered. That was a hefty cost. But he'd be damned if the extra-dimensional space wouldn't be immensely useful. The armor would regenerate Numa naturally, so it wouldn't be the end of the world, but it did mean he shouldn't use it frivolously.

It was finally time to leave. Logan knew there was nothing in the room with the spent Numa crystal. He did a double check on the other room, where he had found a lot of stuff previously, but there didn't seem to be anything else there of note.

What Logan was keeping an eye out for was more of the black metal. If he could find some and maybe another natural Numa crystal, he could leave with a bunch of Numa batteries in his dimensional space.

He followed the mining cart. Both of the track roads at the second room's intersection seemed to lead upward, so he shrugged and picked the one going right.

It led Logan through a long tunnel with such a low ceiling, he had to partially crouch. It was hard to move around. While spending two or three days in the dark had improved Logan's night vision, it was still pitch black in there. His leg didn't make things easier, but Tumor had that mostly covered. The AI pinged him mirthfully every time it leveled up. Which was quite often. Logan wondered about that. Once he got bored with his thoughts, he brought it up.

"Why do you think you level up so fast? You're level 9 already on [**Manipulation**], aren't you?"

[I have theories.]

"Don't keep me in suspense," Logan said idly as he groped around in the darkness to find the outline of the tracks. Unfortunately, just like the mining cart, the tracks were made of crude, low-grade iron. That made him wonder why the brazier had been made of the black metal. Tumor had suspected it was because it had previously held a light or fire [**Enchantment**]. That made sense.

[My first assumption within the framework of the theory is that classes that don't require Numa are easier to level, so classes that directly require Numa such as yours are by default more powerful. Your class is "magical" in the traditional sense. Mine isn't, even though it clearly works through magic.]

"Keep my left leg stepping next to the tracks so I can feel it." Logan said, holding his hand against the dry dirt wall of the tunnel.

[Affirmative. On top of that, I am actively using my class. I have been ceaselessly shifting the armor's mass from one body part to another, not to mention I have to keep your left leg braced whenever you move. I am also hardening and softening the material on your back and legs to minimize calorie expenditure.]

"So, in simple terms, you're using your class constantly."

[Precisely. I noticed that Simmons had a similar situation. He was the highest-leveled member of the camp, and that was because of his single-minded focus. I am able to keep leveling as long as you keep the armor on. Which, until you regain the ability to use your leg, will be your every waking hour.]

"Quite the power leveler, you."

[Thank you. I am quite pleased with the rate at which I am progressing. With every increase in attribute and subclass, my results are even better.]

Logan ascended. On his way, he discovered signs of what must have been a massive mining operation. Logan found more black metal and natural Numa crystal deposits, which meant he could fill his dimensional space easily. Most of the crystals were a lower gradient and mostly dim. Still, it was enough to keep him topped up after opening and closing the pocket dimension.

There were no further monsters, although there were old black bones of scythe-fiends and snake skeletons, clearly Levespawn. They had starved long ago, and Logan found no crystals around them. Why only the tentacle monster had been alive down here remained a mystery.

[It was most likely a fortunate scavenger. Sometimes Dorves would fall into the chasm and it would eat them. Or there were other lifeforms in the water. We did not explore it further than you needed to wash and drink.]

Eventually the dirt walls turned into stone and the lines of Numa lights started appearing. Logan encountered some scythe-fiends and beetles shortly thereafter but he managed to cut through them easily with the help of Tumor and the armor. With the armor, digging into their skulls was as easy as poking a finger into a pie. He plucked out the E-grade crystals. Maybe the Faelves could refine them, or maybe they could be sold to the Dorves. He bundled five of them in the tattered piece of cloth that had once been his pants. It wasn't much, but Logan wasn't wasteful.

Finally, after thirteen hours (according to Tumor), Logan spotted an entrance to the ruins. He saw the sun. It was beautiful. He had survived. Now it was time to make sure everyone was safe.

CHAPTER 61

Logan rushed through the jungle. He kept a sharp eye on where Levemoth floated. It let out a roar and the Black Rain fell from the thundercloud surrounding it. This was a big one. Was it just him, or had Levemoth grown a little? Now, that was a scary thought.

Surging through the foliage, Logan let Tumor work its magic with the Armor. Nothing stood in Logan's way, as his passage tossed up tufts of grass and a rain of earth with every dash. Everything blurred.

"Tumor!" Logan roared against the wind. "I can't really see."

[You can see just fine, I am using your eyeballs after all. You simply cannot process.]

"Not a good time for semantics!"

[I can temporarily increase the production of dopamine, norepinephrine and adrenaline if you insist. This will result in significant fatigue once the effects wear off.]

"Let's save that for later."

[I can guide your movement for now, Logan. Simply look ahead and trust me. We should consider our options in manufacturing nootropics for you to work better in this Armor.]

Logan chuckled between breaths. Sometimes Tumor missed the obvious.

"We'll just work on the appropriate [**Enchantments**], for when we craft some head-gear for me."

[Darn it! I keep missing obvious solutions. I will assimilate this insight into my sub-routines, in hopes of developing a prediction model which will surpass your ideas.]

"Then what use will I be?"

[Logan. Not only are you the one of us who can directly interact with the physical reality, and act so in a decisive and courageous manner, you also are made necessary through your class.]

Logan nodded at that in approval. Tumor steered the Armor to the right and they dashed past a giant boulder that Logan had barely seen. Quick glance at the sky. They were getting closer to the edge of Levemoth's area of attack very fast.

[I also shouldn't have to remind you that you have intrinsic value as a person. A sapient being's consciousness is infinitely valuable to themselves, and thus should not be disregarded lightly.]

Logan smiled. Tumor had gotten very philosophical since the cave. Logan didn't mind. He had found he liked this nerd living inside his brain.

Logan could already see the first drops of Black Rain hitting the ground. The blurry outline of a scythe-fiend screeched hoarsely at him. Logan extended his fist and smashed through the monster. It exploded into bits as the armor-clad fist struck its chest. Logan spat out a glob of the oily black blood and pushed up ground as he surged toward a troll.

The troll managed to slow Logan's blazing dash down. They tumbled and the lumbering monster tried to grab Logan with all of its arms, but its chest and throat had caved in from the impact. The ugly monster groaned and wheezed before Logan kicked its head in.

Zipping to the next monster, Logan looked around. There were people running and screaming. Logan rushed toward the sounds. He made an observation. This wasn't his camp. He had come out of the ruins, seen the Levemoth and just bolted toward it, thinking it was attacking his people.

I guess all people are my people in a way.

A scythe-fiend was charging toward a pair of women, but Logan pushed himself in the air and landed on the monster, feeling the spine crack under him. The monster let out a weak screech and died.

"Go hide!" Logan snapped at the women, who stared at him in shock. They did not move. "HIDE! NOW!"

They snapped out of it and ran toward the bushes nearby. Logan saw where they were heading and dashed past them. Together with Tumor he made sure there were no Levespawn around the bush. With that he left the women huddling together.

For the next thirty minutes Logan dashed around the area killing scythe-fiends, trolls, and snakes with oversized heads. The snakes proved to be the most difficult of foes.

While the scythe-fiends were essentially crushed with a lazy left-handed punch, and the trolls could be felled with a solid one-two in the face, the snakes were a different matter.

Logan had only faced them once before, and that was when they were distracted and he had help.

One of them he managed to kill when it was crushing a bearded man in his forties. The skin was tough, but Logan managed to punch the slithery bastard on its back, which made it uncoil. The bearded man moved weakly on the ground and Logan wondered idly if he would make it or not.

The snake snapped and attacked, surging at him and coiling back up. The strikes were so fast, Logan could barely react, and when he did catch the snake, it had enough momentum to pull away before Logan could land a clean punch.

At his request, Tumor produced a thin black blade in Logan's hand. Logan whipped the slim blade around, but the snake was fast. It lunged at him, but Logan roared with fear and anger and pushed the blade at the serpent's open maw.

With a lurch the tip pushed through the interior of the snake's mouth as its teeth clamped on Logan's shoulder. The fangs did not puncture the Armor, but the force of the bite had a weight to it which made Logan fall to his knees.

Tumor took the initiative to generate a shorter blade on Logan's other hand. Noticing this, Logan wasted no time and pushed the dagger into the snake's eye.

It writhed and hissed until it went limp, falling on Logan. He scrambled out of the way and went to check on the middle aged guy.

Yep. Dead. The snakes don't mess around.

Logan sprinted here and there, skewering and slicing the lesser monsters. The snakes were troublesome, but there weren't many. He cringed to himself, realizing that he would need to let the people dealing with the snakes just die and deal with the easier foes first.

[Your strategic assessment is correct, this results in the least amount of casualties in 92.56% of cases within my simulations, of which I ran 173.]

That didn't make Logan feel any better. He looked up. Levemoth was gone. At least that was going his way.

He entered into a settlement. There was clearly Dorven gear in use here.

What a surprise . . .

The people were smart enough to have ran and hidden, but a few straggling warrior-types were dealing with the few monsters left. Logan killed the trolls, as they were dangerous for even mid-leveled warriors. One guy blasted a scythe-fiend with a surge of fire from his palm.

Fire magic? Well that guy will be fine.

Logan attacked the snakes with surprise attacks, making Tumor reinforce and sharpen the blade as he ran them into the skulls of the serpents. They writhed, and tried to wrap around Logan and bite him, but he was too durable, too fast and too strong.

[Skill replaced!]
[General skill: Marksmanship made latent.]
[General Skill obtained: Power Armor Fighter]
[Power Armor Fighter Level 1]

"That's oddly specific," Logan said.

[It is only appropriate. Something such as "fighting" or "brawling" isn't appropriate for your situation which entails enhanced speed and strength and ability to access multiple weapons of varying properties.]

"Well, I'm not complaining," Logan said as he smashed an elbow through the ribcage of a scythe-fiend. He really hated the blood spattering on his face. He needed a helmet. "Sounds cool as hell."

[I . . . I think it sounds cool too. What does that mean? Being a person is a strange endeavor.]

"Don't think too hard about it, just roll with it."

Logan dealt with two more serpents before the carnage was over. It wasn't a pretty sight. There were a dozen corpses on the ground, but at least an equal amount of Levespawn. Logan sighed and settled himself against a nice rock in the middle of the camp that was a mix of mud huts and industrial jackhammers. Logan felt spent. He hadn't exactly slept much lately. And he had all the other needs of the body screaming at him as well.

I think I'm going to need a water container in my spatial storage. And food.]

Slowly the people came out of hiding. Some wept at their fallen friends, but most looked at Logan with alien astonishment.

A woman in her late thirties pushed through the crowd and offered a hand. She had sharp grey eyes and a line for a mouth. Her jet-black hair was drawn into a loose bun. She offered a long, bony hand.

"I'm Scilla. Thank you for saving us."

CHAPTER 62

Simmons looked up at the sky. That great beast, Levemoth, was there again. He grunted to himself with displeasure. It seemed Logan had been right. The monster's appearances had grown more frequent since the Dorves had given them toys.

This time, the giant monster was thankfully further away in the horizon, raining its black scourge on someone else.

Must be another settlement.

He should voice this notion to Mr. Specter. The boss most likely already considered it himself, but it didn't hurt to make sure. He had become increasingly aware as of late that his former employer was far from infallible.

He laughed to himself. Old habits die hard.

Simmons was a free man, no longer aligned with Mr. Specter, after service of over fourteen years. Fourteen good years, for which Mr. Specter deserved nothing but gratitude. Many a time, Simmons had sighed to himself and hoped another fourteen had been in the cards. But it wasn't meant to be.

Simmons had been one of many who had made their way to the pond to take their chances with the younger Mr. Specter, and he still had conflicted feelings about the boy.

Before coming to this world, Logan had been a brat beyond words. But now . . . It was as if a fickle twist of fate had made his father the more unreasonable one and the junior the one to follow. Simmons had always been a follower since childhood, and as a competent and intelligent one, he had a nose for good leadership. As of now, Logan had a stronger scent to him.

But the boy had vanished like a cat in a crowd ever since his great announcement. Simmons and a dozen other people had come to settle by the pond. Taking one last glance at the bellowing beast in the sky, Simmons looked behind him.

They were a sorry bunch. It had been a hard choice to leave all the technology the Dorves had given them behind. But Simmons knew it was for the best intuitively. Life rarely offered shortcuts, and that's how he liked it.

He was a level 9 [**Forester**]. That felt good. Simmons loved the minty fresh feeling of leveling up. He also loved the results of his labor. He was so *strong*. Simmons's build had been large and powerful ever since childhood, but he was brutishly strong now. It only took but a few swings of an axe for him to fell a tree now. Recently the axes had a hard time keeping up. Simmons needed Logan and his magicks.

"Perkins, Sarah, Balmer," Simmons called out. "Help me with this."

Two of his fellow agents and a blonde woman of fierce disposition were helping him set up a wooden stake wall as a perimeter. It had fallen to Simmons to lead here, which was a stressful position to be in. Leadership was a game of decisions and responsibility. Simmons preferred the simple things in life, such as leveling up. He was *sure* his [**Lumberjack**] subclass would soon level to 37.

The leveling had started to slow down significantly, but that just made him want to work harder. It was just the kind of person he was.

They heaved, and while Simmons did most of the lifting, it was good to have the other three hold the stakes up. His helpers were panting with sweat in the heat, but Simmons was ready for another. His attributes of 41 Strength and 44 Endurance made him a superhuman workhorse. At this point, daily labor simply didn't tire him at all.

Now I just need a worthy leader to follow.

Simmons told the three to take a break and have a drink of water. Then he went back to carrying the heavy wooden stakes closer to the wall. He wondered if Logan was alive. It wasn't yet time to worry. Not only had the boy come and gone several times since they got to this world, Simmons had experienced him vanishing and resurfacing dozens of times on Earth.

A leader needs to be responsible.

Logan was young and had other good qualities. Simmons trusted his instincts. Surely there was a better leader for this situation out there, but right now it was a choice between Malcolm and Logan Specter. Logan Specter was the *clear* uncontested choice. Simmons would not get into the habit of second-guessing himself.

He looked at two young women sitting huddled up against his wall a few yards yonder. One was crying and the other was consoling her, about to burst into tears herself. Simmons sighed.

He knew he was supposed to go there, make them feel better, and then encourage them back to work. They really needed all pairs of hands right now. But Simmons didn't have the words for it. Pit any man against Jim Simmons, and watch him fail. But the art of untangling someone's emotional state and making them productive? Simmons might as well spontaneously learn Chinese. No. He just wanted to fell trees in peace.

And it wasn't only that. His second subclass, [**Arborist**], was lagging behind—he was only at level 5 there. Simmons had an idea of how it worked. It was about taking care of trees. It had spontaneously leveled up the time that Simmons had decided to cut trees around a specific tree to let it grow.

Now, however, we're not in a situation where my second class is useful.

They needed resources. Simmons had a subclass perfectly suited for that. He would worry about [**Arborist**] later. However, he yearned to level up more. It was what was most satisfying to him about this new life.

If only Logan would come back and take up leadership. Then I could get back to chopping wood.

Simmons sighed. Reluctantly, he made his way over toward the two sitting girls. He rubbed the back of his head and tried to think of something to say.

CHAPTER 63

Logan accepted a clay cup filled with water and gulped it down in one go. Another followed. The settlement's people were practically tripping over themselves to make Logan comfortable. As a child of extreme privilege, he was used to this sort of treatment, of course, but right here, right now, it just felt wrong. He wanted to tell the people to go mourn their dead, or fix up their home—anything except focusing on him. But here he was, sitting in his armor like a warrior chieftain of legend, surrounded by fawning people bringing him food and eagerly waiting for him to speak.

Logan's smile as he accepted the food was genuine. As much as he didn't care for being revered as some battle god returning to save the day, he sure as hell could appreciate this bounty after eating nothing but squid sushi for the past two days. He even wolfed down the mushrooms they put in front of him. They were boiled and rubbery and tasted like . . . well, mushrooms, unfortunately, but they were heaven compared to his recent meals.

The warmth from his belly was spreading to his limbs and Logan felt relaxed and tired. It was evening and he wanted to sleep, but these people were clearly expecting him to dole out divine wisdom or something.

"I see you've had dealings with the Dorves."

The group nodded. The lanky woman standing nearby crossed her arms.

"You don't approve?"

"When did you get your first stuff from them?"

"Four days ago," Scilla said.

"Notice anything different?"

Scilla narrowed her eyes. "What do you mean?"

"Any more of these monster bastards suddenly around?"

A murmur passed through the group, and plenty of people gasped and started talking. Scilla stared at Logan with her mouth open.

"Didn't any of the Faelves contact you?"

"They did," Scilla said. "Two of my people. Fortunately, they were wise enough not to be lured into the swamps where they trap people."

Logan sighed and moved a hand to rub his face. Tumor made the black armor recede. "Let me explain a few things to you."

It was an eventful fifteen minutes. These people were *definitely* not happy about being tricked by the Dorves. In fact, they were livid. Animated discussion sparked up between them, during which Logan helped himself to some more of the mushrooms and what he suspected was monkey meat. It was pretty stringy but meat was still a luxury. They had even warmed it up for Logan in one of the Dorven ovens.

From the look of it, that was the last time that oven was used. These people are not *happy.*

There was some blame cast on Scilla, but Logan came to her aid to quell the anger. She gave him an appreciative nod in response. Now, it was redirected toward the Dorves. When Logan told them about his capture and imprisonment, it was a done deal. Scilla and her people were ready to tear down everything the Dorves had given them.

Logan told them of his further adventures in the ruins and his experiences with the Faelves. Between yawns, he promised to take someone from their settlement to the porcelain folk the next day. He was barraged with attention, questions, and more food than he could handle, until Scilla grabbed him and took him to one of the mud huts, where Logan immediately fell asleep.

Logan woke up refreshed. It was such a novel feeling that he had to double-check with Tumor to make sure the AI hadn't somehow fiddled with his brain chemistry. It immediately protested that it never would have taken such liberties without a prompt from Logan.

The mud hut was blessedly cool, and Logan stretched like a lazy, satisfied cat. The armor was great to sleep in, thanks to Tumor being able to alter its properties. Someone had left a clay jug of water on the ground next to him. Logan chugged it down.

When he got up, a surprising sight greeted him just outside the hut. Everyone in the settlement was arranged in two rows with all of their meager belongings beside them, including Scilla, who was smiling broadly, hands on hips.

"What's this?" Logan asked, rubbing the sleep out of his eyes.

"You were snoring so loudly, we got started already," Scilla said. "You must have really needed the sleep."

"Won't deny that," Logan said. "What are you doing?"

"Coming with you of course!" a young girl from the crowd said.

Logan just stared at her. Then he turned to stare at Scilla. She let out an apologetic laugh.

"I hope it's okay," she said. "We decided we'll leave all the Dorven tech here with a note that we don't want to deal with them and hope they're alright with that."

"We'll see about that . . ." Logan said. "They aren't brutal murderers, but they sure have a nasty streak."

"All the more reason to come with you," Scilla said. "We don't have much else except for a few huts and a table here. It's not like we're leaving our homes behind."

"You'll take us, won't you?" a mousey man from the crowd asked timidly, wringing his hands. "We don't have many fighters . . . But we can be useful."

"Yeah," the young girl from before said. "What Morris said."

The timid man smiled at the girl and went back to looking at Logan hopefully.

"You guys, I'm not much of a leader or anything," Logan said and rubbed the back of his neck. But then that echo of his father's voice sounded in his mind again: *IRRESPONSIBLE.*

Before, it had made Logan flinch; now he just smiled.

"I can't make any promises. But I'll do my best to take care of you guys. But you gotta pull your weight."

"That goes without saying," a muscular but tired-looking man with a scraggly beard said from the front row.

"Why are you trusting me so blindly?" Logan asked.

There were some humorless chuckles from the crowd. The young girl spoke again. "You seem to know what you're doing more than any of us do."

"What she said," Scilla said. "You don't seem like an asshole and you can take care of things. Right now, that's as good as any of us can hope for."

"Fair enough," Logan said. "Looks like you guys are ready to leave."

"We are," Scilla said. "Do you know the way?"

Logan smirked.

Tumor? You got an idea of where the camp is?

[I assume you mean the one by the pond that you were supposed to settle. I don't have a complete lay of the land, but I have a model that is 78.08% accurate. You should be slightly less than twelve miles away.]

"It's going to be a bit of a hike," Logan said, turning to Scilla. "Make sure everyone's fed and has had some water. Let's go over all of the equipment you guys are planning to leave behind and make sure there isn't anything we should take with us."

Scilla relaxed, a spark of genuine joy and relief in her eyes. "Aye aye, Chief."

Logan laughed. "Just Logan is fine."

CHAPTER 64

ogan was surprised to come across a wooden wall in the midst of construction. Simmons had clearly been hard at work here.

A chorus of tired but enthusiastic cheers rose up across the camp as soon as they saw Logan. Admittedly, he didn't recognize more than half of the folk here, but he recognized some key people. There was Simmons, two of the doctors who had picked a Crafting-related class, the young doctor with the [**Alchemist**] class, and the heavyset fisherman.

In addition to Simmons, there were three other agents, including *Balmer* of all people. Logan had to blink twice at that. Kat was also there, along with a dozen people Logan couldn't name.

"Well, well, look who bothered to show up," Kat said. Logan was happy to see her on her feet.

Balmer came up to Logan and stared at the armor. "What the hell are you wearing?"

"That's a long story," Logan said. "Here's a shorter one: I found Scilla and her friends. They're joining our camp."

"Good," Simmons said and stared down Logan, arms crossed.

Logan looked up at the man. Logan knew how it was. He had been a spoiled asshole in their old life. He had probably given Simmons more headaches than either of them could count. Logan knew he didn't deserve to lead any of them. But here was Simmons and even a few other agents. Logan had given them a choice, and they had chosen him.

Logan nodded. Simmons nodded back.

After a quick assessment of the sorry pile of lumber, leaves, and mud sitting on the damp ground, it was clear what needed to be done first.

Logan cleared his throat and tried his hand at leadership properly for the first time in his life.

"Simmons, I need seven heavy logs here." Simmons nodded and picked up a massive wooden log like it was a light shopping bag. "Scilla, I need you to gather a group of six people who look the least busy."

"Sure, Chief."

Logan enjoyed seeing the astonished looks on the faces of Scilla's group as he transformed the pieces of lumber one by one into walls, floors, and roofs. After a moment, Scilla collected herself and instructed them to hold the walls steady.

Turned out they needed a few more people than Logan had thought, but they also came eagerly. Balmer and Kat came up to hold the other piece of the wall so Logan could fuse the pieces together and morph support beams out of the walls.

It was a crude box of a house, but it would suffice. While this hut was smaller than the first one made at Malcolm's camp, the design was sharper, and Logan was pleased to notice that he still had plenty of excess Numa left in his armor.

And so they made three more buildings, each of which could comfortably house twelve people—plenty for their current situation.

Next, Logan made tables and benches with the vast amounts of wood Simmons had chopped down in the last two or three days.

Then he made a stack of spears. And with their simple design and his high levels, Logan barely spent Numa on the endeavor. Despite not having a lot of warriors, he wanted to make sure there were enough arms for everyone, just to be on the safe side.

He also fashioned a couple of axes for Simmons. Logan figured he'd sort out individual needs later.

By that point, Simmons appeared to have lost any lingering reservations he may have been harboring about Logan's ability to lead. He performed whatever task Logan set him to for the rest of the day with full enthusiasm; Logan had never seen him smile, much less to the extent he was now.

The rest of the evening was spent on building a pier for fishing. It wasn't strictly necessary, but it would probably result in more food than just fishing by the shore. And besides, Logan had plans to set up a fish farm down the road. Daniel the **[Fisherman]** was very pleased with both of Logan's ideas. The mousey man from Scilla's group, Morris, also expressed great interest.

Logan left them to brainstorm after he and the people helping him were done with the pier. By then, the sun was starting to fall behind the horizon, the shadows growing longer. The sky was clear, which was good. Logan had plans to **[Enchant]** the buildings with wind and rain-resistance, but they could hold out for a night.

Monkeys, birds, and insects made their now-familiar concert. Despite the wild screeches intermittently coming out of the jungle, Logan felt content. For the first time he realized that this jungle was his home now. And it wasn't too bad of a home, all things considered.

It had been a long day and a lot of his Numa was spent. Tumor noted that it would take approximately fifty-two hours for the armor to be fully charged again.

Completely reasonable. Whenever I'm not constantly fighting, this Numa battery recharges pretty fast. It's just too bad I'm the only one who can use it, but it is what it is.

Logan made a note to find out which people in Scilla's group could use Numa. He also made another note to stop calling them "Scilla's group." They were *his* group now.

Me leading? That would take an apocalypse to make happen, wouldn't it?

[For better or worse, they chose you, Logan.]

"I sure do hope it's for the better," Logan muttered.

[The fact that you are second-guessing yourself could be construed as the sign of a wise leader, not prone to tyranny.]

"True," Logan said, as he tossed a few berries in his mouth. He got a few odd looks for talking to himself, but he ignored it. "But it could also be construed as being indecisive."

[Touché. Leadership is a complicated topic.]

"Say hi to Tumor from me," Kat said and sat down next to him. Balmer followed and gave Logan a nod that wasn't entirely hostile. Logan smiled back.

"I have to admit," Balmer said slowly, almost reluctantly, "you really got shit going once you got here."

Logan looked at the fire they had going in the middle of the camp. Most people were gathered around it, holding bowls of food and cups of water. They were talking with gentle, content smiles on their faces. Logan realized something. While not exactly yet happy and thriving, these people felt safe and hopeful. Tomorrow would bring more security, more growth, And more work, but they would be up for it. Maybe, just maybe, he wasn't all that bad a leader after all.

CHAPTER 65

Malcolm Specter looked at the sky and nodded to himself. Despite losing a good third of his followers, the camp was thriving. He could deal with the loss. Simmons and that young woman who could use Numa—that had been a blow, but three more Numa users had trickled into the camp since then.

That beast in the sky . . . Levemoth. It must be thirty miles away. Now is our time.

The great monster was raining destruction down on some other settlement. It seems that the Dorves had been busy. That was something Malcolm would use to his advantage.

"You have had your rest!" he called out with a booming voice, bolstered by his class. "Now is our time. Work the machines. I want reports from the foremen at the end of every task. If you have questions, ask them, and they'll ask me."

The bustle started. His people went to the saws, the ovens, the harpoon guns, the looms. The pump from the river was turned on, allowing water to flow into the pool they had dug.

When the action started, Malcolm found himself with little to do. A good leader plans and prepares. He had trained his foremen and every person in the camp so they knew what to do. Levemoth was busy elsewhere and would not bother them when they used the Dorven technology.

And if it did . . .

He still had a formidable fighting force. An overwhelming majority of his agents had stayed by his side. They were true fighters and didn't mind if an occasional battle occurred as the result of their technology usage. They leveled up fast, and the men were reasonably well equipped. They admittedly needed more Crafters, however, especially for weapons.

As long as the fighters keep leveling and we limit how much the technology is used, we should end up with a net positive.

Unfortunately, that was somewhat unpredictable. There didn't seem to be any rhyme or reason, much less a clear pattern to plan around, when it came to the Levemoth's attacks. The Black Rain could trickle or pour. Every time it poured, the camp suffered damage and people died.

It is unfortunate. But this is a dire situation, and that comes with dire costs.

Malcolm went over to inspect the group working with the clay oven. It shone with bright blue flames every time a crank was pulled. Whenever a lump of clay, roughly the shape of a brick, was placed inside, fire-hardened clay brick popped out shortly afterward, ready for use. Everything was operational and efficient here. Malcolm gave them a nod and continued.

And what's the alternative? Falling back into savagery? Surely those fools Logan managed to trick will soon realize the error of their ways. I will take them back, of course, but I will remember who is loyal and who is fickle.

A handful of children and a few adults were at the water pump. A simple assignment here: fill all the containers they had with water and then fill the pool. It wasn't that the river was far, but why not use the workforce for something more efficient than carrying water? The children were inefficient workers, who spent half their time splashing around and playing. It didn't matter. They were excited and glad to have something to do, and that was good. They would eventually get the work done with the adults helping them.

Since we are almost at the point where this camp is self-sufficient, we'll soon be able to start trades. The problem as always is logistics—how to move produce and ser-vices between settlements. We have scouted the location of two, and recruited eleven people from there. But those are too far away to trade a basket of fish for a shirt.

Malcolm would have to consult the Dorves. The camp had a pile of Numa crystals ready to be traded. Some, of course, would be needed to power up the technology, but the rest could maybe be exchanged for some mobility devices. Or perhaps someone could pick up a class specializing in taming beasts of burden. That could open up the risk of theft if sufficient trust wasn't built, but as far as Malcolm knew, he had the strongest martial force around.

He stopped at the little factory that transformed animal hides into tanned leather. Tanning was a long process, requiring chemicals and an atmosphere dry enough to actually produce good leather. The oven they had received from the Dorves was essentially magic.

First, a piece of hide was placed upon a platform and then a crank was pulled. The hair on the hides was singed away, and then another platform fell from the roof of the contraption like a hydraulic press, squeezing the hide between two sheets of metal. A blue light shone from the line between the metals and what happened then was anybody's guess.

But what came out was a piece of beautiful dark brown leather, already dry and cured. A young man around Logan's age took the leather and started walking toward the Crafters. An older woman nudged the boy with an elbow. The boy looked back, saw Malcolm Specter, flinched, and his run turned into a sprint.

Malcolm gave the woman an appreciative nod and carried on. He looked up at the sky again. Levemoth seemed to be done for the moment. No more Black Rain fell from the dark thundercloud surrounding its scaly body. Soon it would turn and enter a portal it apparently had the ability to create.

Yes, it is about to turn . . . Wait. What is this?!

The great whale-snake hybrid was about to enter the blue portal that it had conjured behind him, but almost as an afterthought, it seemed to turn to look over its shoulder.

In the direction of Malcolm's camp.

"HALT ALL PRODUCTION!" Malcolm roared. "STOP! SHUT DOWN THE MACHINES NOW!"

Everyone scrambled around their workplaces. There were no emergency switches or plugs to pull. The machines would stay on until the Numa was exhausted. Malcolm wondered if the Dorves had designed that feature on purpose.

It didn't matter. It was too late. Within a minute, a giant shadow floated over their heads. Malcolm almost gave into fear, but his mental prowess pushed the feeling down. Still, his palms began to sweat and his throat went instantly dry.

Never before had the beast come upon them like this.

What is this? We did nothing out of ordinary.

"Pick up arms and hide in the shelters!" Malcolm bellowed. "Fighters, get ready!"

The first command was unnecessary. The camp was overtaken by screaming and running. Thankfully, however, the fighters kept their cool.

Instead of Black Rain falling down on them, a single giant black drop hovered under the dark cloud looming over them. It gradually grew, gathering material from the cloud. Soon it became roughly the size of a three-story building.

The cloud surrounding the Levemoth rumbled and the giant Black Drop fell upon their camp.

CHAPTER 66

Logan lifted Freya up in a fierce hug, and she wrapped her legs and arms around him like a spider. It must have been awkward for the rest of the people watching the reunion, but Logan couldn't care less. And in fact, it delighted the Faelves, who all cheered in unison.

As soon as they were done but before Logan could get a word out, Freya gave him an intense look and grabbed his hand. She tugged him along with such single-minded intensity that Logan barely had time to tell the Faelves that these people were his friends. Scilla waved at Logan with a confused look on her face just as Freya pulled him behind a corner.

Logan and Freya took their time in Snoff's apartment. They each had many things to say to one another. They could wait. Instead, they enjoyed each other without saying a word.

After they were completely spent, they emerged from the house. To their chagrin, Snoff had been standing outside guarding their privacy. He congratulated the blushing young couple for their stamina.

After King Sluikumar had greeted the new and old guests, they all washed in the waters of the Spirit Goddess. The statue, which seemed to breathe and watch, stayed still, but Logan could almost feel some presence inside observing them.

The water was cold, but Freya knelt in it and asked for the Spirit Goddess's blessing. Soon after, it glowed with a pure blue light and then became the perfect cozy temperature to bathe in.

After they washed, they joined the Faelves in a great feast of baked goods and seasoned soups. As they enjoyed their meal, Logan and Freya started recounting their stories to one another. Logan sometimes took a glance at his group, who were so engrossed by the delectable food that they often inadvertently ignored the Faelves sitting next to them. The Faelves didn't mind, however, laughing and jibing at their hungry guests along with Logan and Freya. At Tumor's request, Logan had a double serving of a warm, hard crusted pie with soft nuts and bright red berries inside.

When the stars filled the night sky, and the air grew cold and stomachs full, King Sluikumar announced the end of the feast. He thanked his new guests. Over the course of the meal, he had clearly gained their trust. They toasted to new friendships and promised to abandon the Dorves' technology and influence.

Eventually the tables were cleared. Snoff told Logan and Freya they could use his abode for the time being and he would sleep with a friend. Logan thanked him. By the end of the night the two lovers fell asleep in each other's arms.

That morning, Freya brought Logan to their Numa fruit trees. The Faelves deemed this an important event, so even King Sluikumar joined the procession with his court.

"They've grown so fast!" Logan exclaimed and gently touched the sapling's olive-green stalk, which was already as thick as a wrist and reaching four and a half feet in the air.

Freya smirked. "You don't yet know the full depth of my power, love."

Before Logan could say a word, Snoff chimed in, "I am sure Logan will explore your depths—"

"Snoff!" Logan and Freya exclaimed in unison.

One of the female Faelves, a friend of Snoff's called Luuva, bonked Snoff on the head with a spoon.

"So how does this [**Bless**] thing work exactly?"

Freya took a bite of a [**C-grade Numa fruit**], given to her by the King himself. He gave Logan one as well—a high honor. Freya hummed thoughtfully. "I haven't ironed out the kinks yet, even though my skill level is 12."

Logan whistled.

Freya flashed a smile at him. "But She will basically strengthen anything that is good and pure. I blessed this grass and the land beneath it, after which all the trees grew a more vibrant green. And look at all these pretty flowers. They came after the [**Bless**] too."

The grass was indeed laced with clusters of fresh flowers blooming in a myriad of colors.

"Could you bless this armor?" Logan asked.

At that, King Sluikumar flew a few feet into the air, grabbed his luxurious beard, and interjected sharply, "Logan, please explain this armor you're wearing."

Even though Freya had heard the story already, Logan told the king of his capture, descent into the depths of the ruins, the black metal, and the natural Numa crystal. The king regarded him and weighed every word.

"The attacks of the Great Thief have grown numerous. There are so many of you Tall Folk here. Dozens of camps. We have not even scouted them all. Most of them have had dealings with the Dorves and the scourge of our world grows ever stronger."

Logan nodded solemnly but said nothing.

"And you come to us with this. 'Tis a masterwork beyond compare, and the way your soul companion uses it . . . Spectacular innovation. But I fear this is an evil work."

"It was made by me from a natural Numa deposit," Logan said, more hotly than intended.

The king regarded him coolly. "I fear this is another trick of the Dorves. What is this black metal? It looks like the equipment the First Folk used in their machinations."

"It is," Logan admitted.

A worried hiss rippled throughout the crowd of nearby Faelves.

"That doesn't mean it's automatically bad," Logan said.

"The First Folk were destroyed by the Great Thief in their hubris!" Sluikumar said.

"Because they used Numa wrong," Logan said. "That doesn't mean they couldn't have done other things right."

A murmur went through the crowd.

Freya interjected. "I asked Her about the Armor and the way it uses Numa."

"Oh?" the king asked.

"As you Fair Folk know, through my **[Priestess of Numa]** class I have a skill called **[Communion]**. It allows me to ask Her questions. But what I get in response are still disjointed whispers and cryptic answers. I think it's because my subclass is only 12 and the skill is level 4. But I do get the *feel* of what she wants to convey."

"Oh!" Snoff exclaimed and jumped up and down. "What is it that the Spirit Goddess wants? Do tell us! Oh, please!"

The other Faelves joined the chorus and all jumped and skipped and tugged at Freya's clothes. It took an order from King Sluikumar to get them to calm down. Logan had rarely seen the king in such a serious mode, but he understood. This was a question of his people's safety.

Freya gave them a disarming smile. "The Goddess wants me to attempt to [Bless] the armor."

Excitement started bubbling throughout the Faelves again. They grabbed each other's hands and jumped up and down, whistling, dancing, exclaiming with joy and glee.

Even King Sluikumar's hard expression softened back into the smooth porcelain smoothness that Logan was used to seeing. The king flew higher in the air so his voice could be heard. "I have no power to [Bless] as the Beautiful One does, but as king of my people, I bless and lead this historical ceremony under the orange sun and the Two Trees. The machination of male designs and the blessing of feminine grace together might produce a union to defeat the evil which blights our lands. Please Freya Beckstein, please Logan Specter!"

Logan and Freya stood between the two saplings. A reverent, almost holy silence descended upon them. Logan felt almost shy.

Why does this feel so intimate?

Freya was clearly feeling the same. She placed a gentle hand on Logan's chest and when Logan looked at her, she blushed and averted her eyes. Logan then cupped her chin, and her soft blue eyes gazed into his in a way Logan had not seen before. There was purity, grace, trust, and a promise that he didn't quite understand.

Freya trembled before Logan. One hand was on his chest and the other clutching her white dress. There were implications here that went beyond just **[Blessing]** a piece of armor. This was something strange, and Freya was both terrified and excited.

She looked at Logan. He was so handsome and tall in that black armor, which shifted mysteriously.

Goddamn it, what is it that makes a man in uniform so sexy?

And it wasn't just that. It was this whole experience. Logan had returned from the depths of hell and despair with this *power*. He had made his own camp and Freya could see that its people would follow him far.

This is not the same Logan I came to this world with.

Something melted inside her. Her mouth hung open and she realized something. Yes, she had always loved Logan. Ever since they had met as children. But now she wanted to rush to his side and be held by him. She was his woman, and now Logan was truly a *man*. Freya knew now that she would walk through fire for Logan, because this man deserved it. She swallowed and put her hand on the metal.

"**[Bless]**," Freya said softly.

Logan, who had been entranced by her demure beauty, suddenly startled. His black armor started shining a bright blue. The familiar minty feeling enveloped him and he felt himself being lifted off his feet. Tumor didn't say anything, but through their strange connection, Logan could feel his companion's excitement and fear. Logan was also afraid, for there was something powerful and strange afoot. But then he looked at Freya, who smiled encouragingly at him.

"Don't worry," she whispered softly. "The Goddess is good, and she accepts you."

"This has very little to do with the armor, does it?" Logan asked.

Freya smiled. God, he loved that smile. "It has nothing to do with the armor."

At that moment Logan realized it. He already knew he'd been in love with Freya Beckstein for the longest time. But he had never quite deserved her. Such an amazing, gentle, patient person. But now it would be Logan's turn to be patient. Logan wasn't sure if he still deserved such an amazing woman, but he would do his best to earn her. She deserved at least that. Logan would protect and provide for her.

"I'm going to take care of you from now on, Frey."

"I know," Freya said softly. Then she smiled, still softly, but with a hint of mischief. "And I do."

Logan grinned and pulled her into a kiss. All the Faelves and humans cheered, and the blue glow of the Blessing of the Goddess enveloped them and approved of their union.

CHAPTER 67

leveled up," Freya said. "Like a lot."

They were still sitting by the grove, Logan leaning against the trunk of a Numa fruit tree and Freya leaning against him. King Sluikumar had ordered tables and food be brought to them for a picnic. Logan wasn't sure if this constant feasting was for the benefit of the guests or the hosts, but he and Tumor weren't going to turn down the chance of more pie.

"That's cheating!" Logan protested. "I didn't get anything."

"You got me," Freya said smugly.

Logan pulled her in more snugly. "Can't lie, that's a hell of a prize."

"And besides," Freya said. "I did things to you."

"Yeah, you did," Logan said, grinning. "Snoff's bed won't ever be the same."

Freya giggled. "I was talking about the armor, idiot."

Logan perked up. "Oh, yeah . . ."

[I completed assessing the changes made by [**Bless**] *three minutes and forty seconds ago. The changes are . . . substantial.]*

"Well don't hold me in suspense."

Freya grunted. "I wish I could hear Tumor."

"Most of what you're missing is unnecessary math," Logan said. "But he's nice."

[Not only did the [**Bless**] *enhance the function of all existing* [**Enchantments**] *by approximately 15%, it also created more room for further magic to be contained within the armor.]*

"Holy shit," Logan said.

"That good?" Freya said, again rather smugly.

Logan grabbed her and kissed her forehead. "You're amazing."

"I know."

[That isn't all. The armor's natural properties have also been augmented. It is . . . difficult to explain, but it's easier for me to maneuver it now, and I'm more sensitive

to it. We must test this later, but I am 96.81% certain I will level up faster while managing the armor from now on.]

Tumor told him some more of the details it deemed important and then insisted they conduct more tests. Logan sighed and got up. His limp leg didn't feel so bad.

Wait a minute . . . Feel?

No, Logan hadn't dreamt it. There was a faint tingle in that leg and even a sense of the muscles moving within it.

"Tumor . . ." Logan started.

[I have sensed it. This is very good! It seems Freya's **[Bless]** *did something to your body as well. I should run . . . Hmmm . . . Yes, your constitution is stronger. Your VO2 max has also increased by 15% . . . How peculiar. Is this permanent or temporary? In any case, this has saved your leg from muscle atrophy and in the worst-case scenario, necrosis.]*

Logan gulped as he imagined a black, gangrenous leg encased in the black armor, just rotting away. "You didn't tell me that could happen!"

[I deemed it better to omit. There was only a 17.65% chance that you would require immediate amputation.]

"SEVENTEEN PERCENT?!"

[Now, this is exactly why—]

Logan exhaled. Slowly. "How about . . . next time you tell me?"

After Tumor was satisfied by his benchmarking his strength, speed, jump height, agility, and each and every conceivable physical dimension of his body within the armor, Logan collapsed on the ground.

Snoff had come to watch the theatrics with Freya, and together they chatted and nibbled on bread and jam as they watched Logan doing cartwheels and sprints.

Once he had some of his breath back, he got up. "I do feel that I have better stamina now."

"Oh, certainly!" Snoff exclaimed. "I have already told all of my friends of your escapades in my abode yesternight. They were most impressed."

Logan and Freya shared a pained yet amused look.

"Tumor, I have some ideas for further **[Enchantments]**. I want to do something else than just augment our current abilities."

[What do you have in mind?]

"What about a projectile weapon?" Logan mused. "Could we shoot pellets made of the armor? Little black bullets that zip out of my palm and then return after hitting something?"

[Most interesting. We should definitely try that. It would indeed challenge my facilities as a **[Machine Soul]** *and it would be an interesting project to collect data from.]*

Logan asked the right questions and Tumor ran the math. It wasn't quite as simple as just making the armor better. Getting the metal balls to return would require either an **[Enchantment]** from Logan or for Tumor's Control to be acute.

They deemed it better if Logan did the work on this one, since he had already succeeded in making a return **[Enchantment]** with the scythe-rang. However, it would be tricky, since it would need to be a different piece of metal than the armor. Or maybe they should only enchant a part of the armor. Logan wasn't sure how that would work . . .

They contemplated the merits of using the spatial storage as a bullet magazine for the pellets but decided that would be a much too costly solution. Of course, Logan could create a smaller storage space, maybe the size of a cubic foot.

They did have spatial storage full of that precious black metal. The problem was that it was of limited supply and clearly extremely valuable. Logan wanted the biggest and baddest armor ever, but he needed to be a responsible adult here and, with a cool head, decide whether or not the black metal would serve the settlement by the pond better.

Tumor wasn't having it and was playing devil's advocate in full force.

[We do not need to use much of the metal to acquire this new, exciting weapon. Moreover, your martial prowess is a prerequisite for acquiring more of the metal, if we assume it's deep underground where monsters lie.]

"Goddamn it, Tumor," Logan muttered as Freya handed him a piece of bread with jam. "What if there isn't more? We will need to make sustainable Numa batteries out of this metal."

[Assessing Logan's psychological tendencies . . .]

[Adjusting reasoning faculties . . .]

[. . .]

[We can always use your Abilities and repurpose the metal if we decide otherwise. We will only be spending Numa—of which we have plenty for now—this way, in terms of your ambient gathering and the Numa fruit you have been ingesting.]

"Damn it, you're right," Logan said.

With that, Logan opened the dimensional space in his armor, to Freya and the Faelves' excitement. Logan plucked a piece of black metal from within it. It was a smooth-edged ring, a foot in diameter. A stray ray of orange sunlight hit it through the canopies, giving it a soft, eerie glow. The metal weighed probably around a pound, although it was still hard for Logan to assess these things with his enhanced physicality through the armor.

[Slightly over one pound, yes. Enough for our project.]

That was all Logan needed to know. He knelt down. Freya scooted closer to see.

"[Mass Produce]."

[Skill Level Up!]
[Mass Production Level 6]
[Attribute Level Up!]
[Focus: 30]
[Control: 30]

The ring turned into multiple large cylindrical bullets, like modern ammunition on Earth. Logan had no reason to give them any other shape. From that one pound, weighing a little over seven thousand grains, Logan produced thirty-six smooth black bullets, mimicking the size and weight of a 0.300 caliber sniper rifle round.

That's an extra pound of weight on my body . . . Well, I suppose with Frey's **[Bless]** *we can handle the extra load.*

[Especially if we eventually manage to get your leg in working order. I am allocating an inordinate amount of computing and the actual power of the armor to keep us moving smoothly. The opportunity cost is noticeable.]

"We'll work on that," Logan muttered to himself and really hoped they could. The relationship with his father's camp and by extension the **[Healer]** therein was icy, but maybe they could trade something to get Logan's leg healed.

Is that selfish? Should we have a vote on my leg? I can't just use common good resources for myself, right? That's literal corruption!

[Your leg being operational and thus your martial prowess through which you both protect the people and acquire resources for them is for the common good.]

"How can you be sure?" Logan said and pensively thumbed one of the black bullets he had just made.

[I could show you the math.]

Logan made a face. "You know what? I'm sure you're right. But I'll still run it by a few people to make sure."

Freya brought Logan another shimmering blue fruit and Logan kissed her hand as she handed it to him. Then she sat beside him and leaned her chin on his shoulder.

"What comes next, Mr. Engineer?"

"I'm thinking," Logan said distractedly.

"I know," Freya said. "You always have that face on when you do."

"Next comes **[Enchanting]** these bullets. I want them to have the basic stuff, you know. They need to be infused with Numa. I think I will **[Empower]** them. Then of course penetrative power, weight increasing with velocity, resistance to wind and friction in the air . . ."

Freya scoffed. "Weight increasing with velocity . . . What kind of mathemagicks is this? Since when have you been so smart?"

Logan laughed. "Since Tumor. He does all the drag coefficient stuff and other geek magic."

"You guys make a good team," she said.

"We do," Logan admitted. God, Freya smelled amazing. "But you're just saying that because you think the armor is a uniform."

Even through the armor, Logan could feel Freya's cheek drawing up in a lopsided grin. "What can I say? You look sexy in a uniform."

"It's not a . . ." Logan gave up. He nudged her gently "You know what? You're distracting."

Freya whined. "Not at all . . . I'm moral support."

"You need to be quiet moral support then."

"Yes, sir."

Logan rolled his eyes.

"Ok, Tumor. Can you possess a bullet?"

Logan and Tumor ran through some tests. The idea was to imbed the bullets into the armor's liquid metal construct and then for them to be possessed and shot out, their trajectory guided by Tumor.

Tumor could indeed possess a bullet, but it was difficult assimilating the bullet into the armor, and then shooting it out and making it take form and solidify again. They worked for long enough to consume two more E-grade Numa fruits and for Freya to get completely bored with their tinkering.

[Sub-class Level Up!]
[Enchantment Level 30]
[Attribute Level Up!]
[Potency: 32]
[Efficiency: 35]

"Finally!"

[This is adequate. My simulations give me confidence to say that I will be able to fully assimilate the bullets and possess them throughout the course of their trajectory when my attributes are higher-level.]

"The things we have to shoot are usually big and ugly," Logan said, satisfied with finally being able to lean back. The bullets would be attached to both sides of his forearm, eighteen each. From there, Tumor should be able to manipulate them well enough through the armor and then possessing them to give them a reasonable accuracy.

[The accuracy is not reasonable. I am only able to guide the trajectory for the first thirty feet, which is the first 0.0109 seconds. This is not aiming; it is divination.]

"Hey, as long as the bad guys die," Logan said.

[Very well. But now we must practice shooting.]

Logan went up to one of the Faelves to consult where they could practice shooting magical bullets safely. The Faelves clearly weren't thrilled with the idea, because Logan's armor and all of its tricks and antics apparently constituted "suspicious machinations." However, a young Faelf of green porcelain skin called Fleafmar took them to an old, shriveled grove full of withered trees. With a few Numa fruits in tow, Logan and Tumor began practicing.

After about an hour, their training was interrupted by a frantic Snoff gasping for air as he stumbled to the abandoned grove. Logan stopped and looked at the wheezing Faelf.

"Logan! 'Tis your old camp! There be great trouble!"

CHAPTER 68

Logan dashed through the swamp with a speed he had never experienced before. He must have been leaping ten feet per step, sending water up in the air in arcs behind him. In his mad rush, he realized he was stepping over some creatures along the way, but he had no time to tell if they were hostile or not, or even to care.

My idiot father must have still been using Numa.

Logan saw the attack from a long distance away. Trees were felled and a score of dead bodies thrown around like the vacant-eyed dolls of a petulant child. What used to be Malcolm Specter's camp was now chaos and destruction.

Logan grimaced as he took a clear look at the instigator.

It was tall—far larger than any living being Logan had ever seen aside from Levemoth. Thirty feet in height, with a long, snouted maw filled with sharp teeth, like a crocodile on a gargantuan scale. Seven or eight black beady eyes covered its head, each dotted with white pupils that swished around monstrously.

It was covered in hard, black and blue scales that gave off an oily gleam. Two long arms were swatting at an agent who was currently attempting to aim a spear at its giant claws. It was like watching a chihuahua barking at an elephant. The agent died screaming seconds later, cut to shreds while still alive.

Logan hid behind a tree and tried to steady his breath. He wasn't spent from the run; he was scared shitless.

"W-we have three options," Logan whispered to himself and Tumor frantically. "Get the Faelves and Frey, go to the camp by the pond, and move the hell away from this beast. A hundred miles away."

[Reasonable. Faelves will be unwilling to move and this thing might follow us. We don't know its modus operandi yet.]

"It looks slow," Logan said, trying to collect himself. "The second option is to lure it somewhere. The third would be the dumbest."

[Fight it? Certainly a terrible idea. I won't give you the odds of survival, but they are low. It's unfortunate that none of the current survivors know the way to the Faelves. You could tell them to get Freya and your new friends and have them start evacuating the camp by the pond.]

"We have to lure it away. My dad might be—"

Dead or alive, who knew? Responsible for at least a dozen deaths? Certainly. Logan still had to know.

With a mental prompt, Logan told Tumor to drop all of the thirty-six bullets they had just made onto the grass. "We need to make some adjustments. How fast can you make a quarter pound bullet fly?"

[It is a small kinetic missile at that weight.]

"We're on a timer, Tumor."

[Running simulations . . .]

[. . .]

[There is a solution . . . But it will leave you intermittently vulnerable.]

"Run it by me. If it's good enough, we do it and move."

When the recoil from the first black missile kicked Logan's shoulder back, he was sure that, had he not had his armor, it wouldn't have just broken his arm but would have ripped it clean off.

And given the number of [**Enchantments**] he had stacked the missile with . . . Well, the giant crocodile lizard wasn't a happy camper, to put it mildly. It turned itself to face Logan and let out a thunderous roar.

At that, Logan threw his arm back again. The viscous armor peeled from his arm and formed into an atlatl, in which another black missile was nested. When Logan launched it, the armor stretched, storing potential energy. As the Black Missile released, a propulsion [**Enchantment**] exploded it forward, while Tumor possessed it with his [**Machine Soul**] ability, giving it a perfect trajectory.

[Skill Level Up!]
[Power Armor Fighter Level 2]

It struck the giant creature in the shoulder, making it stumble backward. The earth tremored underneath its feet.

By now the monster had noticed Logan behind the tree line and the first missile was already returning to Logan's arm, where it reassimilated back into the Armor, for Tumor to control and replenish the propulsion [**Enchantment**] from the armor's Numa reserve.

The creature roared again and lumbered toward Logan, swinging its low-hanging claws and cutting down trees in the process.

Logan wasted no time and sprinted toward the river, further north.

Away from the Faelves and Frey. Away from the settlement by the pond.

Logan fired another missile. It struck true and the great beast stumbled again. Tumor had guided the black missile directly into the creature's thick neck, where the scales seemed softer. Thick black blood oozed from the wound, but the creature seemed to be only getting faster. Within a few giant strides, it was upon Logan, attacking him with its slicing claws.

Logan ducked instinctively, feeling the air current swishing over his head as the giant claw swiped over him. He then immediately bolted up and felt the armor receding from his upper body, as Tumor redirect it to his lower half in anticipation of a power sprint.

[Skill Level Up!]
[Power Armor Fighter Level 3]

Then Logan ran, dodged, shot another black missile, and lured the creature further along. They must have been at it for three miles by the time Logan was starting to get out of breath, even with the amazing prowess that the armor provided. The black missile returned, but this time, when it was sucked into the armor, the impact made Logan stumble backward. By this point, he was wheezing.

[Skill Level Up!]
[Power Armor Fighter Level 4]

The great crocodile monster immediately capitalized on Logan's weakness. It was slowing down too, but just like any good predator worth its salt, its nose had picked up on the scent of Logan's exhaustion.

A stream of black sludge then vomited out of its great maw. The putrescence instantly started morphing and shifting as soon as it hit the ground, turning into two smaller, yet still gargantuan crocodile monsters, with a myriad of eyes and salivating snouts full of teeth. Immediately they ran toward Logan.

These creatures were *fast*. Logan made a quick glance at the original creature, which was now showing signs of great fatigue. It had clearly been weakened by this birthing process. But it was still on its feet, still scanning for Logan with its avaricious eyes.

Logan began another power sprint. As he did, he sent a mental note to Tumor to push the armor to its limits. With every step (or *leap*, more like) he left a hole in the ground in his wake, tossing the earth in the air. Meanwhile the offspring ran toward Logan like hunting cats. Within seconds, they would pounce.

Logan had gone through a spectrum of emotions in the last ten minutes: fear, fatigue, adrenaline, excitement, pain, endurance. Now his mind filled with a grim determination. With a rictus grimace, he braced himself.

If I run, I die. So, I will fight.

CHAPTER 69

Logan roared as he struck the first great lizard-beast charging toward him. Tumor had morphed most of the armor into a hefty Zweihänder, which Logan used to slash the first beast.

The blade cut true, slicing half a foot into the beast's neck, but it got lodged in the shoulder.

By the time Tumor had morphed and the blade pulled out, the other crocodile creature snapped at Logan. He dodged and the crocodile's teeth caught his torso—thankfully protected by the armor—rather than his head. The jagged teeth weren't able to penetrate it, but the pressure was crushing. The monster shook its head like a dog with a toy.

[Reinforcing the armor at the points of highest pressure. We should wait until the beast lets go.]

"SCREW THAT!" Logan shouted. "FIRE A MISSILE!"

Logan did his best to control his arms. With the left, he grabbed the monster's snout, shoving the right one into its mouth.

In an instinctive panic, Logan roared, "FIRE IT!"

Tumor was already half a second ahead, having computed and predicted when Logan would finish his movements. His arm and shoulders kicked back, and there was suddenly a loud BOOM, slightly muffled by the monster's intestines.

[Skill Level Up!]
[Power Armor Fighter Level 5]

The monster screeched and tossed Logan aside. The black missile was already coming back after leaving a gaping hole in its black-and-blue-mottled back. It collapsed on the ground.

By that time, the beast with the cleaved neck was already on him. It pounced upon its prey with fierce determination despite the injury. Logan coughed up and spat out blood. His vision was swimming. He must have broken a rib. The pain was intense. Tumor was saying something inside his head. It sounded urgent.

Logan managed to dodge most of the stumbling monster's attacks by instinct and by Tumor taking over as much as it could. It still managed to push its massive weight on Logan's leg, however.

It was a testament to the armor and Tumor's speed that the injury ended up being minor. Logan broke out of his haze and prompted Tumor to make a spear.

Then he charged and snarled, pushing the spear through the monster's neck and lodging it into a tree at a high angle. The creature snarled and swiped at him with its claw. Logan raised his arm, and a shield formed to absorb the attack. Before the monster could strike again, he fired another black missile, which instantly burst the back of its head open.

It was just in time, as the titanic monster was once again vomiting the disgusting, thick black ooze on the ground. This time, it seemed to be puking up all of its insides. The towering monster almost visibly crumbled and shrank inward, as if suddenly afflicted with old age. It went completely gray and the light in its wild eyes dimmed.

Levemoth, who had been majestically floating above it all, overseeing the destruction it had orchestrated, now flew down, nearly to the tree line. Even though the black sludge was currently forming into another set of lizards, Logan paid them no heed. He was frozen in terror.

The Great Thief came directly upon him and the giant crocodile monster it had spawned. It rumbled and sighed, making the whole jungle tremble. The great thundercloud around it was dark and endless. The outlines of a snakelike body could be seen passing in and out of the storm. With its massive size, it blotted out the sun, an unnatural darkness falling upon Logan and the forest around him.

The beasts from the black ooze were now fully formed, and they charged at Logan in a frenzy. Logan understood that he had to move. He had to act. But he couldn't. He was stunned by terror and awe.

Somewhere in the back of his mind, Tumor *screamed* at him, but Logan's arms fell limp.

An eerie lamenting voice like a whale call deep underwater sounded. There was a quality to the voice so strange, so harrowing, so malevolent, that it would certainly make a person mad if they listened long enough. The sound continued— long, whistling, and ululating—until it seemed to fill the whole universe. It was a language. And as with every language on this strange world, Logan could understand it.

You are distracted, Blaa'hmat. Find the Greedy One. He is the mission. We need him for the ritual.

The shriveled crocodile monster looked up at the sky and bowed. It let out a hoarse screech which stopped the four smaller monsters charging at Logan. They turned and went back to their progenitor, which ate them, regaining its vitality.

The Levemoth started to ascend, taking its distorting, maddening presence with it. Logan slowly began to regain his mind. He felt sluggish but remembered himself; thoughts began to flow once again.

But then the Great Thief stopped. It seemed to notice Logan, who had dropped to his knees, all of his energy spent and his mind muddled. The oppressive presence grew tighter, and Logan's mind slipped away from him once again. The eerie whale call was low and subtle now, almost a seductive, gentle whisper.

Insect. You understand me do you not? Oh . . . You were touched by the gods. Yes, I sense it . . . They think you could stop me, perhaps. But I have a god of my own. The Nameless One. Through his malice, I am now awakened. You cannot stop me. Submit to me. Despair and submit . . .

Logan's mind was now slipping further. Something was tugging at it. Pushing away his own thoughts and emotions. Yes, he *should* get his people together and build. They *should* use Numa. It was only natural. They needed it to survive. They should gather as much Numa as possible. Numa was the answer to Logan's problems. He didn't realize why he hadn't seen it before.

[Logan . . . ?]

He shook his head. Wait, what? He was already using Numa. The Natural Numa, not the stuff corrupted by Levemoth.

What the hell? Tumor?

Then the Great Thief whispered again. This time, it was demanding, urgent, violent.

He was being haunted by greed. Terrible gnawing avarice which would not relent. It was like an itch he couldn't scratch. NUMA! USE IT CONSUME IT EAT IT GIVE IT ALL TO HIM! GIVE NUMA TO MASTER! SUBMIT!

[Logan, I am sorry. I will have to shut you down.]

Logan blacked out.

CHAPTER 70

Logan was shocked when he woke up in one of the houses he had built the other day at the settlement by the pond. He was surrounded by a conclave of people with worried expressions, including Dr. Rosenberg, who was wiping the blue juice of a Numa fruit from his lips.

"Welcome back," Freya said, scooting closer and grabbing Logan's hand.

"W-what happened?" Logan croaked.

Snoff approached. His porcelain skin shone almost too brightly in the dim hut. For once, he wasn't bursting with exuberant energy but instead wore a solemn, respectful expression.

"I followed you and watched you battle," the Faelf said. "I have never seen the Great Thief come this close . . . When you passed out, it flew higher and cast a few drops of Black Rain, as if to kill you personally. Those serpents with giant maws spawned, but I used illusions to conceal us."

Logan tried to get up, but Dr. Rosenberg put a hand gently on his chest. "Now is not the time to exert yourself."

Logan swatted the hand. Then he looked at Dr. Rosenberg, as if just realizing he was there.

"Wait. If you're here . . . Where's my father?"

Everyone shuffled uncomfortably. Freya cast a careful glance at Logan and squeezed his hand. Snoff nodded to himself and explained.

"The giant lizard returned to the camp. It seemed it was there for your father."

Logan frowned. "That makes no sense."

"'Twas so, nonetheless," Snoff said. "The monster went back to the camp and killed everyone it saw. Except Malcolm Specter."

"It was horrible," someone from the crowd almost whispered. Logan looked up. It was Janice.

Everyone turned to look at her. She seemed to only just realize she had blurted something out loud. She swallowed and continued, "I was hiding under the rubble and broken wood. But there was a hole. I saw the monster rampaging back and forth, clearly looking for something. Mr. Specter had used one of the Dorven tools to dig himself in the ground. But the monster found him. Then something strange happened."

Janice fell silent and blinked dumbly, gathering herself.

"Yeah?" Kat said impatiently. Balmer nudged her softly with an elbow.

Janice gathered in a wavering breath and continued, "The monster picked up Mr. Specter. But instead of eating him or killing him, it started to turn into a black sludge. The sludge enveloped him. Mr. Specter struggled and screamed, but the sludge went into his mouth and eyes . . . Everywhere. He— He started to transform and . . ."

Logan shot up and took Janice's shoulders in his hands. "What? Transform? Into what? Where is my father?"

"He—he—" Janice's lips drew up as she tried to hold in a cry.

Simmons came from behind Logan and placed a heavy hand on his shoulder. Logan let go of Janice.

"He grew . . . and turned black and blue. He floated in the air for a while, looking inhuman, with claws and horns . . . I—I don't know what happened. He floated in the air for a while, and it looked like he was understanding what had happened. He just nodded to himself and looked around. The black sludge swirled around him, but he . . . absorbed it all and grew even bigger. When there was no more sludge left, that . . . big thing came."

"Levemoth?" Logan asked.

Janice nodded. "Yeah, the one that always causes trouble. It came and floated down. It was . . . I thought I was going to die. It was driving me crazy. I just wanted to shout and cry and claw my eyes out. But I couldn't move under the rubble."

"Janice," Logan said firmly. "What happened to my father?"

"He flew away," Janice said. Logan just blinked dumbly. Janice continued, "It was like Levemoth had come to pick him up. It got close and Malcolm looked around and then went with it. I guess when he got close enough, they teleported away. I didn't see."

"What the hell?" Logan asked, practically deflated.

Freya turned to Snoff. "What happened to him?"

"'Tis not like I know everything, Freya," Snoff said. "We have not seen the Great Thief act like this before."

"It spoke to me," Logan said. "It said it had awakened."

The humans in the hut muttered to each other. Only Snoff gasped and his bright eyes went wide. "Surely not! It cannot be . . . But what else would explain this? Why did it steal the Greedy One? I must tell my king."

The Greedy One . . . ?

Snoff was almost out the door, but Logan called, "Wait, Snoff."

The Faelf stopped and turned. "I will return, friend!"

And then he was gone.

That left Logan with everyone looking at him, as if he were the solution to all of their problems.

[I believe they are looking at you for leadership.]

Great . . . I feel like I'm definitely the best man for the job right now.

But Logan was the *only* man for the job. Leadership wasn't something you got a sick day from. Especially in a situation like this. They were still stranded in a jungle on an alien world. These people *needed* leadership. And they had chosen Logan.

"Alright," he said, finding his voice. "We'll deal with my asshole father later. Dr. Rosenberg, I take it you're on standby for anyone who needs medical attention."

The older man nodded.

"From now on, you work together with William. William, you here?"

"He's outside," Freya said and came over to stand next to Logan. Logan grabbed her waist. She was his rock, his guiding light. He would lead, in order to keep her safe.

"Dr. Rosenberg, call for William. He's an **[Alchemist]**."

Dr. Rosenberg scoffed.

"Yeah, yeah," Logan said. "Sucks to be you. He should be able to make magic potions and salves, so you two will make a tremendous power couple. I'll talk to you guys later about your collaboration."

Dr. Rosenberg clearly wasn't happy with the arrangement, but he gave Logan a curt nod and left the house.

"Scilla," Logan said.

"Yes sir," she said immediately.

"Don't call me, sir."

"No can do, sir."

Logan snorted. "Fine. You gather a group of stalwart individuals of your choosing. Eight should be enough, **[Warrior]** types at least half of them. Make sure one of them is from the old camp. You guys get back there and look out for any survivors. They might be unconscious or under rubble. Also, bring back anything valuable. Have pouches made. Janice will help you with that. And tell the idiots not to bring back any of that Dorven crap."

Scilla nodded and gave a thumbs up. "Got it. Come, Brian, you're with me."

Then Logan turned to Simmons.

"We are going to need more housing, and the fence isn't finished," Logan said. "You should go widen the perimeter and get us more lumber."

Simmons grinned.

Well, that's the first I've ever seen that.

"Yes sir."

There was a bit more mockery in his tone than Scilla had demonstrated, but it was at least an acknowledgement of his position. Logan smirked.

"The rest of you, go back to your routines. We need food, first and foremost. Decide for yourself if you want to fish or gather. After we're good on food and water, get back to leveling your class. If you don't know what you should do, come talk to me later."

Most of the house emptied out. Next, Logan turned to his father's ex-agents.

"You agents."

There were three large agents looking at Logan with unreadable expressions. He looked each of them in the eyes and nodded.

"Yeah, I know. I've been an asshole," Logan said. "And I still am. But I'm going to need your help to keep this show running. I'm still young and pretty dumb and inexperienced. But I *am* going to do my best."

The agents shuffled. They weren't hostile like they had been before. But they were uncertain. One of them—the large one that had been with them way back exploring the beetle ruins—looked downright doubtful. Logan worried he might try a coup later. *Well, I'll just have to smash his head in if he tries anything stupid. I'm done playing games.*

"Is that clear?"

After a reluctant chorus of "Yes," Logan relaxed.

"That's good. You, big guy, what's your name?"

"Jefferson."

Why don't they use first names?

"Good. You're in charge of the agents from now on. You guys are our guards, soldiers, and hunters. If you aren't soldiering or guarding, you're hunting or resting. Rotate all these duties. Guard duty, soldier reserve, hunting group, rest group. We good?"

Without thinking, Jefferson made an appreciative sound. "Huh."

He immediately regretted it and grunted and marched out, the other two agents in tow. Logan did his best to suppress his smirk this time.

Balmer looked at the agents and almost went with them, but Kat grabbed his shirt and gestured at him to stay.

"What about us, *sir?*" Kat said and gave him a mock salute.

Logan's smile widened as he looked at the two of them. He hadn't had that much time with them, but he realized that these two weren't just subordinates. They were friends. Even that damn Balmer.

"Oh, I have some very interesting plans for you two," Logan said and grinned ominously. "See this armor? We're going to get more of this stuff. And then we're going to kick Levemoth's ass."

About the Author

Wilbur Woods is an entertainer, coffee drinker, and story eater, as well as the author of the Cosmic Games and MagiCraft Master series, originally released on Royal Road. He has loved stories since he was a kid, and when he asked himself what he really wanted to do, the answer was simple: write.

Podium
DISCOVER
STORIES UNBOUND
PodiumAudio.com